A Study in Seduction

A Daring Hearts Novel

FOREVER

NEW YORK BOSTON

Forever
Hachette Book Group
237 Park Avenue
New York, NY 10017
www.HachetteBookGroup.com

Printed in the United States of America

OPM

First Edition: August 2012
10 9 8 7 6 5 4 3 2 1

Forever is an imprint of Grand Central Publishing.
The Forever name and logo are trademarks of Hachette Book Group, Inc.

For O.P., who is always right.

Acknowledgments

My deepest gratitude goes to Kimberly Witherspoon of InkWell Management for her persistence and belief, and to William Callahan and Nathaniel Jacks for their consistent support. I'm indebted to my excellent editor, Selina McLemore, whose perceptive insights have greatly strengthened this book and my writing. I am so grateful to Franzeca Drouin and Eloisa James, fairy godmothers who make me want to be both a better writer and a better person. F., I will treasure March 28, 2009, as the start of a wonderful friendship. Thank you to my book club and also my critique partners, Bobbi, Rachel, and Melody, with whom I have my best discussions about books and writing. Much love to my husband, Will, and our children, and to my father, who always believed, even if he'd never admit to it.

Author's Note

I relied on a number of sources while researching the mathematical elements of this book, and the following studies form the basis of Lydia's theories about the correlation between love and mathematics. Clio Cresswell, *Mathematics and Sex* (Crow's Nest, Australia: Allen and Unwin, 2003); Sergio Rinaldi, "Laura and Petrarch: An Intriguing Case of Cyclical Love Dynamics," *SIAM Journal on Applied Mathematics*, 58: 4 (1988), pp. 1205–1221; and "Love Dynamics: The Case of Linear Couples," *Applied Mathematics and Computation*, 95: 2–3 (1988), pp. 181–192; S. H. Strogatz, "Love Affairs and Differential Equations," *Mathematics Magazine*, 61(1): 35 (1988). Thank you, brilliant mathematicians, for thinking in ways I never could.

A Study in Seduction

Chapter One

London
March 1854

Every square matrix is a root of its own characteristic polynomial.

Lydia Kellaway clutched the notebook to her chest as the cab rattled away, the clatter of horses' hooves echoing against the fortress of impressive town houses lining Mount Street. Gaslights burned through the midnight dark, casting puddles of light onto the cobblestones.

Lydia took a breath, anxiety and fear twisting through her. She looked up at town house number twelve, the dark façade perforated with light-filled windows. A man stood silhouetted behind one window on the first floor, his form straight, tall, and so still that he appeared fixed in that moment.

Beneath the glow of a streetlamp, Lydia opened her

notebook and leafed through pages scribbled with notes, equations, and diagrams.

She'd written his name at the top of a blank page, then followed it with a numbered list of points, all related to the gossip and suppositions surrounding his family.

As she reviewed her notes, the back of her neck prickled with the strange feeling that she was being watched. She snapped the notebook closed and shook her head. Chiding herself for being unnerved by the shadows, she climbed the steps.

She reached for the bell just as the door flew open. A woman dressed in a vivid green silk gown stormed out, nearly colliding with Lydia on the front step.

"Oh!" The woman reeled backward, her eyes widening. In the sudden light spilling out from the foyer, Lydia saw that her eyes were red and swollen, her face streaked with tears.

Lydia stammered, "I'm... I'm sorry, I—"

The woman shook her head, her lips pressing together as she pushed past Lydia and hurried down the steps.

A curse echoed through the open door as a dark-haired man strode across the foyer, tension shimmering around him. "Talia!"

He didn't cast Lydia a glance as he followed the woman down the steps. "Blast it, Talia, wait for the carriage!"

The woman turned her head to glare at the man and tossed a retort over her shoulder. Lydia couldn't discern the words, but the cutting tone was enough to make her pursuer stop in his tracks. He cursed again, then went back to the house and shouted for the footman. Within seconds, the servant raced down the street after the woman.

"John!" The tall man turned to shout for a second servant. "Ready the carriage now and see Lady Talia home!"

He stalked up the steps and brushed past Lydia. He seemed about to slam the door in her face, but then he stopped and turned to stare at her. "Who the bloody hell are you?"

Lydia couldn't speak past the shock.

Alexander Hall, Viscount Northwood. She knew it was him, knew in her bones that this was the man she sought, though she had not laid eyes on him before now.

Despite the hour and his anger, his clothing was precise, unwrinkled. His black trousers bore creases as sharp as a blade, and shiny gilt buttons fastened his silk waistcoat over a snowy white shirt.

His dark eyes flashed over Lydia. That look—keen, assessing, *close*—caused her breath to tangle in her throat.

"Well?" he demanded.

Every square matrix is a root of its own characteristic polynomial.

The locket. Jane. The locket.

"Lord Northwood?" she said.

"I asked who you are."

His rough baritone voice settled deep in her bones. She tilted her head to meet his hooded gaze. Shadows mapped the pronounced Slavic angles of his face, the sloping cheekbones, the clean-shaven line of his jaw.

"My name is Lydia Kellaway," she said, struggling to keep her voice steady. She glanced at the street, where the footman had stopped Lady Talia at the corner. A carriage rattled from the side of the house and approached. "Is she all right?"

"My sister is fine," Lord Northwood snapped, "aside from being the most obstinate, frustrating creature who ever walked the earth."

"Is that a family trait?" Lydia spoke before thinking, which was so contrary to her usual manner that her face heated with embarrassment. Not wise to insult the man from whom she needed something.

She almost heard Northwood's teeth grind together as his jaw clenched with irritation.

He followed her gaze to where the footman and coach driver had convinced Lady Talia to enter the carriage. The footman gave Lord Northwood a wave of victory before climbing onto the bench beside the driver. The carriage rattled away.

Some of the anger seemed to drain from Northwood, which bolstered Lydia's courage. Although she had no contingency plan for how to handle arriving in the middle of a family quarrel, she couldn't possibly leave now.

Her spine straightened with determination as she faced the viscount. "Lord Northwood, I apologize for the lateness of the hour, but I must speak with you. It's about a locket you purchased."

"A what?"

"A locket. A pendant attached to a chain, worn as a necklace."

He frowned. "You've come to my home at this hour to inquire about a *necklace*?"

"It's terribly important." She gripped the doorjamb so he couldn't close the door and leave her standing on the step. "Please, may I come in?"

He stared at her for a minute, then rubbed a hand across his chin.

"Kellaway." A crease formed between his brows. "Kin to Sir Henry Kellaway?"

Lydia gave a quick nod. "He was my father. He passed

away several months ago." Grief, heavy with the weight of the past, pressed down on her heart.

"My sympathies," Lord Northwood said, his frown easing somewhat as he glanced over her black mourning dress.

"Thank you. How did you know him?"

"We were both involved with the Crystal Palace exhibition in fifty-one." He stood looking at her for a moment, his gaze so protracted she could almost see his thoughts shifting. Then he moved aside and held the door open.

She stepped into the foyer, conscious of the fact that he did not allow her more space to pass, even as her shoulder brushed against his arm. The light contact made her jerk away, her chest constricting.

"What makes you think I have this necklace you seek?" he asked.

"I don't think you have it, Lord Northwood. I know you do. You purchased it from Mr. Havers's shop less than a week ago, along with a Russian icon." Her chin lifted. "It was a locket my grandmother pawned."

Pushing himself away from the doorjamb, Lord Northwood stepped forward. Lydia started before realizing he intended to take her cloak. She pushed the hood off her head and fumbled with the clasp.

He stood behind her, close enough that she could sense the warmth of his body, close enough that her next breath might have been the very air he exhaled.

"Come to the drawing room, Miss Kellaway. You'd best explain yourself."

Lydia followed him into the room and sat on the sofa, making a conscious effort not to twist the notebook between her fingers. Lord Northwood lowered himself into the chair across from her. A stoic footman served tea before departing and closing the door behind him.

Lord Northwood took a swallow of tea, then put the cup on the table and leaned back in his chair. His long body unfolded with the movement, his legs stretching out in front of him. Although his outward bearing was casual, a tautness coiled through him. He reminded Lydia of a bird of prey elongating its wings, feathers ruffling, poised for flight.

"Well?" he asked.

"I found the ticket in my grandmother's desk." She leafed through the pages of her book before finding a small slip of paper. "I hadn't known she'd pawned any of my mother's jewelry."

His hand brushed hers as he took the pawn ticket, the hard ridges of his fingers discernible even through the protection of her glove. She jerked away, curling her hand into a fist at her side.

"Your grandmother had a month to redeem her pledge," Lord Northwood said after looking at the slip of paper.

"I realize that. And I would have attempted to do so on her behalf had I known about the transaction to begin with. I thought Mr. Havers might not have put the locket up for sale yet, or if he had, perhaps it hadn't been sold. But when I arrived at his shop, he informed me he'd sold it last Thursday."

"How did you learn the name of the purchaser?"

Color heated her cheeks. "Mr. Havers refused—rightly so, I suppose—to divulge the purchaser's name," she explained. "When he became occupied with another customer, I saw his book of sales behind the counter. I was able to . . . borrow it long enough to look up the transaction."

A smile tugged at his mouth. She watched with a trace of fascination as a dimple appeared in his cheek, lending his severe, angular features an almost boyish glint. "You stole Havers's salesbook?"

"I did not steal it." She bristled a little at the disagreeable term. "I removed it from his shop, yes, but for less than ten minutes. I gave a boy sixpence to return the book to its proper place without Mr. Havers seeing him. You were clearly listed as the purchaser of the locket. Do you still have it, my lord?"

Northwood shifted, his hand sliding into his coat pocket. Lydia's breath caught in her chest as she watched him withdraw the silver chain, capturing the locket in his palm.

He studied the locket, rubbing his thumb across the engraving that embellished its polished surface.

"Is it a phoenix?" he asked.

"It's called a *fenghuang*, a bird of virtue, power, and grace."

He flipped the locket over to the design on the other side. "And the dragon?"

"When the *fenghuang* is paired with a dragon, the two symbolize the union of... of husband and wife."

His dark eyes moved to hers. "Of male and female."

Lydia swallowed in an effort to ease the sudden dryness of her mouth. "The... the *fenghuang* itself is representative of yin and yang. *Feng* is the male bird, *huang* the female. The bird and the dragon together speak of marital harmony."

"And the woman?" Northwood asked.

"The woman is yin, the bird called *huang*—"

"No." He flicked open the locket, turning it toward her to reveal the miniature portrait inside. "This woman."

She didn't look at the image. She couldn't. She stared at Lord Northwood. Something complex and strangely intimate shone behind his eyes, as if he knew the answer to his question yet wanted to hear the response from her.

"That woman," she said, "is my mother."

He snapped the locket closed between his thumb and forefinger. "She is very beautiful."

"She was."

The sine of two theta equals two times the sine of theta times the cosine of theta.

Lydia repeated the trigonometric identity until the threat of disturbing emotions had passed.

"Why did you purchase the locket from Mr. Havers?" she asked.

"I'd never seen anything like it."

"Nor will you again. My father had it specially made. It is pure silver, though I suspect you know that."

"I do recognize excellent craftsmanship." As he spoke, he lifted his gaze from the locket and looked at her. "And this locket must be very valuable, indeed, if it brought you here in the middle of the night."

Lydia nodded. She slipped her hand into her pocket and closed her fingers around a small figurine. She extended it to Lord Northwood. "My father brought this back years ago from a trip to the province of Yunnan. It's a jade sculpture of an elephant, quite well crafted. I'd like to offer it in exchange for the locket."

"Why didn't your grandmother pawn that instead of the locket?"

Lying would serve no purpose. Not with this man.

"It isn't as valuable," Lydia admitted.

"You expect me to make an uneven exchange?"

"No. My father also has several Chinese scrolls, one or two paintings—if you would consider several items in exchange?"

Northwood shook his head. "I do not collect Chinese art and artifacts, Miss Kellaway, so that would be of no use. As I said, I bought the locket because it was unique."

"Surely there must be something you want."

"What else are you offering?"

Although the question appeared innocent, the undercurrent of his voice rippled through her. Warmth heated its wake—not the tenderness provoked by emotions of the heart but something edged with wildness, lack of control. Danger.

Her eyes burned.

The locket. The locket.

"I...I have not the immediate funds to repurchase it from you," she admitted, "though I've been recently offered a position that involves payment, and I can offer you a promissory note in exchange for—"

"I trust no one to uphold a promissory note."

"I assure you, my lord, I would never—"

"No one, Miss Kellaway."

Lydia expelled a breath, unable to muster any indignation at his decree. She wouldn't trust anyone to uphold a promissory note, either. Almost twenty-eight years of life had taught her that well enough.

"Nor would I accept money that you...earned?" Northwood added.

The statement had a question to it, one Lydia had no intention of answering. If she told him she'd been offered a position on the editorial board of a mathematical journal, he'd likely either laugh at her or... Wait a moment.

"Lord Northwood, I understand you are in charge of a Society of Arts exhibition. Is that correct?"

He nodded. "An international educational exhibition, which I proposed well over a year ago. It's scheduled to open in June. Preparations are under way."

An international exhibition. Lydia's fingers tightened on the notebook.

"Is there by chance a . . . a mathematical element of the exhibition?" she asked.

"There is a planned display of different mathematical instruments used in various parts of the world."

"I see." She tried to ignore the shimmer of fear in her blood. If he did accept her offer, she would have no reason to take on any kind of public role. All of her work could be conducted before the exhibition even opened. Perhaps no one except Lord Northwood would even know.

"Lord Northwood, I should like to offer my assistance with your exhibition in exchange for the locket."

"I beg your pardon?"

"I have a talent for mathematics and am quite certain I could be a useful consultant."

"You have a *talent* for mathematics?"

He was looking at her as if she were the oddest creature he'd ever encountered. Lydia had been on the receiving end of such askance looks since she was a child and had grown accustomed to them. Coming from Lord Northwood, however, such dubiousness caused an unexpected rustle of dismay.

"Unusual, I know," she said, attempting to keep her voice light, "but there it is. I've spent most of my life with numbers, crafting useful theorems into solutions. I can advise you on the efficacy and value of the mathematics display."

"We are already consulting with a Society subcommittee composed of mathematicians and professors."

Lydia's heart sank. "Oh." She chewed her lower lip and flipped through the notebook. "What about the books? Do you need anyone to help with your accounting of the books?"

"No. Even if I did, I would not allow you to work in exchange for the locket."

"Well, I would still like—"

Before she could finish the sentence, Northwood rose from his chair with the swiftness of a crocodile emerging from a river. He crossed to her in two strides and pulled the notebook from her grip. Lydia gave a slight gasp. He paged through the book, his frown deepening.

" 'Alexander Hall, Lord Northwood,' " he read, " 'returned from St. Petersburg two years ago following scandal.' What is all this?"

A hot flush crept up Lydia's neck. "My lord, I apologize, I didn't mean to offend."

"A bit late for that, Miss Kellaway. You've been collecting details about me? For the purpose of retrieving the locket?"

"It was the only way I could—"

" '*A pompous sort*'? Where did you hear I was a pompous sort?"

Lydia's blush grew hotter, accompanied by a growing alarm as she sensed the locket swinging farther out of her reach. "Er... a friend of my grandmother's. She said you were known for moving about in rather lofty circles, both here and in St. Petersburg."

When he didn't respond, she added, "She also said you'd done excellent work building your trading company."

If the compliment mitigated the offense, he gave no indication. He turned his attention back to the book.

"'Scandal involving mother.'" Northwood's expression tightened with anger. "Did your research, didn't you, Miss Kellaway?"

She couldn't respond. Shame and dismay swirled through her chest. Northwood leafed through the rest of the book, his expression not changing as he examined the scribbled equations and theorems.

"What is all this?" he asked again.

"My notes. I keep the notebook with me so I can write things down as I think of them."

Northwood slammed the book shut.

"It's late, Miss Kellaway." His voice was weary, taut. "I believe John has returned with the carriage. If you'll wait in the foyer, he will ensure that you arrive home safely."

Lydia knew that if she left now, he would never agree to see her again.

"Lord Northwood, please, I'm certain we can come to some sort of agreement."

"Are you, now?" He stared at her so intently that Lydia shifted with discomfort. His eyes slipped over her, lingering on her breasts, her waist. "What kind of agreement?"

She ought to have been offended by the dark insinuation in his voice, like the low thrum of a cello, but instead a shiver ran through her blood and curled in her belly.

Yet she had nothing more to offer him.

"Lord Northwood," she finally said, "what do you propose?"

Alexander paused for a moment and stared at the woman before him. Who *was* she? Why did she make him so...curious? And why was embarrassment flaring in him because she knew about the scandal?

"I *propose*, Miss Kellaway," he said, his words clipped, "that you throw your infernal notebook into the fire and leave me the bloody hell alone."

Her eyes widened. "I'm certain you realize that is not an option," she said quietly.

He gave a humorless laugh. So much for attempting to frighten her off. "One can hope."

He could just give her the damned locket back. That would be the gentlemanly thing to do, though he suspected she wouldn't accept the gesture. For her, it had to be done through payment or exchange.

He rolled his shoulders back, easing the tension that lived in his muscles. His earlier frustration with Talia lingered, and now with Miss Kellaway here...it would be no wonder if he concluded women were the cause of all the world's troubles.

Certainly they were the cause of *his*.

"You're correct about this." He tapped the book with a forefinger. "My mother ran off with another man. Younger than she, even. Horrified society. Ever since, people have thought of us as rather extraordinarily disreputable."

"Are you?"

"What do you think?"

"I don't know. I give little credence to gossip. It's not easily proved."

"You require proof, do you?"

"Of course. Mathematics, after all, is built on foundations of proving theorems, deductive reasoning. It's the basis of my work."

"All in this book?" He paged through it again with

disbelief. Scribbled equations, lists, and diagrams filled the pages, some smudged, some crossed out, others circled or designated with a star.

"Those are notes, ideas for papers," Lydia explained. "Some problems and puzzles I've devised for my own enjoyment."

Alexander laughed.

Lydia frowned. "What's so amusing?"

"Most women—indeed, the vast majority of women—engage in needlepoint or shopping for enjoyment," Alexander said. "You devise mathematical problems?"

"Sometimes, yes. May I have my book back, please?" Her frown deepened and she extended her hand. "You needn't find it all so funny, my lord. It can be very satisfying to craft a complex problem."

"I can tell you a thousand other ways to find satisfaction."

Her lips parted, shock flashing in her eyes as the insinuation struck her. He held out the notebook but didn't loosen his grip. Lydia grasped the other end of it and appeared to collect herself, her chin lifting.

"Well," she said, "I daresay *you* couldn't solve one of my problems."

He heard the challenge in her voice and responded as if she'd just asked him to place a thousand-pound bet. He let go of the notebook.

"Couldn't I?" he asked. "How certain are you of that?"

"Quite." She cradled the notebook to her chest.

"Certain enough to wager your locket?"

She wavered an instant before giving a swift nod. "Of course, though I'd insist upon establishing the parameters of a time frame."

The parameters of a time frame.

The woman was odd enough to be fascinating.

"If you can't solve my puzzle in five minutes' time," Lydia continued, "you must return my locket at once."

"And if you lose?"

"Then you may determine my debt."

He gave her a penetrating look that might have disconcerted any other woman. Although she bore his scrutiny without response, something about her demeanor seemed to deflect it, like tarnished silver repelling light.

"Lord Northwood," she prompted, her fingers so tight on the notebook that the edges crumpled.

What would move her? What would provoke a reaction? What would break through her rigid, colorless exterior?

"A kiss," he said.

Lydia's gaze jerked to his, shock flashing in the blue depths of her eyes like lightning behind glass.

"I... I beg your pardon?"

"Should you lose, you grant me the pleasure of one kiss."

A flush stained her cheeks. "My lord, that is a highly improper request."

"Not as improper as what I might have proposed." He almost grinned as her color deepened. "Still, it ought to give you proof of the theorem of my disrepute." He tipped his head toward the notebook. "You can add that to column four."

He knew he was being rude, but he'd spent the last two years holding himself, his words, even his thoughts, so tightly in check that something inside him loosened at the sight of this woman's blush. Something made him want to rattle her, to engage in a bit of bad behavior and see how she responded. Besides, wasn't bad behavior exactly what society expected of him?

"Do you accept?" he asked.

"Certainly not."

"All right, then. I'll tell John to take you home."

He started to the door, unsurprised when she said, "Wait!"

He turned.

"My lord, surely there is something—"

"That's my offer, Miss Kellaway."

Her hand trembled as she brushed a lock of hair from her forehead. The brown strands glinted with gold, making him wonder what her hair would look like unpinned.

Lydia gave a stiff nod, her color still high. "Very well."

"Then read me one of your puzzles."

"I beg your pardon?"

He nodded at her notebook. "Read one to me."

She looked as if she were unable to fathom the reason for his request. He wondered what she'd say if he told her he liked the sound of her voice, delicate and smooth but with a huskiness that slid right into his blood.

"Go on," he encouraged.

Lydia glanced at the notebook, uncertainty passing across her features. He'd thrown her off course. She hadn't anticipated such a turn of events when she'd planned this little encounter, and she didn't know how to react.

"All right, then." She cleared her throat and paged through the notebook. "On her way to a marketplace, a woman selling eggs passes through a garrison. She must pass three guards on the way."

She paused and glanced at him. A faint consternation lit in her eyes as their gazes met. Alexander gave her a nod of encouragement.

"To the first guard," Lydia continued, "she sells half

the number of eggs she has plus half an egg more. To the second guard, she sells half of what remains plus half an egg more. To the third guard, she sells half of the remainder plus half an egg more. When she arrives at the marketplace, she has thirty-six eggs. How many eggs did she have at the beginning?"

Alexander looked at her for a moment. He rose and went to the desk on the other side of the room. He rummaged through the top drawer and removed a pencil, then extended his hand for the notebook.

He smoothed a fresh sheet of paper onto the desk and read her neat penmanship.

An image of her flashed in his mind—Lydia Kellaway sitting at a desk like this one, her hair unbound, a slight crease between her brows as she worked on a problem she expected would confound people. Perhaps it was late at night and she wore nothing but a voluminous white shift, her body naked beneath the . . .

Alexander shook his head hard. He read the problem again and began doing some algebraic calculations on the paper.

Odd number, half an egg more, seventy-three eggs before she passed the last guard . . .

He did a few more calculations, half aware of something easing inside him, his persistent anger lessening. He realized that for the first time in a very long while, he was rather enjoying himself.

Alexander scribbled a number and circled it, then turned the paper toward Lydia.

"She had two hundred and ninety-five eggs," he said.

Lydia stepped forward to read his solution. A perplexing surge of both triumph and regret rose in Alexander when he lifted his gaze and saw the dismay on her face. She hadn't expected to lose.

No. She hadn't expected him to win.

"You are correct, Lord Northwood."

He tossed down the pencil and straightened.

Lydia stood watching him, wariness edging her expression. Her skin was milk-pale, her heart-shaped face dominated by large, thick-lashed eyes. Her cheekbones sloped down to a delicate jaw and full, well-shaped lips.

She might have been beautiful if it weren't for the tense, brittle way she carried herself, the compression of her lips and strain in her eyes. If it weren't for the ghostly pallor cast by her black dress, the severe cut of which could not obscure the combination of curves and sinuous lines that he suspected lay beneath.

His heart beat a little faster. He went to stand in front of her. Lydia swallowed, the white column of her throat rippling. If she was fearful, she didn't show it. If she was anticipatory, she didn't show that either. She merely looked at him, those thick eyelashes fanning her blue eyes like feathers.

He reached up and touched a loose lock of her hair, rubbing it between his fingers. Thick and soft. Pity she had to keep it so tightly bound. He lowered his hand, his knuckles brushing across her cheek. A visible tremble went through her.

"Well, then?" Alexander murmured.

He grasped her shoulders, her frame slender and delicate beneath his big hands. He stared down at her, the muscles of his back and shoulders tensing. The air thickened around them, between them, infusing with heat. His heart thudded with a too-quick tempo and a vague sense of unease—as if whatever strange power vibrated between him and Lydia Kellaway contained a sinister edge.

He inhaled the air surrounding her. No cloying scent of flowers or perfume. She smelled crisp, clean, like starched linens and sharpened pencils.

Her lips parted. Her posture remained stiff, her hands curled at her sides. Alexander wondered if she ever allowed herself to lose that self-contained tension. He continued to grip her shoulders, and for an instant they were both still. Then he slipped his hand to the side of Lydia's neck just above her collar.

She trembled when his thumb grazed her bare skin, brushing back and forth against her neck, the only movement within the utter stillness surrounding them. Color swept across her cheekbones, the same reddish hue as a breaking dawn. Her throat rippled with another swallow, but her expression didn't break; her posture didn't ease.

If anything, she grew more rigid, her spine stiffening. Alexander's thumb moved higher, to that secret, intimate hollow just behind her ear, his fingers curving to the back of her neck. His palm rested in the juncture of her neck and shoulder. Her skin was as smooth as percale; tendrils of her dark hair brushed the back of his hand.

Want. That surge pulsed through him, hot and heavy, the desire to strip her dull clothes from her body and touch her bare skin. As if in response, her pulse quickened like the beat of butterfly wings against his palm.

A soft thud sounded on the carpet as her notebook fell to the floor.

He lowered his mouth to hers. She didn't move forward, but neither did she back away. Her flush intensified, her chest rising as if she sought to draw air into her lungs. Multiple shades of blue infused her eyes. Her breath puffed against his lips. His hands tightened on her shoulders, the side of her neck.

The cracks within him began to smooth, the fissures closing. Instead he was filled with the urge to prolong this strange attraction, to savor the mystery of what would happen when their mouths finally met.

"Later."

His whisper broke through the tension like a pebble dropped into a pool of still, dark water. Lydia drew back, her lips parting.

"What?" Her question sounded strained, thin.

Alexander slipped his hand away from her neck, his fingers lingering against her warm skin.

"Later," he repeated. "I will require the payment of your debt at a later date."

Lydia stared at him before stepping away, her fists clenching. "My lord, this is unconscionable."

"Is it? We never determined payment would be immediate."

"It was implied."

"Ah, that's your mistake, Miss Kellaway. It's dangerous to assume your opponent holds the same unspoken ideas. Dangerous to assume anything, in fact."

He almost felt the anger flare through her blood. For an instant, she remained still, and then something settled over her expression—a resurgence of control, of composure.

She started for the door, her stride long and her back as stiff as metal. Just before she stepped out, she turned back to him.

"Though I prefer a more systematic approach to proving a theorem, my lord, I appreciate your assistance."

He watched her disappear into the shadows of the foyer; then he smiled faintly. He picked up her notebook from the floor and slipped it into his pocket.

Chapter Two

If the linear differential equation were to demonstrate the emotions of two lovers, the equation would be governed by the variables assigned to each lover: $a = Ar + bJ$ and $J = cR + dJ$.

Lydia stared at the page of equations on her lap, then put it aside and wrapped her arms around her waist.

The emotions of two lovers…

Emotions were one thing. Sensations were something else entirely. A memory tried to fight its way to the surface—the memory of how it had once felt to be wild, naked, and unfettered.

She remembered that it had felt astonishing. That all those years ago she'd felt free for the first time in her life—until she learned that the price for indulgence was one no person should have to pay.

…governed by the variables assigned to each lover…

She would never be able to assign a variable to the

sensations that still bloomed through her body after her encounter with Lord Northwood.

Every thump of her heart resounded through her, the slow unwinding of something sweet and rich. Her breasts felt full, heavy, her skin stretched tight over her body, her thighs tense with anticipation.

She closed her eyes. Shame trickled beneath her skin, smothering some of her lingering desire for a man she hardly knew. A man she could never have. Should never want.

Three, four, five: the first Pythagorean triple.

Her heartbeat slowed, her breath stabilizing into a smooth, even rhythm. The unnerving sensations of the previous night began to sink beneath the precise form of a perfectly constructed right triangle.

"You're up early."

Lydia's eyes flew open. Charlotte Boyd stood in the doorway of the study, her hand clenched around her cane. Her white skin was creased with only scant evidence of her age, and her fine features retained vestiges of youthful beauty.

"I couldn't sleep." Lydia pushed her hair away from her forehead, hoping her expression bore no evidence of her thoughts. "Mrs. Driscoll said breakfast will be ready in a half hour."

Mrs. Boyd settled into the opposite chair, her blue eyes sharp. "You're not still upset about the locket, are you?"

Lydia suppressed a rustle of irritation. "Of course I am."

"For heaven's sake, Lydia, I told you to forget the locket. It is a foolish, sentimental thing, and neither you nor Jane should attach any meaning to it except for its value. Mr. Havers gave us quite a bit for it."

"It belonged to my mother," Lydia said, stung by her grandmother's dismissive words. "Surely you understand why that's important to me. Why it's important to Jane. Papa would never have wanted it sold."

"Your parents would have been far more supportive of Jane attending a proper school than they would about keeping a piece of jewelry." Mrs. Boyd frowned. "I'd hope you would be as well."

"You didn't need to pawn the locket to send Jane to school," Lydia muttered.

"You know how expensive Queen's Bridge is, Lydia. We need to procure all possible funds for her initial enrollment. And we do not need an old locket."

I do.

Lydia's hands flexed, her chest tightening as she looked at her grandmother. Now was not the time to fight about Jane's schooling. Lydia had other matters on her mind. "I learned the locket was purchased by Alexander Hall. Lord Northwood."

Mrs. Boyd stared at her with pursed lips, a faintly perplexed expression in her eyes.

"Viscount Northwood? You must be joking."

"I'm not. He bought the locket from Mr. Havers. He said he thought it was interesting."

"You spoke to him?"

"I went to his house yesterday evening. I asked him to return the locket."

Mrs. Boyd's eyes widened. "You went to Lord North—"

Lydia held up a hand to stop the imminent scolding. "Before you chastise me, no one saw me, no one heard. I was careful."

"Really, Lydia, there's nothing *careful* about meeting

a man like that in private! Have you learned nothing over the years? What on earth is the matter with you?"

"You should have known I'd never let that locket go," Lydia said. "Especially after Papa died."

"You've not even looked at it in ages!" In her agitation, Mrs. Boyd rose and began to pace, leaning heavily on her cane. "Honestly, Lydia, now Lord Northwood knows we visited a pawnshop and that we... Oh heavens, what if this becomes known?"

"He won't tell anyone."

"How on earth do you know?"

She didn't. And yet, somehow, she did. "He's not a gossip. He would not deliberately besmirch another person's reputation."

"You're so certain of that?"

"Would *you* do such a thing?"

"Well, I—"

"Of course you wouldn't. Because you know the possible consequences. So does Lord Northwood."

She eyed her grandmother with wariness. Mrs. Boyd's lips pressed together, but she didn't appear inclined to argue. Perhaps because she knew Lydia spoke the truth.

Lydia shivered and rubbed her arms, pushing aside the threatening darkness of the past. Although she lived in dread of any form of gossip, she could not resist the desire to know more about Lord Northwood.

"Is it true?" she asked. "Did his mother run away with another man?"

"Oh, such unpleasant rumors." Mrs. Boyd waved a hand. "It's why most people still want nothing to do with them, even though they're quite wealthy. But yes, as far as I know, the countess, who everyone believed exceedingly proper, was caught having an affair with a young Russian soldier. She ran off with him, and the earl petitioned for a divorce. Quite rightly, I must admit. Northwood returned to London in the midst of the whole thing. Terrible, really, that he had to contend with the aftermath of such a scandal. They've never recovered, that family."

"What happened to the countess?"

"She's been banned from the estates, though I don't think she ever tried to return. I imagine she's still living in sin, probably in the wilds of Russia." Curiosity narrowed her grandmother's eyes. "So what was he like?"

"Lord Northwood?" Lydia searched for words. "Polite, I suppose. Implacable."

Angry.

Compelling. Handsome. Tempting...

Lydia cut short the thought. She must not think of any man in that way, least of all Lord Northwood.

"Hmm." Mrs. Boyd tapped her cane. "From what I understand, Lord Rushton's sons have something in their blood, Cossack ancestors and all. The earl has an ancient family that extends back to the Normans, I believe, pure English lineage there. Not from their mother, though. It accounts for their roughness, that Russian blood. Even before the scandal, Lady Chilton was concerned about the prospect of her daughter marrying Lord Northwood."

Lydia blinked. An unpleasant emotion rose in her chest, something greenish brown, the color of slimy grass beneath a layer of slush.

"Lady Chilton's daughter is going to marry Lord Northwood?" she asked.

"Not anymore, no. They were affianced at one time, but then after Lady Rushton behaved so abominably, Lord

Chilton called off the engagement. He refused to have his daughter associated with the Halls, despite their wealth."

Lydia let out her breath, realizing that her hand was trembling slightly.

"All those brothers, and the sister, too, have spent a great deal of time in Russia," Mrs. Boyd remarked. "It's no wonder they're not much in demand. I've heard they're a bit uncivilized."

Lydia bit her tongue to prevent a retort. Although she was loath to admit it, she thought her grandmother's commentary on Alexander Hall had some merit.

Despite his impeccable appearance, something feral and turbulent gleamed in the viscount's eyes—something that called to mind Cossack soldiers, silver sabers, and the wide plains of the Russian steppes.

Certainly Lord Northwood's behavior had been anything but proper, though Lydia wouldn't go quite so far as to deem it uncivilized.

Yet.

"Sophie!" Jane Kellaway whispered.

The maid turned from the stove, her eyes widening. "Miss Jane, you oughtn't be down 'ere! Your grandmother—"

"Is there another letter? Did the boy deliver one?"

Sophie sighed and pulled a creased paper from her apron pocket. She handed it to Jane and shooed her toward the door.

"If she finds out, I'll be sacked, you know," Sophie hissed.

"She won't find out."

Clutching the letter, Jane hurried upstairs to the schoolroom. Anticipation sparked in her as she broke the seal. She unfolded the paper, which contained a block of precise handwriting that reminded her of black ants marching in a row.

Dear Jane,

Thank you for your recent discourse on fairyflies, which I find a very lovely name for what—as per your description—is quite a disagreeable little insect.

It is, however, interesting that female fairyflies fly more adroitly than males. Perhaps therein lies a lesson for us all.

Enclosed is a riddle called an acrostic. I find myself a bit disgruntled that you solved the last one with such alacrity.

Sincerely,
C

Jane grinned. She'd been rather proud of herself for solving that last riddle so quickly. She slipped the letter behind the second page and studied the latest riddle.

My first is in tea but not in leaf.
My second is in teapot and also in teeth.
My third is in caddy but not in cozy.
My fourth is in cup but not in rosy.
My fifth is in herbal and also in health.
My sixth is in peppermint and always in wealth.
My last is in drink, so what can I be?
I'm there in a classroom. Do you listen to me?

"Jane, have you seen my notebook?"

Jane fumbled at the sound of Lydia's voice, tucking the letter under her arm. She glanced at her sister to see if she had noticed the clumsy movement, but Lydia was looking distractedly around the room.

"Your notebook? You've lost it?"

"I've misplaced it," Lydia corrected.

Jane glanced out the window to see if pigs were flying, because surely the universe had gone mad if Lydia Kellaway had misplaced her notebook. "When did you have it last?"

"Oh... last night." Lydia bit her lip, an odd distress appearing in her eyes. "Well, no need to worry now. I'm certain it will turn up." She gave Jane a smile. "Mrs. Driscoll says there will be Savoy biscuits for tea."

"That will be nice." Jane injected a note of enthusiasm into her voice. She liked Savoy biscuits, but tea was dreadfully boring—even more so since Papa was no longer here to play Chinese tangrams.

"Perhaps we can even persuade her to let us have some of her precious strawberry jam." Lydia smiled again, though the tension remained in her expression—likely because of the lost notebook, but also because it was just always *there*.

Jane remembered a lesson in geology during which they'd studied rock veins—lines of quartz or salt that split through the middle of a rock. She thought her sister contained a vein like that, except with Lydia it wasn't shimmering and shiny. The vein running through Lydia was made of something hard and brittle, a material that appeared on the surface only in unguarded moments.

Jane still didn't know its cause—never had—but she suspected it had something to do with their mother.

"Did you water the fern?" Lydia asked.

Still clutching the letter underneath her arm, Jane went

to the small bell glass on a table beside the window. A scraggly fern, the edges of the fronds turning brown, grew from a bed of rocks and soil. She removed the glass and poured a few drops of water around the base.

"It's a bit pitiful, isn't it?" Jane remarked, plucking a few dead fronds.

Lydia joined her to peer at the plant. "Perhaps we ought to move it somewhere else? Or does it need more air or a different soil? I must say, Jane, I've never quite understood how ferns are expected to thrive while encased in glass."

Jane pushed open the window a crack to let the breeze in. She and Lydia studied the fern for a few moments.

"I suspect we need to do more research," Lydia said. "I'm going to the library tomorrow, so I'll see if they have any books about fern cultivation. Now shall we continue our work on long division?"

Lydia began spreading a workbook and papers out on the table that dominated the tiny room first set aside for use as Jane's nursery and then as the schoolroom.

While Lydia was distracted, Jane picked up a book and tucked the letter between the pages, then pushed the book onto a shelf between two encyclopedias.

She was struck with the sudden urge to tell Lydia about the other letters that lay folded and hidden on the bookshelf, but the purposeful way her sister was moving about the room made her lose courage.

Besides, she didn't want to disobey the sender's instructions about secrecy—these anonymous letters and the accompanying riddles had been a welcome distraction after Papa's death, and she didn't want them to end.

She went to join Lydia at the table. "Is everything all right?"

"Of course. Why wouldn't it be?"

"You seem a bit upset."

"I'm not upset. Now come and sit. We'll review dividends and divisors."

Jane sat and picked up a pencil. "Is it Grandmama?"

"Jane, honestly, nothing is the matter."

But Jane saw the irritation rise in Lydia's eyes. She didn't know what Lydia wished their grandmother would or wouldn't do, but *she* wished everyone would stop being so stern and start to enjoy things a bit more.

Every day it was the same—breakfast, lessons, lunch, an outing, tea. And it wasn't as if the outings were anywhere terribly interesting, only to the park or library or shops.

"Jane."

Jane glanced up. "Sorry. I wasn't paying attention."

"Do you remember what a remainder is?"

"A number left over."

"Good. This problem will have a remainder, but start with the whole number, then multiply it by the divisor. See, what's so interesting about long division is that you're able to do division, multiplication, and subtraction all in the same equation."

"Lyddie?"

"Hmm?"

"Is it wrong to keep a secret?"

Lydia looked almost startled. "A secret? What kind of secret?"

"Oh, nothing that would hurt anybody. Just... you know. A secret. Something no one else knows. Like that you've got a bag of bull's-eyes tucked beneath your bed."

"Well, I... I suppose it depends on what the secret is. But if it doesn't hurt anybody to keep it, then no. I don't think it's wrong." Lydia reached out and pushed a lock of hair from Jane's forehead. "Do you have sweets stored away somewhere?"

"No." Jane gave her sister a winning smile. "If I did, I'd share them with you."

"Lovely." Lydia gave Jane's cheek a gentle pinch. "But you'd still have to figure out how to share them equally. And for that, you need to learn how to divide."

Jane made a face of mock irritation before turning her concentration to the problem. Although she liked mathematics, the way her sister sometimes talked, one would think the world revolved around numbers.

Jane supposed in some ways it probably did, though she had the sense the world was driven by something far more mysterious than sums.

Something like riddles, conundrums, puzzles.

Secrets.

Chapter Three

The locket swung back and forth, sunlight captured in the silver casing. Alexander lifted the chain to study the engraving. Edging his thumbnail into the seam, he opened the little compartment.

The miniature image of a woman with sparrow-brown hair stared back at him, the hint of laughter that curved her lips mitigating the imperiousness of her pose. The other side of the locket's casing bore a picture of a man, his features narrow and strong, a neat beard covering his jaw and a serious expression in his eyes.

Alexander had a sudden image of Lydia Kellaway wearing this locket around her neck, enclosing it in her hand every so often as she thought of her beloved parents.

Not an emotion he would ever have extended to his own parents—his iron-fisted father, his cold-as-glass mother, who'd shocked them all with her shameful affair.

Sometimes Alexander still couldn't believe it. The Countess of Rushton, imperious to a fault with her dulcet tones and porcelain skin, debasing herself with a common soldier.

At least she'd had the sense to run off, Alexander thought. Otherwise he'd have thrown her out himself after the affair came to light.

A grunt made him look up. His twenty-nine-year-old brother Sebastian slumped into a chair, his eyes heavy lidded and his jaw unshaven. He dragged a hand through his messy hair and yawned.

"Late night?" Alexander asked, his voice tight.

Sebastian shrugged, staring at the table as if he expected breakfast to appear. He yawned again and headed to the sideboard and the coffeepot.

"Where did you go?" Alexander asked.

"Concert at the Eagle Tavern. Their pianist canceled, so they asked me to fill in. Thought I'd sleep here so's not to disturb Talia or the old bird."

"You thought performing at the Eagle Tavern was a good idea?"

Sebastian groaned and took a swallow of coffee. "It's a respectable enough place. Besides, no one cares, Alex."

"I do."

"You're the only one, then."

Frustration tightened Alexander's chest. For all his efforts following their parents' divorce, his siblings had failed to do a single thing to help restore the family's reputation. Sebastian cared nothing for what others thought, and if Talia had the choice, she would seclude herself at their country estate and never visit London.

Alexander, on the other hand, lived within the thick of it—attending social events, clubs, and business meetings as if nothing had gone wrong, as if their mother had not left them in disgrace. As if their deep association with Russia were not an increasing burden.

"I sent word to Father yesterday that I wish to speak with him about the management of the Floreston estate," he told Sebastian. "There's been some discrepancy between income and expenditure, and I've several tenant issues with which to contend."

"If you wish to speak with Lord Rushton, I suggest you call upon him." Sebastian scrubbed a hand over his face. "He can be found at Forty-five King Street, Piccadilly, in the event you've forgotten. Likely he's spending the morning in his greenhouse."

"And Talia? What are her plans for the day?"

"I think she's got a meeting with the Ragged School Union." Sebastian eyed him over the rim of his cup. "Told me yesterday you were haranguing her about marriage again."

"I was not haranguing her. She needs to understand that a good marriage will help not only her, but also the family. Both financially and socially."

"She'd be more civil if you let her alone," Sebastian said. "Moreover, you'll do better to worry about your own state of matrimony rather than Talia's."

Alexander scowled. "You think I've got time to find a suitable wife?"

"All you need do is find yourself a sweet, empty-headed young chit, Alex. God knows there are plenty. Better still if the girl's father has found himself with pockets to let. You needn't do much except wed her and bed her." Sebastian arched a mocking eyebrow. "Neither of which ought to take you much time."

"Blackguard," Alexander muttered. "It wouldn't take

much time because a young chit would faint with shock before I'd even got started."

Sebastian grinned. "You needn't pay a wife regular visits, so long as she produces a son. Then Mrs. Arnott will be happy to keep you entertained. Word is she favors you for more than just your money."

Alexander sighed. His infrequent patronage of the brothel was due to the need for discretion and his lack of interest in the complications of an affair.

Not to mention his distaste for marriage to a "sweet, empty-headed young chit"—no matter how beneficial such a match would be to the earldom. The very idea brought back the ugliness of his experience with Lord Chilton and his daughter.

"Wed and bed, Alex. All you need to do."

Alexander shook his head and left the dining room, somewhat gratified at restoring his brother's good humor—if one could call it that.

Despite their different temperaments, of his three brothers, Alexander had always been closest to Sebastian. Partly because they couldn't compete with the bond their twin brothers shared, but also because Alexander always secretly appreciated Sebastian's relaxed, devil-may-care approach to life.

An approach Alexander had never been able to cultivate.

And as much as they'd sparred over Sebastian's cavalier attitude about the scandal, Alexander couldn't help the sting of envy he felt. Sebastian did what he pleased, everyone else be damned.

He wasn't the one who had been forced to sacrifice all his plans. *He* wasn't the one who'd had to return to London to contend with the detritus of their mother's abandonment and the subsequent divorce. *He* wasn't the one who'd borne the humiliation of a broken engagement to a society debutante.

None of his brothers were.

Alexander rubbed the back of his neck to ease the persistent tension caused by the weight of responsibility. After he had finished dressing, he had picked up Lydia Kellaway's notebook from where he'd left it on a table.

She was no sweet, uninspiring daughter of a rustic peer. If her writings were anything to judge by, she knew far more about prime numbers and differential equations than fashion and etiquette.

Perhaps that alone was the reason Alexander hadn't met her before now. Though her father, Sir Henry Kellaway, had been a scholar of considerable repute in Chinese history and literature, he'd always been something of a recluse.

Had that been because of Lydia?

Alexander frowned at the thought. He ordered the carriage brought around, then gave the driver an East Street address that was written inside the front cover of the notebook.

As he rode, he paged through the notebook. There appeared to be no organization to the scribbles—just pages and pages of algebraic equations and geometrical diagrams.

This happens when r is the greatest of the solutions of $a + ar = b + \beta r$, $a + ar = c + \gamma r$, *&c. Let* $(k - a) : (a - \kappa)$, *which we call* ρ, *be the greatest in the set—*

Alexander gave a short laugh. Odd, he'd called her? Miss Kellaway was more than *odd* if her brain not only comprehended such convolutions, but also actually produced them.

A few words on the following page caught his eye.

Variables as the measure of love.

The word *love* was heavily underlined. This was followed by a series of equations and notes that made little sense to Alexander, aside from his recognizing the structure of differential equations and scrawled references to the *Iliad, Romeo and Juliet,* Petrarch.

He closed the notebook, not having any idea what to make of it. But rather wishing he did.

A short while later, Alexander descended the carriage across from a modest brick town house. A newspaper boy, his trousers tied with a length of rope, paced in front of an iron fence. At the corner, a fruit seller set up her stand and shooed away a dog pawing for scraps.

The door of the town house opened, and a woman emerged, her arms laden with at least half a dozen books. No, not *a* woman. Lydia Kellaway. In a black dress, her torso as rigid as a tree branch above the billow of her skirts.

Yet despite her clothes, her body appeared both slender and quite deliciously rounded, intensifying Alexander's conviction that an unclad Lydia Kellaway would be lush, soft, and as tempting as sin.

He crossed the street, his heart slamming against his ribs with every step.

A brown-haired girl, perhaps ten or eleven and as neat as a pin in a starched pinafore, appeared at Lydia's side to hold the door open.

"Jane, please, could you take—" Lydia's gaze slid to Alexander as he approached. She straightened, fumbling with her books, her lips parting with surprise.

"Miss Kellaway."

"Lord Northwood."

God. Even the sound of her voice made his blood hot. Lyrical, with just the slightest bit of a rasp, like a good brandy that slid rich and warm down one's throat. He wanted to hear the sound of his Christian name in her voice, wanted it to melt against his skin.

"May I?" He stepped forward to take the books from her. His fingers brushed against her arms, her gloved hands. His head filled with the scent of the air surrounding her.

"Thank you." Lydia lifted a hand to straighten her crooked hat. Exertion flushed her pale skin, and a few locks of dark-brown hair spilled around her neck and forehead.

She placed a hand on the girl's shoulder and bent to whisper in her ear. The girl shot a curious look at Alexander before going back into the house. He looked after her with a slight frown.

"My sister," Lydia explained. "You'll forgive me for sending her away. I don't wish her to know of recent... events."

"Events?"

"Yes, the... Lord Northwood, please come inside." She preceded him into the drawing room.

As he unloaded the books onto a table, Alexander let his gaze sweep across the room, the worn brocade sofa and chairs, the peeling wallpaper, the faded Chinese scrolls. Not a speck of dust appeared on any surface, but the furnishings bore the evidence of age and wear.

"I intended to contact you today, my lord." Lydia turned beside the window, tugging off her gloves. "Have you got my notebook? I'm afraid I left it the other night."

Alexander lifted his gaze from her slender white hands and tapered fingers. He slipped the notebook from his pocket. Relief flashed across Lydia's face as she started forward.

"Oh, thank you. I've got so many notes written there that if I were to—" She stopped a short distance from him as she realized he wasn't extending the book to her.

A frown creased her forehead, and she gave an irritated huff. "Please don't tell me you're going to make an entirely improper request before you give me my notebook back."

"Hmm. Hadn't planned to, but it's an intriguing thought."

"Lord Northwood!"

Alexander grinned and handed her the book. Their hands touched as she took it. She pulled her arm back, a faint flush coloring her cheeks.

Her reaction wasn't coy. He knew that. It was as if she simply had no idea what to do with him, and her lack of knowledge caused her embarrassment.

Lydia looked at the front of his shirt, her white teeth biting down on her lower lip. He took the opportunity to study her in the light streaming through the window, noticing details he hadn't the other night.

The smooth arch of her eyebrows, the faint freckles sprinkled over the bridge of her nose, the delicious fullness of her lips—no, that he *had* noticed when he'd been close enough to feel her breath. But now he could see the color of her bare, unpainted lips, like the blush of an apricot. She'd taste that way, too, all sweet and juicy and pink.

Hell.

Alexander took a step back, fighting to rein in his arousal. He forced himself not to skim the rest of Lydia Kellaway's body, to rake with his gaze the curves of her full breasts, the slope of her waist, her round hips…

Stop.

For no other reason than to stop looking at her, Alexander turned his attention to the books he'd dumped on the table. For a man who prided himself on his self-control, he was reacting like a lusty greenhorn.

As he forced aside his reactions, his vision focused on the title of the topmost book. *Introductio in analysin infinitorum.* He pulled the books from the stack and glanced at the other titles. *The Mathematical Analysis of Logic. Thoughts on the Study of Mathematics as Part of a Liberal Education.*

Alexander restacked the books before lifting his head. She was watching him, her thick-lashed eyes wary, her lower lip still caught between her teeth.

"Do you read anything else besides texts on mathematics?" he asked.

"The occasional magazine or book, yes."

"Petrarch?"

She blinked. "I beg your pardon?"

"You read Petrarch, don't you? Shakespeare? The *Iliad*?"

"How did you—" She drew back, her lips parting on a shocked gasp. "You read my notebook?"

"Hardly. If I'd *read* your notebook, that would imply I understood it. Which I did not. I did, however, notice your writing about romances."

"Lord Northwood, you have violated my privacy!"

"Mmm. Like you did mine when you invaded my house at midnight? Or when you hunted up gossip about me? Or when you skulked about unlawfully procuring my name from Havers's salesbook?"

"Well, I—" Twin circles of pink stained her cheeks,

and Alexander wondered if any other woman in the world blushed as much as Miss Lydia Kellaway.

She cleared her throat and fumbled with a brooch pinned to her neckline. "That is to say, I didn't intend—"

"In any case," Alexander said, "I fail to see what's so private about scribbling a few names and equations. Now, if you'd written erotic poems or—"

"Lord Northwood." Despite her intensely pink complexion, she lifted her head and looked him in the eye. "I happen to believe there is a mathematical basis for romantic relationships."

He stared at her. He couldn't have been more surprised if she'd told him she actually *did* write erotic poems—just in a different notebook.

"A mathematical basis for relationships?" he repeated, not understanding at all.

"Yes. A pattern of behavior. I am using historical examples such as Romeo and Juliet, Tristan and Isolde, Helen and Paris, etcetera, to test my theories and establish proofs."

She was serious. She stood there clutching her infernal notebook, her blue eyes blinking without guile.

"Proofs of... of *what*?" Alexander asked.

"Patterns of attraction and rejection. For example, although Laura was a married woman who spurned Petrarch's advances, he continued to pursue her through his sonnets. I believe I can describe their relationship by assigning variables to their emotions and creating differential equations."

Alexander was dumbfounded. The woman was trying to quantify love.

"Lydia, I thought you were going to—"

Both Alexander and Lydia turned as an elderly woman

entered, her steps accompanied by the click of an ivory-handled cane. She stopped.

"Grandmama, this is Viscount Northwood." A hint of dismay colored Lydia's voice. "Lord Northwood, my grandmother, Mrs. Charlotte Boyd."

"Mrs. Boyd." He nodded in greeting, suppressing his annoyance at the interruption. How in the name of heaven did one quantify love? "A pleasure."

"Lord Northwood." Mrs. Boyd looked at Lydia and back to him again. Something calculating sharpened her assessment. "Lydia has confessed she . . . disturbed you at your home."

She did, indeed.

"I do apologize for her impertinence," Mrs. Boyd added.

"No need, Mrs. Boyd. Miss Kellaway and I have come to an agreement." He cast a quick glance toward Lydia before returning his attention to Mrs. Boyd.

"Have you?" The woman's gaze narrowed. "Might I inquire what kind of agreement?"

"It's nothing, really," Lydia broke in. "I'm working on some accounting for Lord Northwood in exchange for the locket."

Alexander studied the older woman to see if she saw through the lie, but rather than appearing suspicious, Mrs. Boyd seemed oddly pleased.

"Well, I don't think it's quite proper for a woman to work on accounting," she admitted, "but I do know that Lydia will be most accurate and thorough. She's always had a head for numbers, my lord."

"So I've discovered." He glanced at Lydia. "I'd best be on my way. I'm expected at the Society of Arts offices within the hour."

As he returned to the carriage, Sebastian's words echoed through his head.

Find yourself a sweet, empty-headed young chit.

Alexander wouldn't call Lydia Kellaway sweet. She was sharp and peppery, not sweet. As for empty-headed... he almost laughed. If anything, that woman's head was crammed with far too many thoughts and suppositions. And young? She must be nearing thirty.

He stared out the window. No. Miss Kellaway was too forthright, too opinionated, too prickly. Not to mention downright odd. She did not come from a prominent family. Society would think it a strange match. It wasn't what people would expect of him.

Yet he hadn't been as intrigued by a woman in ages, if ever. He didn't understand all she was about, but he was determined to try.

He made her blush. Blush! How many years had it been since she—Lydia Kellaway, mathematical prodigy who at eight years of age studied differential and integral calculus—had blushed? At least, in a way that elicited a tingle of pleasure and the urge to smile.

And when Lord Northwood looked at her, her heart fluttered like petals in a breeze.

She wondered what he thought when he looked at her. Did he like what he saw? The heated look in his eyes suggested he did, but he was far more experienced in such matters than she was, so perhaps it was all a game to him.

Or perhaps not.

She pressed her hands to her cheeks, even now feeling them warm with color. Somewhere deep inside, in a place she rarely allowed herself to venture, Lydia remembered what carnal desire had felt like. She remembered the heating of her blood, the tension swirling in her belly.

But this... the lightness, the surge beneath her heart... this was all new. Welcome. Lovely.

Dangerous.

Lydia closed her eyes, hating the whispered warning, the reminder that not even in her imagination should she allow herself to acknowledge, let alone enjoy, the sensations Lord Northwood aroused.

"Lydia."

Lydia's eyes flew open at the sound of her grandmother's voice. She sat up, folding her arms across her breasts. Shame clawed through her, even though she had done nothing wrong.

"Would you please join me in the drawing room?" Mrs. Boyd asked. "I'd like to speak with you."

"About what?"

"I've several matters I wish to discuss before my meeting at the bank tomorrow morning. Ten minutes, please."

She turned and left, her statement freezing any memory of Lord Northwood from Lydia's mind. She smoothed the wrinkles from her dress, then scraped her hair away from her face and neck, ensuring any loose tendrils were tightly contained by a ribbon.

Apprehension rippled through her as she went to the drawing room. Her grandmother stood beside the fire, her arms crossed.

"Please," Lydia said. "What is this about?"

Mrs. Boyd tapped her fingers against her arms. "How many times have you seen Lord Northwood?"

"Seen him? Twice, I think. Why?"

"You're to see him more often, I imagine, if you're

working on his books," Mrs. Boyd continued. "My friend Mrs. Keene claims he's been intent on restoring honor to his family. It's one reason he's working so hard with the Society of Arts and the organization of the educational exhibition. He's vice president of the Society and director of the exhibition. He's also been attempting to arrange a suitable marriage for his sister."

Ah. Likely that had something to do with why the young woman had been so upset the other night.

"I'm certain he'll prove successful," Lydia said. She couldn't imagine Northwood being unsuccessful at anything.

"However," Mrs. Boyd continued, "word is that he's not expressed interest in finding a wife for himself."

"And?"

"Odd, don't you think? He's the one who must produce an heir, after all. Though I suspect he knows that no high-ranking family wants their daughter wed to him, not after his mother's deplorable behavior. And especially not after Lord Chilton insisted his daughter break off her engagement to him."

Tension crawled up Lydia's spine. "What are you implying?"

"I'm implying nothing, Lydia," Mrs. Boyd replied. "I'm merely giving you the facts about the man, considering you took it upon yourself to visit him *unescorted*. I should hope that Jane's education means as much to you as that foolish locket does."

Lydia blinked at the sudden shift in topic.

"Of course," she said. "Jane and her education mean everything to me. You know that." The tension tightened around the base of her skull. "Why would you think otherwise?"

"I know you care about her, Lydia. And you've—"

"*Care* about her?" Good Lord. Did her grandmother not know that she loved Jane more with every breath, every heartbeat?

"You have done well with her," Mrs. Boyd continued. "She's still a bit careless, but for the most part she is a well-behaved, respectful girl. However, she is ready for a different type of schooling. The kind that will secure her a place in polite society."

"She's doing beautifully under my tutelage. We've started reading the *Odyssey*; we're studying the countries of the empire; she's learning fractions and basic algebra—"

"Lydia, Jane requires guidance from teachers who possess far more intuitive social grace than you do. She must learn proper etiquette if she is to marry well."

"She's not yet twelve," Lydia protested. "I didn't give etiquette or, heaven forbid, marriage a thought until I went to boarding school."

"Perhaps you should have started earlier." Her grandmother paused; then her voice sounded like the clip of scissors. "The discipline might have done you good."

Lydia flinched, her hand clenching around the back of a chair.

The cosine of theta plus gamma equals the cosine of theta times the cosine of gamma plus the sine of theta times the sine of gamma.

"I know we've talked about her attending Queen's Bridge, but even with the funds from the locket, it's too expensive..." Lydia's voice faded. Something in her grandmother's expression caused a flutter of panic.

"I have discussed the matter with Mrs. Keene, whose

opinion I implicitly trust," Mrs. Boyd said. "Mrs. Keene has a widowed aunt who resides in Paris, a baroness whose late husband left her with both a fortune and his good name. Mrs. Keene has corresponded with Lady Montague about a girls' school she recently opened in the Quartier St. Germain."

"No."

Mrs. Boyd's mouth compressed. "I am not asking your opinion, Lydia."

"You cannot send Jane all the way to France for her education." The flutter of panic began to grow, beating hard against her chest. "You can't do this to her."

You can't do this to me.

"I am not doing this to her, Lydia," her grandmother replied. "I am doing it *for* her."

"No. It's too far. She won't—"

"Heavens, Lydia, it is Paris, not the wilds of Africa," Mrs. Boyd interrupted. "As you pointed out, we cannot afford to send her to any of the better London schools, least of all Queen's Bridge. Lady Montague, however, owing to my friendship with Mrs. Keene as well as her wish to have a strong initial enrollment, has very kindly offered to provide Jane with a scholarship."

"And you accepted?"

"I intend to, yes." Mrs. Boyd sighed, her hand moving to fuss with her lace cuffs. "Lydia, I don't wish to see Jane leave us either. But unless we can find a way to send her to a school in London—an exclusive school, mind you, one that will give her the education we cannot—I have no other choice."

She lifted her head. For a long moment, they looked at each other. Lydia's heart constricted, shrank. A thousand years seemed to fill the space between them, overflowing with regret and the pain of loss.

She wished her mother were here. Not the woman of the haunted, twisted mind, but the mother she remembered before the descent of darkness. The Theodora Kellaway of laughter and calm, of soft hands and long hair as thick and shiny as wheat.

And she wished her father were here. She needed his calm, serious approach, his perspective. Despite everything, he'd only ever wanted the best for both her and Jane.

"You still want to punish me, don't you?" The question broke from her lips, coarse and crumbled.

"This is not about you," her grandmother said. "This is about Jane."

"It is about me! You'll never let me forget what happened when you sent *me* away, will you?"

"Lydia!" Mrs. Boyd thumped her cane on the floor. "How dare you suggest this is in any way related to your folly? Lady Montague's school is new, but it will certainly provide Jane with a place that is both highly instructive and *properly* supervised."

Lydia stared at her. Mrs. Boyd's mouth clamped shut as she appeared to realize what she'd said. Lydia trembled with a flare of outrage.

"No." Her fists clenched, her eyes stinging with hot, angry tears.

"Lydia—"

"No. I won't let you do this. I will not let you take Jane from me!"

Lydia crossed the room and slammed the door behind her. She drew in a long breath, her fingers tightening on her skirt, her blood racing through her veins.

The clock in the foyer ticked. Shadows swept across the stairs, reflected in the mirror, an ominous blend of dark and light.

Anger and hurt churned through Lydia, dredging up remnants of shame. She yanked open the front door. Once outside, she walked faster and faster until she was running, the night air stinging her face. She ran until her lungs ached, and then she slowed, gasping, pulling her arms around her body to hold in the hurt and block out the cold.

She sank onto the steps of a darkened town house, fighting to catch her breath and calm her racing heart.

Memories surfaced, but she ruthlessly shoved the images away, not wanting to see her mother's emaciated frame, her father's sallow, despairing expression, her grandmother's fury.

Not wanting to see a pair of cold green eyes that could still cut her like glass.

She shuddered. The chill spread to the center of her heart.

After what seemed a very long time, she lifted her head from her knees. A layer of fog coated the sky, suffocating the moon and the light of the stars.

She rose and walked to Dorset Street. Several black cabriolets waited at a stand for hire.

A driver looked at her with mild curiosity before giving a short nod at her request. He ushered her into the cab and slammed the door shut.

Lydia closed her eyes as the cab began moving toward Oxford Street.

If p is a prime number, then for any integer a, $a^p - a$ *will be evenly divisible by p.*

The derivative of uv equals u derivative v plus derivative u times v.

"Twelve Mount Street, miss."

Lydia opened her eyes. Light glowed in several windows of the brick town house. She was foolish to come here again. She knew that, and yet she asked the driver to wait, then approached the door and rang. No response. Her heart clenched. She rang again.

The door opened to reveal a straight-backed footman. "Yes?"

"Lord Northwood, please. I am Lydia Kellaway."

"One moment." He stepped aside to allow her to enter, then disappeared soundlessly up the stairs.

After a moment, a square of light appeared from the upper floor, and Lord Northwood strode toward her, each step so certain he appeared to be securing the ground beneath his feet. His lack of hesitation, the strength that radiated from him, made Lydia ache with the wish to possess such assurance.

"Miss Kellaway?" He frowned, glancing through the half-open door at the cab. "Are you all right?"

"I...I don't have any—"

"Come inside. I'll take care of it." He gestured to the footman to pay the cab fee before turning back to Lydia. "What are you doing here?"

"I've come..." Lydia took a breath and lifted her head to meet his gaze. "I've come to settle my debt."

Did she feel the same?

She didn't look the same. She was older, of course, the edges of her face harder, the curiosity, the anticipation extinguished from her eyes, from her movements. Replaced with tight composure.

Only once since Joseph had returned to London did

he notice her falter—just after her father's funeral when she'd been standing outside the church with the girl, who'd turned to wrap her arms around Lydia's waist and sob.

Then Lydia had visibly struggled with her own tears. A crack in her self-possession.

Before the girl had pulled away from her, a mask of calm, of reassurance, had descended over Lydia's face.

The girl. Jane. A plain name, though she was pretty enough. She was intelligent, too, if her letters were anything to judge by. However, he required more time to probe the actual depths of her mind.

"Sir? We're here." The cabdriver was peering at him.

He nodded, then flicked his hand to indicate the driver should return to his seat. "Back to Bethnal Green."

As the cab rattled away, he watched Lydia Kellaway disappear into the Mount Street town house, the tall silhouette of a man at her side.

Joseph chuckled. She might be older, but apparently her needs were the same. She was rising above her station, though, if the neighborhood was anything to judge by.

Or was she?

He knew the Kellaways had been in financial straits, even before Sir Henry's death. What if Lydia had found a way to earn money using the talents of her body rather than her mind?

Fancy town houses here on Mount Street. Belonging to wealthy people. He would soon find out who lived at number twelve.

Chapter Four

After ordering tea, Alexander watched as Lydia sank onto the sofa in the drawing room. Her hands trembled as she lifted them to smooth back her disheveled hair, confined only by a ribbon at the back of her neck. Red blotches marred her smooth skin, and puffy circles ringed her eyes. She stared at the floor, her chest hitching with every breath.

A surge of something fierce and protective rose in Alexander. He stood behind a chair, his grip tight on the polished wood.

He wanted to pull Lydia hard into his arms, to feel her slacken against him, to fix whatever it was that caused her such distress. The realization, the intensity of the feeling, startled him. He dragged a hand over his hair, unable to stop looking at her.

"Miss Kellaway." He forced his voice to remain steady, not wanting to frighten her away with the urgency of his need to know. "Has someone harmed you?"

She laughed, a bleak, harsh sound. "Not in the way you think."

"You can tell me the truth."

"That is the truth."

"You're certain."

"Yes." She nodded, her fingers twisting and untwisting the folds of her skirt. "I'm not... It's not what you imagine."

"Then what is it?"

"A personal issue, a... It doesn't matter."

"It does to me."

"Does it?" She lifted her head, her blue eyes dark with anger and frustration. "Don't you merely want the payment of my debt? That's why I'm here. Take it. Kiss me."

Alexander shook his head. "Not like this."

"There was no condition attached to your request."

"There is now."

A knock at the door preceded the footman's entry with a tea tray. Alexander nodded his thanks as Giles turned to leave. He waited until the door had closed before reaching to pour the tea, adding sugar to one cup before pressing it into Lydia's hands.

"What condition?" she asked.

"I will not kiss you when you are in evident distress. Aside from the fact that such an act would be misguided, if kissing me were to intensify your misery... well, I don't believe my pride could withstand such a blow."

The shadow of a smile curved her lips. "Your pride appears quite capable of withstanding much worse, my lord."

"Perhaps. Though I've no intention of finding that out." His eyebrows drew together as he watched her take a sip of tea. Her lips closed around the thin edge of the cup, her throat rippling.

Alexander waited an interminable few minutes for her to further compose herself. Then he asked again, "What happened?"

Her eyes darkened to the color of lapis lazuli. She shook her head, tendrils of thick hair moving against her neck. When she spoke, sorrow weighted her voice.

"I sometimes feel . . . very powerless."

Alexander had no idea how to respond to that simple statement. On the one hand, it made no sense coming from a woman with as brilliant, as perceptive, a mind as hers. On the other hand, she spent her time devising equations about love, a task Alexander knew would lead nowhere.

Silence stretched, flexed between them like a living entity.

He cleared his throat, wishing for a fleeting instant that Sebastian were here. Sebastian would know what to say. His brother possessed a natural ability to make women feel safe, protected. They confided in him, trusted him. Not like Alexander, whose reputation for remoteness had some basis in fact, especially after the catastrophe of his failed engagement.

Lydia's mouth twisted as she set her cup on the tray. "But that's neither here nor there, is it?"

"What sort of power do you seek?"

"None that I might obtain, so why bother naming it?"

He studied her, the bend of her neck, the way her eyelashes made shadows on her cheekbones. "I know you possess a fine, sharp mind. That your aptitude for numbers has earned you respect among the highest academic echelons."

"How did you come by such knowledge?"

"I asked about you. Your name carries respect, Miss Kellaway."

"My name carries curiosity, my lord. Like that of a South American tapir or a circus performer."

He shook his head. "You're wrong."

"Am I?" She lifted a hand to smooth her hair away from her forehead. "I don't mean to sound as if I pity myself. Or as if I don't value my own mind. I merely ask that you don't attempt to convince me that my abilities endow me with authority over anything except equations. They don't. I learned that long ago."

"Yet mathematicians and university professors consult you about their work."

"Yes. Exactly that. The work. Our discourse is purely academic." Something appeared to harden within her as she met his gaze again. "My point, Lord Northwood, is that my mathematical skill is quite a distinct entity from the rest of my existence. Command over one area of life does not translate to another."

"It can."

"Not in my case. I feel a great sense of power in solving equations, in proving theorems. But it ends within the restricted world of mathematics."

Alexander let out a breath. "I can't admit to being the most productive student. However, even I know that mathematics is hardly a restricted world. In school I learned about the mathematical formulas applied to Renaissance art. There are connections between music and mathematics I couldn't begin to understand. Managing an estate the size of my father's requires a constant balancing of income versus expenditure, of figuring rent and—"

Lydia held up a hand. "That's very well and good, my lord, but please understand that my experience bears out quite differently. In my world, mathematics is indeed restricted."

Like you.

The two words punched through his head. He stood, restless anger stirring in his gut, and began pacing.

"What do you want, Miss Kellaway?"

"I don't...I didn't have anywhere else to go. I thought of—"

"No." The word came out hard, abrupt. He spun to look at her, his hands clenching at his sides. "What do you want?"

"From you?"

"For you."

"I don't understand."

"What do you want? What would help you obtain this elusive sense of power?"

She blinked. Her expression seemed to close off, as if she sought to suppress a myriad of surfacing thoughts. "I don't know."

"You do know. What is it?"

"Sir, I am not a fool. I know my place, my position. Dreaming of what can never be is illogical and senseless."

"What makes you think it can never be?"

Amusement shone in her eyes, faint and yet sparkling with the promise of brilliance. If Lydia Kellaway ever allowed herself to experience full, unrestrained laughter, it would be a thing of beauty.

"You're a romantic, are you, Lord Northwood?" she asked. "Believing things might happen merely because we wish them so."

"Or because we make them happen."

"Easy enough for you to say."

"What does that mean?"

"Even before we... before I made your acquaintance, I'd heard about you. Though I meant it when I said I dislike gossip, I can still determine some elements of truth."

"And what is the truth about me, Miss Kellaway?"

"That you've sought for two years to restore your family's reputation in a very public and unapologetic manner." She glanced down at her cup and quietly added, "Unlike your father. Your work with the Society of Arts, trade regulations, numerous charities, lectures, clubs, and now an international exhibition... it all speaks to your philosophy of generating change."

She looked resigned, as if the condensed report of his efforts had somehow dispirited her. As if she spoke of something she wanted and yet would never possess. Alexander began to pace again, aware of a nagging discomfort.

"That is all true enough," he finally allowed. "Though I've had little choice in the matter. If I didn't do something, no one would."

"Oh, you had a choice, Lord Northwood. We always have a choice."

"No. Given the current difficulties with Russia, my family's ties to the country are increasingly maligned. What choice do I have in that?"

"You've a choice in how you respond to such intolerance."

Alexander turned his head to look at her, struck again by the sense that Lydia Kellaway's composure was something both durable and imperfect, like a solid Greek amphora marked with cracks and flaws.

"What was your choice?" he asked.

For an instant, she didn't speak, though some fleeting, raw emotion passed across her features.

"Not one I care to elucidate." She took another sip of tea and stood, smoothing the wrinkles from her skirt. "I do apologize for intruding upon you yet again. It was reckless and very imprudent."

"I think you ought to be reckless and imprudent more often, Miss Kellaway."

"Then your thoughts are extremely mistaken."

"Are they?"

"Yes." Her jaw tightened with irritation, her chin lifting. "I'm no longer a young woman, my lord. My days of recklessness are long past."

"In all honesty, I find it difficult to imagine you ever had days of recklessness."

"Good." She started toward the door.

"Tell me what you want, Miss Kellaway."

She stopped. Her back stiffened, her shoulders drawing back. "I will not have this discussion."

"Tell me what you want and you can have the locket back."

She spun around, her skin reddening with anger. "How dare you manipulate me!"

"It's a fair trade."

"It is not. No trade is fair when the winner also loses."

"What does that mean?"

"It means you haven't a care for either of the things being exchanged," Lydia said. "The locket means nothing to you and everything to me. My wishes mean nothing to you and everything to me. So I tell you what you want to hear and win the locket back, but I've still lost, haven't I? You've still gotten what you want."

"Forget the locket, then. Just tell me."

"Why do you want to know?"

"Because I refuse to believe the answer is *nothing*."

"You want to know what I want? What I can never have?" She stalked toward him, her body rigid. "Fine. I'll tell you what I want. Then you'll realize what an unproductive act of futility it is for a woman like me to want anything beyond what she has."

Alexander didn't move. "Tell me."

Her eyes flashed. "I want my mother's locket back. I want my mother back. I want her to be whole and well and never to have suffered the horrors of her own mind. I want my father to have had the career he deserved. I want my sister to live the ordinary, happy life I never did. Is that enough? No? There's more. I want my grandmother to stop trying to set Jane's future. I want to prove Legendre's prime number theorem. I want *to do something*. I—"

Alexander stepped forward and captured her face in his hands. He stared at her—the fire of pain and anger blazing in her eyes, the flush of her skin. An ache of want speared through him again, powerful enough to break his own vow. Before she could draw another breath, he lowered his head and kissed her.

She trembled beneath his hands, a hard, edgy tremble of anger. But she did not pull away. Alexander pressed harder, heat spreading through his chest as he sought to invade her mouth. Soft, soft, soft. Her mouth was so full, so pliable, such a contrast to the rigidity of her body. He flicked his tongue out to lick the corner of her mouth. She shuddered in response, and though her shoulders remained stiff, her lips began to slacken, to open.

The taste of tea and sugar, of Lydia, swept through

Alexander's blood. His hands tightened on her shoulders, pulling her closer so the curves of her breasts brushed against his chest. She gasped, a choked, throaty sound that made him ache to know what kind of noises she'd make if she were splayed naked and willing beneath him.

The image burned in his brain. He pressed himself against her. He lowered his hands to her tight waist, his fingers digging into an impossibly stiff corset. He wanted to strip it from her body, to feel her bare skin against his, to cup her breasts in his hands and hear her moan with pleasure.

Hot. Christ, she was hot. He could almost feel her skin burning through the material of her gown. She kissed him back, her delicious tongue sliding across his teeth, her hands fisting in the front of his shirt. It was neither a gentle kiss nor one of seduction. Her kiss was angry, frustrated, her lips fierce against his.

She pushed herself closer to him, one hand unclenching from his shirtfront to splay over his abdomen. Her palm slid over him in a heated and urgent caress, her fingernails scraping against his chest. She pulled his lower lip between her teeth. A mild twinge of pain went through him, only heightening his arousal.

Yet even as his body began to ache for her, a sense of unease began to dilute Alexander's uncoiling lust. His brain fogged too thick for comprehension, but he knew instinctively that something was wrong.

With supreme effort, he lifted his head, his fingers digging into Lydia's shoulders as he set her away from him. Her eyes blazed indigo blue into his, her reddened lips parted as she drew in a sharp breath.

"Not reckless enough for you?" she asked, her voice as tight as spindle-pulled yarn.

"Miss—"

"You think I'm a spinster, don't you?" she snapped. "Dried up like a piece of leather. Unused, lonely. You think—"

"Do not tell me what I think." The words came out harsh and frustrated. His hands clenched as he stared into her eyes. He couldn't shake the unease, the odd apprehension. The sense that he was falling into something far more complex than he had ever anticipated.

"You believe I'm destined for a life of solitude," Lydia continued. "My only companions textbooks and equations and formulas. A cold, intellectual life of the mind."

"I don't—"

Lydia stepped closer, a visible shudder racking her slender body. "My lord, it would be for the best if you simply continued to believe that."

"Why?" he demanded.

"Because it is far too dangerous for either of us to believe otherwise."

Before he could move, before he could speak, she was gone, the door shutting with a hard click behind her.

Chapter Five

"Miss Jane, you've got to stop coming down 'ere!" The maid Sophie turned from the kitchen sink, pushing a lock of hair away from her damp forehead with the back of her hand. The scents of toast and bacon drifted from the dining room.

Jane shifted from one foot to the other, anxious to return to her room before Grandmama and Lydia came down for breakfast. "Has he arrived yet?"

"I'm expecting 'im any minute now, but—"

A knock on the door interrupted her. Sophie cast Jane an exasperated look and went to answer it. The delivery boy, a freckle-faced lad with coppery hair, stood there with a box of goods.

"Mornin', Sophie, yer looking quite the beauty, ain't you?"

"Hush now, Tom." Sophie glanced at Jane with embarrassment and held the door open to let Tom in.

He pushed the box onto a table. "Miss Jane, isn't it?"

Jane nodded, stepping toward him. "Have you got a letter for me, Tom?"

"Indeed." He pulled a wrinkled letter from his pocket and handed it to her.

Jane took it, eyeing the scrawled name on the front. "Who gives these to you, Tom?"

"You don't know, miss?"

"Should I?"

"I... well, I thought you knew who was writing 'em, miss. I get them from Mr. Krebbs. He owns a lodging house over in Bethnal Green near's where I stay. Gives me a letter sometimes to bring to you and a tuppence as well. Dunno more than that, miss."

"Mr. Krebbs surely doesn't write the letters."

"Don't think so, miss."

"That'll be all, Tom, thank you." Sophie gave the boy his coin and shooed him out the door before turning back to Jane. A worried frown creased her brow. "You sure it's all right, then, miss? The letters and all?"

"It's fine, Sophie. Just a game."

She hurried from the kitchen, tearing the letter open.

Dear Jane,

So I might have guessed that riddle would prove too simple.

Teacher, yes, of course that is the answer. Here is another.

I shall assume that since it is shorter, it will also be more difficult:

A word there is, five syllables contains
Take one away, no syllable remains.

Till soon,
C

A word with five syllables...

"Jane, do watch where you are going."

Jane looked up at her grandmother, who was striding down the corridor. A frown etched her face.

"What are you doing?" Mrs. Boyd continued. "Where is Mrs. Driscoll?"

"Oh." Jane fumbled to fold the letter and tuck it against her side. "I don't...I don't know. I went to speak to Sophie."

"What for?"

"I wanted to see if...if we had any jam for our toast." Jane almost winced at the feebleness of the excuse.

Her grandmother's frown deepened. "We always have jam for our toast. What is that in your hand?"

"This?" Jane looked at the letter as if she'd only just noticed it. "Just a...some mathematical problem Lydia gave me to solve."

"Well, I suggest you do so in your room rather than wandering about the house."

"Yes, ma'am." Jane scurried past her grandmother and up the stairs.

As she returned to the schoolroom, she wondered where this was going—who *C* was and what he wanted from her besides correspondence.

Perhaps she ought to start making more inquiries of the delivery boy and Sophie—learning the letter writer's identity would be like solving a puzzle in and of itself. Perhaps that was the point of this whole game. Perhaps she was meant to solve the most mysterious puzzle of all.

The pleasure of being loved. *R = Return.*

The reaction to the partner's appeal. *I = Instinct.*

The process of forgetting. *O = Oblivion.*

If she made certain assumptions on the behavior of the individuals and assigned variables to a positive linear system, and the linear model of $x_1(t) = -\alpha_r x_1(t) + \beta_r x_2(t) \ldots$

The pleasure of being loved.

Lydia dropped her pencil. She lifted her head to stare out the window, her heart vibrating like the strings of a violin. No equation could quantify that kind of pleasure. No theorem could explain Lord Northwood's intent to touch her, which had been so palpable she'd felt it from clear across the room.

She pushed her papers aside and went downstairs. Her own fault, this restless trembling in her veins, the heat of memory. She pushed the longing down deep, alongside the other mistakes that lay buried beneath the crust of time.

The door to her father's study sat half-open, and Lydia knocked before entering. Her throat constricted at the sight of Sir Henry's cedarwood desk, the bookshelves crammed with works of Chinese history and literature. She imagined she could still detect the fragrant scent of his pipe smoke. The walls held calligraphic scrolls and Tang dynasty paintings with images of lively horses and riders, mist-covered mountaintops, graceful kingfishers.

Jane sat curled on a sofa by the window, a book on butterflies spread open on her lap. Lydia slipped into the seat beside her and drew the girl close, bending to press a kiss against Jane's soft brown hair. The bands around her heart loosened as she breathed in the scent of Pears soap.

"You're all right?" she asked.

"I just miss him."

"So do I."

The comfort of shared memories wrapped around

them—Sir Henry patiently teaching them how to write Chinese characters, telling them stories of his youthful travels, playing puzzles and games together.

Throughout Lydia's childhood, her father had spent much of his time either traveling or working, but his dedication to her, his support of her education, had never wavered. And after Jane was born, he ceased traveling in favor of teaching and studying. His placid, serious presence had been so very, very welcome after the loneliness of Lydia's childhood and the death of Theodora Kellaway.

And Jane—to Lydia's utter, complete gratitude—had known only Sir Henry's unwavering love and devotion.

Jane closed the book and rested her head against Lydia's shoulder. "Do you think Grandmama really will send me away?"

Lydia looked at her sister. "How did you find out?"

"I couldn't sleep and came downstairs for a glass of milk. I heard you talking in the drawing room."

"You oughtn't have listened."

"Wouldn't you have listened if you overheard someone talking about you?"

Lydia chuckled and conceded the point. "I suppose."

"Do you think she'll do it?" Jane asked. "Do you think she'll send me to that school in Paris?"

Lydia searched for a proper response. She could not undermine her grandmother's authority, but neither could she lie. She opted to evade the question.

"How would you feel if she did?"

When Jane didn't respond, Lydia's heart sank. She wished Jane would immediately say she didn't want to go, but of course her sister didn't respond to anything without thinking it through.

"I don't know," Jane finally said. "I'd miss you, of course, and the house. But it's not as if... I mean, it isn't as if we ever *go* anywhere, d'you know?"

"That's not entirely true. We—"

"It is true, Lydia." Frustration edged Jane's voice. "The only place I've been outside of London was that trip we took to Brighton. At least Paris would be interesting."

"Yes, it would," Lydia admitted, though her heart began to feel like a rock.

"And honestly, I'd like to learn piano and French." Jane turned her head to look at Lydia's face. "Oh, Lyddie, I didn't mean to upset you."

"You didn't." Lydia hugged her sister. "I understand what you mean. When I was a few years older than you, I went away to school as well. To Germany."

"Did you like it?"

Lydia's stomach knotted. That single year was like a diamond inside her—bright, cold, and hard. In some ways it had opened her to things she could never have anticipated, and in other ways... it had destroyed both her and those closest to her.

"I liked learning new things," she said. "Everything was different and interesting. But it wasn't easy. I spoke little German. I didn't make many friends. I missed home. I often felt alone."

I was alone.

Even before Sir Henry had agreed to send her to Germany, Lydia had been alone. With her grandmother caring for her mother and her father either away or working... solitude had been Lydia's sole companion.

Until *him.* The man with the cold green eyes and twisted heart. She shivered.

"What happened when you were there?" Jane asked.

"What—"

"I heard you say something to Grandmama about punishing you for something that happened. Was that in Germany? What was it?"

Panic quivered in Lydia's chest. She tightened her arm around Jane and kissed the top of her head again. "Nothing you need worry about. It was a very long time ago."

She released her sister to stand. "Would you like to see the diorama in Regent's Park this afternoon? It just opened last week."

"Yes, let's." Jane brightened.

"Good. Go upstairs and finish your geography report. We'll go after lunch."

Jane hurried from the room.

Lydia picked up the book her sister had left on the sofa. Bright, multicolored butterflies sprang from the pages, each illustration created with meticulous detail. A folded piece of paper stuck out from the back of the book. Lydia slipped it back into place.

She tried to imagine what her life would be like without Jane—and couldn't. She had her work, yes, but almost everything she'd done for the past eleven years had centered around her sister.

She couldn't lose Jane. Not yet. Not even if Jane *wanted* to go.

Talia's hand tightened on Alexander's arm, her fingers digging in hard as they descended from the carriage into the cold night air. He ignored the pang of regret as he turned to his sister. In a pale blue silk gown, her chestnut-brown hair perfectly coiffed, she looked lovely and brittle.

She'd applied a slight excess of rice powder, which gave her a cold, masklike expression.

He put his hand over hers. "Talia, it won't do any good to look as if you're heading to the gallows."

"Five hundred pounds, Alex. I told Mr. Sewell of the Ragged School Union to expect your bank draft on Monday."

"If you act as if you're enjoying yourself, I'll add a hundred pounds to that."

She flexed her fingers on his arm as if making an effort to relax. "If Lord Fulton is here, I'm leaving straightaway."

"What about Fulton?" Sebastian asked, clambering out of the carriage after them.

"Last week, Alex suggested to his lordship that I would be amenable to a marriage offer," Talia replied.

Sebastian let out a noise that was a half snort, half laugh. "Fulton? Good God, Alex, what are you trying to do? Send our Talia running to a nunnery?"

"A far more attractive prospect than Fulton, I daresay," Talia agreed, turning to Sebastian. "Your brother took it upon himself to make the suggestion to Lord Fulton before discussing it with me." She threw Alexander a withering glance. "Likely because he knew what my response would be. So I found myself the object of some great joke since everyone at the theater knew about it except me. It was humiliating."

"You could do worse," Alexander muttered.

"Oh, could I? Did you know Lord Fulton believes no one else will offer for me because of my Russian blood? That *he's* the only one willing to overlook such a travesty?"

Alexander frowned. "He said that?"

Talia gave Sebastian an exasperated look. He winked at her.

"You're the one who's got to say yes, old girl. Not him."

He nodded in Alexander's direction. "Though I do hear Fulton's sister is getting a bit desperate. Long in the tooth, you know, and wide in the hips. Muddled in the head, too, no doubt."

"Sounds an ideal prospect for *you*, Alex." Some of Talia's tension eased a little as she and Sebastian exchanged wry grins. "Considering you're thirty-two, perhaps you'd do well to focus on your own marital prospects rather than attempting to control mine."

Alexander turned away as they entered the foyer, not knowing whether his irritation was a result of his siblings' behavior or Fulton's alleged comments. He sighed. Bribing his sister to attend a ball with him was not the way he wished to move about in society, but the stubborn chit gave him no other option.

After the butler greeted them, they entered the ballroom, which was crowded with well-dressed men and women circling the room like ships in a harbor. Music, laughter, and conversation mingled in the air.

"Why, Lord Northwood. Lady Talia and Mr. Hall as well." The Marquess of Hadley, who was the president of the Royal Society of Arts Council, and his wife approached. "We weren't expecting you."

"The Society did intend some of the ticket proceeds to fund the educational exhibition, my lord."

Hadley coughed, and his wife's smile wavered a bit.

"Yes, of course," Hadley replied. "It's just, you know, this dreadful business with Russia. Seems to be coming to a head now."

Lady Hadley waved her hand and stretched her smile wider. "But never mind all that. It's so nice to see you all here. Do enjoy yourselves."

Not likely, Alexander thought. "Go along with Lady Hadley, Talia," he suggested.

His sister gave him a mild glare but, along with Sebastian, accompanied the woman toward a group by the hearth.

"What about the *dreadful business*?" Alexander asked Hadley.

"The council wishes to convene a meeting to address the, er, specter of war with Russia," Lord Hadley said. "They're concerned about its effect on the exhibition. Announcement of the meeting is expected at the end of the week."

"Where does the concern lie?"

"The French commissioner to the exhibition, Monsieur Bonnart, has indicated there's a growing anti-Russian sentiment among the French public. He does not wish his country's involvement in the exhibition to indicate any contrary sympathies."

Alexander frowned. "This is not a Russian exhibition."

"I know, Northwood, but it's the inclusion of the Russian section that is causing a bit of consternation. The French are giving quite a bit of financial assistance to the Society for this. Just don't want any trouble, you know?"

"I shouldn't think there will be," Alexander said. "Lord Hadley, tell the council members I will prepare a speech on the matter that will allay their concerns."

He gave a nod of dismissal and went to get a drink. He'd been aware of the growing anti-Russian sentiment over the course of the year, especially after the Russian navy obliterated a Turkish fleet last November. The event caused a wave of antipathy toward the czar and strengthened the push for a declaration of war, which appeared likely any moment now.

Alexander swallowed some brandy, disliking the

unease evoked by Hadley's remarks. As vice president of the Society of Arts, he'd proposed this exhibition to celebrate the Society's one hundredth anniversary, but he'd had an ulterior motive as well.

The educational exhibition would focus on the positive aspects of British education and include international displays to promote the necessity of free trade between Great Britain and other countries. Yet the exhibition would also be Alexander's triumph—a display of brilliant ideals that would reflect back onto him and thus remove shadows of scandal from the earldom.

But if his ties to Russia were to be linked to the political climate... well, he refused to allow the council to use that against him or let it affect the exhibition. Not after all he'd done.

He went to refill his glass but stopped, his gaze moving to where a handsome blond man stood speaking with Talia. Stiffness lined Talia's posture, her entire body drawn back as the man stood too close.

Alexander tensed and started forward, only to be stayed by a hand on his arm. Sebastian shook his head.

The blond man grasped Talia's arm. When he bent even closer to speak to her, she tried to pull away, her features tightening. Alexander shook off Sebastian's hand and strode toward their sister.

Before he reached her, a tall man with sun-streaked brown hair stopped beside Talia. With one movement, Lord Castleford gripped the blond man's arm and twisted him away. He stepped between them, shielding Talia with his body. He muttered a few words that caused the younger man to hunch his shoulders and skulk away.

In almost the same movement, Castleford pressed a

hand to Talia's lower back, guiding her onto the dance floor as the music began.

Alexander glanced around, realizing Castleford had accomplished his mission with such stealth that no one except them had noticed the unpleasant little scene.

"I saw him approaching," Sebastian explained, "and he's far more discreet than you would have been. Care to tell me again that I don't give a whit for society's opinion?"

He arched an eyebrow and strode away. Alexander waited until the music stopped before approaching his friend and clapping a hand on his shoulder. "Welcome back, you old bohemian. It's good to see you again."

"Good to be back, North."

Alexander looked at his sister. She gave an almost imperceptible shake of her head, as if to indicate the incident with the other man was of no consequence.

"How long were you gone this time?" Alexander asked Castleford.

"Over a year, but I'm planning another excursion to Malay in the fall. Lady Talia tells me you've organized the Society of Arts' educational exhibition?"

"I have."

"Alexander, Lord Castleford would be a great help with the display focusing on Chinese education," Talia said. "He traveled extensively in China, you know. He's also agreed to help me rework my curriculum proposal for the ragged schools."

Alexander eyed his friend. "I'd no idea you were so interested in education, considering your penchant for playing cricket over studying."

Castleford grinned. "We can't all be as industrious as

you, North. You've still got your *Eton Latin Grammar*, haven't you?"

"And I consult it regularly," Alexander replied. "I'd wager you couldn't decline a noun to save your life."

"*Salva animum tuum.*"

"*Abi.*"

"Boys," Talia said. Although her voice was stern, she looked amused for the first time that evening. "Pay attention. We've the children's festival next weekend, Alexander, the one to benefit the ragged schools. I've invited Lord Castleford to attend, and I'd hoped you would as well."

"It's on my calendar, yes."

Talia smiled. The expression almost startled Alexander. His sister hadn't directed a smile at him in an age. It was as if a light had been lit inside her and shone onto him.

"Lord Northwood?" A young woman in a green silk gown paused at the edge of their circle and looked up at him. Her lips curved with pleasure. "We were hoping you would be here tonight. We've heard so much about the exhibition."

"Miss Cooper. Allow me to introduce—"

"Lord Castleford, yes, we're acquainted." Miss Cooper's cool gaze passed over Castleford and came to rest on Talia. "And good evening to you, Lady Talia."

Talia gave the other woman a stiff nod. Castleford curled his hand around Talia's elbow, murmured an excuse, and guided her toward the refreshment table.

Alexander turned to Miss Cooper, who was looking at him with expectation. He swallowed a sigh.

"How are your parents, Miss Cooper?" he asked.

"Very well, thank you. Mother is leaving for a trip to Paris next week. She plans to visit a renowned modiste, having been recommended by her dear friend Lady Dubois. I do so wish I could accompany her, but I've already several social engagements here in London. Will you be attending Lady Whitmore's ball?"

"I've not yet decided," Alexander replied. "Please convey my best regards to your parents."

He stepped back, intending the remark as a polite closure to the conversation, but Miss Cooper moved forward into the slight distance he'd created.

"I do hope you'll be there," she continued. "And I believe Mother would like to invite you for tea one afternoon before her departure."

She blinked up at him. Alexander gave a half bow.

"Thank you, Miss Cooper. I shall look forward to receiving the invitation. Do enjoy the remainder of the evening." He walked away before she could respond and headed for the card room.

Tension stiffened the back of his neck as he wove through the crowd. He ought to have asked Miss Cooper to dance. He ought to have asked her if he could fetch her a glass of champagne. He ought to have told her she looked beautiful. He ought to have bloody well flirted.

A week ago, he might have.

Before he'd met Lydia Kellaway.

He stopped inside the card room. Crossing his arms, he drummed his fingers against his biceps. An image of Lydia appeared in his mind: flushed cheeks, angry eyes, and hot desperation.

"She's far prettier than Fulton's sister." Sebastian stopped beside him.

"Of course she's prettier than... Oh." Alexander cleared his throat. "You mean Miss Cooper. Well, yes. She is."

Sebastian gave him a shrewd look. "Who else would I have been referring to?"

"Any number of young chits, I'd imagine." Alexander steeled himself against his brother's curiosity. He'd told Sebastian about his encounter with Miss Kellaway, about the locket, but he hadn't divulged his growing interest in the woman.

"You ought to take up with one of them," Sebastian continued. "Plenty around like Miss Cooper. Pretty and a bit idle headed. I assure you such women are a delight to keep company with. Lady Welbourne's niece is new to town, and word is she's quite lovely. You ought to attend her ladyship's dinner party tomorrow, make her niece's acquaintance."

"I've other business to contend with tomorrow. A meeting with Father's solicitors. Letters to dictate regarding Floreston Manor."

Sebastian was quiet for a moment, then moved in front of him. Alexander suppressed the urge to take a step back, to try to deflect whatever it was his brother intended to say.

"Being the firstborn doesn't mean you need surrender to duty, Alex," Sebastian said. "It doesn't mean you need to put responsibility above all."

Alexander looked past Sebastian's shoulder to the numerous card games in progress.

"If I do not," he said, his voice stiff, "who will?"

Sebastian didn't respond. Alexander shifted his gaze to meet his brother's eyes. They were both thinking of Rushton. Alexander smothered a rush of frustration directed at their father.

"And you," he continued, "are the one who suggested

I marry. What other reason would I have if not for the future of the earldom? If not for duty?"

Sebastian stepped back. An odd flash of disappointment crossed his features. "You could do so for *you*."

"Don't be foolish."

"For Christ's sake, Alex, duty doesn't mean you need to be wound tighter than a clock." Sebastian scrubbed a hand through his hair. "There's no law against you having a good bit of fun. Why don't you come with me to the Eagle Tavern later tonight?"

Alexander hesitated, temptation warring with the ever-present fear of *what people would say*. He shook his head. Sebastian's disappointment visibly deepened.

"All right, then," he said. "Do whatever makes you happy. Oh, no, you'll never do that, will you? You'll always do what you have to do instead."

Alexander watched his brother walk toward a card table. For all his efforts and work in recent years, Alexander wasn't even certain what he truly wanted to do.

He did, however, know what he did *not* want to do. He did not want to marry a woman like Miss Cooper whose life revolved around the latest fashions and social functions. He did not want to enter into a union reminiscent of his parents' marriage, one of brittle formality and coldness. He did not want to be bored.

Well. Perhaps he did know what he wanted to do, after all. He wanted to marry a woman who was interesting and clever. Who made his blood run quick and hot. Who challenged him and forced him to look beyond the boundaries of his own life. A woman whose beauty was only enhanced by the keen intelligence in her eyes.

A woman who hadn't been far from his thoughts since the day she walked into his life.

A woman like Lydia Kellaway.

Alexander watched Sebastian as his brother sat at a card table, laughing at something one of the other men said. Perhaps he ought to take his brother's advice, see what happened.

Alexander didn't know what would come of pursuing Lydia Kellaway. He didn't know if she would reject him. He didn't know what his father would say. But he did know he would enjoy the pursuit immensely. And he dared to believe it might even make him happy.

Chapter Six

The sun burned low and bright in the sky, casting pale light onto the bare trees just beginning to bud with leaves. Street vendors selling flowers, oranges, penny pies, tarts, and hot green peas shouted out the quality and price of their wares. The calls of a fruit seller drew Lydia to a cart to purchase two apples.

"We'll also have an iced lemonade at the gardens," she promised Jane as they continued down New Road for their Tuesday afternoon outing.

"D'you think the hippopotamus will be out?" Jane asked. "And the orangutans?"

"We'll have to see. I hear they also have a new animal from Africa, though I can't recall what it is."

She placed her hand on Jane's shoulder to steer the girl away from a sleek black carriage that came to a halt near them. An old fear curled through her, and she quickened her pace without looking back.

"Miss Kellaway." The deep voice stopped Lydia in her

tracks. She turned to look at the man who descended from the carriage.

Lydia's hand tightened on Jane's shoulder. "Lord Northwood."

He approached, the sun shining on his dark hair like a halo, his black coat stretching across his broad shoulders and chest. Lydia almost felt the awe radiating from her sister as the viscount neared.

"Good morning to you both." He smiled at Jane. "You must be Miss Jane."

"Yes, sir."

"This is Lord Northwood," Lydia told her sister, though she knew she couldn't even begin to explain how she'd made his acquaintance. She glanced at him.

He was looking at her. With purpose. Her heart thumped.

What do you see when you look at me, Lord Northwood?

"What brings you here, my lord?" she asked, her voice sharper than she intended.

"I thought I might convince you to accept transport to whatever destination you intend." He tilted his head toward his carriage.

"Actually, we're rather enjoying the walk, and—" Lydia paused when Jane tugged on her hand.

She glanced at the girl, resignation sweeping through her when she saw the pleading look in Jane's light green eyes. Neither of them had ever had the opportunity to ride in such a luxurious carriage.

"We're going to the zoological gardens," Lydia said.

"Excellent. If you don't mind my companionship, I'd be delighted to accompany you. Can't remember the last time I visited the zoological gardens. I suppose Drury Lane doesn't qualify."

Jane giggled. "Can we, Lyddie? Please?"

"Only if his lordship doesn't consider it an inconvenience."

"I wouldn't have offered if it was." Lord Northwood opened the door and handed them both up into the velvet interior before issuing instructions to the driver and climbing in after them. The instant he sat opposite them, the space in the carriage seemed to shrink, making Lydia far more aware of his presence than she wished to be.

"You've an interest in animals, Miss Jane?" he asked.

"Yes, sir. More insects than animals, though."

"Insects?"

Jane nodded. "Our father used to take me to exhibitions of the Royal Entomological Society. The first was about butterflies; then we went to one on spiders and another on insects from North America. We even went to an exhibition of tamed fleas. You wouldn't imagine fleas could be tamed, but they can, you know."

Northwood regarded her thoughtfully. "You might be interested in a section of a Society of Arts exhibition I'm organizing. We plan to have an extensive display of flora and fauna, including some new species of exotic insects."

"Can we go, Lydia?" Jane asked.

"Of course. Perhaps you can write a report on the new discoveries."

Jane rolled her eyes at Lord Northwood, who grinned. "Never lets up, does she?" he asked.

"Hardly. She's been my tutor since I was little." Jane's expression closed off a bit. "But our grandmother says I need a broader education, so I'm to be sent away."

Lydia felt Northwood's gaze settle on her, as tangible as the brush of his fingers. She shifted, pressing a hand to her abdomen as a twinge of pain went through her.

"Sent away," Northwood repeated. It wasn't a question, but Jane nodded in response.

"She thinks I need more instruction in... What was the word she used, Lyddie?"

"Propriety."

Northwood smiled at the girl. "Propriety is overrated, if you ask me."

"Our grandmother thinks I need more of it."

"And you can't provide that?" Northwood asked Lydia.

"Jane is of an age when it's necessary that she learn more about etiquette and social graces. So our grandmother is sending her to a school in Paris where she can learn French and take proper music and dancing lessons."

Northwood continued to look at Lydia as if he knew quite well that her grandmother's dictate stung like nettles beneath her skin. As if he knew it was the source of her despair the night she had wanted to settle her debt. The night she had wanted to go nowhere else but to him.

"London has no shortage of music and dancing teachers," he said. "In fact, my brother Sebastian teaches the piano. I'd be pleased to introduce you to him next week, should you wish your sister to start lessons straightaway."

Lydia felt Jane tug on her arm, felt the plea radiating from her sister's eyes.

"Well, I... thank you, my lord." Lydia chanced a look at Northwood. "Most generous. I will discuss it further with our grandmother."

Northwood and Jane exchanged glances. He winked, and she grinned in response.

A tendril of unease curled through Lydia's heart at the evident rapport between her sister and Northwood. She pushed it aside with ruthless determination. Nothing would ever come of her association with Lord Northwood, except perhaps piano lessons for Jane, so there was no need for further anxiety.

They rode around the outer circle of Regent's Park, the coach coming to a halt at the Carriage Drive entrance. Northwood descended to assist Lydia and Jane, then instructed the driver to see to the admission fees.

They walked past the entrance lodge to the terrace walk that led into the lush landscape of the gardens and the new glass-roofed aviary. Flowers and trees bordered the walkway, which branched off into gravel paths leading to different animal enclosures and houses.

Jane hurried ahead, her steps light.

"She's a lovely girl," Northwood said as he and Lydia followed Jane toward the meadows where deer, pelicans, alpacas, and several gazelles grazed. Movable trellis houses dotted the grass, birds flitting around inside.

"Yes, she is. She has a quick mind and a good heart."

"Like her sister."

Lydia couldn't prevent a smile. How long had it been since someone complimented her, no matter the motive? "You're a flatterer, my lord."

"I never say anything I don't mean."

Lydia paused, bringing him to a halt beside her. As much as she enjoyed his company, the oddness of the situation—the sheer improbability of running into him and the even greater unlikelihood that he would actually want to visit the zoological gardens—struck her hard.

She leveled her gaze on him. "Why are you really here, my lord?"

"My sister Talia—you, ah, encountered her the other night—does quite a bit of work with the ragged schools."

Lydia blinked at the non sequitur. "Oh. That's good of her."

"Yes. Are you familiar with the ragged schools?"

"I've heard of them, but I don't know their intent."

"The schools attempt to reclaim children from the streets," Northwood explained. "Their students come from impoverished families whose fathers are either in prison or committing crimes that will eventually land them there. It's a cause that's very dear to Talia."

"It sounds like a worthy cause, indeed."

"It is. Talia and several of her friends have arranged a charity event on Saturday next. It's a children's festival with games and such, all to benefit the schools. I'd be obliged if you would attend."

Anxiety began to simmer inside Lydia. "Oh, I don't know if—"

"I'm certain your sister would enjoy it," Northwood said. "I believe there's also kite flying, dancing, wagon rides. Talia has spent several months helping organize it. She's even talked Sebastian into playing the piano." Before she could protest, he added, "I'll have my carriage pick you up at eleven. I'll return you home whenever you like. Really, you might even enjoy it yourself."

Lydia chewed on her lip for a moment. She glanced at her sister, who was walking ahead of them toward the animals' enclosures, then nodded. "I would enjoy it, my lord, and I know Jane would too. We don't often attend such events."

She realized the impact of her hasty comment when Northwood frowned.

"Why not?" he asked.

"I just don't...I haven't got a great deal of time for

such things." *Never did.* Pain sliced through her chest as she recalled her own dark childhood, where frivolities like festivals and kite flying didn't exist.

She knew Jane's childhood had been nothing like hers—she'd seen to that—but she also hadn't actively sought many amusements for her sister.

"Because you're too busy with your equations?" Northwood asked.

The edge to his voice cut her a little, and she looked away. "I'm not made of numbers, Lord Northwood."

"Then why do you foster such notions?"

"What does that mean?"

"You want people to believe you're made of nothing more than mathematical brilliance."

"I do not—"

"Don't you? Less than a fortnight ago, you attempted to tell me what I believe about you."

"Quite frankly, that is what everyone believes about me."

"I don't."

Startled, she looked up at him. "You don't?"

"No. It isn't true. Your destiny is not one of cold intellect. And I do not for an instant believe you are happy with only textbooks and numbers as your companions."

Lydia swallowed. He was gazing at her with more than curiosity, more than puzzlement. He looked as if he knew that beneath her thick shield lay something vulnerable and painfully tender. Something he was more than capable of protecting.

"Why would you believe such a thing?" Her voice shook.

He stepped closer. So close that the cool air began to heat around them, so close that she felt the intent radiating from his body. His voice dropped lower, sliding like a caress against her skin.

"If you were content with such a life, you would not have kissed me, touched me, as if you longed for more," he murmured.

Her face burned. "I exhibited an appalling lack of judgment."

"You exhibited what you felt. What you want."

"I've told you what I *want*. And that was not it."

You are not it.

She couldn't bring herself to say the words, knowing they would be a lie to the tenth power. Her shoulders tensed as she stepped away from him.

"You may think what you wish of me, my lord. I only ask that you remember one thing. I said it would be for the best if you believed what I told you, if you left me to a destiny of intellectual solitude. Anything else would most certainly be for the worse."

She turned away from him. He grasped her arm, his fingers tightening with a possession that caused her heart to jolt.

"Nothing between us will ever be for the worse, Miss Kellaway." He spoke with absolute certainty. "*Nothing.*"

"Shorten your statement, my lord, and you'll have the truth." She pulled her arm from his grip. "Nothing between us will ever be."

"You're wrong."

Her throat tightened. How she wished she could be wrong. How she wished she could unlock the closed part of herself and let him in. The more time she spent in his presence, the more she imagined how glorious it would be to discover the potential of what they could be together.

Even if it were for only one night.

Shaken by the thought, Lydia turned away. Without looking at the viscount, she went toward her sister. "Jane!"

Jane waved her hand to urge Lydia closer. Lydia quickened her pace, hoping against hope that Northwood would leave.

"Look!" Jane gestured at the screened terrace containing six dens for housing lions, tigers, cheetahs, and a jaguar. "Lord Northwood, did you know the lions are from a place called Nubia? It's in Africa. And, look, the leopards. I think they're from India. Isn't that right, Lydia? One of them is, anyway. Lord Northwood, did you know the ancient Greeks believed giraffes were a mix between a leopard and a camel?"

He stopped beside Lydia. "I did not know that. I've ridden a camel, though."

"Really? Where?"

"When I was a boy, my father took our family on a trip to Egypt. Camels are as common as carriages there."

"What was riding it like?"

"Like being on a boat about to capsize. It was decidedly one of the oddest things I've ever done."

Jane grinned and turned her attention back to the lions' den. Lydia and Northwood stopped to watch as the huge felines plodded around their enclosures, pawing at the ground and stretching their sleek muscles.

"Why Paris?" Northwood asked.

Lydia sighed. "You are relentless."

"All the more reason for you to answer me."

"This isn't your concern, my lord."

"I know. But I am curious. Why Paris?"

"Because we can't afford to send her to one of the London schools, and Lady Montague has offered Jane a scholarship."

"And why does your grandmother feel you are not suited to such instruction?"

Lydia gazed at her sister. Jane trailed a stick across the ground as she began walking toward the bear pits. Her long hair glimmered in the sunlight, falling across her shoulders like a swath of silk.

Northwood thought he knew her destiny, did he? He thought he knew what she wanted, what she needed, what kind of life she ought to lead? Perhaps he'd change his perceptions if he knew of her past.

"Because I never received it myself," she said.

"Not even from your mother?"

Although the question was not unexpected, it caused a sharp pang to spear through Lydia. She stopped, trying to ease her hitched breath.

"Miss Kellaway?" Northwood cupped a hand beneath her elbow. "Are you all right?"

She nodded, glancing in Jane's direction to ensure the girl was still within sight. "My mother wasn't capable of taking care of herself, let alone providing etiquette instruction."

"What happened to her?"

Lydia stilled. His hand remained on her arm, the warmth of his palm burning clear through his glove and her sleeve. He stood close, too close, his gaze on her face as if he sought to solve a complex puzzle. His presence was big, strong, unmoving.

Lydia experienced the sudden and unwelcome thought that a man of his formidable nature could easily withstand whatever truth she flung at him. He could bear without effort whatever confessions she sought to unload from her heart.

"She had...trouble." Lydia lifted a shaking hand to touch her temple. "Here. She developed a disease of the brain. The strangest veering between melancholia and mania. She started having episodes of rage, of profound darkness. Until I was about five years of age, she'd always seemed fine. But then...later my father told me she'd lost several children through miscarriages and a stillbirth. That...that broke something within her.

"She began locking herself in her bedroom, refusing to come out. She'd become furious with me over the smallest things, like a grass stain on my dress. She'd never done that before. She'd leave the house for days, and no one would know where she was. My grandmother came to live with us to help take care of her. That helped for a time, but then it became too horrific even for her. She convinced my father to send my mother to a sanitarium for proper medical attention."

His grip tightened on her elbow. "Did it work?"

"At first it seemed to." Lydia kept her gaze on Jane, who had paused outside the bear pit to study a massive brown bear. "She'd come home for a time; then it would get worse again. So my grandmother would arrange for another institution, another doctor. Another course of treatment. They traveled constantly throughout the Continent. Finally when rumors began to mount, my grandmother requested permission to remove her from London permanently. They went to a place in France she'd heard of through her church. Outside of Lyons. My mother was there for almost three years."

"Did it help?"

"She seemed content there for a time. My grandmother stayed with her. My father visited when he was able. That was where my mother died."

An odd emptiness widened within Lydia as she said the words, even as she felt Northwood's body vibrate with shock.

"I'm sorry."

"Don't be. She was a prisoner of her own mind for so long that it almost seemed as if she were finally free. But of course it nearly destroyed my grandmother. To lose a child, a daughter, even one as ill as my mother had been..."

She eased her arm from his hold, sensing his mind working, furrowing through all she'd told him. She turned away and began walking toward Jane.

"Lydia."

She stopped. The sound of her name in his baritone voice thudded right up against the walls of her heart.

"Where were you when your mother was in France?" Northwood asked.

She didn't look at him. "Not with her."

Alexander Hall. Viscount Northwood.

Lydia was indeed moving up in society. The question was whether she was merely the man's whore or if she aspired to be something more.

Did it matter?

Joseph watched as the girl Jane climbed back into the viscount's carriage, Lydia close behind her.

Yes, it did matter. Now that Sir Henry was dead, perhaps Lydia was no longer concerned with the consequences of her actions, the possible damage to her character.

In which case, his plan might not work.

If, on the other hand, Lydia was pursuing Lord Northwood for more than money... well, that would be of benefit to all involved.

Especially himself.

Chapter Seven

Jane swung her leg back and forth, staring at the dramatic oil painting that hung above the fireplace. A hunting scene with a tiger as the quarry. She didn't like it at all. An arrow protruded from the tiger's side, blood dripping over its fur, its face twisted into a snarl.

She swung her other leg and wondered if thc delivery boy had given Sophie another letter this morning. Lydia had been rushing Jane around getting ready, so she hadn't had a chance to speak to the maid privately.

Lydia's hand came to rest on Jane's leg, stilling her nervous movement. Jane let out a breath and reached for another slice of tea cake. Mr. Hall's piano, black and so shiny she could probably see her reflection if she got up close, stood in a corner of the vast drawing room. What if she left smudges on the keys?

She rubbed her hands over her skirt. First she got to ride in a viscount's carriage, and now she was sitting in an earl's drawing room about to have her first piano lesson with his son.

Quite a bit to have happened in the past week.

She glanced at Lydia. "Where did you find it?"

"What?"

Jane gestured to the notebook resting on Lydia's lap. "I thought you'd lost...er, misplaced it."

"I found it in...well, I'd left it somewhere and it was returned to me. Fortunately."

"Terribly sorry for the delay." The door flew open and a man strode in, his dark hair messy and cravat askew. He hurried to them, extending his hand. "Sebastian Hall, Miss Kellaway. I hope you haven't been waiting long."

"Not at all. We arrived early. This is my sister, Jane."

"Miss Jane, a pleasure." Mr. Hall gave her an easy smile. She liked the fact that he wasn't all staid and proper. "Have you had piano lessons before?"

"No, sir." She shifted a little, suddenly not certain she wanted piano lessons anymore. Mr. Hall seemed very nice, but this room was too big, too fancy. And she didn't like that painting at all.

"I hope you'll find them enjoyable," Mr. Hall said. "If we could review the program and schedule, we'll get started right away." He looked at Lydia, who nodded and followed him to the piano.

Jane trailed after them as Mr. Hall opened a book and began explaining his theory of music and what Jane could expect to learn in the first few weeks.

She glanced at the painting again and thought of all the animals they'd seen at the zoological gardens. Why would anyone want to kill a tiger?

A bank of windows lined the wall on the other side

of the room, sunlight streaming through them. Jane wondered if they overlooked the garden.

When Lydia and Mr. Hall started discussing which books to procure, Jane crossed the room. An alcove was next to the windows with a door presumably leading outside. Metal trays sat on several tables, filled with dirt and sprouting green seedlings. She stepped closer, peering at the little shoots.

The door opened and a tall, big-shouldered man entered, his black hair sprinkled with gray like a coating of frost. He was fiddling with an apparatus in his hands, his head bent. He looked up at Jane and frowned.

She startled. The earl! She knew it. His face was austere and hard, lined with creases around his eyes and mouth.

Jane's heart pounded. She couldn't move.

"Who are you?" the Earl of Rushton demanded in a deep voice.

"Er . . . Jane Kellaway, sir . . . my lord. I'm taking piano lessons with Mr. Hall."

"What are you doing here, then?"

"He's . . . he's discussing things with my sister."

"Is she taking piano lessons?" His words were short and clipped, like bullets.

"No, si— my lord."

"Then oughtn't he discuss things with you?"

Jane scratched her forehead, then stopped. Likely it wasn't polite to scratch in front of an earl.

"I . . . well, I'm certain Mr. Hall knows what he's about."

The earl stared at her for a second, then gave a laugh that sounded rusty and humorless, as if he hadn't laughed in ages. "Certain of that, are you?"

Jane glanced back to where Lydia and Mr. Hall were

still conferring, then shrugged. The earl frowned at her. He looked like a cruel knight Jane had once seen in a picture book of verses.

"Be gone, girl," he ordered. "I've work to do."

His gruff tone made her insides quiver, but she didn't move. "Are those your plants?"

"Whose else would they be?"

"What's that?" Jane indicated the apparatus he held.

The earl lifted it a bit. It was a long metal tube with what appeared to be a handle at one end. "Water syringe. Meant to spray a mist of water on seedlings. Useful, if one can get the blasted thing to work."

He pushed the handle, but it stuck halfway down the cylinder. The earl scowled at the thing as if it had deeply insulted him. Jane fought a smile.

"That's the way it is, isn't it?" she said. "Most things are useful only if they work."

"That so? What do *you* plan to do, then?"

Jane wished she knew. "I haven't decided yet."

The earl grunted and turned to his plants. Jane watched him for a moment.

"I like to study insects," she finally said.

He barked out one of his rusty laughs again. "You like to study the scourge of my garden? Find a way to get rid of them—then you'll be useful."

His tone implied that until that day, she would be nothing more than a bother. A twinge of hurt went through Jane, though she didn't quite know why. It wasn't as if it ought to matter what the man thought of her, even if he was a peer. Papa had always said a man's character mattered more than his stature.

"My lord, do you know anything about ferns?" she asked.

He looked as if she'd asked him if he knew how to be an earl.

"Of course I do," he said. "Why?"

"I've got a fern that's a bit tattered. Turning brown and such. Can't think what I'm doing wrong, but perhaps you might tell me?"

Lord Rushton harrumphed, then ordered, "Bring it the next time you come round."

"Jane?" Lydia's voice, threaded with tension, came from behind her. "Are you…Oh." She stopped, resting her hand on Jane's shoulder.

"My father, the Earl of Rushton," Mr. Hall said.

Lydia's fingers tightened. "My lord, a pleasure to meet you."

The earl glowered at her from beneath bushy eyebrows, gave a gruff nod, and turned away. Jane tried to ease away from Lydia, whose grip was beginning to hurt.

"Come along, then." Lydia steered Jane back to the piano, bending close to her ear. "I do hope you didn't disturb him."

"His bark is worse than his bite," Mr. Hall said without concern, his voice almost amused. "Unless you're his own child. Sit down, please, Miss Jane, and we'll begin."

Jane sat at the piano but glanced toward the alcove at the earl. The outside door shut with a click as he left.

She turned her attention to the piano, obeying Mr. Hall's instructions as she tried to convince her fingers to cooperate with her brain. After an hour of learning the keys and starting scales, Jane followed Lydia from the town house with a lesson book and a sense that she might not have an exact talent for music.

"It'll take some time," Lydia assured her as the cab

rattled toward home. "Once you start learning songs and such, I'm sure it'll become more interesting."

"Did you ever take piano lessons?" Jane asked.

"No." Lydia looked out the window. "Too busy with other things."

Jane glanced at the notebook Lydia still held on her lap. As much as she loved her sister, she couldn't help wondering why Lydia never seemed to do anything beyond mathematics and tutoring. She'd never married, she didn't have friends over for tea, and she attended social events rarely and only when Grandmama insisted upon it; she didn't even like shopping or going to the theater.

Seemed to Jane there ought to be more to life than numbers. Certainly there ought to be more to *Lydia's* life.

"Where did you meet Lord Northwood?" she asked suddenly.

Lydia gave her a startled look. "Oh...I can't remember. Why?"

"His father is a bit stern. Lord Northwood didn't seem that way. Neither did Mr. Hall."

Lydia made a murmuring noise. "What did you say to him? Lord Rushton?"

"I asked him about his seedlings and what might be the matter with my fern. Seems he's got an insect problem. He wasn't as...as *earlish* as I thought he might be."

"What did you think he'd be like?"

"Rather majestic, I suppose, as if he'd just come from meeting with the queen. Instead he was more grumpy than regal. I don't suppose he's invited to court often."

"Because of his temper?" Lydia smiled. "Papa was once received at court, you know. When he was knighted. That was years before you were born."

"Did you attend the ceremony?"

"No, but Mother told me about it. She said it was magnificent, if a bit severe. I'd the sense that she would have liked to tell a rude joke or something simply to see what would happen."

Jane grinned. "Was she fond of jokes?"

"She was fond of laughter." A soft, bittersweet affection flashed in Lydia's eyes. Jane knew that though their mother had died a decade ago, shortly after Jane was born, Lydia had lost her long before that. And yet Lydia rarely spoke of their mother's illness—she told Jane only of the days when she was whole and well, the way her eyes lit with happiness and her laughter sounded like bells.

"She wanted everything to be light," Lydia said. "Cheerful."

"Not like Papa," Jane said, then added, "Or you."

"No." Lydia slipped her arm around Jane, drawing her closer. "I've always been like him. Serious, academic. But secretly I wanted to be more like her."

"Why?"

Lydia brushed her lips across Jane's temple. "Because I thought life would be easier."

"But her life wasn't easy at all," Jane said.

"No, that's true. I was wrong."

Lydia's arm tightened around Jane with sudden urgency, and she pressed her cheek against Jane's hair. Jane started a moment, then slipped her arms around Lydia's waist and hugged her.

"Do you still miss her?" she asked.

"All the time."

"I wish I did." Jane's voice grew smaller, colored with a hint of shame. "But I didn't even know her. I mean, I wish she were still here, but I didn't know her at all, or what she was like...Is it wrong that I can't miss her?"

"Oh, no. No. And you did know her. For too short a time and not as any of us would have liked, but you knew her."

"Everything would be different if she hadn't died, wouldn't it?" Jane asked. "If she hadn't gotten sick."

Lydia's grip tightened. Jane heard her sister's heart beating beneath her cheek, a rapid thumping that made her look up.

"Yes." The word was tight, strained. Lydia looked over Jane's head out the window. "Everything would be different."

Tension threaded through her sister's body. Jane frowned, then reached over to squeeze Lydia's hand.

An odd, uncomfortable feeling rose in her—the sense that Lydia didn't want to imagine just how different things might have been if their mother had lived.

Hot, damp air filled the greenhouse, making Alexander's collar too tight, his coat too heavy. Resisting the urge to pull at his cravat, he passed rows of flowering plants to where his father stood examining a pot of soil.

"Sir." Alexander stopped a short distance away. An old, familiar feeling rose in him—a strange combination of pride and inadequacy whose layers Alexander never wished to examine. He'd experienced that feeling in the Earl of Rushton's presence for as long as he could remember, a fact that made his recent aggravation with his father all the more unsettling.

Rushton looked up. "Northwood. What brings you here?"

"What have you heard about the war?"

"Whatever you have."

"In the event of a declaration, the Earl of Clarendon has emphasized the right to consider anyone residing in Russia an enemy," Alexander said. "I've sent word to Darius in St. Petersburg, though I suspect he already knows."

The earl pushed the pot away with a grunt of annoyance and went to pick up a watering can. His big chest and shoulders were encased in a plain black coat and waistcoat—never one for fripperies, Rushton—and comb marks furrowed his metal-gray hair. Although he still appeared formidable, his frame had grown thinner over the past two years, his face gaunt and creased with lines of stress.

"Your brother won't alter his plans," he said.

"I know. But if you wrote to him, he'd be more inclined to consider the ramifications."

"If he continues to reside at the court," Rushton said, "he will be in less danger there than here."

"I've little doubt Darius can and will take care of himself whether he resides at the court or not. However, I'm concerned about the consequences this could have for us here."

"Such as?"

"Talia, for one. She's of marriageable age, and she—"

"As are you." His father shot him a pointed look.

"But Talia is—"

"Let the girl alone, Northwood. It's your own lack of prospects that ought to concern you, especially after the Chilton debacle."

Frustration swelled in Alexander's chest. They'd all borne the embarrassment that followed his broken engagement. Between that and his mother's desertion, even

Alexander admitted it would be difficult to believe any of the Halls could contract an advantageous marriage.

Since he had no rebuttal to his father's remark, he chose to change the subject. "Talia has expressed a wish to visit Floreston Manor again."

Rushton's expression darkened. "Ought to have got rid of the place years ago."

"She wouldn't forgive you if you did." Although none of them had visited Floreston Manor since their mother left, Alexander knew it was the one place Talia had been happy as a child.

His sister had been a mystery to him then—a bronze-haired child who flitted through the corridors of Floreston Manor and the gardens of St. Petersburg like a wood sprite.

He sighed. Talia was even more of a mystery to him now, though her faint otherworldliness had become weighted beneath a layer of shadows.

"Sebastian has agreed to accompany us, if you're willing to reopen the manor," he said. "And we'll invite Castleford."

The earl didn't respond, clipping dead leaves from a plant.

"It would do Talia some good," Alexander persisted. *You, as well.* "She doesn't enjoy being in London during the season."

Rushton finally gave a short nod. "Very well."

"Good. I'll leave the arrangements to you, then?" Anything to get the old bird to do something besides tend to his blasted plants.

He turned to leave when his father's voice stopped him. "What of the Society exhibition, Northwood?"

"The council has expressed concern about the Society's connection with France and the substantial Russian component. However, I do not anticipate any difficulties yet."

His father glanced at him, his mouth turning down. Alexander's final word seemed to echo against the damp glass of the greenhouse.

Yet.

Chapter Eight

Alexander paced to the hearth, then swiveled on his heel and went to the windows and back to the hearth. Sebastian hunched over the piano, pencil in hand, looking at a sheet of music as if it were an earwig.

After his third trek across the carpet, Alexander stopped. Through three layers of fabric, he felt the heavy weight of the locket pressing into his chest. He hadn't looked at it closely for the past three weeks, had only dropped it into his pocket every morning for reasons he couldn't quite comprehend.

He tugged it out now and stared at the silver surface, the intricate engraving.

"You wouldn't have that grim look about you if you'd got rid of it," Sebastian remarked.

Alexander shook his head and replaced the necklace. He'd told his brother the whole tale in the hopes of obtaining some words of wisdom. Instead, Sebastian had strongly advocated that he simply give the locket back to Lydia.

Alexander had been unable to explain why he knew she wouldn't accept it.

"Her mother was mad," he said.

"Mad?"

Alexander paced back to the windows. "It happened when Lydia was a child. Sir Henry was forced to institutionalize his wife several times. She died at a sanatorium in France after giving birth to Jane."

"What has that got to do . . . Oh."

Alexander's shoulders tensed as he stared at the garden. "I assume it caused a stir at the time, though no one appears to remember. Or if they do, they don't care. Perhaps that speaks to the Kellaways' lack of importance."

"Then you oughtn't be concerned about gossip should you"—Sebastian cleared his throat—"pursue her."

Pursue her. Alexander hadn't told his brother that was exactly what he wanted to do. And despite his near-constant thoughts about Lydia, his determination to unravel her complexities, his memories of her soft mouth, Alexander hadn't devised quite the right approach. He could pursue any other woman in the world with flattery and attentiveness, but those alone would not work with Lydia.

He had yet to determine what, exactly, would.

He sank into a chair and rubbed his forehead. A knock came at the door, and the butler stepped into the room.

"Pardon, my lord, but there's a woman to see you."

Alexander and Sebastian exchanged glances. "A woman?"

"Miss Lydia Kellaway."

Sebastian laughed.

"Send her in, Soames," Alexander said.

Soames nodded and slipped from the room. Alexander experienced a gleam of anticipation as they waited. He smoothed his hair away from his forehead. He straightened his collar. He brushed his hand against his breast pocket and allowed it to linger over the locket.

The door opened again. Soames stepped aside to let Lydia enter the drawing room. Both Alexander and Sebastian stood.

Alexander's body tightened at the mere sight of the woman. God only knew how those severely cut dresses managed to give her such allure, but they did. This one fitted her form with such precision that once again he couldn't help wondering what those rounded breasts would look like bare and quivering under his hands.

He grimaced and shifted, forcing away his lustful thoughts. "Miss Kellaway."

"Lord Northwood." Her gaze slanted to Sebastian. "And, Mr. Hall, a pleasure to see you again. Jane greatly enjoyed her first lesson."

He smiled. "Pleased to hear that. She's a lovely girl."

Lydia returned his smile, her blue eyes bright. Alexander smothered an irritating surge of jealousy.

She looked at Alexander again. "Your footman told me you were here, my lord, if you've a moment?"

Alexander made a point of consulting the clock. "A moment, yes. Sebastian, go find out what time the Society meeting starts this afternoon."

"Soames already—"

"Then ensure John knows to order the carriage."

"But—"

Alexander turned on his brother. "Go do *something*."

Sebastian gave Lydia Kellaway a charming grin before pushing himself away from the piano and strolling out the door as if walking through a meadow of wildflowers.

Alexander's teeth came together as he gestured for Lydia to sit.

"I won't stay long." She shook her head, her blue eyes unnerving in their directness. "I have another proposition for you, Lord Northwood."

His interest stirred. He moved closer to her, stopping when she was within arm's reach. "And once again I find myself intrigued."

She withdrew a piece of paper from her notebook and extended it to him. Alexander took it, glancing at her again before looking at the paper. Written in a neat, precise hand, the numbers and final question caused a wave of sheer puzzlement.

The sum of three numbers is 6, the sum of their squares is 8, and the sum of their cubes is 5. What is the sum of their fourth powers?

Alexander scratched his head. "Ah, would you care to explain? What is this?"

"A mathematical problem."

"I can see that. Why have you given it to me?"

"I want you to solve it." There was an amused glint in her eyes, a slight curve to her mouth—all evidence of a wicked side that Alexander hadn't seen before now. "I believe my puzzle about the woman selling eggs was too simple for you. This one is more complex."

Alexander stared at her. A weight seemed to descend on his heart at the realization she hadn't sought him out just for *him*.

"You want me to solve this problem," he said, "in exchange for the locket."

"Yes. I don't like to put all my eggs in one basket, you know."

Alexander barked out a laugh. "I imagine you still wish to establish the parameters of a time frame."

"Yes. If you are unable to solve the problem in two weeks' time, with no help from anyone else, mind you, then you will promptly return my mother's locket."

Alexander continued staring at her. Her expression still contained that wicked gleam—quite appealing, if he were to be honest with himself, seeing as how it made her eyes darken to the color of a dawn sky—but other than that, she appeared utterly serious.

He looked at the problem again. "You wrote this?"

"You needn't sneer, my lord. You know I enjoy devising puzzles, but the one you solved was just that—a puzzle. This is a problem."

"And you don't think I can solve it."

"I didn't say that."

Despite his irritation, Alexander experienced a prickle of anticipation again, a feeling aroused only by this particular woman. It was sharply pleasant, like the taste of Russian black bread, fragrant and tart.

"You implied it," he said; "otherwise you wouldn't have made the offer."

"Yes, well..." Her lips curved—lovely, tempting; he wanted to put his mouth over hers and feel her yield...

"Perhaps implications aren't so vague after all," she said.

Alexander tossed the paper onto a table and planted his hands on his hips. Lydia Kellaway stood there looking like a little black rabbit in her charcoal dress, her blue eyes and flushed skin the only sources of color on her person.

For a fleeting, unexpected instant, he wondered what

she'd look like in bright blue or green, ostrich plumes flowing from her hat, her cheeks and lips enticingly painted with rouge.

No. He didn't like that image. At all.

He cleared his throat. "Miss Kellaway, it appears I've behaved unfairly with regard to your mother's locket. And if you ever tell Sebastian I said that, I'll deny it to the end of my days. However, you've made your desire for the locket quite clear, and as I've no wish to cause you further grief, I will return it to you immediately."

A brief flicker of surprise crossed her face before her smile curved again. "*You* don't think you can do it."

"I beg your pardon?"

"You don't think you can solve the problem."

"I do not think that."

"And I've no desire for pity, my lord."

"I do not pity you," Alexander snapped. "I'm trying to behave like a gentleman, which I don't find an easy fit."

"A gentleman conducts business in a fair and just manner."

Alexander tried not to grind his teeth together. "Which I am attempting to do."

"Returning my mother's locket out of pity is neither fair nor just. However, if you wish to concede defeat, then I will gladly accept the mantle of victory and claim my winnings."

Alexander stared at her. Then he crossed the room in three long strides and grabbed her by the shoulders, pushing her up against the wall so swiftly that she gasped. Without giving her an opportunity to resist, he lowered his head and captured her lush mouth, driven by a sudden burning intent to sear her with a kiss.

Her body stiffened beneath his grip, her hands fisting against his chest. He pressed harder, moving his mouth across hers, urging her to let him in. Heat swept through his blood, and though she began to soften, her closed lips did not yield, did not open for him.

A mathematical problem, for God's sake. The only problem he wanted to solve was the soft, supple one currently in his arms.

Alexander growled with frustration. He pressed one hand against her lower back, pulling her as close as he could. His frustration mounted when his desire to feel her body was thwarted by a morass of skirts and petticoats. He darted his tongue out to lick the corner of her mouth, and when her lips parted on an indrawn breath, he delved inside with one heated stroke.

Ahhh.

A pure male satisfaction rose in him as he felt her surrender, the relaxing of her hands, the opening of her pliant lips. He cupped one hand around the back of her warm neck, angling her head for more thorough access.

Her hands spread over his chest, the warmth of her palms burning through his shirt. One of his fists clenched in her skirts as he fought the urge to drag all the damned layers up and *feel* her. To strip every blasted article of clothing from her and expose her sweet-scented skin and rounded breasts.

He groaned. He pressed his lower body against her, knowing she'd feel him if it weren't for the barrier of her clothing. He grasped her wrist. Her pulse beat swift and hot beneath his fingertips as he dragged her hand down the front of his shirt lower...lower...lower...

He stopped. Used inhuman willpower to ease his hold.

Waited with a thudding heart for her to pull away. She twisted her wrist from his grip, lifting her head to stare at him.

Seconds passed. Her breath steamed hot against his lips. Heat flared in her blue eyes. And then she splayed her hand flat against his belly and slid it down to his groin.

Alexander swallowed, his gaze locked to hers as her fingers brushed against the bulge in his trousers. A hint of trepidation appeared in her expression, but then her fingers curved with tentative curiosity until his erection pressed against her palm.

She sighed, her lips moving to his jaw, her cheek rubbing over his. He winced, desire churning through him. He placed a hand against the wall behind her in an effort to master his rapidly diminishing control.

Lydia paused, her breath still hot against his jaw. He grasped her wrist again. For an instant, neither of them moved, and then her hand slipped from him.

He stepped back, moving away to allow her to gather her composure while he did the same. He dug into his pocket and removed the necklace, turning back to extend it to her—and realizing his mistake too late.

She stared at the locket nestled in his palm, two spots of color high on her cheekbones. Alexander swallowed a rising tide of shame.

"I'm sorry, I—"

"I require no payment for services rendered," Lydia said coldly.

"I didn't mean—"

"You've made it quite clear what you *mean*. And I believe I've made my intentions equally clear. I will not accept your charity."

His fingers tightened around the locket. "Your pride will be your downfall, Miss Kellaway."

"Do you think so? Tell me, if you were in my position, would you take the locket back simply because I felt sorry for you?"

Alexander didn't respond. He gave a curt nod and tossed the necklace onto the table beside the paper she'd given him. His shoulders felt stiff enough to break, his blood still flaring with desire unfulfilled.

"And should I solve your damned problem?" he asked through a clenched jaw.

"If you manage to do so by the end of two weeks, you may once again determine my debt."

"And you will abide by it?"

For an instant, a glimmer of apprehension appeared in her eyes. "As long as it remains within reason."

"Meaning?"

"No requests for a kiss or... anything else of that nature."

"Very well."

She blinked. "You agree?"

"Yes." His mouth twisted. "You're surprised?"

"Considering your—*our*—behavior of late, I suppose I am."

"And disappointed?" He smiled without humor.

"Certainly not."

"Good. There's no need to be, you know." He approached her again, his booted steps silent against the thick Aubusson carpet.

Lydia didn't back away from him, but her wariness visibly deepened. "Why... why not?"

Alexander reached out to slide his thumb across her full lips, a renewed surge of arousal filling him at the sensation of her warm breath. "Because the next time we engage in something *of that nature*, debt will not be an issue."

Lydia swallowed, her finger twisting around a lock of hair that clung to her damp neck. "There will not be a next time, my lord."

"Oh, yes. There will. Not because you owe me, but because you want it."

She swiveled on her heel and strode to the foyer. Alexander followed, ensuring she was safely in the cab before turning back to the drawing room.

He stopped. His father stood at the door of his study, his expression unreadable.

"Miss Kellaway, wasn't it?" he asked.

Alexander nodded, not knowing what to say and not liking the feeling of having been caught doing something wrong.

Rushton's gaze flicked to the drawing room and back to the front door before he turned and disappeared into his study.

Chapter Nine

The sun hung like a golden ball in the sky, burning away the last of the late-morning fog. A gentle breeze rustled through the trees. Beside Lydia on the carriage seat, Jane peered out the window as the festival came into view.

"There it is!" Jane almost bounced up and down.

Lydia smiled. Her sister had spent the past week and a half chattering about the festival, and her excitement solidified Lydia's belief that she had done the right thing in accepting Northwood's invitation.

She took her sister's hand as they descended the carriage and walked toward the field amid a crowd of well-dressed men and women, all accompanied by eager children.

Flowers, streamers, and balloons decorated the field, and several booths sat around the perimeter. A wooden platform demarcated an area for dancing, and musicians were tuning up their instruments. Sebastian sat at a cottage piano, in consultation with another musician over a sheet of music.

Before Lydia and Jane reached the entrance, Lord Northwood approached with a young woman at his side.

Lydia's heart gave a little leap. Dear heaven, he looked magnificent. The points of his collar emphasized the hard angles of his face, and he walked with an easy, masculine grace that made Lydia want to gaze upon him for hours.

"Good morning." He stopped in front of them and removed his hat, his dark eyes slipping over Lydia. Her skin prickled with awareness. "A pleasure to see you again."

He made the introductions, and Lady Talia Hall greeted them with warmth.

"I'm glad to meet you properly, Miss Kellaway." Though the young woman had more delicate, refined features, she and her brothers shared a resemblance in their dark eyes and high cheekbones that lent them a foreign air. "I apologize for the . . . chaos of our initial encounter."

She threw Alexander a pointed look. He had the grace to look somewhat abashed.

"There is no need to apologize, Lady Talia," Lydia assured her as they handed their tickets over at the entrance and went into the festival grounds.

"Miss Jane, I'd be honored if you'd accompany me to the game booths," Northwood said. "And there's a display of dioramas that I think you'll find quite fascinating."

He extended his hand to her. Jane glanced at Lydia for permission, and for an instant Lydia didn't want to let her go. There were too many people, too much activity . . .

Stop it. Northwood would never let anything happen to Jane.

She nodded. Jane gave Northwood a brilliant smile

and took his hand. Trepidation slipped through Lydia as she watched them melt into the crowd.

Much to Lydia's gratitude, Talia remained by her side as they walked around the festival and met various people, including Lord Castleford—a man whose tall, imposing appearance might have been intimidating were it not for the welcoming twinkle in his eyes and the broad smile creasing his tanned face.

"Miss Kellaway's father was Sir Henry Kellaway," Talia told Lord Castleford. "He was a scholar of considerable renown on the subject of Chinese history. Perhaps you knew of him?"

"Indeed. I had the pleasure of making his acquaintance several times, Miss Kellaway. His lectures were brilliant."

Lydia smiled, warmed by the evident admiration in Lord Castleford's voice. They spoke about her father's work and travels as they continued through the festival grounds, before Lydia turned to see Northwood approaching with Jane.

Her heart twisted at the sight of them—her Jane, as sweet as cake even in her mourning dress, her hands gesturing as she spoke and laughed, her green eyes sparkling. Northwood walked beside her, his hand on her shoulder, his head lowered to better listen to her chatter. His smile flashed every so often, or he responded with gestures and laughter of his own.

They could not have appeared more opposite—the tall, dark-haired viscount and the pale, brown-haired girl, but somehow they looked entirely natural. Somehow they fit.

Lydia's throat constricted. She couldn't let this happen. She couldn't allow herself to feel this way about

Lord Northwood. Moreover, she couldn't let Jane become attached to a man with whom Lydia had no future.

She had no future with any man. Despite what she'd told Northwood, she knew her destiny—she was fated to live a spinster life, fulfilled by her work and her love for Jane. And while Lydia sometimes could not deny her longing for more, she had to be content with her fate. It could have been so much worse.

"Lydia, you must see the dioramas!" Jane hurried forward. "They've got one that shows the Aurora Borealis and another the changing seasons in Paris. It's lovely. My favorite is the one of Africa, though, with the sun rising and the lions actually moving. Isn't that right, Lord Northwood?"

Northwood watched Jane affectionately as the girl turned away to answer a question Talia asked. Then he glanced at Lydia.

"Have you solved the problem, my lord?" she asked in an effort to remind herself of the only thing she wanted from him.

He scowled. "I doubt Pythagoras himself could solve the blasted thing."

Lydia suppressed a smile. "So you concede defeat?"

"Never. I've still over a week, yes?"

She inclined her head in acknowledgment, experiencing a small surge of admiration for his persistence. "Shall I give you a hint?"

"That will not be necessary." He gave her a mock frown. "You don't think I can do it."

"I didn't say that."

"That doesn't mean you aren't thinking it." His frown eased into a smile, the corners of his eyes creasing in a manner so appealing that Lydia's heart pattered like raindrops. "Never mind. I take great pleasure in changing people's preconceived notions."

He winked at her before turning to Jane. "Shall we show your sister where we can procure an ice cream?"

Jane nodded, grasping Lydia's hand. Her heart still warm from Northwood's gentle teasing, Lydia allowed herself to absorb the girl's enthusiasm. There was no harm in having a bit of fun—in fact, it would do both her and Jane a world of good to enjoy the lovely day.

They spent the next couple of hours with Talia and Northwood, playing games, watching a troupe of jugglers, eating ice cream. The laughter and happy shrieks of children resounded throughout the festival grounds. Jane and Talia went to procure tissue-paper balloons from one of the booths.

Lydia smiled at the sight of Northwood—his hair in disarray from the wind, his coat wrinkled, and his fine linen shirt smudged with grass stains—joining a group of children in a game of hoops.

Which person was he—the formidable viscount who strode through the world with determined pride or this seemingly carefree man who liked ice cream and knew how to talk to an eleven-year-old girl and remembered how to roll a hoop?

Which man did Lydia want him to be?

Both.

The answer slipped like a whisper just beneath her heart.

A warning followed, but she chose to ignore it and allow the warmth and pleasure of the day to submerge her persistent unease.

Jane came hurrying back to fetch Lydia and Northwood for the start of a puppet show, and after a helping of lemon ice, they went to the area where the musicians had begun to play. The lively tunes swam above the sounds of laughter as a number of children and adults began dancing.

"Will you honor me with a dance?" Northwood asked, pausing beside Lydia.

"Dance? I—"

A grin tugged at his mouth. "You're about to tell me you can't dance, aren't you?"

"Of course I can dance, Lord Northwood. I'm not ill-bred." Lydia lifted her chin a fraction. "It's simply been some time. I'm a bit out of practice, I fear."

"Then I'll enjoy teaching you again." He curled his hand around her wrist, his fingers skimming the pulse beating too rapidly beneath her skin.

As they stepped onto the dance floor, Lydia expected him to draw her closer, but instead he wove a path around the couples who danced to a brisk country tune. He guided her into the easy rhythm of the dance. His grip remained firm on her waist, the warmth of his hand burning through her glove, his gaze so attentive it seemed as if he wanted to look nowhere else but at her.

And all of it, everything about him—his touch, his eyes, his grasp, the movement of his body mere inches from hers—incited a response of pure pleasure in Lydia, a pleasure undiluted by guilt or shame.

They parted several times to dance with others—Northwood with Jane and then Talia, Lydia with Sebastian and then Lord Castleford. After an energetic Scotch reel, she paused to sit on a bench and catch her breath.

Then Sebastian began playing a waltz, and Lydia watched as Northwood stopped to look around. For her.

She waited, expectant, ready. Surprised at the happiness that filled her blood.

Alexander approached, his dark eyes twinkling. At that moment, Lydia wanted nothing else in the world. She put her hand in his and went out to dance again.

He watched her from his position hidden in the crowd. He remembered when he'd first laid eyes upon her.

She had arrived on a train. Not pretty at first glance—pallid skin from being indoors all the time, too serious, her forehead marred with frown lines. She'd barely said anything either, let her grandmother do all the talking. Then after they'd gotten home and she'd removed her coat and hat, he'd noticed the way her dress fitted her, the thickness of her hair, her dark eyelashes.

That was when the seeds of lust had sprouted, though it had taken many months of cultivation before they'd borne fruit.

All that time he'd spent—leaning over her shoulder at the table to point out an error in her equations, standing beside her at the blackboard, watching her at her desk, sitting across from her at the dinner table—all leading to that one afternoon when he'd summoned his courage and made his move.

And she had responded. Like a cat in heat.

Even now, remembering, he became aroused. He wanted that Lydia again. Not this one, not the hardened, older Lydia of today, but the young Lydia who'd arrived in Germany so quiet and serious. The Lydia who, contrary to every expectation he'd had about her, had blos-

somed under his touch—until that stupid girl had ruined everything.

Anger subsumed his arousal, tightening his chest. His hands curled into fists.

She owed him. She'd instigated his downfall from a prestigious career. She'd lost him the respect of his peers. She was the reason he'd returned to the filth of London. For well over a decade, Lydia Kellaway had owed him—and now the time had come to pay.

Chapter Ten

Alexander paced outside the building. A horse clomped past, pulling a wagon filled with broken furniture, rusted bits of metal, and a pile of greasy rags. The sun burned through the layer of yellowish fog permeating the city streets.

He flicked open his watch and gave a mutter of impatience. He had allowed four days to pass since the festival—days during which he'd stayed up well past midnight attempting to solve Lydia's damned problem—before devising another excuse to seek the woman's company. When he'd gone to her town house, Mrs. Boyd had told him Lydia had a meeting with the editorial board of some mathematical journal, but she ought to have been finished by now.

Alexander paced several more steps before the door opened and Lydia stepped onto the street, followed by a half dozen men.

"He is the Hollis professor of mathematics and natural philosophy at Harvard University," one of them grumbled.

"That doesn't mean he applied the method correctly, Dr. Grant," Lydia replied, adjusting her hat against the sun. "I'll write the letter of amendment this week and present it at our next meeting."

"He won't take kindly to that," Grant muttered.

"Better we ask him for a revision than publish a flawed paper," another portly man remarked. "Miss Kellaway is correct about the application. I suggest we allow her to see this matter through."

"Agreed," a third man said. "We've also your paper on our next agenda, Miss Kellaway. If you could send it along in advance, that will give us time to review it prior to discussion. It's the Euler equation paper, correct?"

Lydia nodded, and the little group commenced a discussion of Euler—a Swiss mathematician whose work involved calculus and graphing. Alexander waited a few more minutes before clearing his throat. Loudly.

They all looked up. Lydia blinked.

"Lord Northwood?"

"Your grandmother told me where to find you, Miss Kellaway," he said. "She anticipated your meeting would be concluded by now."

"Well, yes, we've just finished." Lydia gestured to the men, who had clustered in a half-circle stronghold behind her. "These are my colleagues on the editorial board."

She stepped aside to make introductions. Alexander greeted the other men, aware that they were eyeing him with suspicion.

"What are you doing here, my lord?" Lydia asked.

"I'm going to oversee the exhibition preparations at St. Martin's Hall and thought you might like to accompany me."

"The Society of Arts exhibition, my lord?" Dr. Grant asked, stepping forward. "Haven't you got a number of mathematical instruments on display?" He glanced at the others. "Lord Perry is on the consulting committee, you know, and he said it's quite an impressive array of items they've got. Yes, indeed, let's all go and see how things are progressing."

The other mathematicians murmured their agreement. Alexander frowned.

"Will it be all right, my lord?" Lydia asked, a glimmer of amusement shining in her blue eyes.

"Er... certainly." He nodded toward the group. "Gentlemen, I welcome your thoughts and opinions."

A bustle of activity ensued as Drs. Grant and Brown announced they would ride with Lydia in Alexander's carriage while the others procured a second cab.

Alexander tucked a hand beneath Lydia's elbow to help her into the carriage. A rigid shock coursed through her, stiffening her body.

"Miss Kellaway?"

The color drained from her skin, and unmistakable fear flashed across her face. Alexander followed her gaze to where she was looking across the street, but aside from the usual array of passersby, there appeared to be no cause for such alarm.

"Lydia!" He shook her a little. "Are you all right?"

She jerked back. "Y-yes. I'm sorry. I thought I saw..."

"What? Who?"

"Nothing." She pressed a hand to her forehead. "We... The meeting room was a bit stuffy, and I'm afraid I needed some air. I'm fine now, thank you."

She pulled her arm from his grip and climbed into the

carriage. After the other two men entered, Alexander followed. Lydia stared out the window, her hand at her throat, her breathing quick.

"You've got cause for concern with the start of war, my lord?" Dr. Grant peered at Alexander through the filtered light of the carriage interior. "Your mother was Russian; isn't that right?"

"You are correct, Dr. Grant, yes. And no, I've no cause for concern."

He kept his gaze on Lydia as the carriage rattled to a start. Color returned to her cheeks, but her unease appeared to linger even when they arrived at the hall.

Alexander fell into step beside her as they walked inside. Noise filled the air—the shouting of orders, hammers banging as workers constructed displays, crates screeching open.

Alexander bent closer to Lydia. "What is it? What happened?"

She shook her head and pressed her lips together. "Nothing, really, my lord. I'm dreadfully sorry. Just a bit of fatigue. Now please do explain to us how your exhibition is organized."

For her sake, he allowed her the temporary escape but didn't intend to let the matter drop. He gave the mathematicians a brief tour of the main part of the exhibition, which contained general objects of education—full classifications of paper and notebooks, inkwells, engraved alphabet slates, blackboards, portable chemical laboratories, lesson stands, mathematical instruments, and countless other implements for classroom use. A section just beneath the long gallery held dozens of floor, table, and pocket globes.

The subdivisions of the exhibit comprised items from

foreign countries—models of Swedish and Norwegian schoolhouses, zoological specimens for teaching natural history, maps, sample drawings, writing frames for the blind, and musical instruments.

As much as Alexander had hoped to have Lydia to himself this afternoon, he admitted the mathematicians' responses were gratifying—they expressed their interest and admiration over the array of objects and made several useful suggestions of how to improve the displays.

"How did you manage to obtain permission for all of this?" Lydia asked after the others had drifted off to various sections of the exhibit.

She was watching the activity with a hint of awe. Pride coursed through Alexander. He wanted the exhibition to impress society, the government, the *world*, but right now this one woman's admiration surpassed the need for anything more.

"All the articles for display were brought in duty-free," he said. "When I first applied for the exhibition, I assumed it would be small. I knew it was a good idea, but I wasn't certain how people would respond. Displays of writing books and maps aren't quite the same as displays of ancient sculptures."

"Yet people did respond," Lydia said. "Emphatically. You ought to be very proud, my lord."

He was. Not only of himself, but also of the Society, the members who had supported him despite everything, the people who had worked for almost two years to bring the idea to fruition.

"Would it be all right if I brought Jane here to see the preparations?" Lydia asked. "I think she'd especially enjoy seeing the insect cases."

"Of course. Your grandmother is welcome to visit as well."

"She'll be delighted. She's heard quite a bit about it already. Your reputation precedes you, my lord." A flush colored her cheeks as she appeared to realize what she'd said.

"Not always in a positive manner," Alexander said. He leaned his shoulder against a display case and studied Lydia. "What have you heard about me? Other than the usual rumors."

"That you run a company trading in . . . cotton and flax, I think?" She examined a display of pocket globes, her eyelashes dark against her high cheekbones. "That you were once engaged to Lord Chilton's daughter, but he insisted on breaking off the engagement after what happened with your mother."

Alexander waited for the inevitable questions. Threads of old hurt and embarrassment wove through him, but they were now ancient and frayed, too tattered to be binding.

"Did you love her?" Lydia's question was quiet, her voice steady.

His hands dug into his upper arms, his spine stiffening. Lydia didn't look at him, though her jaw appeared to tense as silence filled the space that should have contained his abrupt denial.

She rested her hand on a globe, lifting her gaze to him, her blue eyes concealed behind a shield of wariness.

"I had known Miss Caroline Turner for several years before proposing," Alexander said. "She was everything I thought I wanted."

"And what was that?"

"She was elegant, lovely, perfect for a peer. Polished as a diamond. And she was a good person, kind and without artifice. No one ever had an unkind word to say about her. I knew she would make an excellent wife." He paused, then pushed the words through his constricted chest. "Before the scandal, yes, I loved her."

Until this moment, he didn't think he'd even made the admission to himself. And yet his sole concern was how Lydia would react.

She was quiet for what seemed a very long time, the tips of her fingers resting against the glass-covered surface of the miniature world.

"You must have been so hurt," she finally said. An undercurrent of emotion tugged at her voice.

He wondered at its source, wondered how Lydia Kellaway had the capacity to experience pain over *his* loss. It was true—Lord Chilton's severance of the engagement had sliced Alexander to the bone. But the humiliation had only deepened cuts already bleeding from his mother's scandal, his father's shame, his family's disgrace.

"I can't say I was surprised," he told Lydia. "I knew what I'd have to contend with when I returned to London. I knew what I'd face. I'd other plans I didn't want to give up, but I had to."

"What were your plans?"

"I was preparing for a lengthy trip throughout Russia. I'd been planning it for years. Siberia, the Urals, Vladivostok. I'd proposed to Miss Turner before I left, and we agreed to marry upon my return."

The frustration of a thwarted ambition rose in him. "The trip was intended to expand my company."

"And you never went?"

"I couldn't. The scandal, the divorce...I had to come back and attempt to repair the damage."

"And Miss Turner?" Lydia asked.

Alexander rubbed a hand over the back of his neck, his muscles tight and pinched.

"What of her?" he asked.

"What will happen when you've restored your family's reputation? Will she wish to reopen the question of marriage to you?"

Alexander might have laughed if Lydia hadn't sounded so grave. He shook his head.

"Miss Turner married the son of a viscount over a year ago. She has thus far borne him one daughter, and by all accounts they are quite content."

Lydia's blue gaze sharpened, the clouds of wariness dissipating. "Did that disappoint you?"

"God, no." He might have loved the woman at one time, but now his affection for Miss Turner seemed inconsequential and misguided. "If all had remained status quo with my family, I'd have had a good marriage to Miss Turner. But as things transpired . . . she hadn't the constitution to withstand the ugliness of it."

He pushed himself away from the display case and moved closer to Lydia, drawn into the clean, crisp paper smell that belonged to her alone. "And the past month has made me realize I owe Lord Chilton my deepest gratitude for not allowing me to become shackled to his daughter."

He stopped in front of her and lifted a hand to that single loose tendril of hair against her neck. He wrapped the soft strands around his forefinger.

"Because if I had been," he continued, "I couldn't do this."

Her lips parted as if she expected him to kiss her. Instead he rubbed his thumb across her mouth, the ridges of her lips both soft and slightly rough. Her breath tickled his hand, her cheeks darkening with a crimson flush.

Aware that anyone might see them, Alexander fought the almost overpowering urge to kiss her. He stepped back. If she were his wife, there would be no barrier, either self-imposed or external, to prevent him from touching her, kissing her, lov—

Well. He needn't go that far.

"We'd best go," he said. His voice sounded hoarse. He cleared his throat. Must have caught a chill. "The hall will be closing soon."

Dear Jane,

Monosyllable, yes. Clever girl. Here is another riddle:

A word of one syllable, easy and short.
Which reads backward and forward the same;
It expresses the sentiments warm from the heart
And to beauty lays principal claim.

Frankly I'm reaching the end of my riddle repertoire, so I will have to procure more complex challenges. Perhaps I'll send along some mathematical problems to further test your skills.

Best of luck with your comprehension of long division; it sounds as if you've a most excellent tutor in your older sister.

Sincerely,
C

The riddle ran through Jane's mind as she walked with Mrs. Driscoll toward the house for her piano lesson. *A word of one syllable...*

She glanced to the side as a movement caught her eye. Lord Rushton was striding along one of the side paths toward a large glass house.

"Sir...my lord!" Jane let go of Mrs. Driscoll's hand and almost ran to catch up with the earl, her heart beating with a combination of fear and excitement over her own audacity.

He turned with a frown. Did the man ever smile?

Not that she expected him to smile at her.

"I've brought you something." She thrust a book at him. "It's a treatise on insects that are most harmful to a garden. It's got pictures and everything. If you can identify them, you can figure out how to rid your garden of them. There's all sorts of things you can try, like tobacco water or lime water for aphids, fumigation...you can trap snails and slugs with raw potato...and there's a whole section on insects that injure greenhouse plants..." She paused to catch her breath.

The earl's frown returned as he paged through the book. "Why did you bring this to me?"

"I thought you might find it useful. I did tell you I like to study insects, if you recall."

He glowered at the pointed note in her tone.

"I also like puzzles and riddles," Jane added. "I even know one about insects. Part of a tree, if right transposed, an insect then will be disclosed."

"What on earth are you going on about, girl?"

"It's a riddle. Part of a tree—"

"I heard you," the earl grumbled. "Foolishness, riddles."

Jane flushed. "Er, did you figure out what's the matter with my fern, my lord?"

"Yes. Not enough moisture and perhaps too much direct sunlight."

"I water it every day."

"Mist it every day. Don't water the roots every day. They ought to dry in between watering. I've got your fern in the greenhouse. Come and collect it after your lesson."

"Yes, sir. Thank you, sir."

Jane turned and hurried back along the path to where Mrs. Driscoll stood waiting.

"Leaf," the earl called.

Jane stopped.

"Leaf?" she repeated.

"Leaf. Transposed it's *flea*. The answer to your riddle." He almost smiled. *Almost.* "Bastian tells me your sister's fond of puzzles as well."

"Oh, yes, my lord. But Lydia's are more difficult than mine. All about numbers and sums and such." A rush of pride in Lydia filled her, and she added, "My sister is brilliant, Lord Ruston. There isn't a puzzle in the world Lydia can't solve."

"Is that a fact, Miss Jane?" A faint air of challenge crossed his expression. "We'll just see about that."

Chapter Eleven

He was *here*. He was coming up the front step right this moment. Lydia gripped the heavy curtain in her fist, trying to remember if her grandmother had left the house. Yes, she had; she'd taken Jane to attend one of her charities with Mrs. Keene.

Relief mixed with a combination of fear and anticipation as Lydia hurried down the stairs to the front door. Before the bell rang, she pulled the door open. "Lord Northwood."

He scowled. He looked terrible. Dark circles ringed his eyes, his jaw sported coarse whiskers, and his clothing was abominably wrinkled, as if he had been in the same coat and trousers for the past two days. If she didn't know better, she'd think he was Sebastian Hall rather than the impeccable Lord Northwood.

But of course she knew it was him. She knew it by the way her skin warmed, her heart thumping like a metronome. She knew it by the way his gaze slid over her as if he were a man starved and she a warm, soft muffin. And she knew it by the way her entire being flooded with something suspiciously close to joy.

She smiled. Ridiculous, really. The man had caused her nothing but trouble, and yet here she stood, unable to deny this sheer happiness at the sight of him. It made no sense, but at this stage in her life, she knew that emotions had little sense to them.

She couldn't stop smiling, which only intensified Northwood's scowl. "What is so blasted funny?" he growled.

"I'm not laughing." Lydia stepped aside to allow him entry. "Come inside. You look as if you could use a good strong cup of tea. Or perhaps whiskey or brandy would suffice. We have—"

"Nothing, thank you."

Lydia closed the drawing room door behind them, watching with curiosity as he reached into his coat and removed several sheets of creased, smudged paper. He thrust them toward her.

"Your bloody problem, Miss Kellaway."

Her eyebrows rose. "You've solved it?"

"I've no idea."

"I don't understand." Lydia took the papers and smoothed them out. Her original question was grubby almost beyond recognition, the other pages filled with a scrawl of numbers, letters, and numerous erasures. Heavy black lines crossed out several of the equations.

Northwood folded his arms across his chest, his jaw tightening. "I think I have the solution, but I can't be certain."

Lydia stared at him, knowing to her bones that it cost him dearly to admit his doubt about his own abilities. She ran her hand over the pages, imagining that they still contained the heat of his touch, the intensity of his thoughts.

"I... It will take me some time to figure out your—"

He pointed to a small secretaire near the window. "Do it now."

"I beg your pardon?"

"Sit down, Miss Kellaway, and tell me if I've got it right or not."

"Right this very moment?" The slight teasing note to her voice did nothing to ease his scowl.

"Yes. The *parameters of your time frame* end this evening. I intend to know who has won this particular wager before then."

"Very well." Lydia crossed to the table and sat, spreading the pages on the desktop. The back of her neck prickled with awareness when he moved to stand behind her.

She picked up a pencil and began reviewing the process of his solution.

"This page is next." Northwood leaned over her shoulder and shuffled the pages into order. "This is the problem, isn't it? I've got the cubic equation wrong."

His arm brushed her shoulder as he pulled back. Lydia suppressed a tremble of response.

"No, this part is correct," she said, attempting to concentrate on the task at hand. "But you didn't need to actually calculate *a*, *b*, and *c* to determine the sum of their fourth powers. They are roots of x^3 minus $6x^2$ plus $14x$ minus C equals 0."

She removed a clean sheet of paper from a drawer and wrote several equations equaling zero. "And it would have been easier if you'd found the constant term *P* first. Like this." She wrote out several more equations determining the roots of the numbers. "Then you can identify *a*, *b*, *c* as roots of this." She wrote $x^3 - rx^2 + \frac{1}{2}(r^2 - s)x + [\frac{1}{2}r(3s - r^2) - t]/3 = 0$ and tapped the paper with her pencil.

She turned the page to show him how she'd worked it out. His eyes flashed with self-directed anger. "That's not what I did."

"I see that. Fortunately, there is often more than one way to solve a problem."

Lydia ran her finger over the scribbles and cross-outs that constituted his work. When she came to the last page, a black circle ringed the solution he'd reached. Lydia looked at the number *0* with a curious combination of dismay and elation.

Schooling her features into an expression of impassivity, she turned to look at him. He stood right behind her, his hands loose on his hips, his expression still dark as he stared down at his messy work.

"You've got it," she said.

His gaze went to hers, his eyebrows lifting. "I beg your pardon?"

"You solved the problem." Lydia tapped her pencil on the page. "The sum of the fourth power of the numbers is zero."

"It is?" Northwood blinked with surprise.

"Yes."

"You're sure?"

"Positive. Congratulations."

"I'll be damned." Northwood shook his head, a grin breaking across his whiskered face. He slapped his hands together in victory. "You're not putting me on, are you?"

"Of course not." Lydia couldn't prevent another smile, her disappointment over losing the locket yet again fading underneath a sudden rush of pure pride. In *him*.

Northwood chuckled, his fatigue dissipating with his well-deserved satisfaction. He ran his hands over his face and through his disheveled hair.

"And you wrote that." He shook his head. "Good lord, woman, you've got a sharp mind, though I admit to occasionally believing you'd given me an unsolvable problem."

"I wouldn't have done that." Lydia gathered the papers and slipped them into the desk drawer. The secret place in her heart knew she would always treasure them. "I do play fair, Lord Northwood."

"You not only play fair, but you also play well."

Lydia closed the drawer and stood, turning to face him. Apprehension twisted through her as she realized that his solving the problem meant that, once again, she owed him an undetermined debt.

He looked at her, his gaze intent on her face as if he were trying to see beneath the surface. Her hand curled around the back of the chair.

He continued looking at her, scrutinizing, assessing. "Women very rarely receive an education in advanced mathematics."

"True."

"So how did you?"

A black cloud threatened at the edge of Lydia's consciousness. She pushed it aside, refusing to allow it to darken her pleasure over Northwood's victory, over his admiration of her abilities.

"My grandmother," she confessed. She rubbed her finger over a crack on the surface of the desk. "She was...I told you that my mother became quite ill when I was just a girl. But even then I had a fascination with numbers. My grandmother recognized my aptitude and convinced my father to hire a mathematics tutor. Mr. Sully. He taught me for about four years, everything from algebra to geometry and basic calculus. Then when my mother's illness worsened, my father sent me to boarding school so I wouldn't have to contend with her condition."

"Did you have to put mathematics aside then?"

"On the contrary. It wasn't part of the curriculum for girls, but again my grandmother insisted that the headmistress bring in a special tutor for me. My father paid an extra fee to ensure I had at least two sessions per week. Mr. Radbourne this time. He wasn't as amiable as Mr. Sully, but he was brilliant. Neither one of them ever treated me as some sort of abomination. Without them—without my grandmother and my father—I never would have sought to explore my intellectual capabilities."

"Did you continue studying with tutors after boarding school?"

"I went to Germany, actually, when I was fifteen." Her chest tightened. She stared at the floor, at the intricate pattern spreading through the worn carpet. "Mr. Radbourne knew of a mathematician at the University of Leipzig. After I took several exams to prove my competence, he agreed to become my professor."

"And your father allowed you to go?"

"He was reluctant at first, owing to the distance," Lydia admitted. She pressed a hand to her chest, feeling the beat of her heart beneath layers of fabric. "But he agreed after my grandmother argued that it would be an unmatched opportunity for me. She accompanied me until she found a woman who served as a suitable chaperone."

"Your grandmother knew you possessed an exceptional mind."

"She did." A sting of tears burned Lydia's eyes so unexpectedly that she had to turn away. "Both she and my father did. Throughout my childhood, my grandmother was my greatest champion, my strongest supporter. And my father never tried to stifle my abilities."

Silence filled the space behind her, though she felt Northwood's disquiet, his sense that something was terribly wrong. She pressed her fingers against her eyes, swallowing old tears, fighting to keep the cloud at bay.

"What happened?" His voice was a low, quiet rumble.

She shook her head. Not even for him could she ever, *ever* answer that question.

"Lydia."

Oh, God, he was closer. And that delicious, fluid sound of his deep voice speaking her name sent a wave of pleasure through her blood. He was right behind her. She knew if she took one step back, she would encounter the hard plane of his chest. Her fingers curled into her palms as she fought the urge to do just that.

His hands settled on her shoulders, heavy and solid. Her breathing grew shallow, even as her body stiffened under his touch.

"What shall it be, my lord?" Gathering her strength, Lydia pulled away, turning back to face him.

"What shall what be?"

"My debt. You solved the equation. Now I owe you something once again."

Northwood frowned. "I will not hold you to a debt."

"I insist that you do."

He muttered a curse under his breath and reached into his pocket. He cupped the locket in his palm, looking down at it for a moment.

"I wish you would just take it back," he said.

"I know you do. But, like you, I have my pride." She followed his gaze. Her locket appeared small, the chain delicate, engulfed by his large hand.

She wanted the necklace back. Needed it back. And yet if she accepted his offer, she would have no further excuse to seek him out. She would have no reason to see him again.

The very thought made her heart ache in a way she had never before experienced.

Northwood shoved the necklace back into his pocket and paced restlessly across the room. "All right, then. The debt. In late June you will deliver a lecture at St. Martin's Hall on the subject of mathematical education."

Lydia looked at him as if he'd asked her to fly to the moon. "I beg your pardon?"

"I'm the head of a subcommittee in charge of planning a lecture series to coincide with the educational exhibition. The lectures will focus on educational theory and practice. I've already confirmed several speakers who will discuss educational models, such as the use of the microscope in schools, music, education and the poor, and botanical and economic science." Northwood stopped pacing and looked at her. "I want you to deliver a lecture about mathematical instruction in schools."

"I... I don't... do you mean to say that women will be giving lectures?"

"No. At least, no women have been asked to do so. Until now."

"Why me?"

"I know of no one else more suited to the task."

Lydia curled her fingers around the pencil she still

held. "I'm sorry." A shadow spilled over her brief pleasure at Northwood's compliments. "I can't."

He frowned. "Why not? These lectures will be attended by prominent scholars from throughout the world."

"I don't want their audience. I haven't delivered a lecture in months, and I publish my papers infrequently. I consult with a select few colleagues who do not divulge our association. They are the ones who invited me to be part of the journal editorial board, which is the first professional position I've taken in years."

"Why did you take the position now, then?"

"Because the meetings are with only a few other mathematicians who I consider friends. I don't attend large symposiums or correspond with scholars on the Continent."

"Why the bloody hell not?"

The vehemence of his tone startled her. Her grip tightened on the pencil, her heart hammering as she struggled for a way to explain.

"Being a mathematician, an academic, is not fitting for a woman," she finally said. "You know that. And while my father and grandmother encouraged my education when I was younger, it soon became clear that people viewed me as an oddity, someone to be avoided or whispered about. Such a perception affected our family, especially coming on the heels of rumors about my mother. We concluded it would be best, especially for Jane's sake, if I were to pursue my studies more anonymously."

Northwood was quiet for a moment. His expression remained hard and unmoving, but his eyes flashed like the surface of a lake disrupted by sweeping wind.

"That is utter foolishness," he said. "A mind like yours, to—"

"No." Lydia stopped him with a raised hand. "Please don't try to convince me to do anything differently. You will not succeed."

The currents in his eyes heightened, the winds intensifying, but to Lydia's mild surprise, he didn't press the issue. Instead he gave a swift nod, his arms folding across his chest.

"All right, then," Northwood said, his voice like stretched leather. "Next weekend my father, Talia, and I are going to visit our estate in Devon. Haven't been there in ages. Castleford is also invited. Sebastian is going because he's got nothing else to do. You will accompany us."

"Why?"

"Because I would welcome your company. I'll send a carriage to pick you up Thursday afternoon for the train station."

With that, he began striding toward the door.

"Lord Northwood!"

He stopped. Lydia's heart pounded hard.

"You...you would welcome my company?" she repeated.

A faint amusement lit his eyes. "Is that difficult to believe?"

"Well, no, but I...I really don't think—"

"You intend to renege on a debt?" A wicked glint appeared in his eyes as he approached her again. "My lady of such honor and pride?"

Lydia straightened her spine. "I did say I wished for the debt to be within reason."

"Nothing unreasonable about a short visit. Floreston Manor is always enjoyable."

"I don't doubt it. I...I merely think it would be best

if we maintained a business relationship, such as it is anyhow."

"Are you implying this visit could result in something more?" He stepped closer, close enough that she could see the flecks of gold in his irises, could sense the storm brewing in him.

Lydia swallowed. "I . . . I would merely prefer not to create the illusion of impropriety."

"All right, then. We'll dispense with the illusion and engage solely in the impropriety."

Her eyes flew to his in shock, but before she could utter another word, he closed the distance between them. His big hand slid around the back of her head, and he brought her mouth to his in a kiss as sweet and delicious as a ripe apple. Her hands came up to flatten against his chest, her arms tensing with the simultaneous urge to push him away and pull him closer.

Heat bloomed through her body. His mouth moved with urgency over hers, setting flame to the desire she'd kept banked for so very long. His hand moved to her neck, his fingers tangling through her hair. He slipped his other hand around to her lower back, pulling their bodies closer.

Lydia closed her eyes. Colors of crimson and gold swept behind her eyelids and began whirling through her blood.

Alive. Lord in heaven, he made her feel so incredibly *alive*.

Every beat of her heart echoed in her head, and a delicious, melting sensation spread through her lower body. Her fingers moved across his chest, trembling at the feeling of the hard muscles beneath his shirt. He was tense, vibrating with want, his tongue sliding across her lower lip in a possessive move that made her shudder with the urge to be taken.

Her lips parted beneath his. With a mutter of satisfaction, he slipped his tongue into the hot cavern of her mouth, the invasion unbearably intimate. Their breath danced. Lydia remembered their last encounter when she had been bold enough to cup his heavy groin in her hand. With a gasp, she did it again, slipped her hand down his torso to find the source of his arousal.

He swore, his body tightening with need. Triumph flitted in Lydia as she moved her fingers over him, her heart tripping over itself, her tongue darting tentatively past his lips. His hand tightened on the back of her damp neck, his breath coming faster.

Then, in a gesture that seemed oddly contradictory to the heat sparking between them, he slid his mouth away from hers and pressed a kiss to her cheek.

Something broke inside Lydia, the cracking open of a fragile eggshell. Unwanted, painful memories clouded the eruption of intense pleasure and desire. She shut her eyes tight as if to block out the darkness, desperate for the brilliant, sweet sensations to regain supremacy.

She knew it then. She knew that if she were ever to allow her true self to emerge once again, if she were ever to acknowledge the suppressed part of herself, it would be with Alexander Hall. No other man in the world would ever make her want—no, *need*—to take such a dangerous, breathtaking risk.

She moved her lips to his ear, loose strands of her hair sliding across his cheek. Her voice sounded hoarse, heavy with need. "I want to see you."

"Christ, Lydia—"

She tightened her grip on him. Northwood sucked in a breath. He shoved himself against her, burying his face in her thick hair. Blood rushed through her veins, as hot and fast as a firestorm.

"I won't last," he hissed in her ear, his voice taut.

"I don't want you to," Lydia breathed. She drew back, her skin flushed with heat and her body filled with a longing so intense she didn't know if it could ever be sated. "But I want..." She shifted against him, sliding a leg between his thighs, her hips rocking. "I want more, Northwood, please—"

With a groan of surrender, he grabbed her skirts, pushing them up around her waist to expose her long slender legs encased in cotton drawers. Lydia's gaze jerked to his. He stopped, his chest heaving. Then she grasped his hand and pulled it down between her legs to the opening of her drawers.

Dear God. One kiss and she was so ready. Everything in her ached to feel him naked and heavy between her thighs, to grip his powerful shoulders and wrap her legs around his. Her body surged with swirling heat.

"Wait. Oh, wait." Lydia looked down, her fingers trembling as she struggled to unfasten his trousers. He didn't help, instead staring down at her as she bit her lower lip in frustration. "Northwood, I can't... I'm shaking... oh, there... let me..."

She gave a breathless little laugh as the buttons yielded. She hastened to push his trousers over his hips. Her gaze flew to his. Need filled his eyes with heat.

Trembling, Lydia lowered her hand again and took him in her palm. The sensation of his rigid, pulsing length against her cool fingers caused her heart to jolt.

"Tighter," he muttered, reaching down to wrap her fingers around him. "Like that, Lydia. Just like that."

He pushed his hips forward and slipped his hand to her drawers again, finding the opening and parting the material for access to her bare, intimate flesh. When his fingers touched her, she moaned, her back stiffening against the wall.

"I need... oh, please."

He lowered his head to her ear, murmuring soothing noises as he stroked his finger against her. At the same time, Lydia caressed him, sliding her thumb across his length.

What little restraint she had left evaporated under the need to make him lose control. His body tightened as the pressure mounted and spilled, his low groan vibrating against her mouth. Her grip on him loosened as her own pleasure spiraled upward, her legs parting and thighs trembling.

He stroked her with his thumb and eased a finger into her. A moan stuck in her throat as she closed around him. She came apart almost instantly, her arms tightening on his neck as pleasure shot to every corner of her being.

Northwood braced one hand against the wall to hold both himself and her upright as they recovered. She tucked her head beneath his chin, her whole body shaking and her skin hot. He held her until her trembling abated before he eased away and lowered her skirts. He adjusted his own clothing, his gaze on her.

Lydia lifted her head. His eyes contained a strange light, a mixture of fading shock and lust. Her skin heated with a flush, but she could not muster up even the slightest twinge of regret. Not for something that felt so unbearably good. So right.

He continued looking at her. Then he reached out to cup her face with his hand, his thumb brushing across her lower lip.

"You..." His voice tightened.

He swallowed, his fingers moving to the pulse still pounding hard at the side of her neck. He rested his hand there for a moment before lowering it to his side. Then he turned away, appearing rather uncharacteristically discomfited.

Lydia sagged against the wall, pressing her hands to her heated cheeks as she waited for her lingering arousal to ease. Warm, pulsing sensations continued to throb in her blood, between her legs.

Silence stretched between them; then the noise of horses' hooves and carriage wheels came from outside.

Lydia pushed loose tendrils of hair away from her face and went to take the pages of his work from the desk drawer. Holding them close to her chest, she preceded him into the foyer just as the front door opened.

"Ah, Lydia. I'm glad you're home."

Lydia winced as her grandmother entered, followed by a petite blond woman with delicate features and peach-blushed cheeks peeking out from beneath a fashionable hat.

Lydia became acutely conscious of the dampness on her drawers, the material clinging to her thighs. The musky scent of Northwood on her body. She glanced at him. He appeared entirely composed, only the wrinkles on his shirt evidence of their behavior.

"Good afternoon, Lord Northwood," Mrs. Boyd said as Sophie came to take the women's coats. "Lydia, this is Lady Montague. She just arrived from Paris yesterday for a visit. My lady, this is my granddaughter Miss Lydia Kellaway and Viscount Northwood."

"A pleasure, Miss Kellaway. Lord Northwood."

He responded in kind, stepping forward to greet her.

My God, Lydia thought—or rather, *mon Dieu.* What if the two women had walked in fifteen minutes prior?

A bubble of laughter worked its way up her throat. "Yes... yes, and you as well, Lady Montague."

"Jane is still at the church with Mrs. Keene, but Lady Montague was kind enough to agree to come and meet you," Mrs. Boyd explained. "Please tell Mrs. Driscoll we're here, and then you can join us for tea." She frowned. "What is so amusing?"

"Nothing. I..." Lydia pressed her lips together.

"You're welcome to join us of course, my lord."

"I was just leaving, Mrs. Boyd," Northwood said. "Miss Kellaway and I had several accounting matters to discuss. And I wished to invite her to visit my father's estate next weekend."

"Oh." Mrs. Boyd glanced at Lydia. Anticipation sparked in her eyes—though Lydia knew quite well it had nothing to do with the proposal and everything to do with the fact that Viscount Northwood had extended her an invitation.

"You're welcome to join us, Mrs. Boyd," Northwood added. "Jane as well."

"Oh, thank you, my lord, most generous. But I must decline. Jane will be starting dance lessons, and I've several charities of my own I must attend to. But Lydia would be delighted to accept, wouldn't you, my dear?"

"Delighted."

"Delighted," Mrs. Boyd echoed. She flashed a brilliant smile at Northwood. "Thank you, Lord Northwood. We are much obliged. You know, Mrs. Keene has spoken quite highly of you and the good works in which you are engaged."

"Oh, yes," Lydia agreed. "Lord Northwood is very generous with his endowments, which are indeed considerable."

Northwood laughed.

Chapter Twelve

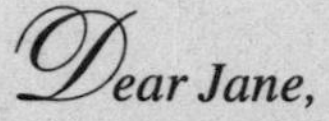*ear Jane,*

Another excellent riddle. I am still working on my response.

I did not know that worms have the ability to replace lost segments of their bodies. What an odd characteristic, though certainly a convenient one.

Here is a word problem for you, since it appears your cleverness exceeds the complexity of my own riddles:

Find an odd number with 3 digits such that all the digits are different and add up to 15. The difference between the first two digits equals the difference between the last two digits. The hundreds digit is greater than the sum of the tens and ones digits.

Perhaps you might ask your sister for help. If necessary, of course.

Sincerely,
C

The door clicked open. Jane pushed the letter between the pages of sheet music and turned to greet Mr. Hall. Except that it wasn't Mr. Hall who entered the fancy drawing room, but Lord Northwood.

"My lord." She smiled as she pushed herself up from the piano bench and gave a little curtsy. "I was waiting for Mr. Hall. Mrs. Driscoll's just gone for tea."

"Hello, Jane." With an answering smile, Lord Northwood closed the door behind him and approached the piano. He paused beside her, running one finger across the pristine keys. An F-sharp sounded.

"Sebastian had this specially made by a piano manufacturer in Germany," he said. "Cost a fortune. The man who made it accompanied the delivery himself to ensure it was intact and properly tuned when it arrived."

"We just... we have a little cottage piano at home," Jane explained. "I think my mother used to play it when she was alive. But no one plays it anymore. Well, I do now sometimes for practice. We had it recently tuned."

"Do you like piano lessons?" Lord Northwood asked.

Jane hesitated, her flush deepening. She liked Lord Northwood a great deal and didn't wish to lie to him. But neither did she want to sound as if she didn't appreciate Mr. Hall's lessons.

"I like Mr. Hall," she finally said. "He's quite a good teacher. And he's kind. But I just don't think I've much talent for music."

He continued looking at her, his fingers still idly playing with the keys.

Jane glanced at his hands. "Do you play, sir?"

His mouth quirked. "No. I know I don't have talent for music, though I do still recall one tune."

He sat down, flexing his hands and fingers in an exaggerated imitation of the exercises his brother did before playing. Jane giggled and edged a little closer to the piano. Lord Northwood plucked out a tentative version of "Greensleeves" before stopping and turning back to her with a grimace.

"That's all I remember," he confessed. "I had lessons for a time as a child, but it appears my brother hoarded all natural musical ability for himself. Always thought that was a bit unfair."

Jane smiled again. A strange sense of relief flowed through her, though she didn't quite know why. "It's funny, isn't it, sir? That some people are so effortlessly good at something that's not at all easy for others."

"Mmm. Very odd, that. Though you've got your encyclopedic knowledge of insects."

"That's not exactly a talent, though. Anyone can learn about insects. Not everyone can learn to play the piano the way Mr. Hall does. Or solve algebra problems the way Lydia does. Not everyone has something...inside them to offer."

Lord Northwood looked down at his hands resting on the keys. "Everyone has something to offer, Miss Jane."

"I don't." She winced, worried she sounded self-pitying when she meant to merely state a fact. But Lord Northwood only gave her a considering look.

"Why do you say that?"

"I don't have something like Mr. Hall or Lydia. Or my father. He had such an instinct about his translations. Few people could do what he did."

"Someday you might study insects in depth. Write books. Give lectures. Discover things about entomology that no one has learned before."

Jane had never considered such a thing. A little tingle of excitement went through her at the idea of discovering something that no one else in the world knew—and at the idea that Lord Northwood believed she could.

"Well." Jane gave him a wry smile. "Quite difficult to discover things when one is busy learning to dance and hold a fork properly. Not at the same time, of course."

Lord Northwood laughed. He had a wonderful laugh, deep and booming, his face creasing and eyes twinkling.

"Ah, Alexander, you've finally consented to let me teach you a thing or two." Mr. Hall stepped into the room. "Rather than the other way around."

Lord Northwood rolled his eyes conspiratorially at Jane. She grinned at the mischievous look.

"On the contrary, Bastian, you've got a lovely young woman to instruct about the fine art of piano." Lord Northwood pushed himself to his feet. "See you don't bore her to tears."

He picked up a coat that lay over the back of a chair near the piano. As he shook out the creases, a thump sounded on the carpet, the glint of metal flashing.

Jane bent at the same time as the viscount to retrieve the item. He reached it first, scooping the object into his hand, but not before Jane recognized the *fenghuang* engraving on the silver locket.

She straightened, confusion filling her chest. Lord Northwood and Mr. Hall exchanged glances, Mr. Hall clearing his throat with an awkward sound.

Jane scratched her head, the sudden tension in the air adding to her bewilderment. She knew the locket had belonged to her mother, that Papa had had it specially made as a wedding present. After Theodora Kellaway died, the locket was tucked away in a box with several other pieces of jewelry. As far as Jane knew, it hadn't been taken from the box in years.

So the fact that the necklace was in Lord Northwood's pocket was utterly baffling.

The viscount stepped toward her and extended his hand. The locket looked delicate and small against his big, rough palm.

Jane took it from him and rubbed her thumb over the engraving. She'd only seen the locket, held it, once or twice. Her chest hurt a little.

"It was my mother's," she finally said.

"I know." Lord Northwood's deep voice sounded tight. "Your sister told me."

"Did she give it to you?"

"No. I'd never intended to keep it."

"But why do you have it at all?" Jane asked.

"Through a rather odd set of circumstances that are perhaps best left unexplained. I have every intention of returning it to your sister."

"I see," Jane said, though she didn't really.

She stared at the dragon engraving on the back. Something was happening between Lydia and the viscount. Jane sensed it now more than ever. Something ominous yet inevitable, like the darkening of a sea before a storm, long shadows of dusk spilling over the streets, flower buds closing to the night. A dragon spreading its wings.

She twisted the chain around her fingers and opened the locket. She stared at the picture of her lovely, smiling mother, and Papa, his expression serious, his face so dear, so familiar. Tears stung Jane's eyes.

The voices of Lord Northwood and his brother created a deep hum. Jane glanced up to find they had stepped away from her to speak in lowered tones.

She started to close the locket, then noticed that the casing seemed oddly thick—too thick to house mere paper images. She closed the compartment and examined the edges.

The case hinging appeared thick as well, almost as if it were holding together a double seam. Jane pulled the case open again to reveal the pictures, then turned it to look at the seam. She wiggled her fingernail into the edge again, blinking with surprise when the casing popped open to reveal a second compartment hidden behind the first. An object dropped from the case to the floor.

Her gaze flew to the brothers, who remained half turned away from her in conversation. Jane bent to peer at the carpet, running her hand over the thick pattern. Her fingers brushed against a small piece of cold metal. She picked it up and laid it flat in her palm.

A tiny brass key. She'd never seen anything like it before. Smaller than the length of her little finger, the key had a scrolled end and a rectangular bit pierced with decorative holes. It looked like something a mouse might use.

The thought made her smile to herself.

"Miss Jane."

Starting at the viscount's voice, Jane looked up, her fist closing around the key.

"I'd be very much obliged if you would return the locket to your sister," Lord Northwood said. "Though I must warn you she might not be entirely pleased."

Jane thought the warning had something to do with the *circumstances best left unexplained* of which he'd spoken.

"Sir, if Lydia knows you have the locket, it's not my place to return it to her." She moved forward and held out the necklace. "And I'd rather not have her displeased with me."

After a long hesitation, Lord Northwood allowed her to drop the locket into his palm. Jane started to return the little key as well, then stopped. Her fingers tightened around it, the thin edges digging into her hand.

"Right." Mr. Hall clapped his hands together and moved to the piano. "We'd best begin our lesson, Miss Jane. I thought you might like to learn a little song called 'Pretty Bee.' "

Lord Northwood gave Jane a bow, the locket still enclosed in his fist. "We'll meet again soon."

"Thank you, sir."

She watched him walk to the door, her nerves stretching as she tried to make herself call him back. The key made an imprint against her palm. Lord Northwood left, the door closing behind him.

Jane's heart thumped as if struggling to push blood through her veins. She turned to Mr. Hall, who was rifling through the sheet music.

"Come and start the scales, please, Miss Jane."

Jane approached the piano. She dropped the key into her pocket, where it burned through her skirts for the entirety of the lesson.

Chapter Thirteen

Floreston Manor sat nestled among the hills of Devon, the grounds spreading out from the house like a vast green ocean. The ivy-covered brick-and-stone house appeared well suited to the landscape, as if the two were a married couple living out their years in peace and happiness. Spring blossoms perfumed the air.

Alexander breathed in the clean, fresh scent as he followed his father from the carriage onto the circular drive.

"Is the girl coming along? Jane?"

Alexander looked at Rushton in surprise. "No, she's staying in London with her grandmother."

The earl made a noise that sounded like displeasure.

"How do you know Jane?" Alexander asked.

"Met her when she came for a lesson with your brother. Pleasant girl. Bit interfering, but clever enough."

"One might say the same of her sister."

He and Rushton exchanged glances; then they both chuckled. A knot loosened at the base of Alexander's neck as they walked toward the manor, where a line of staff stood waiting to greet them. The place was ready and gleaming for their arrival.

"Isn't Lady Talia to have come as well?" the housekeeper, Mrs. Danvers, asked with a worried air.

"She's arriving on a later train with Miss Kellaway, Sebastian, and Lord Castleford," Alexander explained. "They'll be here in time for supper."

He preceded his father into the drawing room. They both stopped as a large portrait of Lady Rushton looked down at them from above the mantel. The image was one of cold beauty, the woman's eyebrows arched, her mouth curved into a hard smile.

Rushton coughed. "Have Weavers remove that at once. Any others as well."

Alexander went to convey the request to the butler. When he returned, his father was pouring two glasses of sherry at the sideboard.

"Not like her, is she?" Rushton asked without turning. "Miss Kellaway. Not like your mother."

"God, no." Alexander spoke before thinking. His mother had been beautiful in a cold, detached way, like a pane of stained glass against an empty wall. No warmth, no light, no illuminated colors shone through. In all his years, Alexander rarely had the sense there was more to his mother than her beauty and manners.

But with Lydia . . . he thought forever would not be long enough for him to discover the depths of her complexity, her inner life.

"Not like Chilton's daughter either?" Rushton asked.

A humorless laugh stuck in Alexander's throat. "No. She is not."

A speculative gleam entered Rushton's expression. That, combined with the line of questioning, caused a rustle of both anticipation and apprehension in Alexander.

"Sir Henry was a good man, if I recall," Rushton continued.

"He was."

"Owned no properties but was well regarded as a scholar. No scandals in the family, except for the mother..." Rushton's voice trailed off as he shook his head. "Brackwell recalls her having been rather daft."

At least she didn't run off with another man.

"Mrs. Kellaway's illness was a misfortune," Alexander said. "Difficult for both her daughters."

An image of Lydia and her sister came to Alexander's mind—their almost identical smiles, the sharp intelligence in their eyes, their tangible affection. The way Jane seemed to absorb everything around her, filled with endless curiosity, whereas Lydia approached the world with caution, guarding herself against it.

Rushton reached for the decanter and refilled his glass. "What is she like?"

"I beg your pardon?"

"Miss Kellaway. Not like your mother, you say. Not like Chilton's chit. So what—or who—is she like?"

"She's like... like no one I've ever met."

Alexander didn't even know how to explain Lydia to himself, let alone to his father. In the past weeks, she'd slipped far beneath his skin. He couldn't stop thinking of her haunted blue eyes, the seething frustration in her kiss, the way she'd responded to him. His need to touch her was becoming a physical ache.

And the feelings she roused in him—a maddening

combination of lust, tenderness, affection, fascination, a near-overwhelming protectiveness…

He flexed his fingers, resisting with effort the urge to stand and begin pacing.

"Do you find her interesting enough to sustain a marriage?" Rushton asked.

More than that. Alexander found her interesting enough to sustain *him*. He'd never imagined he would find a woman he could marry for reasons beyond what was expected of him. For reasons that were his alone.

And while he knew to his bones he wanted to make Lydia his wife, he wasn't yet prepared to confess his intentions to his father.

"What makes you think I've got marriage in mind?" he asked.

Rushton laughed. To Alexander, it was a foreign sound, one he'd heard little throughout his life.

"I'm getting old, Northwood," Rushton replied, "but I'm not a fool."

When she arrived at Floreston Manor with Talia, Sebastian, and Lord Castleford, Lydia was enraptured by the beauty of the estate and the countryside. The bright, flower-filled house and fresh air seemed to wash away the grime and noise of London. Lydia thought it might even lessen the shadows clinging to her heart.

As she stood on the terrace looking over the vast grounds, she decided that for the next three days she would enjoy herself. She wanted to walk along the riverbank, pick flowers, breathe the sweet-smelling air, feel the sun warming her face.

"Lydia!" Talia called. "Have you seen your room?

Come along, I'll show you. Sam has already brought up your things. It's the nicest room in the house, really."

With a lighter heart, Lydia followed the younger woman inside. Being back at Floreston Manor also brightened Talia's entire demeanor, and she rushed around issuing orders, ensuring her guests were well situated, and conferring with the housekeeper about the weekend's menus.

The men had the good sense to stay out of the way—Rushton disappeared into the garden, Castleford went off to check on the stables, and Sebastian took the buggy into the village.

After Talia declined her offer of assistance, Lydia sat on the sofa in the upstairs study, her head down as she wrote in her notebook.

"Why are you always carrying that thing?" Northwood asked.

"Because if I don't write down my ideas as they come to me, I fear they'll come out my ears." Lydia looked up and smiled as he stepped into the room.

Not returning her smile, he gestured to the book. "What is it this time?"

"Wha— Oh. One of the papers I'm working on relates to the dimensions of the roots of equations. When we were on the train, I had the idea that the theorem might be simplified by the extrication of a lemma." She studied her book. "That is, if the lemma were to give all the values of *r*... it could represent the dimensions of the roots."

"I have no idea what you're talking about."

"I know. And that's rather gratifying." Lydia closed the book. "Though I suppose it's impolite to work when I've been invited here as a guest. The manor is lovely, my lord. Thank you again for the invitation."

He was still frowning at her. Apparently the travel hadn't done his temper any good.

"Why are you in such an ill humor?" she asked. "Will a walk in the garden lighten your mood?"

She rose to pass him and, as she did, he turned to her so suddenly that Lydia took a step backward and came up against the wall. Before she could move aside, he put his hands on either side of her, trapping her between the wall and his body.

Lydia gasped, her gaze flying to the study door, which stood half open.

"No one is near," Northwood murmured.

He shifted his hips against her, making her pulse stutter. "Still, you... you must release me."

"Make me laugh, and I will." His lips touched her temple.

"What?"

"Make me laugh, lighten my humor, and I'll release you."

Make him laugh? Despite her remark, she wasn't exactly a fountain of hilarity.

Lydia searched her brain for an amusing anecdote. She could think of theorems and proofs with no effort at all—surely some witticism or conundrum would spring to the surface.

"I'm waiting." Northwood shifted against her again, his knee beginning to push between hers. Lydia flushed, curving her hands around his forearms as she fought the urge to allow him access, to press herself against the hard length of his thigh.

"At what time was Adam married?" she blurted.

"Adam who?"

"*Adam*. The first man. Adam."

"Oh." Northwood lifted a brow. "At what time was he married?"

"Upon his wedding Eve." She gave him a weak smile.

Not a spark of amusement flashed in his eyes. He shook his head. His knee pressed with more insistence, causing her legs to part. Air wafted up beneath her skirt and petticoats. She shuddered.

"What..." Her breath caught. Her mind whirled. "What...er...what is the proper length of a lady's skirt?"

"What?"

"A little above two feet."

"Hmm. Not funny. Not true, either." His hands fisted in the folds of her skirt, his eyes darkening. "The proper length is well above her knees, as far as I'm concerned."

Oh good heavens. He was drawing her skirt up, and her petticoats along with it. The material of his trousers brushed against her calves, his knee sliding upward between her thighs. Heat bloomed through her, a tightness centering in her sex and making her want to writhe against him.

She swallowed. Some faint but still rational part of her mind reminded her anyone could walk into the study.

"What..." She squirmed, trying to avoid the insistent caress of his leg. "What is that which can be right but never wrong?"

"An angle," he replied. His lips skimmed her forehead. Her skin tingled.

"No."

"Then what?"

"Me."

He laughed. His eyes creased at the corners, his teeth flashing white in the pale light of the sun coming through the windows. The deep laugh rumbled through his chest, causing a shiver of pleasure to ripple over her.

"You...you ought to release me now." Lydia tried to bring her legs together, tried to quell the intense arousal that this man could spark with a mere touch.

Amusement still glinted in his eyes as he gave a slow nod, the movement bringing his lips in line with hers.

"You're right," he murmured the instant before his mouth met hers.

Although her mind warned her against it, Lydia sank into the kiss as if nothing else mattered. And in that moment, nothing did. His tongue caressed hers, his teeth sliding across her lower lip. She drew in a breath as her pulse began a low, heavy throb that echoed in her head.

She curled her hands around Northwood's arms, pressed herself down onto his hard thigh, felt his fingers digging into the stiff lines of her corset. A tremble ran through his body. His knee shifted, his thigh beginning to rub against her with delicious friction.

Then without warning he was moving away from her, his palms smoothing down her skirts as he positioned himself between her and the study door. Lady Talia's voice began to penetrate Lydia's fog of desire.

She pressed her hands to her cheeks, attempting to regain her composure. Northwood leaned toward her, putting his mouth close to her ear, one large hand sliding beneath her breast.

"Why is a good woman like dough?" he whispered.

"Why—"

"Because a man kneads her." His lips touched her ear before he moved away, his dark eyes filled with a combination of humor and desire. "And make no mistake. You are a good woman."

Lydia pulled herself from his grip so swiftly that her heel caught on the edge of a rug. She grasped the back of a chair to steady herself, all amusement evaporating like steam.

"As you once told me, Lord Northwood," she said, "it's dangerous to make such assumptions."

"That, Miss Kellaway, was not an assumption."

Dear Jane,

Hah, I've perplexed you, haven't I? Did you ask your sister for help? Though I suppose that might be a bit like cheating, considering her apparent talent for numbers.

Don't feel badly that you haven't got the same facility as Lydia—not everyone is capable of grasping certain concepts with ease. I'd wager that she doesn't see the insect world in quite the same way as you do, which is rather unique.

Sincerely,
C

Jane lowered the letter. She looked out the rain-spattered window, down at the street, where pedestrians bustled back and forth, umbrellas blooming like mushrooms. A damp bird flitted onto the surface of the iron fence across the way.

Jane's fingers tightened on the letter. For the life of her, she couldn't remember if she'd ever told *C* her sister's name.

Chapter Fourteen

Lydia looked at the equation, unable to muster any interest whatsoever. Even though she'd slept well and eaten a hearty breakfast, a headache pressed between her eyes. She couldn't concentrate. Likely because one dark-haired, compelling viscount kept pushing his way in between her theorems and equations.

A good woman. *Good.*

Did he really believe that? And even if he did, did it matter? Although her grandmother had expressed a calculated interest in Lord Northwood, Lydia knew nothing substantial could come of their association. So it oughtn't matter at all what kind of woman he presumed her to be.

And yet, of course it did matter. A great deal.

She shook her head and focused on her paper.

A knock sounded at the door. Lydia dropped the pencil with a frustrated sigh and pushed back her chair. Her eyes widened at the sight of Northwood standing in the corridor holding... a fishing pole?

"What on earth..."

He held up the pole. His dark eyes twinkled with something she'd never seen in him before. "Angling," he said. "Ever been?"

"No."

"Come on, then. Great fun."

Lydia glanced back to her desk, where her paper awaited her return. Northwood made an impatient noise.

"Five minutes, Lydia," he warned. "If you must, you can calculate the ratio of fish to water drops or something foolish like that. We're waiting in the garden."

He turned and headed back downstairs. Lydia remembered her promise to herself that she would enjoy her short stay here. A pleasant sense of anticipation tickled through her at the thought of fishing—one of many sports in which she'd never imagined herself participating. She put on her wrap, hat, and gloves, checked her reflection in the mirror, and went out to the garden.

Talia, Sebastian, and Castleford waited by the rose bed, with Talia and Castleford each carrying an array of fishing gear. Sebastian had both his arms wrapped around a rather enormous picnic basket.

"Ah, glad you could join us, Miss Kellaway," Castleford boomed. "You're certain to keep Northwood from lying about the size of his catch."

Lydia laughed at the thought of Northwood lying about anything. Least of all the size of his catch. He flashed her a grin, the warmth of which caused a lovely glow to fill her chest.

The three men began walking toward the river, chatting about the wind, the weather, the possibility of trout. A sense of cheer and good humor surrounded them.

Northwood's shoulders were relaxed, his stride long and easy. Sunlight glinted off his dark hair.

Something loosened inside Lydia at the sight of him. Her headache melted away, and her heart lightened. She liked seeing him cheerful, smiling, hearing his laughter rustling through the tree leaves. She liked it a great deal. Perhaps too much.

"They've been friends for ages." Talia fell into step beside Lydia, adjusting her hat against the sun as she nodded toward the three men. "They were in school together, though of course Sebastian was two years behind. After they graduated, Castleford went off to travel and expand his father's company. He's got enormous energy. He's rarely been in London the past five years."

A faint wistfulness in the younger woman's voice made Lydia glance at her. Talia gazed into the distance at the curling ribbon of the stream.

"He did come back after... what happened, though," she continued. "Lent his support to our family both in private and very publicly. Made things easier, actually. We're indebted to him for that."

It had been only two years, Lydia realized, since Talia's mother had run off to parts unknown.

"It's not easy, is it?" she asked before she could think.

Talia looked at her. "What?"

"Losing your mother."

Talia stared at her for a moment, her green eyes wide. Lydia swallowed, color rising to her cheeks as she realized she had deeply insulted the other woman.

"I'm sorry, I—"

"No." Talia reached out to squeeze Lydia's arm. "No, don't apologize. You're right. It's not easy. In fact, it's one of the most horrid things I can imagine. The worst part is that even though I'm so terribly angry with her, I still miss her." She laughed, a hollow sound. "Silly, isn't it?"

"Not at all. I miss my mother every day."

"What happened to her?"

Lydia told her about Theodora Kellaway's illness and subsequent death. Sympathy darkened Talia's eyes.

"It's been nearly a decade," Lydia said, "but I don't imagine I'll ever stop missing her. Thankfully I have Jane, though, and my grandmother."

"That helps, doesn't it?" Talia said. "I've been fortunate to have a few good friends. They've made things easier for me as well. Now if only my brother would leave me be, I think I might actually get through this."

She gave Lydia a wan smile. Castleford shouted a distance in front of them, waving at them to hurry. Talia grasped Lydia's hand as they quickened their pace to the river.

"All right, now. This is yours." Northwood handed Lydia a pole and tied something furry onto it.

"It's a Royal Trude," he said.

"A royal prude?"

"*Trude*. It's meant to imitate a stone-fly."

Talia took her pole from Castleford and began fixing the line with an expert touch. She grinned when she saw Lydia staring at her.

"Don't forget I grew up with four brothers," she said. "I could tie a fly before I could walk."

"Not to mention roll a hoop, ride a horse, and climb a tree," Sebastian added.

"And she was often the fastest," Northwood said. He held a lure out to Lydia. "Now, watch, because you're going to learn how to make a proper backcast."

He moved with deft precision as he showed her how to strip line and whip the fly backward and forward until he had it just where he wanted. Although Lydia became a bit breathless from his proximity, she was able to focus enough to get a handle on it.

Northwood stood behind her and grasped her wrist to show her how to cast, his fingers warm and strong. She knew he could feel her rapid pulse. His hips brushed hers. Her knees went a bit wobbly.

"Concentrate," he ordered, his breath caressing her temple.

He spoke to her with that husky voice and expected her to concentrate?

"I *am*," she muttered, flinging her rod back with a little too much force. Her line ended up tangled in the reeds at the side of the river.

"You've got to establish a rhythm," Northwood said. "It's the same tempo as breathing. Match the two. Back and forth, in and out."

"I can't establish anything with you standing so close," Lydia whispered irritably.

He chuckled and moved away, but not before she swore he patted her backside. She wished he'd do it again—only at a time when she could actually feel it.

She cast again and landed her line in the middle of the stream. Castleford, Talia, and Sebastian all expertly cast and retrieved their lines, though they caught only one or two small trout, which they unhooked and tossed back in. Lydia found herself thoroughly enjoying the company and spring air, which filled her with a sense of warmth and lightness.

After a couple of hours with little reward, they settled

underneath a tree to indulge in a delicious picnic lunch of cold roasted fowl, cheese, fruit, crusty bread, cider, and pastries. The men ate so much that after lunch, they tipped their hats over their faces and stretched out to nap.

Lydia and Talia exchanged amused glances over the three long, recumbent bodies. Faint snores filtered up into the tree leaves.

"Like beached whales," Talia said.

Lydia smiled. As they packed up the remnants of the picnic, she allowed her gaze to dart every now and then to Northwood. His broad chest moved with heavy, even breaths, one big hand resting over his stomach.

As she moved the basket aside, she felt Talia's hand on her arm. She turned to meet the other woman's gaze.

"Lydia, I just want you to know that he's a good man." Talia's words came out in a tumble, two spots of color appearing on her cheeks. "I... Alexander, I mean. He's had a hard time with... with all that happened, and the broken engagement, and he does have a terrible tendency to want to control everything, but he... he means well. He's honest. I just want you to know that."

"I do know that." Although she spoke with soft certainty, Lydia felt a rustle of discomfort.

Why was Talia trying to convince her of Northwood's worth?

Talia nodded and sat back, looking faintly relieved. She reached into another basket and removed an embroidery hoop. "Despite what my brothers think, I do enjoy more feminine pastimes. Do you embroider?"

Lydia shook her head, watching as Talia's needle flashed in and out of the cloth. She stood and dusted off her hands.

"I'll just go for a walk, I think."

"I'll stay and safeguard our priceless bounty." Talia tilted her head toward the slumbering men.

Lydia picked up her rod and started down the riverbank. The cool, fresh air wiped the lingering stress and fatigue from her body. She breathed deeply, enjoying the stretch of her muscles, the warmth of the sun against her face.

A splash sounded in the water. She peered out as a large fish broke through the glittering surface of the river and flopped back in. Excitement—and the lure of competition—sprang through her.

How she'd love to catch a big, fat fish while her three strapping male companions snored the afternoon away. She'd return in triumph and—with Talia's full support—tease them all without mercy.

She looked at the Royal Trude. It didn't look at all edible to her, but then she wasn't a trout. Lydia decided she would give the fish something they couldn't refuse.

A cluster of trees sat near the riverbank, one of them broken and half-submerged in the water. She crouched beneath the base and began digging through the soft dirt. At least eight worms wriggled from the pile.

Lydia winced. Jane would love this. Her sister would collect all the worms in a glass container and bring them into the house for further study.

With a grimace, Lydia plucked a worm from the dirt and tried to ignore its writhing as she impaled it on the hook. She wiped her hands on her skirt and cast the line out. The hook tangled in the reeds.

Lydia muttered an oath and tried again. The line fell short and caught on the grass. She yanked it free and inspected the hook. The worm was gone.

Suppressing her squeamishness, she dug for another worm and attached it to the hook. She cast again and watched the hook plop into the reeds.

Match the tempo to your breathing, she thought. *Balderdash.* What she needed was to get farther out to the middle of the river where she'd seen the fish.

She reeled the line back in and climbed onto the tree trunk that jutted out into the water. It was slippery with moss but jagged enough that she could maintain her balance by digging her feet into the grooves of bark and holding on to the branches with her other hand.

Clutching her rod, she inched her way to the end of the trunk. The fish flopped through the water again, spurring her determination. She reached the end of the trunk and straddled it, then ensured the bait was still attached before casting the line out again.

The rod bobbed almost instantly. Lydia gave a squeak of excitement and tried to pull the line in, but it slackened before she cranked two turns. She reeled in quickly and cast out again.

The hook caught. She gasped and tightened her hands on the rod. *Reel! Reel!*

She leaned forward, her heart hammering as she began to turn the spool. The fish yanked at the line.

She had it! She just had to—

Her weight shifted. She tried to stick her foot against a branch to steady herself, but it slipped on the moss. Horrified, she felt herself begin to slide.

The fish pulled on the line, hard. She clutched the rod with both hands. If she could—

Lydia shrieked. She tipped forward and fell off the branch like an otter sliding across the ice. Freezing water hit her, soaking through her clothing. Her breath stopped in her lungs and her throat constricted.

She heard the faint shout of her name before the water closed over her head. Slick weeds brushed across her face like tentacles. She opened her mouth to scream, and water choked her. She kicked toward the surface, struggling to find something to grab.

Oh, God, she could see it now—the police constable filling out a report: *Mathematician drowned due to miscalculation.*

She kicked harder, her right hand closing around an underwater branch before the current pulled her down again. Her lungs expanded, her chest feeling as if it were about to burst.

Suddenly two strong arms clamped around her waist and hauled her upward. Her head broke through the surface, her mouth opening on a huge, choking gasp that filled her lungs with blessed air.

After another push, she landed on the hard surface of the riverbank, the smell of grass pungent in her nose and the sun hot on her face.

"Lydia!" Alexander's urgent voice cut through the pounding current still ringing in her ears.

She opened her eyes, swiping water off her face as she stared upward. Four faces crowded above her, their expressions lined with concern and anxiety.

"Are you all right?" Talia pushed Lydia's wet hair away from her forehead. "I heard you scream, and we all came running—"

Lydia blinked and nodded, so grateful to be breathing air that she didn't want to waste it by speaking.

Alexander frowned. "What the bloody hell did you think you were doing?"

Lydia tried to remember.

"Alex, don't shout at her." Talia pushed the men away and helped Lydia sit up. She wrapped her in the picnic blanket and tried to dry her hair off a bit.

"I was f-figuring just how far I could creep out onto that log," Lydia said, her teeth rattling together. "I weigh nine stone, and... and that boulder there, see... that's the pivot, but I m-miscalculated the moments of inertia."

Everyone fell silent and looked at her with bewilderment. Except for Alexander, whose mouth appeared to be twitching.

"Well, we all make mistakes like that, don't we?" Talia said brightly. "Were you—"

She looked at Lydia's hands. Lydia looked too. She was still clutching the fishing rod in her left hand, and the line was still tight.

"Oh!" The word came out a croak. Her fingers shook with cold as she reeled the line. "There was a fish... a fat rainbow trout, five pounds if it weighed an ounce. It'll be wonderful for dinner! Perhaps we can have it with melted butter. It put up such a fight, fairly pulled me right off the tree. You wouldn't believe—"

She yanked the rest of the line out of the water and pulled the still-hooked fish onto the bank. Triumph surged through her. The misery of being wet and cold faded.

She'd done it! She'd caught the—

Northwood started laughing. A deep, booming laugh that made Lydia's stomach flutter with something rich and pleasant and... Why was he laughing?

She stared at him—the sun sparkling off his wet hair, the water dripping off his face.

Then Castleford chuckled. Then Sebastian. Northwood bent to grasp the end of Lydia's fishing line and held it up. A small silvery fish, no more than three inches, writhed on the end of the line.

"Behold, my dear fisherwoman," Northwood said, "your whale of a catch."

The men exploded with laughter.

"Perhaps it might serve as a nice appetizer," Sebastian suggested.

"Or we've a cat who could gobble it whole," Castleford said, sending all three men off into another fit.

"Now, stop it, you three," Talia scolded, though her green eyes danced with amusement. She patted Lydia's hand. "It's quite impressive for Lydia's first catch. Now we must get her home before she catches her death. Alex! Stop it and help."

"I did help," he said, between guffaws so deep he ought to have been clutching his stomach. "I'm the one who rescued her from the raging current, remember?"

Talia gave a huff of exasperation and looked at Castleford pleadingly. Still grinning, he took a gallant step forward and began to lift Lydia off the ground before Northwood shouldered him aside.

"Watch yourself, old chap," he muttered. His smile flashed white and striking as he gathered Lydia up and lifted her against his chest. He shifted her in his arms, as if testing her weight.

"Nice catch indeed," he said in a low voice meant for her ears alone.

Her flush warmed her to the bone. She pushed halfheartedly at his chest. His very solid, very broad chest.

"I can walk," she protested. "You'll get all wet."

"I'm already all wet," he reminded her. "I dove in after you. It was quite masterful."

"Come on, then," Sebastian called. "Our bountiful dinner awaits!"

Sebastian flung Lydia's rod over his shoulder, the poor hapless fish still dangling from the line, and strode forward to lead the party back to the house. They trooped along the riverbank—the men still as merry and amused as a band of jesters—and Talia trying to hide her traitorous smile every time Lydia shot her a glower.

Even through her humiliation, however, Lydia couldn't deny the pleasure of being held against Northwood, feeling the smooth rhythm of his long stride, his strong arms tight around her.

After a minute, she allowed herself to rest her head against his chest. His lingering chuckles vibrated through him. Despite the wetness and the cold, the heat of his body seeped into her. He glanced at her occasionally, looks of such amusement and warmth that her blood shimmered.

Even with the pathetic little fish dangling mockingly in front of her, Lydia never wanted this walk to end.

"Out! Out!" Talia waved her hands to shoo Northwood and Castleford from Lydia's room. "Anne, draw a hot bath for Miss Kellaway, quickly, then fetch her some hot tea. No, better yet, brandy. No—both! Yes, both. Susan, help me get these clothes off her. Oh, and tell Jim to bring up some wood for a fire."

The maids fluttered around, clucking like hens, as Talia closed the door firmly behind the two men. Between the three women, Lydia found herself stripped to the skin and soaking in a hot bath in no time at all.

Lydia washed the river water from her hair, sighing with pleasure as she scrubbed herself with soap that smelled of honey. She dried off and dressed in clean clothes, combing the tangles out of her long hair as she returned to the bedchamber.

"How do you feel?" Talia asked, her brow creased with worry. "I do hope you don't fall ill."

"I'm fine." In fact, Lydia hadn't felt this good in a very long time. She smiled and squeezed the younger woman's hands. "Really. Go on. I'm sure you want to change as well before supper."

"My room is one floor up, so call if you need me," Talia insisted. She pressed a kiss to Lydia's cheek and hurried out.

Lydia sank into a chair beside the fire. Although it was warm outside, flames danced from crackling logs. Lydia fanned her hair out around her shoulders and continued combing it in the hopes the heat would dry it quickly.

A knock sounded. "Come in!"

Her heart gave a little leap when Northwood entered, a tray of tea and biscuits in his hands. He looked somewhat startled to see her, pausing two steps into the room.

"Well, come in, then." Lydia nodded to the chair across from her. "Since you've all had a good laugh at my expense, you might as well make amends by pouring my tea."

Leaving the door open behind him, he moved to sit. He looked rather lovely—all clean and fresh with a crisp white shirt and his hair still damp from his own bath. He continued staring at her with an odd expression.

"What is it?" Lydia asked with impatience. "Have I got rushes stuck in my ears?"

Northwood blinked. He gestured to her head. "I don't

think…" He cleared his throat. "I've never seen your hair like that."

"What, wet?"

"No. Entirely…unpinned."

"Oh." The comb caught on a tight knot. Lydia swallowed hard and yanked it free. She shifted under his stare.

If he'd been looking at her with…well, *heat*, she might not have been quite so disconcerted. That intense, knowing look of his still embarrassed her, but she was becoming accustomed to it. In fact, she was starting to like it.

This, however, this was…what was it? Wonder? *Awe?*

Lydia grabbed the heavy length of her hair in two fistfuls and pulled it away from her face. She hurried to the dressing table and found several pins, which she used to secure an untidy knot at the back of her neck.

"Not quite the done thing, is it?" she asked with a wan smile, though her heart was suddenly racing. "Seeing a woman in such disarray."

He didn't take his eyes off her. "Very appealing. The disarray. To me, at least."

He splashed a bit of brandy into her cup and crossed the room. He pressed the cup into her hands, his dark gaze intent. The desire was there now—unmistakable, making her pulse throb—but there was something else, something warm and tender and…affectionate.

A response swirled in her. This wasn't like before, all those years ago when a man had awakened her body but left her soul unmoved. With Northwood—only with him—she felt a restless stirring, like something rousing, breaking open, coming to life.

"Stay and rest before dinner," he said. "No one expects you to join us downstairs."

"I'm really not—"

"I insist." He pushed a damp strand of hair away from her neck, his fingers lingering at the base of her throat.

Then, before she could move, before she could even breathe, he pressed the lightest kiss to her temple. "I never imagined it, you know."

Lydia almost couldn't speak. "What?"

"This." His hand slid across her neck, his lips moving to her cheek before he released her and stepped back.

He smiled—beautiful, rakish, gentle—and left.

Oh, my heavens, Lydia thought as light spilled through her in waves of silver and gold. She wanted him to smile at her like that forever.

In that instant, she realized what she'd been feeling in his presence. She could name the gentle surge beneath her heart, the lightness that eased the ancient, persistent tension in her chest.

Young. Alexander made her feel young again.

No, that wasn't quite right. He made her feel young for the first time ever.

Chapter Fifteen

Lord Castleford and Sebastian Hall nearly tripped over themselves getting to Lydia when she arrived for dinner. Shame-faced apologies tumbled from their mouths.

"So terribly sorry, Miss Kellaway...absolutely meant no offense...just having a bit of fun, you know...certainly didn't intend to insult a very delightful guest...our deepest, *deepest* apologies..."

Lydia almost put a halt to the barrage of words before glancing past to where Talia stood watching, her arms firmly crossed. After the men had expressed their voluminous contrition, they both turned to look at her. She gave a satisfied nod, and relief flashed across the men's faces.

Seated in a chair beside the fire, the earl watched the proceedings with a faint smile.

Castleford turned back to Lydia. "Really, we do hope you weren't offended, Miss Kellaway."

"One who is foolish enough to clamber onto a log over

a river... well, that person has no right to be offended at the consequences of her actions, Lord Castleford."

He grinned, his brown eyes twinkling. "And you know, your fish wasn't quite so small when we looked at it more closely."

"Under a microscope," added a deep voice just behind Lydia.

She turned to give Northwood a glare. He smiled in response. She forgave him.

He extended his arm. "Shall we?"

They went into the dining room and indulged in a lovely dinner of oxtail soup, veal cutlets in tomato sauce, sautéed potatoes, and green peas—the fish having gone to the appreciative household cat.

After dinner and coffee, Sebastian provided piano music while the others engaged in card games and conversation. Lydia found herself sitting with Lord Rushton beside the fire, at his request, explaining a recent puzzle she'd devised.

While he worked out the solution, Lydia stood to study the contents of the bookshelf where an abacus sat on display. She extended a hand to touch the shiny frame and beads but withdrew at the sound of Talia's voice.

"That was a gift from Lord Castleford several years ago," Talia explained, pausing beside her. "He brought it back from a trip to China. Did you ever travel there with your father?"

"Oh, no." Lydia curled her fingers into her palm. "I'd have loved to accompany him, but with Jane... well, it wouldn't have been possible. I've always loved the idea of travel, though."

A faint smile tugged at Talia's mouth. "You, Castleford, my brothers... even my father used to love travel once upon a time."

Lydia looked at her curiously. "And you?"

"I enjoy travel, yes, but since... well, lately I've become a bit of a home-bird, I'm afraid."

Sensing Talia was leaving much unspoken, Lydia wondered whether she ought to pursue the conversation when Talia gave her a smile and patted her arm.

"I'm glad you came, Lydia," she said. "It's lovely to have a new friend."

Warmth filled Lydia's chest as she watched the other woman walk away. Yes, it was lovely indeed to have a new friend.

She returned to Lord Rushton's side to discover he'd solved the puzzle with both accuracy and care. They discussed his solution, then joined the others for a final game of cards.

It was past midnight before everyone said their goodnights and headed upstairs to bed. Feeling content and sleepy, Lydia went into her bedchamber and saw her papers spread out over the desk. She looked around for her notebook and realized she'd left it downstairs.

She returned to the drawing room and found the notebook beside the fireplace. After tucking it beneath her arm, she looked at the abacus again, the beads glowing in a shaft of moonlight.

Her heart constricted. She picked it up, smoothing her fingers over the bamboo frame.

"Your father must have been familiar with the abacus." Northwood's voice drifted into the stillness of the room.

Lydia turned as he approached and stopped beside

her. Her skin prickled with delicious awareness of his presence.

"Yes, he was," she said. "I am as well. My father brought me an abacus from China when I was quite young and taught me how to use it. Jane and I devised several games as part of her lessons. We stopped playing years ago, and I believe my grandmother sold the abacus at some point."

She ran her hand over the beads, listening to the soft clicking, the slide of the wire. A clear, sharp-edged picture came to her mind—her father crouching on the floor of the schoolroom to present her with the abacus, explaining its history, its use. *It's called a suanpan, used to express numbers by the position of the beads...*

"It's the use of one's hands, I believe, that makes the abacus so effective," Lydia said, stroking her palm across the wood. "Touching the smooth beads, the tight brass wires, the polished frame. It adds a very tangible dimension to abstract concepts."

Northwood stepped forward and drew his forefinger across a row of beads. Lydia's hands tightened on the frame.

He had moved closer. She could smell him, a delicious combination of earth and sky that clung to his clothes, a faint tinge of smoke, as if he were composed of the very elements.

She cast an uneasy glance over her shoulder toward the open door.

She could feel the heat radiating from his body. His hands began to move over the frame of the abacus, toward where she continued to hold it in a tight grip. She was cloistered with him in a space that began to feel unbearably close. Intimate. Secret.

"Russian shopkeepers use it, you know," Northwood said, his hands sliding closer and closer to hers. "The abacus."

"Do they?" Her breath was uneven.

"Mmm. It's called a *schoty*. They use it to tabulate both simple and complex calculations. I imagine several of my Russian ancestors were shopkeepers. So it must be in my blood."

His hand reached hers, his fingers sliding across her knuckles.

"What must be in your blood?" she asked.

His thumb rubbed back and forth, back and forth, over her hand. "The effectiveness of touch."

A tremble coursed through her, little shivers raining up her arm. He hardly needed an abacus to prove that to her. Or, she suspected, to any other woman.

She drew back. "My lord."

"Alexander," he murmured. "I want you to call me Alexander."

Her gaze flew to his. "I beg your pardon?"

"Alexander," he repeated. His breath stirred the tendrils of hair at her temple. "Say it."

She wanted to. The urge filled her mouth like warm cream. She wanted to give voice to this man's name, to listen to it flow through the thick, dusty air. She wanted to say it aloud, the sharp *X* sound slicing the elegant vowels like a knife through soap-soft leather. She wanted to hear the acute consonants scarring the liquidity of the word.

She loved *Alexander*. Loved the name's imperfection, the melting of soft and hard sounds, the way it trailed off into a purr at the end. She could never think of him as *Alex*, could never cut short the silver ribbon of his name.

"Lydia." In his deep voice, her own name acquired new depth, like poetry that only he had the power to explain.

In that instant, Lydia had the strange, profound revelation that if she were to say his Christian name, it would be like severing the rope leading her from a maze. She would be left within a complex yet utterly compelling labyrinth with nothing but Lord Northwood's hands wrapped around hers and his breath on her skin.

She would not be able to find her way out. She would not want to find her way out. She would belong to him forever.

Her hands tightened on the abacus. His hands tightened on hers. She lifted her head, seeing herself reflected in the glossy dark surface of his eyes. Her voice was a steady, unfurling whisper.

"Alexander."

Chapter Sixteen

Jane peered out the window at the man standing across the street. Something about him seemed familiar, though she couldn't figure out what it was.

She turned away and paced. With Lydia gone, Jane didn't quite know what to do with herself—Grandmama had taken her to the park this morning, but then had gone off shopping with a friend and left Jane in the care of Mrs. Driscoll.

Jane glanced out at the man again. He appeared tall and thin, his hands in his coat pockets, his hat pulled low over his forehead.

A knot pulled just beneath Jane's chest. She wondered what Lydia was doing at Lord Rushton's country estate.

She slid her hand into her pocket, where the locket key still rested. She hadn't yet tried the key in any lock, though she knew of only one or two places where the little thing might fit.

"Would you like some tea, dear?" Mrs. Driscoll appeared in the doorway.

Jane shook her head and muttered that she wasn't hungry.

She slipped past the housekeeper and went downstairs. Unaccountably, her insides began to twist with nerves. Before she lost courage, Jane crossed to the closed door of her father's study and went inside.

The box sat on a shelf near the cedarwood desk. *Copper,* Jane thought as she ran a finger over the floral engravings. She'd seen the box numerous times, noticed the little lock holding it closed, though she'd never wondered about its contents. Until now.

She glanced over her shoulder, then inserted the key into the lock and turned. A faint click echoed through the room. She lifted the lid to reveal a padded velvet interior.

In an odd contrast to the rich-looking material, there was a worn brown envelope with frayed edges. A tattered string held the envelope closed. Jane picked it up and examined it. No writing or stamps marred the smooth exterior.

She hesitated. This was wrong. This was obviously private, or her father wouldn't have locked it away.

Jane put the envelope back in the box and started to close the lid. She looked at it for a moment, her heart beginning to thump a heavy beat inside her head.

She had the sudden feeling that the contents of the envelope were of the utmost importance.

Her heart hammered more loudly. Before she could change her mind, she grasped the envelope again and tore off the string. Her hands shook as she opened the flap and removed a piece of paper, yellowed with age, the sheet divided into separate boxes, each enclosing a few words.

She studied the page, the scrawled, loopy handwriting

that exceeded the boundaries of the printed boxes, only realizing after a moment's perusal that most of the words were in French.

French. Her mother had lived in France for years... a convent or sanatorium run by Dominican nuns. She'd died there, too, so perhaps this was a certificate of death or...

Jane gasped.

"My father visited Russia several times at the behest of the czar," Lord Rushton said, slicing into the filet with one stroke. "He always spoke of the country with great affection, and I often went along when I was a boy. He was quite pleased when I was appointed ambassador to St. Petersburg. Of course, that was a long time ago."

Lydia could have sworn she saw wistfulness pass across the earl's face before he gestured for a footman to pour more wine.

"Do you go back often?" Lydia asked, glancing at Sebastian, who sat to her right. "To St. Petersburg, I mean?"

His expression clouded. He shook his head and reached for his glass.

"Like Papa, we visited quite often when we were children," Talia said, her voice a bit too bright. "It was a second home to us. Our brother Darius still lives there. Lovely city, Miss Kellaway. You must visit one day. You'd find a number of fellow scholars, I'm quite sure."

"What is it like?" Lydia asked.

Silence fell. The three siblings exchanged glances, as if each waited for the other to speak. As if none knew how to answer her simple question. Alexander shrugged.

"Cold winters." His voice vibrated with something distant, foreign. "That's what it's like. A bitter cold that steals your breath. Snow piles everywhere, ice covers the windows, the river and canals freeze layers thick. Polar winds are as sharp as glass and drive gusts of snow through the streets. Darkness sets in midafternoon and doesn't lift until morning. The ice doesn't thaw until May. Sometimes it seems as if winter will never end."

"Not all that pleasant, eh?" Castleford remarked. "D'you know I've never been?"

"Really?" Talia looked at him. "Haven't you been everywhere?"

"I prefer warmer climes, my lady, especially if St. Petersburg is buried under a layer of ice six months out of the year."

"That's when you learn another way of living," Alexander said. His gaze came to rest on Lydia, and then it seemed as if he spoke only to her. "In winter, the sound of troika bells replaces summer birdsong. Candlelight fills the churches, and well-tended stoves keep the houses warm. The theaters host concerts, plays, and operas. There are sleigh races on the frozen Neva. The city holds festivals with music, dancing, skating, puppet shows, ice palaces, vendors selling hot tea and pastries. You can lose yourself in the Hermitage, the cathedrals, the academies. And when you don't want to be lost, you can find yourself in the white darkness. In the silence."

An emotion passed across his face that Lydia did not recognize, something solitary and bleak, as if he had lost something of value and had no idea where to begin looking for it.

"Quite right, Northwood," Rushton muttered.

"Well." Alexander forced a smile. "I suppose one can find similar amusements anywhere."

"No." Talia put her hand over his, her voice soft. "Not anywhere."

Rushton cleared his throat and stood, clapping his hands to break the solemn mood. "Coffee in the drawing room. And let's find out if Miss Kellaway is truly the brilliant scholar she claims to be."

Lydia looked at Alexander, but he only shrugged and indicated that they should accompany the earl. After they were seated in the drawing room, Rushton rummaged through a stack of books on a table and produced a folded paper.

"And now, Miss Kellaway." The earl placed his reading glasses on his nose and peered at her over the rims. "Your sister recently informed me that the puzzle does not exist that you cannot solve. So I set forth to find one of substantial difficulty, which took me no small degree of research. I daresay, without meaning to impugn your intelligence, this simply cannot be done."

A hush fell over the company, as if the earl had just thrown down a gauntlet. A sense of pride—of challenge—rose in Lydia.

She extended a hand to Lord Rushton. "May I see the problem, my lord?"

The earl gave the paper an irritated shake but allowed her to take it from him. "You cannot solve such a puzzle with mathematics. This is a trick of some sort."

"Read it aloud, if you would, Miss Kellaway," Sebastian suggested.

"Take a number of persons not exceeding nine," Lydia read. "After you leave the room, one person puts a ring upon his finger. Upon returning, you must determine the wearer of the ring, the hand upon which it rests, and the specific finger and joint."

The earl spread his hands. "I swear it cannot be done."

Lydia studied the problem, her mind working around the idea for several minutes before she looked up. "Actually, my lord, this is an application involving the determination of a number fixed upon. It's a bit of a trick using the principles of arithmetic."

"Show us." Alexander stood, extending a hand to Talia. "Might we borrow a ring?"

"My rings won't fit any of your fingers, which isn't fair for the puzzle." Talia glanced around the room and went to a vase from which a spray of spring flowers bloomed. She removed a primrose and broke off the flower, then twisted the stem into a ring. "There."

"All right, then," Lydia said. "You must all sit in a specific order, and I will assign numbers."

The company moved to sit in the places she indicated. Lydia designated the earl as number one, Lord Castleford number two, Talia three, Alexander four, and Sebastian five.

"Your right hand is also numbered one," she continued. "Your left is number two. Your thumb is number one, your forefinger number two, and so on. The joint nearest your palm is number one, the next number two, and the last is three. Now I'll leave the room while you determine who will wear the ring."

She stepped outside the drawing room until Talia called for her to return. Lydia went back into the room, where everyone sat with their hands behind their backs.

"Now, then, Miss Kellaway," Rushton said with a challenging look of his own. "How will you use arithmetic to determine the wearer of the ring?"

"I'll require your help, my lord," Lydia said. "Without telling me anything yet, would you please double the number of the person who has the ring?"

The earl nodded. "Done."

"Then add five and multiply the result by five."

"Done."

"Add ten, plus the number denoting the hand bearing the ring."

"Do you require pencil and paper?" Talia asked her father in a sweet tone.

"Only to extract you from my will," the earl retorted.

Sebastian and Castleford both chuckled. Even Alexander grinned.

"What next, Miss Kellaway?" the earl asked.

"Multiply your result by ten, then add the number of the finger holding the ring. Then multiply that sum by ten and add the number of the joint."

"All right."

"Then add thirty-five and tell me the sum you've reached."

"Seven thousand six hundred fifty-seven," Rushton replied.

Lydia performed a quick calculation in her head and turned toward Alexander. Her heart did a little twist as she saw the intense way he was looking at her.

"Lord Northwood," she said, her eyes locking with his, "is wearing the ring on the second joint of the forefinger on his right hand."

Silence descended over the company, so swift and hard that for an instant Lydia feared she'd made a mistake. Then Lord Rushton laughed, a big booming sound that echoed against the walls and ceiling of the elegant room.

A slow, beautiful smile spread across Alexander's face

as he extended his right hand to reveal the flower stem wrapped around his forefinger.

Talia turned an astonished stare upon Lydia. "How on earth—"

"It's quite simple, really, if you assign each part of the problem a fixed number and know the equation." Lydia's face heated slightly at the realization they thought she'd performed some astonishingly complex feat. "If you subtract three thousand five hundred thirty-five from the final number Lord Rushton provided, you have the solution. Seven thousand six hundred fifty-seven minus three thousand five hundred thirty-five is four thousand one hundred twenty-two. Lord Northwood was designated number four. And he wore the ring on his right hand, on the second joint of the second finger."

"Miss Kellaway, you're a marvel." Rushton stood and clapped his hands. "I'd have sworn it couldn't be done."

"You did swear it couldn't be done," Sebastian replied, throwing Lydia a grin. "Impressing the earl can be an insurmountable task, which makes its achievement quite an event."

Lydia glanced at Alexander. He was watching her with a curiously intent expression—his brow creased, a slight frown pulling at his mouth, as if he were attempting to reach a conclusion that still eluded him. Then he stood and approached Lydia with determination.

Her skin prickled with the sudden anticipation that something momentous was about to take place. Something both thrilling and devastating. The back of her neck dampened with perspiration, the candlelit room suddenly cloying and hot.

"I...I need to take some air." She stepped back to

escape his increasingly imposing presence, attempting not to hurry as she went toward the doors leading to the terrace. "If you'll excuse me—"

He followed her outside. The cool evening air bathed her skin. Her heart beat with unaccountable speed.

Alexander stopped beside her, resting his hands on the railing. For a moment, he stared out into the darkened garden as if it held the answer to a question with which he'd been struggling. In the ambient light, his profile appeared rough and shadowed, his eyes shimmering beneath thick dark lashes.

The sound of a Beethoven sonata drifted from the piano, mingling with the chirps of insects and night-bird calls.

"My father has not engaged in company for a very long time," Alexander finally said. "He only agreed to come this weekend because of Talia."

"She's a lovely young woman."

"Yes, she is. She could marry astonishingly well if she'd—" He broke off with a shake of his head.

Tension infused his shoulders, the line of his body. Lydia swallowed, a surge of anticipation and apprehension mingling in her chest.

"Alexander?"

His forehead creased, and his jaw appeared to tighten. Lydia's apprehension intensified. "What is it?" she asked.

"We've not known each other long," he said.

"No."

"And forgive me, but neither of us is in the bloom of youth."

"True."

He looked at her, his dark eyes direct as always, but

with a trace of uncertainty that troubled her. In the short time she'd known him, she'd come to think he would never be uncertain about anything.

"For several years, my father has expressed his wish that I marry and produce an heir," he said. "I haven't done so in part because I've been occupied with my business and family matters, but also because I haven't found a woman I could imagine marrying." He paused. "Until now."

Lydia pressed a hand to her chest. Her heart thumped wildly against her palm like a leaf whipped by a strong wind. She tried to speak, but her voice tangled around the words and stifled them.

"I believe we are well suited for each other," Alexander said. "I find you interesting, if somewhat baffling, and your family maintains a respectable status. We are... ah, physically matched, if recent events are any indication."

He cleared his throat and tightened his hands on the railing. Lydia realized with a start that he was more than uncertain. Alexander Hall, Viscount Northwood, was actually nervous.

"My—," she began.

"There is, of course, the issue that your consent might give rise to renewed gossip surrounding your mother," Alexander continued. "Though it is of little consequence to me, I do not wish for possible rumors to cause you or your family further distress."

A sheen of unexpected tears stung Lydia's eyes.

"However, I can promise you that marriage to me would not be disagreeable," Alexander said. He paced away from her a few steps, heading toward the door, then circled around back to her. "You will be free to pursue your interests, to continue your work in mathematics."

"I'm sorry, I—"

"You may run the household as you like," he continued. "I pledge my fidelity. I do wish to travel again, though I would welcome your company should you—"

"Stop." Lydia held up her hand, the tears spilling over. Her breath hitched, her chest tightening to the point of pain. "Please, please, stop."

He looked at her, the uncertainty in his expression evaporating into concern. "Surely it's not that horrid a thought."

"No. It's not that.... I'm sorry." Lydia pressed her hands against her eyes. Her heart swam beneath a surfeit of emotions that she couldn't even begin to comprehend. "I'm so terribly sorry."

His warm fingers curled around her wrists, pulling her hands away from her face. "Sorry about what?"

"I can't marry you." Lydia swiped at her eyes, regret and outright fear slicing through her. A sob rose to flood her throat, and her knees began to buckle.

Alexander caught her before she could fall. His breath heated the side of her neck. The warmth of his body spread through her. His heart beat heavy and strong against her. His arms were like taut, secure ropes preventing her from sinking beneath a wave-lashed surface of darkness.

Lydia pulled in a breath, her emotions twisting, her mind wrestling for an equation, a theorem, a proof—but she could seize nothing, not even a simple sum. The sheer and complete feeling of Alexander overpowered coherent thought, and she lost all ability to anchor herself with numbers.

She took another breath and placed her hands on Alexander's arms, urging him to release her. He did, though not without reluctance, his palms sliding flat against her midriff.

Lydia stepped from the circle of his arms.

He was cold suddenly without the warmth of her body against his. Alexander fisted his hands as he watched Lydia pace away from him.

"Lord Northwood, I wish to...to apologize..." Her voice wavered, her hand coming up to coil a stray lock of hair around her fingers. "I can offer you no detailed explanation, but—"

A look of defeat overcame her, her rigid shoulders slumping, her eyes brimming with tears.

Alexander fought the urge to enfold her in his arms again but allowed his tone to soften. "You've no need to apologize. Believe me, I'm not worth this much distress."

Lydia managed a faint smile through her tears. She wiped her eyes and looked up at him. "You must understand. I cannot marry you because I will never marry anyone. Ever. But please know that I'm deeply honored by the offer."

"You've an odd way of showing it, Miss Kellaway."

Lydia gave a watery laugh. "Oddness appears to be my modus operandi, Lord Northwood."

He moved forward, lifting a hand to brush it over her hair in a gesture that first made her flinch before she stilled and let him touch her. He smoothed a few tendrils of hair from her forehead, then lowered his hand.

Her smile faded. "I owe you more of an explanation—I know that—but there isn't much else I can tell you."

"I cannot believe that."

"I'm sorry."

The air between them thickened. She pulled back. He gripped her shoulders.

She stared at him, those blue eyes searing through him like a slice of the sky. He put his hand on the back of her head and pulled her to him, pressing his lips to hers in a kiss that made them both shudder. He drew her lower lip between his as he eased away, every part of his being aching for her.

She lifted a trembling hand to his mouth, sliding her finger across his lips. Something seemed to open inside her, a spilling light, a fateful certainty.

"I can't marry you," she whispered. "Please never ask me that again. But I will... I want to be your lover."

Alexander's heart slammed against his ribs. "I will not compromise you."

"No, you won't."

Confusion rose hard and fast, frustrating Alexander with his ever-present urge to fully understand this woman.

"Why?" He tightened his hands on her shoulders. "Why engage in something so scandalous when there is another way? If you would—"

"Don't. Don't ask me again." She put her lips against his cheek, her hand sliding across his chest, her whole body curving into him. "Take what I'm offering you, Alexander. Please."

Alexander fought a hard but brief battle with his conscience. God knew he wanted her more than he'd ever wanted a woman. Yet he knew the cost of scandal, and it was a price he never wanted Lydia to pay.

He forced his fingers to uncurl from her shoulders, to release her.

"Go back to your room," he said, his voice strained from the tension pulling between his mind and his body. "I will leave for London first thing tomorrow morning."

She stared at him for an instant, then turned and fled back into the house.

Chapter Seventeen

Lydia wanted to breathe. She wanted to pull great gulps into her lungs, to feel her body filling, her ribs expanding, her blood singing with sweet, delicious air. And she wanted to exhale, to slacken, to sink into a chair with repletion. Then she wanted to do it again, inhale, exhale, inhale, exhale. Over and over and over.

She closed her eyes. An hour had passed since she'd left Alexander on the terrace. She feared he might never return, that perhaps he'd decided to return to London that very night...

"God."

The whispered oath made her turn. Alexander stood in the doorway of his bedchamber, staring at her. She was clad in her corset and underpetticoat, her dress and overpetticoats in a crumpled heap on the floor. Lydia's blood thundered in her ears, nerves and fear twisting through her belly.

"I told you to go to *your* bedchamber." His voice was unsteady.

Lydia shook her head. Although he hadn't acquiesced to her offer, she knew he wanted her. He would not—could not—resist her blatant invitation.

She waited for a heart-stopping instant for his reaction to her undressed state but saw not the faintest hint of aversion cross his features. Only a desire so deep, so seething, it stole her breath.

She almost couldn't speak. "Y-you're really leaving tomorrow? Because of me?"

Lydia took a tentative step toward him, but he held up a hand.

"Don't."

"But—"

"You look..." His throat worked as he swallowed. "The fire behind you... like you're filled with light."

Light. No.

Once perhaps, many years ago, when she'd clambered over the pebbled beaches at Brighton. When her mother was whole and well and laughed with Lydia's father as the salty wind nipped their faces and the sea swept up to meet them. Then Lydia was whole too. Then she was filled with a light bright enough to illuminate the blackest of caves.

"The fire. I...I was getting cold." Her voice sounded unnatural, hoarse. She forced a smile, reaching a trembling hand to tuck a lock of hair behind her ear. Gooseflesh skittered over her skin.

Alexander closed the door, his boots soundless as he crossed the room to her. With every step that brought him closer, Lydia drew back into herself, her hands moving to rub her bare arms.

She expected him to grasp her shoulders, to pull her to him, but instead he stopped several inches from her and looked at her, his hot gaze settling on the generous swells of her breasts above her corset before moving back to her face.

Lydia shifted, her corset chafing against her torso, the place between her legs warming with Alexander's proximity. She watched him warily, questioning for the hundredth time the wisdom of her boldness.

"You make it impossible for me to withstand you," he said.

"That was my intention." A faint smile pulled at her lips. "And you did once say you thought I should be reckless more often."

"It appears I was correct."

Despite her admission, nerves continued to spiral through her. She stepped back toward the fire, the heat burning through her chemise and drawers. "Alexander, I..."

She looked at the buttons of his shirt, unable to meet his gaze. How could she ever tell him? How could she confess to the utter sordidness of her past and the horrific price she'd had to pay?

Perhaps she didn't have to. It was *her* past, fixed in her soul like a fossil—but there was no need for Alexander to know the full truth. She would never agree to marry him. Perhaps they would be lovers for a time, but their relationship would not extend beyond that. She owed him nothing except the loyalty due any lover.

At least this time, she knew the terms.

"I've done this before." Her murmur was almost inaudible, even to her own ears.

"I know."

Lydia jerked her gaze to his. "You do?"

He nodded, his features expressionless as he continued to watch her.

"H-how do you know?"

"No woman responds so swiftly to a man's touch, to passion, without having experienced it before."

A sting of tears blurred Lydia's vision for an instant.

It's not merely a man's touch, she wanted to cry out. *Not a nameless passion. It's you. You, you, you.*

Alexander stepped closer, catching her arms in his hands as he pulled her away from the fire. "Much as I wish to see you go up in flames, I'd rather it be in the metaphorical sense. And by my hand rather than an errant spark."

Her skin grew hot. Alexander slipped his hand beneath her chin and drew her head up. He frowned, brushing a stray tear from her cheek.

"I'm really not so horrible."

"I never thought you were. Quite the opposite, in fact." Lydia managed a smile as she brought her hand up to his coarse-whiskered jaw. She moved her thumb across his mouth, tracing its shape, feeling the slightly dry ridges of his lips. His breath on her fingers.

"Kiss me," she whispered.

His eyes darkened. Sliding a hand around the back of her neck, he pulled her to him, his mouth hovering over hers for a breathless instant before he closed the distance. Lydia shut her eyes and sank into the feel of him, parting her lips as he swept her mouth with his tongue.

Flowers of heat bloomed deep inside her, dispelling the last threads of cold. She could never be cold in Alexander's arms. She would never feel a bitter chill, not even from the depths of her own soul—not while wrapped in his all-encompassing warmth.

He angled her head, his tongue sliding across hers, his teeth gently biting down on her lower lip. Lust sparked and caught. She spread her hands over his shirt, feeling the hard ridges of his chest through the linen, his heart pounding against her palm.

He stroked his hands down her back to her buttocks, cupping them and lifting her against him. The bulge in his trousers pushed against her thigh, eliciting a renewed firestorm of arousal. Lydia squirmed, her breath coming faster and faster as she slid her lips across his cheek to his ear. She moaned. Alexander muttered something into her hair, his fingers kneading and parting her bottom so that she was splayed against his hard thigh.

Lydia gasped, her hips moving involuntarily as she strove to release the tension beginning to wind through her lower body. She pressed down, pushed forward and back, her fingers tightening on his shoulders. Alexander urged her movements with the grip of his fingers before he gave a hoarse laugh and eased them apart.

"Sweet Lydia, you'll be the death of me." His voice was uneven, edged with roughness. "A fate I'd gladly suffer a thousand times over."

He turned her around to unfasten her petticoat, letting it fall to the floor. Lydia's body surged with desire, her nipples tightening painfully against her corset.

"Help me take it off," she whispered in a husky entreaty, her hands tugging ineffectually at the front. "Oh, please, Alexander, take it off."

He fumbled with the laces, his big fingers clumsy as he sought to unfasten the expert ties. After a few muttered oaths, he finally yanked at the laces to loosen them, then turned her again to unhook the front.

Lydia moaned, her body vibrating with relief as Alexander tossed the garment aside. He stared at her breasts beneath her chemise, the heavy weight freed from confinement, her nipples pressing against the thin fabric.

A hard shudder racked Lydia's body when he reached out to fondle her, rubbing his hot palms over her breasts, sliding his fingers into the damp creases below.

She breathed, her chest filling with air, pushing her breasts against Alexander's adept hands. A restless churning started in the pit of her belly, making her press her legs together with the increasing urge for release.

"I want to see you," he said. "Now."

Hands shaking, Lydia grasped her chemise and pulled it over her head, baring her naked torso to his gaze. Alexander groaned at the sight of her, his hands now rough as he pulled her against him and crushed her mouth with his. A frantic urgency lit between them, hot and thick. Lydia rubbed her breasts against Alexander's chest, gasping as he slid his hands beneath her bottom again and lifted her.

Without hesitation, she wrapped her legs around his waist, the opening of her drawers parting. She fought the urge to squirm and writhe, wanting this delicious torture to go on and on and on until the world fell away beneath exquisite, unending pleasure.

"Alexander. Touch me. *Please*." She could hardly speak past the cascade of arousal coursing through her body. Every part of her being ached for the touch of his hands, his lips, the slick glide of his skin against hers.

"I knew you'd be this beautiful, this soft. Knew it." Alexander lowered her to the bed, moving to kiss the slope of her shoulder. He slid his lips across her throat, flicking his tongue into the damp hollow before moving lower.

Lydia arched at the first sensation of his lips on her sensitive flesh, her fingers tangling in his dark hair. Need streamed through her, a torrent of sensations as if multi-hued colors had replaced her blood. As Alexander moved to stroke her other breast, his fingers caressing, Lydia closed her eyes against another unexpected sting of tears. She hadn't known until now, until Alexander, that she was capable of feeling such pleasure.

He lifted his head to look at her, his eyes burning. Lydia's tongue darted out to lick her dry lips. She parted her legs. Still holding her gaze, Alexander slid his hand down her naked torso to the opening of her drawers.

"Oh." Her hips bucked upward at the first touch of his long fingers. "Oh, Alexander, yes . . ."

He lifted the length of his body alongside hers, lowering his head to kiss her. Lydia quivered, shook, vibrated like a viola string as his tongue delved into her mouth and his fingers eased into her.

"Come, Lydia." Tension thickened the command. "For me. Now."

She did, surrendering to the unbearable pressure as his thumb rubbed at the pearl of her body. Alexander captured her scream with his mouth. Undiluted rapture swept through her veins as she convulsed beneath his expert manipulations.

Before the pleasure had even abated, Lydia fumbled for the front of Alexander's trousers, her breathing ragged. "Let me see you."

Alexander bent to remove his boots, then unfastened his trousers and pushed them off. Another sweet tremor shook Lydia as she took his shaft in hand, the sleek warmth pulsing against her palm. She imagined all that malleable hardness filling her, stretching her, pressing against her in the most intimate way possible.

Alexander grasped her wrist, his jaw clenching. "Lydia—"

She hurried to unfasten the ties of her drawers and pushed them to the floor. Unashamed of her nakedness, basking in the glow of Alexander's hot gaze, she opened her thighs and grasped the front of his damp shirt to pull him to her.

"I want you inside me," she whispered, rubbing her lips across his jaw, his neck, his shoulder, her hands skimming over his chest through the shirt. "Fill me."

A groan tore from his throat. Standing beside the bed, he adjusted her position to align their bodies. Then he moved between her legs, pushing hard against her, finesse and tenderness lost in the onslaught of consuming need.

Lydia grasped his forearms, rolling her hips upward, choking out a cry when he began to fill her, hot, smooth, and heavy. Alexander stared at the juncture of their union, his gaze scorching as he watched himself disappear into her.

And then he was seated fully, the pulse of his body in rhythm with hers. She expected him to lever himself over her, to press their mouths together in time to that delicious plunging that would drive them both to rapture, but instead he placed his hands on her raised knees and watched her.

A blistering flush swept over Lydia's already overheated skin. Never had she expected a man to watch her so intently while he thrust into her, to stare at the quiver of her breasts, the jostle of her body, the roll of her hips. Never had she anticipated that a man would look at her face as if he wanted to witness the renewed arousal tensing her features.

She closed her eyes. Then she put her hands over her face, her nerves stretched to the breaking point, her mind awash in unfathomable sensations. Alexander's grip tightened on her knees, spreading her farther apart. The sound of flesh against flesh, of rough breathing and broken moans—his and hers—filled Lydia's ears. She was hot, so hot, sweat dripping down her neck, her breasts, her thighs.

He grasped her wrists again, pulling her hands away from her face, forcing her to look at him. He was close, she knew it, saw it in his hard features, felt it in the tension vibrating from him. And still he surged forward and back, again and again, stroking her and pushing her arousal ever higher.

She broke for the second time, bliss sparking through her veins in a delicious torrent. Alexander pressed his fingers to her sex to draw out every last pulse of pleasure, but as the burst of light began to fade, Lydia remembered.

"Alexander." Her voice cracked. She had to tell him, should have told him earlier.... Panic began to claw at her insides despite the lingering pleasure. "You can't..."

With what must have been enormous self-control, he pulled from her before surrendering to his own release. Lydia's body slackened with both pleasure and relief as she watched him ride out the final spasms. Her heart continued to thump hard, her blood pounding in her ears. Then Alexander collapsed onto the bed beside her, reaching a hand to urge her closer.

Lydia turned to curl into his side, trying to push away

the uncertainty, the tension, the doubts beginning to crawl like insects back into her consciousness.

Alexander's hand slid over her back, a warm stroking that brought her back to him. She rested her cheek against his chest, closed her eyes, and breathed.

Chapter Eighteen

He was asleep, and beautiful in his slumber. Lydia's heart tightened. His dark hair was a stark contrast to the white pillow. His chest moved with deep breaths. And though even in sleep his features remained set, a faint softness eased the angles of his jaw and cheekbones. If she looked at him long enough, she might believe he possessed more than a touch of vulnerability.

Lydia dragged her gaze from Alexander's face and reached for her chemise. The embers of the fire burned low and red, emitting wisps of smoke and little heat. She pulled on her shift and reached for her corset just as he spoke.

"Lydia."

His baritone voice rumbled into the cold. She stopped. Apprehension skittered across her skin as she turned to face him. Her breath caught at the sight of his naked body burnished in the pale light. All traces of softness gone from his expression, he swung his legs over the side of the bed and reached for his trousers.

Arousal tugged at Lydia as she watched him hitch the trousers over his hips, his muscles shifting as smooth as cream beneath his taut skin. Her fingers tingled with the urge to slide her palms over his shoulders again, to feel the flexing of his body, the tense grace that coiled through every one of his movements.

"Where are you going?" he asked.

"Back to my room."

Anger flashed in his eyes as he moved to stoke the fire, jabbing at the smoldering logs as if they had somehow wronged him. Sparks cascaded onto the hearth. He stabbed harder. The wood split beneath the poker.

"You'll go nowhere until we've settled this." The poker clattered back onto the stand. He paced to the bed and back again, pulling a hand roughly through his disheveled hair. "The risk of an affair is too great. I will not tolerate it."

The irritation in his tone stung her. "You appeared to *tolerate* it quite well several hours ago."

He glowered, even as heat flared in his eyes. "No man could resist a woman half undressed as you were."

Her stomach twisted. She'd known enough to expect this reaction, not that she could blame him. "If you believe it was a mistake—"

"It wasn't a mistake," Alexander interrupted. "It was inevitable. The minute I saw you, I knew I would have you in my bed."

The beat of her heart increased, the sound pulsing into her thoughts and masking the admission that she had known the very same thing.

Before she could respond, he crossed the room to her and gripped her wrists in his hands.

"But this stops now," he said. "I will give you two weeks."

"I beg your pardon?"

"Two weeks," Alexander repeated. "If at that time you don't agree to marry me, our relationship is over."

Her heart thumped. "Is that a threat?"

"It is a fact. I will not risk an affair."

"Why two weeks, then?" She struggled to infuse her voice with steel. "Why not pose the ultimatum now?"

"Because two weeks gives you time to prepare."

She stared at him in astonishment. "You think I'm going to agree, don't you?"

"Of course you're going to bloody well agree," Alexander said, a muscle throbbing in his jaw. "You *will* be my wife."

"I will not."

Anger and something else—desperation?—split through his expression like lightning. "For God's sake, I'm heir to an earl, you foolish woman."

"I am well aware."

"We've weathered scandal, yes, but my fortune alone is considerable."

"That alone is not reason to marry you."

"I've told you you'll have plenty of freedom, funds, time. You'll continue your work, do whatever you want during the day."

He moved closer, his eyes burning into hers and filled with remembrances of past lusty encounters . . . and promises of many more. His hot breath brushed her lips.

"And at night," he said, the words almost a growl, "you will be mine, wholly and utterly. Without reservation."

Lydia's arousal heightened, pulsing against her skin, between her legs. Her cheeks darkened with a flush, her chest rising with increased breaths. "I don't mean to imply that sounds unacceptable—"

A trace of amusement flashed in his expression. "Of course it's not unacceptable. It's a goddamned paradise."

Hardly a poetic sentiment, and yet a deep happiness flowered in her soul because he believed—he *knew*—a marriage between them would be a thing of glory.

Lydia stared at the beautiful, strong column of his throat, the damp hollow where she had tasted the salt of his skin. She rested a trembling hand against his chest, felt his heart pound against her palm and reverberate through her arm. His fingers closed around her wrist.

All the hopes and dreams and wishes of her life flooded through her—the goals realized, the opportunities missed, the chances taken. The strange combination of happiness and despair that pulsed through her blood.

The deep-seated knowledge that she would change nothing about her life, *nothing*, not even if it meant possessing the freedom to accept his proposal, to embrace all the glorious advantages of being Alexander Hall's wife.

"If I were ever to marry," she said, "I would wish for no other husband except you."

"Then say yes."

Frustration slammed hard against Alexander when Lydia didn't respond. He tightened his grip on her wrist until her wince made him realize he was hurting her.

Muttering a curse, he released her and stepped back. He felt her gaze on him. He fought the urge to pace. Instead he picked up the poker again and stabbed at the burning logs. He reined in his anger, knowing it was hardly the most effective way to convince her to accept him.

Lydia sank into a chair beside the fire, wrapping her arms around her knees.

Silence fell between them for what seemed a very long time before she spoke.

"It's required of you, isn't it?" she asked. "That you marry well. I can see why the daughter of a baron would have been an excellent match for you."

Alexander tightened his fist on the poker.

"She was nothing of the sort," he said. "And you are not the daughter of a baron, but I still—"

"Exactly," Lydia interrupted.

"What?"

"There are vast differences between your former intended and myself." She rubbed her hand over the arm of the chair and studied the pattern of the upholstery. "I know nothing about society, Alexander. I've not the faintest notion what style of dress is fashionable or how to conduct an afternoon tea."

"Talia can assist you with that sort of thing, if it's a concern."

"But that's not enough." She lifted her head to look at him. "I would not be an asset to either you or the earldom. Can you not see that?"

"You're wrong. You're well regarded, Lydia, as your father was before you. I learned that shortly after meeting you. Your talent for mathematics is cause for fascination rather than disapproval." He took a step toward her, willing her to believe in his sincerity. "And you would be an asset to me. Yes, I've a duty to marry well, but beyond that we are undeniably compatible. Never have I met a woman like you. A woman with whom I wish to spend my life."

An unbearable sorrow darkened Lydia's eyes. A sorrow

Alexander had seen before. One whose source he could not fathom.

She ran her forefinger over the floral design of the upholstery, tracing the leaves up to the open flower. Her head was bent, her tumble of long hair partially obscuring her features, her lashes lowered.

"Mutually inverse functions," she said.

"What?"

"That's what marriage should be like," she continued. "Mutually inverse functions. Suppose a function travels from point A to point B. An inverse function moves in the opposite direction, from B to A, with the idea that each element returns to itself, so if you were to—"

"Stop."

She looked up at him, her dark-fringed eyes wide. "It's a mathematical way of—"

Alexander strode forward and grasped her shoulders, pulling her from the chair and against his body. "No. There are no *mathematics* to this, Lydia."

Her generous breasts pressed against his chest, firing his blood all over again. He gathered the folds of her shift and pulled it up to expose her legs, her rounded hips. Lydia softened, her palms splaying against his chest as her breathing quickened.

"You can't formulate an equation to explain this," Alexander whispered, stroking one hand along the slope of her waist, the curve of her hip, down to the warmth between her thighs. "You can't find a pattern in love, in desire. You can't calculate what makes a man want a woman. You can't quantify attraction and passion. All you can do is *feel* it."

Lydia gasped as his fingers explored farther. Her blue eyes darkened, her hands tightening on his shoulders.

"I . . . I just meant that if you—"

"Feel it, Lydia." Alexander cupped his hand beneath her chin and lowered his mouth to hers. "Just feel it. Do you?"

"Yes," she whispered, her body fitting with ease against his, as graceful as an elongating flower stem. "Oh, yes."

Hot anticipation seeped into Alexander's blood, inundating the growing awareness that this woman had filled a place inside him he hadn't even known was empty.

And when she was beneath him, her body lush and supple under his, her broken gasps hot against his ear, he fought the urge to demand her surrender again, fought the compulsion to make her admit she belonged to him. That she would only, could only, ever be his.

Chapter Nineteen

The faint sound of hammers and saws echoed through St. Martin's Hall and against the walls of the Society of Arts meeting room. Five men sat opposite Alexander at the council table, each reviewing papers and occasionally marking them with a pencil.

Alexander didn't want to be here. Didn't want to be back in London. A week after returning from Devon, he'd received notification about the Society of Arts' urgent meeting. And he had a sinking feeling he already knew the reason for the council summons.

He fisted his hands on his knees as he waited for the Marquess of Hadley to speak.

"I'm afraid we've increasing cause for concern, Lord Northwood." Hadley's frown slashed across his face, wrinkled his forehead. He looked up from his notes. "You've two brothers still residing in St. Petersburg, do you not?"

"One." *I think.* He didn't know where Nicholas was,

couldn't remember the last time they'd received a letter from him. Alexander tried to keep his voice level. "I fail to see what this has to do with the exhibition."

"Then you'd best look more closely, Lord Northwood." Sir George Cooke thumped a fat finger on the table. "Your *brother* is considered an enemy of the state."

"My brother is not a soldier, not in politics—"

"You think anyone cares what he does?" Lord Hadley asked. "We've already received numerous objections to the extent of the Russian display in the exhibition, and we've not even received most of the objects yet."

Lord Wiltshire coughed. "And, forgive me, Lord Northwood, but no one has forgotten the unfortunate circumstances surrounding your mother and the divorce of your parents. Owing to your support and the strength of your work with the Society, we've been willing to overlook it up to this point, but I'm afraid the increasing hostilities with the Russian Empire force us to take it into account once again."

Alexander's back teeth snapped together. "What my mother has to do with—"

"Lord Northwood, please." Sir George held up his hand. "You are not on trial. We are not asking you to defend yourself or your family. We are simply stating the facts, and I venture to suggest that even you yourself cannot disagree with them."

Alexander sat back, detesting the helplessness that swamped his chest.

"There is a great deal of anti-Russian public sentiment in France," Sir George continued, "and it is beginning to flourish here. We dare not risk causing tension with the French and other foreign commissioners to the exhibition by suggesting that we sympathize with the czar."

"A despotic ruler, if ever there was one," Lord Wiltshire added. "We must be united with our allies against him, Northwood, and in all areas of society. That's really the crux of the matter."

"And your own business of trading with Russia—fibers and such, isn't it?—is also an issue, Northwood," Sir George said. "It's not been declared illegal, per se, but we can't discount the possibility that it will be soon. Or at the very least that it will arouse public sentiment."

"What would you have me do?" Alexander asked. "Remove the Russian display from the exhibit, limit trade with—"

"Lord Northwood, there's not much you can do." Faint sympathy glimmered in Hadley's expression. He and Sir George exchanged glances. "We've got to... well, we'd need support of the union representatives and there are bylaws to consider, but I'd suggest you prepare yourself for the eventuality."

Alexander's fists tightened. "What eventuality?"

"I'm afraid we've little choice but to consider replacing you as director of the exhibition."

Alexander stormed from the room. All the work he'd done for the Society, the exhibition, his family, his company... slipping like water from his fist. He let the door slam shut behind him as he strode into the exhibition space of St. Martin's Hall.

Workers teemed through the great room like insects over a field. The hall itself, and the staircases, galleries, and passages, were crowded with tables, shelves, cases, and partitions to demarcate various displays. The air filled to the paneled ceiling with the sounds of shouting voices, hammers, the scrape and thump of crates.

His doing. None of this would have been possible if it weren't for him, and now they could strip him of his duties as if—

Alexander stopped at the section devoted to the countries of Asia. Lydia stood near the China exhibit, her head bent as she examined a shelf of books. A surge of joy swelled beneath Alexander's heart at the sight of her, diluting his anger.

Even with all the frustration she'd caused him, he could not deny the sheer pleasure he found in just looking at her. He had a constant longing to hear her voice, to feel her gaze on him, to bask in the warmth of her smile.

Christ in heaven.

He loved her. He wanted to marry Lydia because he loved her. He needed to marry her. He needed *her.*

He took a few breaths to calm his turmoil before approaching her. Talia and Castleford were also there, deep in conversation.

"Hullo, North." Castleford lifted a hand in greeting. "We were just going over the final details here."

Alexander kept his gaze on Lydia. An image of her flushed and naked beneath him flashed into his brain. He drew in another lungful of air and forced steadiness into his voice. "A pleasure to see you, Miss Kellaway."

She smiled. His blood warmed.

"You as well, my lord," she said. "I received word that several mathematical texts have arrived. You wanted my opinion on whether they should be included in the exhibition?"

Hell. Now Alexander didn't even know how much

longer the decisions would be his to make. He gave a short nod.

"If you would accompany me, please?" he asked.

Lydia stepped away from the exhibit, falling into pace with him as he walked toward the offices at the back of the hall.

"Er, is that Miss Kellaway?" A male voice interrupted them.

Alexander muttered an oath as Lydia turned to face the two men who were approaching. Alexander frowned, straightening his shoulders to convey an air of intimidation. It worked, as the two men stopped a distance away, their eyes going uncertainly from Lydia to Alexander.

She stepped forward with a delighted smile. "Lord Perry, Dr. Sigley, how wonderful and unexpected to see you here."

Heartened by her enthusiasm, the men approached with their hands extended—the gesture being the only similarity in their respective appearances. One of the men was small and sprightly with inquisitive eyes that brought the image of Queen Victoria's late pet spaniel, Dash, to mind. His shuffling, big-shouldered companion sported ears like Staffordshire oatcakes and a lackadaisical expression mitigated by keen dark eyes.

"And our utmost pleasure to see you, Miss Kellaway," Dash the Spaniel said, grasping her hand in both of his and pumping it heartily.

"Yes, it's been far too long since we've had the opportunity to match our wits with yours." Oatcakes sidled between his companion and Lydia to take her hands.

Alexander cleared his throat. Lydia turned to him with a smile.

"Lord Northwood, these gentlemen are renowned mathematicians," she said, gesturing to Dash. "This is Dr. Sigley, Fellow of the Royal Society of London and editor of the *Cambridge and Dublin Mathematical Journal.* And Lord Perry is a professor at King's College whose election to the Society is expected this month. Isn't that correct, my lord?"

"Indeed it is, Miss Kellaway. Thank you for remembering."

"Of course. But what are you both doing here?"

"The committee in charge of collecting mathematical and scientific instruments asked us to be advisors," Lord Perry said, scrutinizing her with the attentiveness of a jeweler examining a rare gem. "We'd hoped to call upon you for assistance, but knowing you prefer... er, that is, seeing as how you cherish your privacy... ah, in the sense that—"

"We know you prefer to avoid the recognition," Dr. Sigley put in.

"Yes," Perry agreed. "Much as recognition would like to cast its radiant light upon you, my dear Miss Kellaway."

He and Sigley fell silent in a moment of reverent admiration. Alexander coughed.

"Forgive me, gentlemen." Lydia turned to Alexander. "This is Alexander Hall, Viscount Northwood. He is the director of the exhibition."

Alexander's back teeth came together hard. He nodded. "Gentlemen."

"My lord." Perry shuffled his feet together, casting a glance at his companion. "Miss Kellaway, are you involved with the exhibition?"

"No, I'm just giving his lordship my opinion about several mathematical texts."

"And will you attend the symposium week after next?"

Sigley asked. "I received the paper you sent for review, the one about the rotation of a body around a fixed point. You claim it can be solved by six meromorphic functions of time?"

"Yes, provided all six have a positive radius of convergence and satisfy the Euler equations as well."

"Genius," Perry murmured. He grasped Lydia's hand in both of his and spoke to Northwood while continuing to stare at her. "Lord Northwood, you've got a most extraordinary...Miss Kellaway is deeply admired. Very deeply admired."

Sigley moved to ease Perry away from Lydia, who appeared amused rather than affronted by the man's evident devotion.

"You've several fascinating ideas in your paper, Miss Kellaway," Sigley agreed. "I've some questions about the integrals but need to study the equations a bit more. Perhaps we can discuss it further at the symposium?"

"Of course. I look forward to it."

"As do I," Sigley said. "Pleasure to see you again, and to meet you, my lord."

"Yes, and...and we do hope that you will make yourself more...er, available to us in the future." Perry gave an awkward little bow before he and Sigley moved off toward the display of mathematical instruments.

"What symposium?" Alexander asked.

"Oh." Lydia waved a hand in dismissal as they left the great hall and went to an office at the back of the building. "One focusing on recent studies in mathematics. I received an invitation last month and accepted. I haven't been to a symposium in an age, and I thought I might like to hear the latest theories."

After picking up several books from the desk, she started to walk back to the corridor. He stepped in front of her and closed the door.

Lydia stopped. "Alexander?"

"Why haven't you attended symposiums and such recently?" he asked.

"I don't—"

"And why did both those men know you'd rather avoid recognition?"

"I just have something of a reputation for preferring to conduct my work in private. It doesn't mean anything, Alexander. It's just the way I am. How I've always been."

"Why?"

"What do you mean, why?"

"Why is it that *you*, a woman with a mind even Euclid himself would admire, are so determined to be anonymous?" Frustration flashed through him at the notion that her talents had been muted... and he'd no idea why. "And don't use Jane as an excuse. Why did you spend so many years pursuing mathematics if you intended to stop using your talents?"

Lydia pressed her lips together, a mixture of irritation and sadness flaring in her eyes. "I never intended to stop using my talents. Where mathematics is concerned, I've always wanted to contribute to its body of knowledge, to see my work published and debated, to write books, to study identities and equations. That's all I've ever wanted to do."

"Prove it."

"What?"

Alexander stepped closer, the urge inside him intensifying. He hated it, hated the idea that his brilliant, stunning Lydia had been locking herself away for years upon years, that she had been alone with her own thoughts, closed off from a community of academics who *wanted* her theories, her ideas, her intelligence.

"Deliver a talk for the educational exhibition lecture series," Alexander said. "The topic will be your choice. Practical instruction in schools, use of the abacus, mathematics and science... I don't care. Whatever you want. Whenever you want. But *do it*."

She was so still that even the air around her seemed to stop moving. She clasped her hands in front of her, her blue eyes guarded.

"I—"

"Deliver a lecture," Alexander interrupted, "and you will finally have the locket back."

A smile ghosted her lips. "Another wager?"

"Not a wager. An agreement. The payment for your locket is one lecture. My final offer."

"Alexander, I—"

"No." He took two steps toward her and grasped her shoulders. "Do *not* tell me you can't. That will be a lie. And we have no place for lies."

To his shock, a flood of sudden tears swamped her eyes as her fingers curled around his arms. He loosened his grip on her, prepared to step back, but her hold on him tightened.

"Wait." She swiped at her eyes with her sleeve. "Wait. Alexander, I'm sorry. I'm so sorry."

"You needn't be sorry, Lydia. You need only do what you were put on this earth to do."

"You... you believe that?"

"Of course I believe it. You were meant to impart

knowledge, Lydia. It's why you were granted such intelligence." His mouth twisted. "Though you might have suffered a lapse in said intelligence when you rejected my proposal."

Lydia gave a watery laugh, but the sound was hollow. She moved closer to him, her grasp so tight that the warmth of her fingers, her palms, burned through his coat and shirt.

"I'm sorry, Alexander. Please believe it's not... I didn't decline because I don't love you."

Alexander's breath stopped. He stared at Lydia, her blue eyes clear and direct, her cheeks flushed, the ends of her eyelashes still damp. His heart thumped, an odd, discordant beat that resonated with everything Lydia—her maddening, luscious presence in his life, her naked abandon, her crisp, fresh-pencil scent.

"Then why?" he asked, his voice tight.

She shook her head.

Frustration spiraled through him again, winding into his chest. "I will not tolerate this, Lydia. You have one more week."

"This is not like solving a mathematical problem, Alexander."

"Isn't it? Aren't you studying this sort of thing, figuring out equations to explain emotions? Love plus love equals marriage, doesn't it?"

She drew in a sharp breath, a hard tremble racking her body. He tightened his grip on her, inhaled the perfume of her thick hair.

"Say *yes*," he whispered, not knowing if he was referring to his marriage proposal or the lecture series, or both.

Lydia stiffened in his arms, her fingers clutching the lapels of his coat. "No."

Something broke inside Alexander as that single word rose between them. His brother's words from so many weeks ago echoed in his head.

Do whatever makes you happy. Oh, no, you'll never do that, will you?

But Alexander had tried. God in heaven, he'd tried.

He let Lydia go as she pulled away from him. She went to collect the books, tucking them into the crook of her arm. He stared at her profile, the graceful curve of her cheek, and the way a loose tendril of hair spilled over her neck.

Determination swelled anew. He wasn't finished yet. If Lydia still refused to recognize they were meant to be together, he would find another way to convince her. He needed an ally.

Chapter Twenty

Pencil marks, notes, and scribbled equations marred the pages of her notebook. Lydia leafed through them, attempting to muster the desire to pursue her ideas, to prove that Alexander was wrong. She *could* quantify love. She could explain attraction through a differential equation, could establish patterns of intimacy.

She just no longer wanted to.

She looked at all the notes she'd made about Romeo and Juliet, Tristan and Isolde, Lancelot and Guinevere, Helen and Paris, Petrarch and Laura. Her equations could never explain the one common element of those relationships—the fact that none of them ended well. For all their passion and emotions and desire, none of the couples lived a joyful, fulfilling life together.

So $dr/dt = a_{11}r + a_{12}j$ mattered not a whit since, ultimately, it equaled unhappiness. Not to mention a frequent untimely death.

I propose, Miss Kellaway, that you throw your

infernal notebook into the fire and leave me the bloody hell alone.

A faint smile tugged at Lydia's mouth. She snapped the notebook closed and stared at the fire. With a flick of her wrist, she tossed the notebook into the flames.

It fell open, pages fluttering in the heat before the paper caught and began to burn. Her writings, her numbers, her equations, blackened and curled in the fire.

She watched until the book burned to ashes. A sense of freedom spun through her. She'd get another notebook—she was, after all, a mathematician to the bone—but no longer would she devote her time and intellect to fictional relationships that ended in tragedy.

Life was too valuable, love too precious, to be measured.

She turned away and swiped at a stray tear. When Alexander had first held the door open for her all those weeks ago, she hadn't imagined so many subsequent doors would open as well. Without him, she never would have ventured forth again. Not in mathematics. Not in life. Certainly not in love.

She tried to imagine agreeing to his suggestion, presenting her ideas to an audience of her colleagues. Her prime number theorem or the lemma of—

Oh, Lydia. Stop being foolish. What have you been telling Alexander all this time?

Strengthening her resolve, Lydia brushed off her skirts and went upstairs to the schoolroom. Jane stood beside the fern near the window, a metal apparatus in one hand, while their grandmother busied herself organizing Jane's books.

"It's looking lovely." Lydia stopped to examine the

fern, which had grown green and lush in the past few weeks. "What is that?"

"It mists water onto the fronds. Lord Rushton told me how to care for it." Jane put the bell glass back over the plant and turned away. "What are you doing here?"

"I thought we might go over long division again."

"I've actually got something else to do." Jane dropped the apparatus onto the windowsill and left the room.

"Is she all right?" Lydia asked Mrs. Boyd.

"As far as I know, yes. Why?"

"I've hardly seen her since I returned from Floreston Manor." Lydia frowned. "You don't suppose she's upset that she wasn't able to come along?"

"I shouldn't think so." Mrs. Boyd straightened from the bookshelf and dusted her hands. "I told her she could accompany you the next time you go."

Lydia's heart lurched. "What... what makes you think there will be a next time?"

"Of course there will be." Her grandmother stacked a pile of books on the table, then bent to retrieve several folded papers that fell to the floor. "Lord Northwood didn't ask you to his country estate because he wished to end your relationship." Her eyes narrowed. "Did he?"

Lydia's throat tightened. She shook her head.

"Well, then," Mrs. Boyd said. She glanced at the papers and replaced them on the shelf. "I must say, Lydia, I never imagined things would come to this when you went to retrieve that locket. Have you gotten it back, by the way?"

"Not yet."

"Good. All the more reason to keep his lordship's acquaintance." Mrs. Boyd's lips curved into a smile. "Had

I known this would happen, I might have pawned the foolish thing years ago."

She swept the books into her arms and left the room. Lydia went to the window, staring down at the street, where wagons and pedestrians passed.

She couldn't find it in her to be indignant over her grandmother's attitude. Despite Charlotte Boyd's manipulations, she had always wanted the best for Lydia. Like Alexander, her father and grandmother had always believed in her abilities, her intelligence. They believed she had something important to offer the world.

The difference was that Alexander also wanted her to believe in herself. Because he loved her. He loved her in ways she had never been loved before, in ways she hadn't even known existed.

Longing sliced through her, cutting through thick layers of resistance. She couldn't stop herself from envisioning what her life would be like if her wishes came true.

She sank into a chair by the window, resting her forehead against her hand. She would be Alexander's wife, she would stand before a crowded lecture hall to explain her theories, she would pour her heart out to Jane and give the girl everything Lydia never had. She would be free—mind, body, soul.

Perhaps one day...

The little whisper of her heart brought tears to her eyes because her mind knew that *one day* would never come. Never.

Enough.

Alexander flexed his fingers in an effort to ease the tension hardening his every muscle. He'd worked too hard for everything—the Society, the exhibition, his family, his company—and it was all slipping from his control. He would not allow the same to happen with Lydia.

With unshakeable resolve, he descended the carriage on East Street. The housekeeper answered the door of the town house, her eyes widening at the sight of him.

"Lord Northwood! We weren't expecting your—"

"Never mind, Mrs. Driscoll. Is Mrs. Boyd at home?"

"Yes, milord, she's in the morning room."

"Good. Tell her I am here."

"One moment, please, yer lordship. Miss Kellaway is—"

"At St. Martin's Hall. I know."

"Just a moment, then, milord." Mrs. Driscoll scurried off.

Alexander waited impatiently before she returned to usher him into the morning room. Mrs. Boyd stood, smoothing the wrinkles from her skirt as she approached. She had an imperial quality that he admired, and he intended to use her calculated interest in him to his advantage.

"Lord Northwood, to what do I owe this honor?"

"Mrs. Boyd, has Lydia spoken to you regarding my intentions?"

"Your intentions?" A gleam of interest appeared in her eyes. "No, my lord. Might I inquire as to what they might be?"

"I requested her hand in marriage when she visited Floreston Manor."

"Oh." Her eyes widened, her hand going to her throat. "Oh, Lord Northwood, I had no idea. Lydia never said anything to me."

Alexander paced to the windows and back. "Perhaps because she refused the offer."

"She *refused*?"

"Yes, but she gave me no satisfactory reason for doing so."

"I'm sorry, my lord." Mrs. Boyd's fingers trembled a bit as she brushed a lock of white hair from her forehead. "I've no idea what to say, except that clearly my granddaughter has behaved in a very foolish manner."

"Quite contrary to her usual nature," Alexander agreed. "And I must explain that I told Lydia she can continue her work, that she will lack for nothing. You may be assured I will take both you and Jane under my protection as well."

"I'm deeply obliged to you, my lord. I... May I ask if the offer still stands?"

"For one more week, yes, though Lydia gives no indication of changing her mind."

"This is why you've come to me?"

"I hope you might be able to talk some sense into her."

"My lord, *please* have patience. Lydia is... different, you know. She always has been. She did not have a normal childhood, though of course she would make an excellent wife and do nothing to—"

Alexander held up a hand. "You needn't vouch for Lydia, Mrs. Boyd. I am well aware of her qualities."

He paused as the truth of the statement struck him. Everything about Lydia complemented him—her intelligence, her wit, her passion. Even her stubbornness suited his nature, as if it were a gentler echo of his own inflexibility. And her genuine goodness, her kindness, reminded him with every heartbeat of what he should strive to be.

"Lydia has many traits that I deeply admire," he continued. "However, my offer does not stand much longer."

"Of course not. I'll speak with Lydia straightaway, my lord. Thank you ever so much. You honor our family with your consideration."

Alexander took his leave and returned to the foyer. As he was putting on his coat, he stopped and glanced toward the stairs. Jane stood on the bottom step, her hand curled around the newel post.

Alexander straightened and buttoned his coat.

"Did you mean it, my lord?" Her voice quavered. "You really want to marry Lydia?"

He nodded and approached her. Her green eyes swam with tears, which made him uncertain what to do.

"You dislike the idea of me marrying your sister?" he asked.

Her tears spilled over. She shook her head.

"Then what is it?"

Her chest hitched as she swiped at her cheeks with the back of her hand. Alexander gave her shoulder an awkward pat, discomfited by her reaction. He suspected Jane couldn't imagine someone taking Lydia away from her, that the very idea caused her pain.

"You would continue to see Lydia as often as you like," he said.

She sniffled.

Alexander reached into his breast pocket and removed the locket. He took Jane's hand and put the necklace in her palm, closing her small fingers around it. "This belongs to you. Lydia always intended for you to have it. If she does accept my offer, I'll be most pleased to have you as a sister-in-law."

Jane's fingers tightened on the locket as a fresh course of tears spilled down her pale cheeks.

"It's not that I dislike the idea of you marrying Lydia." She gulped. "It's that I don't want *her* to marry you."

She turned and ran up the stairs, leaving Alexander staring after her in utter bewilderment.

Chapter Twenty-One

"He told me you *refused*." Her grandmother's voice shook with anger. She stood beside the windows of the drawing room, her hand clutching the knob of her cane. "Why would you do such a thing?"

Lydia twisted the folds of her skirt. Mrs. Boyd had been waiting for her when she returned from a brief meeting with Talia at St. Martin's Hall. Her heart ached at the discovery that Alexander had gone to her grandmother without her knowledge, even as she could not deny a thrill at the evidence of his persistence.

The man *wanted* her to be his wife.

"You know quite well why I refused," she told her grandmother.

"It doesn't matter anymore, Lydia! Have you forgotten your position? That you were responsible for ruining your own future? That once Jane leaves this house and begins her own life, you have *nothing*?"

"I could...I couldn't agree to his proposal without

telling him the truth." Lydia forced away the tears beginning to fill her chest, to choke her throat. "He has... has a reputation, I know, his family does, but he's a good man. He has a good heart. And if he were to take a wife who..."

"A wife who what? Who is a mathematical genius? Clearly he finds that an asset rather than a detriment. And have you thought about what this could do for us?" Mrs. Boyd moved closer to Lydia. "Everyone with whom I have spoken has been conciliatory about the viscount. Oh, several have mentioned the scandal, of course, but really, Lord Northwood is not to blame for that. His own reputation remains intact, as long as one does not punish him for the sins of his parents. Which I am not inclined to do."

"And what of *my* reputation?"

"You have no reputation, Lydia, not in such lofty circles. That is why Lord Northwood chose you—he doesn't want a titled woman who fears the scandal will reflect upon her family. With you, the man has a respectable woman who is admired for her intellect and will prove a good and honorable wife."

"I am not honorable."

"You can be." Her grandmother thumped her cane hard on the floor. "Idiot girl! This is your only chance to better yourself, Lydia, to better the pathetic life you lead. You don't even have your work anymore, do you? Not the way you'd wish for it to be. Do you want to spend the next twenty years hiding, wasting away to nothing?"

"What makes you think marriage to Northwood would prevent that?"

"You'd at least have a good life, Lydia! Yes, he has difficulties, but even two months ago did you imagine you would ever be in this position? He's a viscount! He has a fortune. Imagine what you could do if he allowed it."

The horrible thing was, Lydia could imagine. She'd thought about little else ever since Alexander first proposed.

She imagined working with Talia on the ragged schools' educational program, helping establish mathematical curricula for girls' schools. She could imagine teaching governesses how best to approach mathematical instruction, funding symposiums, lectures. She could even see herself at Alexander's side with the Society of Arts—exhibitions of inventions, award programs, judging panels.

And, of course, she could envision *him*—talking with him, touching him, kissing him, feeling his hands on her body, his gaze warm on her face.

Whenever she wanted. All the time. Without reservation. With him.

Imagining all that, picturing it in her future, caused a longing so deep, so sharp, that Lydia almost couldn't breathe.

"Is this what you wanted?" Her grandmother's voice was closer.

Lydia turned to look at her, into the blue eyes so like her own, so like her mother's. Mrs. Boyd's expression softened with regret. She put her hand on Lydia's cheek.

"Did you really expect your life would turn out like this?" her grandmother asked.

Lydia swallowed past the lump in her throat, her heart squeezing painfully. "What will you do if I accept him? What about Jane?"

"Oh, Lydia." Her grandmother's eyes glistened with a sheen of tears. "We'll be here. We'll always be here.

You'll see Jane as much as you do now, if not more. And do you think Jane's feelings for you will change one whit simply because you're married to Lord Northwood?"

Lydia's tears spilled over, rolling so fast that she tasted salt on her lips. She grasped her grandmother's hand where it rested against her cheek. "How can I not tell him?"

"Because you can't." Such a simple response, and yet so tangled, so twisted. "It isn't as if anyone will ever know."

"Everything will change," Lydia whispered.

"Only for the better."

"I've already refused." She struggled to hold on to her resolve, but she could feel it weakening, breaking, the light of a possible new future showing through the cracks. The shadows would always be there, but maybe now, finally, the brightness would overpower them.

If she allowed it to.

"Lord Northwood told me the offer stands for one more week," Mrs. Boyd said. "He wants to marry you, Lydia. He wouldn't have asked otherwise. You mustn't allow this opportunity to pass. For Jane's sake, if for no other reason. Do for her what your parents were unable to do for you."

A thread of candlelight wove through the darkness. Lydia approached the bed where Jane lay beneath the covers, staring at the pattern of shadows across the ceiling.

Lydia paused and looked at the girl. She saw no resemblance to Theodora Kellaway in Jane's rounded features, her soft, full mouth, her dark eyebrows. And as much as she wanted things to have been different with her mother, Lydia was glad—fiercely glad—that Jane bore no similarities to a woman whose mind had filled with darkness.

She sat on the edge of the bed and rested her hand over Jane's. Jane tried to pull away, her body stiffening.

"Jane?"

Jane turned her head, studying Lydia with a peculiar intentness, as if she'd never seen her in this light before.

"What did Grandmama say?" Jane asked. "Did she tell you Lord Northwood came to her about the proposal?"

"You knew about that?"

"I heard them talking."

"What do you think of the idea?" Lydia waited, hoping for a faint flicker of interest, of *something*, to cross Jane's expression, but the girl's face remained as unreadable as a china plate. "Does it upset you?"

Jane shrugged. "Do what you like. I won't be here much longer anyway, at least once Grandmama makes the arrangements for Paris."

A faint accusing tone underscored her voice. Lydia tightened her clasp on Jane's hand.

"I should like to go to Paris," Jane continued. "And I like Lady Montague."

Unease constricted Lydia's heart. "She seems kind, doesn't she? Certainly very... very refined."

"Grandmama's right, you know. My education has been a bit lacking. I ought to learn French and that sort of thing."

Lydia forced a smile. "Well, Paris is the place to do that."

Jane sat up so quickly that Lydia released her hand. The candle flame flared across Jane's pale features.

"That's it?" she snapped. "You don't even care that I'm going away?"

"Of course I care, Jane. I'll miss you terribly."

"No, you won't! You'll be glad to get rid of me, won't you, now that you've got Lord Northwood."

Shocked, Lydia watched a flood of tears fill Jane's eyes. "Jane—"

"No." Jane pushed at Lydia's hands when she tried to reach for her. "Leave me alone. Is that why you gave him the locket, Lyddie, so he'd ask you to marry him?"

The locket?

"Jane, how . . . how did you know he has the locket?"

"I saw him with it when I went for a piano lesson. Then he . . . yesterday when he was . . . Oh, never mind." Jane glared at her, her chin set with mutinous stubbornness. "Is this why he had it? Because you wanted to marry him?"

"No." Lydia pressed her hand to her throat, unable to absorb exactly what Jane was telling her. "No. The locket . . . Oh, it's such a long story, but it's true. Lord Northwood never intended to keep it. It was always meant to be yours one day."

"I don't care. I don't want it."

"Why would you say such a thing? And why would you think I'd trade the locket for marriage?"

"So you could get away from the boredom of *this*." Jane flung her arm out as if to encompass their lives together. "So you could live the life of a viscountess. So you wouldn't need to do whatever Grandmama says and you'd no longer have to bother with me."

"What gave you the notion I've ever considered you a bother?" Lydia tried to reach for her again, but Jane rolled away and curled herself into a tight ball. "I love you, Jane. I love our life. If I did marry Lord Northwood, it wouldn't be because I was trying to escape."

Lydia rubbed her burning eyes, exhaustion falling

over her. She bent to wrap one arm around Jane, ignoring the girl's stiffening rejection as she pressed her lips to Jane's hair.

"I'm sorry," she whispered. "None of this was intended to hurt you. Just the opposite. I only ever wanted to protect you."

"From what?" The pillow didn't muffle the crack in Jane's voice.

"From…from living a life you didn't want. From being unhappy."

"Like you are?"

A lump clogged Lydia's throat. "You think I'm unhappy?"

"Aren't you?"

"Not when I'm with you. Never."

"But other times? You seemed so. At least until you met Lord Northwood." Jane shifted, turning to peer at Lydia over her shoulder. "Why is that?"

Lydia's heart wrenched. She thought of Alexander, that beautiful man with his sunlit black hair, angular features, and formidable build that contained the strength of a thousand ancestors.

She tightened her arm around Jane.

"Because, my dearest girl," she whispered, the confession falling like drops of water from a leaf, "I love him."

Chapter Twenty-Two

*ear C,*

How, exactly, do you know Lydia Kellaway?

Sincerely,
Jane

Alexander didn't move. He watched Lydia as she stood inside the doorway of his drawing room, her hands twisted in front of her, her skin as pale as milk. A dark storm brewed in her eyes.

He cleared his throat. "I beg your pardon?"

"I said I accept your proposal, my lord," Lydia repeated. "I will marry you, should...should you still desire the union."

I will marry you. The words he'd longed to hear since the night he'd proposed. A cautious hope began to form.

He approached Lydia, his boots soundless on the carpet. She drew back closer to the door.

"What has brought on this change of heart?" he asked.

"You told my grandmother." An accusatory tone sharpened her voice.

"Because I knew she would see reason."

"Well, then? You've got what you want. I said I'll marry you."

Alexander scraped a hand through his hair. Although she spoke the words he desperately wanted to hear, unease twisted through him. He'd wanted Mrs. Boyd to convince Lydia to marry him, but something was still wrong—and he'd no idea what.

"Why?" he asked.

"I don't wish our relationship to cause suspicion of impropriety. I take full responsibility, of course, as I'm the one who initiated...things. And because of that, I must do what I can to rectify the situation."

"So you'll marry me to stifle a scandal of which there is yet no evidence."

Her eyes flew to his. "I don't mean to imply that's my only motive, but I know you understand the necessity of avoiding gossip."

Alexander was silent. He studied her for a moment, attempting to read beneath the surface of her contained demeanor.

"Two weeks ago you were adamant in your claim you would never marry," he said. "You were equally adamant that you would never marry *me*. Now because I've spoken to your grandmother, you stand here not only willing to marry me, but also claiming your acceptance is a protective measure."

"I...I refused before I knew that rumors were—"

"You refused because you did not want to marry,"

Alexander interrupted. "Why did you allow your grandmother to change your mind?"

"I realized there is a possibility of damaging rumors."

"That wasn't enough to deter you from asking me to be your lover."

A crimson flush bloomed across her cheeks. "I...I fear I behaved quite irrationally. I apologize. I should have maintained my sense of decency."

Alexander stepped closer to her so she was backed against the door; then he cupped his hand beneath her chin and brought her face up. She still didn't meet his gaze.

"You think"—his tone dropped dangerously low— "you think what we have done is indecent?"

Her jaw tightened against his palm. "A respectable woman does not engage in affairs."

"That doesn't answer my question."

He moved his hand to the side of her neck, resting his thumb against the pulse that beat just underneath the surface of her skin. The movement of that little pulse revealed her emotions far more acutely than her words did. In a purposeful reminder of their very first encounter, right here in this room, he began to stroke her throat with slow movements of his thumb.

Lydia swallowed. A tremble coursed through her. Alexander stepped even closer, so close that not an inch separated them, so close that their bodies touched. So close that her clean scent filled the air he breathed.

He pressed his lips against the gentle hollow of her temple. Her pulse increased against his palm. He put his other hand against the door behind her. He moved his mouth lower, over her cheek to her ear.

"You think it's been indecent, Lydia?" he whispered.

"That you haven't behaved respectably? Writhing naked in my bed? Letting me kiss your bare skin, touch your—"

"Alexander..." Her voice was strangled.

He inhaled the scent of her, brushing his lips across the soft skin of her neck. "Why didn't you accept my first offer?"

"I...I should have."

He pulled back to look at her, his breathing rapid. "Why didn't you?"

Something appeared to harden within her—a resolve, a determination—and she lifted her eyes to his.

Alexander stared down at her, watching with a trace of fascination as Lydia's mind worked behind her lovely blue eyes. It was like gazing at a clock, knowing all the gears, weights, and springs were operating in complex unison behind the perfect, pristine face, yet still having no idea how everything fitted together.

"Our finances are in a state of decline," she said, her voice unwavering and her gaze steady. As if she had rehearsed this speech. "They have been for some time. My grandmother insisted on very costly treatments for my mother, private practitioners, trips to spas and institutions throughout Europe. The charges drained my father's funds."

She took a breath and continued. "My mathematics career has not been lucrative in terms of income. And my grandmother's husband left her with little. So in recent years we have existed in a state of flux with regard to our finances. Lately, the situation has been deteriorating."

Alexander frowned. "And that is why you refused my proposal?"

"Yes."

"That makes no sense."

"My lord, you have proven yourself to be a man of... of generous spirit, and I knew that if we married, I would have to reveal our financial difficulties. Just as I knew you would offer whatever assistance you could. And I... I did not wish for you to think I was marrying you for your money. That is why I declined your initial proposal."

She paused, lifting her chin, a faint relief appearing in her eyes as if convinced her explanation was more than adequate.

For Alexander, however, it was not even passable. His brain worked to recall their conversation on the terrace at Floreston Manor.

"Then why did you tell me you would never marry *anyone*?" he asked.

"Because my grandmother would not allow a union in which my family did not gain financially," Lydia said. "And I did not wish to impose upon any man in such a manner."

"So what has changed now?"

"As I said, I accept your proposal so that we both might avoid scandal. And I must rely on your... belief in me when I tell you that my acceptance is quite honestly *not* an effort to better my family's financial situation or social ranking."

"Though both of those will be an inevitable consequence of our union."

"And welcomed by my grandmother, I must confess."

"But not by you."

She didn't respond. Apprehension plagued Alexander. Lydia's reasoning made intellectual sense—he knew well that her pride would never allow her to reveal her family's weakness—but there was more to it. Something that festered behind her discourse and explanations. Something she wasn't telling him.

He pushed against the door away from her, putting half the room's length between them—though for her sake or his own, he didn't know. After dragging a hand through his hair, he turned back to face her.

She hadn't moved, a rigid, quiet bird with eyes that flashed all the colors of the sea, a mind as complex as celestial navigation, and an unbridled sensuality that would make him ache with desire for the rest of his life.

"Very well," he said. "We will be married before the month is over."

"You've made a good match."

Alexander turned to find Talia beside him, looking like a combination of sea and sky in a dark blue dress with pearls woven through her hair. He searched her face for some hint of irony, of smugness, but there was only approval. Acceptance.

He followed her gaze to where Lydia sat with Jane at a table beside the window. Jane was poring over the eight-volume collection of John Curtis's *British Entomology* he'd given her as a gift after the announcement of the engagement.

"Not a match I expected when I first met her," he admitted.

"But one you wanted." It was a statement, not a question. "Sebastian likes her a great deal. So does Papa. I know Darius and Nicholas will too."

"And you?" Alexander asked.

Talia was quiet for a moment, and in that space of time,

a burn of fear lit in Alexander. Her response meant more than he'd anticipated.

"I would wish no other woman for you." Talia rested her hand on his arm. "You could not do better than Lydia. I know our mother would agree."

An image of Lady Rushton appeared in Alexander's mind, followed by a wave of sorrow beneath his heart that almost undid him. He'd spent so long being angry with his mother that he hadn't realized her desertion and his parents' divorce had caused him deep sadness. This grief, the sense of loss, must be what made Talia hurt so deeply. What made her so brittle.

He turned to his sister, but she moved away, ducking her head as she hurried back to Rushton's side. Alexander turned his gaze to Lydia.

Although unease still simmered in him over Lydia's reason for changing her mind, and although her acceptance hadn't been as he would have wished, he was thankful for it. He wanted to marry her. He knew to his soul they were well matched, knew he would always treasure her intelligent, considerate presence, knew she would enhance the respectability of his family. He knew he would always love her.

He set his glass down and went toward Lydia and Jane, expecting conversation to hum between the two sisters.

Instead, he was met with silence. Jane stared intently at the engraving of a beetle, while Lydia stared at Jane as if she were trying to figure out an equation. Alexander paused, unaccustomed to tension between the two sisters.

Jane looked up from her book and gave Alexander a smile. "I can't thank you enough, sir. I never thought I'd own such a collection."

"It was Lydia's idea," Alexander said. "I wanted to get you something you could use, and she suggested the books. You are one of the few people I know who will use them for their intended purpose rather than to fill a bookshelf."

Jane glanced at her sister. Lydia reached out to squeeze Jane's shoulder before standing. Without making an excuse, she headed to where Talia and Rushton stood.

Alexander nodded toward the open book. "The only condition attached to the gift is that you study the books well."

"Oh, I will," Jane assured him. "I've only seen part of the volume on *Lepidoptera*, but nothing of the others."

Alexander looked at her for a moment, then placed his hand on the table and bent to her level.

"You've no idea how much you have to offer the world, Jane. Never doubt that. Never doubt yourself."

To his surprise, a veil of tears shimmered in her eyes. His stomach knotted at the sight of her distress, at the memory of her reaction to the idea of his marrying Lydia.

Jane blinked rapidly to banish her tears and gave a quick nod. "Yes, sir."

Alexander stepped away, then stopped when Jane spoke his name.

"Lord Northwood?"

"Yes?"

"What about Lydia? Will she still... being Lady Northwood and all, will she still be able to study mathematics and write papers? To work at the ragged schools?"

"Yes, of course. I never intended to prevent her from continuing her studies. Did you imagine I would?"

"No, sir." She looked back at the beetle engraving.

"That is, I'd hoped you wouldn't. She needs her work like she needs air."

Alexander didn't know what to say. The edge of bitterness to Jane's voice confused him, augmenting the sadness in her eyes. An uncomfortable emotion reawakened in him, one he hadn't felt since Talia was a child. The sense that the girl expected something from him, and he had no idea what it was.

"You know your sister well," he finally said.

Jane turned the page of the book. "No, sir. I don't really know her at all."

Chapter Twenty-Three

Silence filled the drawing room of Alexander's town house, the scents of coffee and fresh-baked cake still lingering in the air. Lydia sat by the fire, paging through a book of puzzles.

She turned at the sound of the door opening. Her heartbeat increased as she watched Alexander cross the room to her. He paused beside her chair, warmth radiating from his body, his intent as clear as if he'd spoken the words aloud.

"Is it wicked if we're engaged?" She shivered as his big, warm hand came to rest on the back of her neck.

"Most definitely." His voice was low and husky against her ear. "Let's start a wealth of rumors about our depraved erotic activities."

Arousal bloomed through her. She stared down at the book. After the betrothal party, her grandmother and Jane had left for one of Jane's dance lessons, and she and Alexander finished a game of cards with Talia, Rushton, and Sebastian, who'd also left. A bit pointedly, Lydia thought.

Not that she minded.

She ought to go as well.

Her fingers tightened on the book. "Alexander, I... I have work to do."

"Mmm. So do I."

"I've got to submit my paper before the end of... oh..."

His lips touched the back of her neck. "A paper on how to quantify love?"

"No, I'm explaining a method of representing curves."

"You already do that most successfully." He cupped her breasts, then moved his hands up and began removing the pins from her hair.

"Alexander, I—"

"Go on, then." He continued to unpin her chignon, dropping the pins to the floor and easing his fingers through the long strands of her hair. Pleasure skimmed down her spine.

"Explain your method," Alexander said.

"Well, it's called tangential polar coordinates, which differ from a system of ordinary polar coordinates where the position... Oh."

He captured her earlobe between his teeth. His warm breath brushed her neck. He slid his fingers against the back of her head, rubbing slowly. She melted under the exquisite sensations.

"Alexander, I really ought to—"

"No. You ought to do nothing." He took the book from her, then turned her to face him. A dark gleam appeared in his eyes, making her heart skip. "Except come to me with both abandon and unrestrained enthusiasm."

Lydia almost gasped as her blood went into full boil. She didn't have even a second to respond as Alexander wrapped one arm around her waist and pulled her against him for a kiss so heated and thorough that she lost the ability to think.

"So?" he said as he led her up to his bedchamber. "Ordinary polar coordinates?"

"You were listening?"

"And finding it rather arousing."

Lydia laughed. "Lord Northwood, I'd no idea you were stimulated by my theories."

"I'm stimulated by everything about you, especially your theories."

Lydia slipped her hand over his shirt to cup the evidence of his arousal. "Well, in this theory, the pole is a point that determines a certain position—"

"Fascinating." He lowered his lips to her neck, his hands moving to fumble with the clips binding her hair. "Take off your clothing."

Instead she worked the buttons on his trousers. "And a given line through the pole is the prime radius..."

"What about the curves?"

"They're the locus of an assemblage of points—"

"Take *off* your clothing."

Lydia smiled. After shedding her clothing and corset, she stepped into his arms. Closing her eyes, she pressed her cheek to his shirtfront and breathed him in. The tension dissipated from his body as heat swept over them. She sank into his touch, into the heat of his body. Her thin cotton chemise allowed her to feel every inch of his hard frame, the delicious crush of her breasts against him.

He pulled back to look at her, reaching to brush her

hair away from her forehead. Something flashed in his eyes—questions, uncertainty, doubt—that made Lydia's heart quiver.

"I love you," she whispered. She touched his roughened cheek and slid her hand around to the back of his neck. "Please believe that. I love you."

She drew him down and locked her lips to his. In this, at least, she could be honest. She could love him with every inch of her body in the full knowledge that there was no deception in her overwhelming desire for him.

He grasped her chemise, pulling it upward until the heat from the fire stroked her bare bottom. With a whispered oath, his fingers smoothed and kneaded her taut flesh, moving lower to part her thighs. A fierce shudder tore through her.

He gave a hoarse laugh, his hips pressing against her belly. Lydia sighed, sliding her lips down his rough throat, flicking her tongue out to taste the delicious hollow where his pulse throbbed. She wanted to dissolve into him, to feel the heat of his body merge with hers, his heart pounding against her breasts.

Her fingers trembled as she unfastened his shirt, baring his chest to her questing hands. She loved all the different textures of him, the combination of coarse hair and smooth, muscled skin, the hard ridges of his abdomen.

"Sit down," she whispered.

His eyes darkened to the color of ink. After divesting himself of his trousers, he sat naked in a chair beside the fire. The firelight caressed his body like a lover—long, sweeping shadows that intensified the hot desire in his eyes and bronzed his taut skin.

Lydia's breath caught as she looked at him, and a tight

pain began to coil around her heart. A chill skimmed over her, causing her skin to prickle with gooseflesh. A moan escaped her dry throat as she went down on her knees in front of him, her hands settling on his thighs. He speared a hand through her tangle of long hair, drawing her toward him with an insistence both firm and gentle.

Lydia closed her eyes. Alexander's grip tightened on her hair, his thighs tensing beneath her hands as she drew in the length of him. The taste of him spread into her blood.

A log split in the fire, casting a shower of sparks onto the marble hearth, flames catching the fresh wood and escalating higher. Heat spilled against Lydia's skin. She clenched her thighs together to stem the rising wave of need.

"All the way." Alexander drove his other hand into her hair. His voice grew hoarse with urgency. "Take it in all the way."

The rough command elicited a thrill of excitement. Perspiration broke across her flesh. The glide of Alexander in and out of her mouth, the tightening of his fingers against her head, the sounds of his ragged breath, heightened her stimulation to immeasurable peaks.

Her hands skimmed up his thighs and smoothed over his flat belly before she eased back and released him from her mouth. A gasp escaped her lips as she met his hot gaze, her chest heaving and her body so aroused she feared she might come apart with one flick of his finger. Bracing herself on his knees, she rose and grasped the folds of her chemise. In one movement she pulled it over her head and bared herself to him.

"Ah, Christ..." Alexander's eyes moved with lust over

her naked breasts, the curves of her hips. He started to stand and reach for her, but Lydia placed a hand on his chest and pushed him back.

"Wait," she whispered, her voice throaty with promise.

Alexander winced, the planes of his face glistening with sweat and flickering shadows. "Can't wait much longer."

Lydia turned as his hands gripped her hips and drew her toward him. She reached behind her to find him, then spread her legs apart and began to ease herself down. Lydia closed her eyes as her inner muscles clenched around his thick, delicious length.

"Stop."

His command stopped her movements. "What?"

"Turn around. I want to see you."

Lydia's teeth sank into her lower lip, her heartbeat escalating to thunder inside her head. For an instant, she didn't know if she could do it, didn't know if she could face him, look into his compelling dark eyes.

Alexander's fingers tightened on her waist as he eased her away from him. Lydia turned, grateful for the veil of loose, tangled hair falling over her face and shoulders. She settled her hands on Alexander's upper arms, straddling his thighs again.

"Lift them," he said.

With a shiver, she cupped her hands beneath her breasts and lifted them to him. He captured one hard peak between his lips, tugging lightly, his tongue swirling over her flushed skin. Lydia shook with arousal as he lifted his hand to cup her other breast. The heat of his breath against her nipple, the glide of his long fingers into the moist crevice below the heavy globes, rained shivers through her body.

She poised herself above him, then sank down in one movement, a cry ripping from her chest as he filled her with inexorable, exquisite pressure. His thighs tightened beneath her bottom, his hands sliding over the curve of her waist.

"Do it." An edge of desperation cut through his deep voice.

Lydia lifted her hips and brought them down again, pleasure jolting through her. She rose again, straining to find a rhythm, a cadence that would build slow and steady to rapture. Alexander groaned as she engulfed him again and again, her movements increasingly fraught with urgency.

Gripping her hips, Alexander muttered another oath and thrust upward as she sank down, creating an explosive friction that made Lydia's blood throb. She grasped his sweat-slick shoulders and tried to temper the riot of sensations coursing through her. "I'm going to—"

"Now."

She cried out, awash in the sensations of his hands on her breasts, his body in hers. Pleasure erupted through her, causing her to tremble, even as she became aware that Alexander was nearing his own climax. She tensed, absorbing the ebbing cascade of bliss as she lifted away from him. She grasped his shaft as his rough shout struck the fire-heated air.

A renewed flow of sensation shivered through her as she watched him ride out his own pleasure. She sat back on his thighs as his body began to slacken. She stared at him, mesmerized by how his damp skin shone in the flickering light, the intense repletion in his dark eyes.

Her husband-to-be.

A violent upwelling of love filled her chest—love and utter wonderment that this man had broken through her well-constructed shell. That she had allowed him in, let him fill every inch of her heart.

He lifted a hand to brush the tangles of hair away from her face. His gaze searched hers, his hand sliding down to cup her cheek. Lydia leaned into his touch. She closed her eyes and anticipated spending a lifetime with this beautiful, complex man who had the power to make her heart soar and her body sing.

A faint but palpable tendril of hope spiraled through her.

Was it possible? Could she have a blissful married life with Alexander? Could she be a good wife to him and still give Jane all she wanted? Could she continue her work without living in constant fear?

Could she be truly happy?

"Is it too late to agree to your other proposition?" She opened her eyes to find him still watching her. Her heart beat with nervous anticipation. She took a breath. "I'll give a lecture for the exhibition. I'll do it for you."

Something dark flickered across his expression, a resurgence of his previous uncertainty. "I want you to do it for you."

"All right." She curled her hands around his in promise. "Perhaps I'll even divulge my thoughts about love and differential equations, though at the risk of shocking my esteemed colleagues."

"Your colleagues could stand a shock or two."

Lydia smiled and pressed her lips against his. "Do I get my locket back now or after the lecture?"

"I don't have it anymore."

"Where is it?"

"I gave it to Jane."

"What?" Lydia yanked her hands from his, shock freezing her blood. "When?"

"The day I went to speak to your grandmother." Alexander frowned. "What's the matter? You said it was to be hers."

"One day, yes! Not now, not until..."

Her breath stopped. Anxiety cut into her. She pushed away from Alexander and fumbled for her clothes. Through her fear came a memory of Jane's strange, distant behavior the night Lydia had told her about the potential marriage.

"Lydia?" He started toward her, concern etched on his forehead.

You'll be glad to get rid of me...

She froze in the movement of fastening her corset. "Oh, God, Alexander. What have you done?"

Chapter Twenty-Four

Lydia hurried into the foyer of her grandmother's town house. Her fear rustled harder, ominous, about to take wing. "Mrs. Driscoll!"

The housekeeper hurried from the kitchen. "Yes, miss?"

"Is Jane at home?"

"Yes, she and your grandmother just returned from Lady Montague's tea. They're in the schoolroom, I believe."

Apprehension pounding in her blood, Lydia went into her father's study. The copper box sat in its customary place beside the window, the tarnished metal glowing in a thin shaft of sunlight. She grabbed the box and shook it. Her heart plummeted when no thud of the envelope came from inside. She twisted the lock, but it was fixed shut.

Without thinking, she lifted the box above her head and slammed it hard against the edge of the windowsill.

From the foyer, Mrs. Driscoll let out a startled cry.

Lydia fumbled with the lock, then angled it against the sill and brought it down again and again, so hard that dents appeared on the wood.

The lock broke. Lydia pushed the lid open. Though she already knew the contents were gone, a moan escaped her at the sight of the empty velvet interior. She dropped the box to the floor.

"Lydia!"

Her grandmother's voice was sharp, heavy like an ax. Lydia began to shake. She forced her head up, watching her grandmother's eyes sweep across the room, comprehending the implications of Lydia's distress, the broken lock, the empty copper box.

Then . . . silence. A dry, parched cavern desperate to be filled.

"She . . . he gave her the locket . . . I'd hidden the key inside it months ago . . ."

The words flared and died in Lydia's throat. She covered her face with trembling hands.

"Did . . . Has she said anything to you?" she asked her grandmother.

"No." Mrs. Boyd glanced at the housekeeper, who hovered with anxious confusion in the background. "You may return to your duties, Mrs. Driscoll."

"Yes, madam." Mrs. Driscoll hurried from the room, closing the door behind her.

Lydia stared at the box as her grandmother's shadow moved across it. "Where is she?"

"Upstairs." Mrs. Boyd nudged open the box with the end of her cane. "Where is the paper?"

"She . . . she must have it."

"If she's told no one, we might still be able to rectify

this." Mrs. Boyd nodded to the door. "Go speak to her, Lydia."

"If Alexander comes here, keep him away."

Lydia picked up the broken box and climbed the stairs with a sick feeling of dread. The door to the schoolroom stood half-open, and she knocked before pushing it the rest of the way. Jane stood at the window with one hand flat against the glass.

"Jane."

The girl turned, her gaze going to the empty box. Lydia moved into the room, her hands tightening so hard on the box the copper edges cut into her palms.

"How...how was Lady Montague's tea?" Lydia's voice shook.

"Proper, of course." Jane lifted her chin and faced the window again. Her slender shoulders tensed. "Delicious. She offered meringues, macaroons. A *pain d'épices*, she called it. From Rheims. It had orange-flower water and aniseed."

"It sounds quite lovely."

"Everything about Lady Montague is lovely."

"True." Lydia approached Jane cautiously, then stopped in the middle of the room. "Jane."

The girl whirled around so fast that her hair fanned around her shoulders. Her mouth compressed, her green eyes hardening. "I hate you, Lydia. I *hate* you."

"No." Terror seized Lydia's chest. Her hands started to tremble, and she dropped the box onto a table. "Please, let me explain."

"You lied to me! All this time, you've lied!"

"I know, but—"

"Why?" Jane pushed a stack of papers off the desk and

grabbed the one that had been locked in the copper box for so many years. "You kept this hidden from me when I had every right to know the truth!"

"No one knew the truth, Jane. No one except Papa and Grandmama." Tears stung Lydia's eyes as she reached for the girl, but Jane evaded her grasp and went to the door.

"Why not me, then?" she snapped.

"You would have been taken away from us," Lydia said. She swiped at her eyes, hating the way Jane looked at her with such animosity. And yet she couldn't blame her father or grandmother either, for they had only done what they thought was best. They had done all they could to ensure Jane would stay with them. "We couldn't tell you, didn't want you to—"

"You could have," Jane retorted. "You didn't want to because you knew I'd make things horrible for you. Lord Northwood would never marry you if he knew! But if you kept it a secret from me, you'd have everything you wanted and I'd be left with nothing."

Lydia's heart constricted. "Oh, Jane. You'd never have nothing—you know that. I didn't keep this from Northwood because I wanted him to marry me. I didn't tell him because *no one* could know."

"Why? Why did you have to keep it such a secret?"

"It...it was too dangerous." Lydia stared at Jane. Flashes of memory appeared—a sculptured face with eyes as cold as glass, the glimpse of a slender, blond man from across the street, the eerie feeling of being watched.

The terror returned, scratching like claws up Lydia's throat. "Jane, if anything—"

"Dangerous for you, you mean," Jane retorted. "I know why you haven't told anyone, Lydia, and it's got nothing to do with me. It's because your life would be ruined if anyone knew the truth!"

She spun and stormed out of the room, slamming the door behind her. Lydia choked out a cry, her tears flooding over in waves as she sank into a chair and buried her face in her hands.

In that instant, Lydia knew she had to choose between Alexander and Jane. And in the end, there could be no choice at all.

Dear C,

If Lydia was a student of yours, why have you started a correspondence with me and not her?

I confess I have found a document that has caused me no end of questions—all of which lack answers.

I have not asked Lydia for answers. I would first like to speak with you. So I would like to propose a meeting as soon as possible. I am planning a visit to St. Martin's Hall on Tuesday.

I do not intend to ask Lydia anything. If one has concealed the truth, then one is not owed the truth. Don't you agree?

Sincerely,
Jane

Chapter Twenty-Five

The sine of two theta equals two times the sine of theta... The thought dissolved like salt in boiling water.

Lydia grasped the driver's hand as she descended the carriage to the bustling street. As she walked toward the lecture hall, she attempted to focus on the identity again, but her effort was halfhearted at best. Her mind was too knotted to think about sines or cosines or polynomials or square roots.

"I received your letter."

Lydia spun at the sound of the low, male voice. Alexander stood a short distance away, his expression grave, his eyes simmering with suppressed anger.

Lydia swallowed hard and clutched her satchel tighter. She knew she'd been a coward by sending him a letter, but having to tell him in person—

"I'm sorry," she said.

"The banns were posted last week," Alexander snapped. "I will not withstand another broken engagement."

"You don't want to marry me, Alexander," Lydia said, her throat nearly closing over the words. "Believe me when I say a broken engagement is a far better course for you than marriage to me."

He stepped forward to grip her arm, his dark eyes flashing. "Why?" he hissed, lowering his head closer to her. "Why have you refused to see me for the past three days? What the bloody hell is going on? If you don't—"

"You all right, miss?" Two men paused in passing, glancing from Lydia to Alexander.

With a muttered curse, Alexander relaxed his grasp and stepped away from her. Lydia gave the men a brief nod, then hurried toward the Greco-Roman façade of the lecture hall. Her chest tightened when Alexander fell into step beside her.

"Where are you going?" he asked.

"This is where they're holding the mathematics symposium."

"I'll go with you." He took her satchel from her. "And afterward we will continue this discussion."

"Alexander, I—" Her heart sank at the mutinous look on his face, and she knew she'd have no immediate chance of escaping him.

They went into the auditorium, which resounded with the rumble of male voices, the rustle of papers, and the scrape of chairs. Lydia searched the crowd until she found Dr. Sigley standing amid a group of men. He gave her a wave and pushed his way toward her.

"Miss Kellaway, you've arrived." Dr. Sigley stopped before her and took her gloved hand. "And, Lord Northwood, a pleasure to see you again."

He extended a hand to guide them into the main room

of the lecture hall. As they sat down, Lydia took her satchel from Northwood and removed a sheaf of papers. She tried to concentrate on what she wanted to tell the professor, knowing she had to present a front of cool competence even if her heart broke a little more with every breath she took.

"This... this is my response to your question about the integrals," she said, handing the papers to Dr. Sigley, who spread them out and reached for his spectacles. "The general systems have only three. There must be a fourth. And if you normalize the units, then choose the axis in which all moments of inertia are equal, then you find this unit." She pointed to the pages. "So the fourth integral can be written in complex form like this."

"Ah." The single word conveyed understanding and satisfaction. "Now, this makes perfect sense. I do hope you intend to publish this, perhaps even lecture about it."

No. No chance of that anymore.

The gaslights dimmed. The symposium coordinator banged a wooden pointer on the podium to gain everyone's attention. Lydia sat back as he announced the series of lectures, the first starting with a discourse on symbolic logic and theory. As the lecturing professor began organizing his notes, Lydia fished for a pencil and spread a new notebook on her lap.

She listened as best she could, took copious notes for later review, and engaged in whispered consultations with Dr. Sigley.

And yet the entire time, her skin prickled with awareness of Alexander beside her—his tense posture radiating his frustration and anger.

What a fool she'd been to believe, even for a moment,

that they might have a life together. That they could be happy. She'd reached too far beyond her grasp... and now she had to bear the fall.

It was one o'clock before the first half of the symposium concluded, with the coordinator inviting the participants to lunch in the adjoining hall prior to the start of the afternoon session.

"Will you lunch with us, then, Miss Kellaway?" Dr. Sigley asked, absently rubbing his belly. "Lord Northwood?"

"No, I hadn't planned to stay for the afternoon," Lydia admitted as they made their way along with the tide of men toward the exit. "But you and Mrs. Sigley must come to dinner soon."

"Will do, then. A delight to see you again, and when I've got my thoughts on your paper in order, I'll call upon you." Dr. Sigley gave her hand a light squeeze of farewell and nodded at Alexander before joining the men heading into the dining hall.

"You're coming home with me," Alexander said.

Irritation prickled the back of Lydia's neck at the implacable tone in his voice.

"Alexander, if you hadn't divulged your intentions to my grandmother, we would not be in this position," she whispered. "If you had listened to me when I first declined and..."

Her whole body rippled with a sudden chill.

"Lydia?" Alexander stopped at the sound of her strangled voice. "What is it?"

Someone bumped into Lydia from behind, forcing her to move forward. Her eyes locked on to the back of a blond man, his hair cropped short against an elegant neck, his shoulders narrow beneath a dark suit coat.

She shook her head. *No. Don't be silly. It couldn't be, of course; there's no way in the world...*

He turned. She gasped.

"Lydia?" Alexander clutched her arm and used his body to push through the crowd, pulling her along beside him. When they reached the lobby, he eased her back away from the men still streaming through the doors. "Lydia, what's the matter? You've gone sheet-white."

Lydia swallowed through a parched throat, her eyes skimming the crowd. He was gone, his sculpted features obliterated by the crush of people heading for the adjoining room.

"Alexander, would you... would you bring me a glass of water, please? I feel a bit faint."

He didn't look as if he wanted to leave her. "Come with me."

"I'm fine." Lydia pressed her hand against the wall. "Please. Just... hurry."

Alexander released her arm with reluctance and moved past her. As soon as he was gone, she looked toward the doors.

She had to get out. Even if she'd only imagined him, even if she'd seen something that wasn't there... she had to get out. Now. Gathering in a breath, she turned and started through the lobby.

"*Guten tag*, Lydia."

She fought down a scream.

"*Bitte setzen Sie sich.*" He drew a chair against the wall and gestured with a long, elegant hand.

She didn't take the seat, not because her legs weren't about to collapse underneath her but because she wanted nothing he offered. She didn't look at him, her gaze fixed on some blurry point beyond his shoulder.

"What... what are you doing here?" Her voice sounded thin, vibrating with tension.

"*Ich bin—*"

"I don't speak German."

She felt rather than saw his smile; then he spoke in fluent English. "I came to hear the symposium, of course. I received notice last month."

"Lydia."

A choking combination of relief and terror rose in Lydia as Alexander crossed the lobby back to her. His gaze slanted to the other man, his expression hardening with a dislike that seemed instinctive rather than rational.

Alexander stopped beside Lydia and handed her a glass of water, then slipped his hand around her arm and pulled her quite deliberately to his side.

Lydia grasped the glass. "Thank you. I... Would you give us a moment, please, my lord?"

He frowned. "I'd rather not."

"Please."

"I am Viscount Northwood," he told the other man, his voice flat and cold. "Miss Kellaway's fiancé. You are?"

The man's mouth twisted into a semblance of a smile. "I am Dr. Joseph Cole. Miss Kellaway and I are old friends."

"Odd. She doesn't appear to think of you as a friend."

"I'm fine, Northwood." Lydia infused a forceful note to her voice. "Please go."

She willed him to hear the plea in her voice. He hesitated, then stepped back—barely. "I'll wait over there."

He jerked his head toward the other side of the lobby,

not taking his eyes from the man beside her as he backed away.

Lydia sipped the water and placed the glass on the chair. She sought the courage she didn't know she possessed, then turned her head to look at Dr. Cole.

Her heart thumped hard against her rigid corset. Her eyes narrowed as she studied him, the analytical part of her brain submerging the emotions threatening to wreak havoc upon her soul.

She assessed him with a clinical eye, noting the gray strands threading his thinning blond hair, the wrinkles furrowing his forehead and the sides of his mouth. Behind his spectacles, his eyes looked the same—a pale green like ocean ice, thick spiky lashes.

"What do you want?" She forced the question through numb lips. "Why are you here?"

He reached into his coat pocket and removed a folded, sealed letter that he pressed into her hand. "Do not open it now. At your convenience, please."

She tried to push the paper back to him. "I don't want to read anything you have to say. And I have nothing to say to you."

"Yet you ask what I want. Do you not wish the answer?"

He moved a little closer, his presence seeming to thin the air around her. Lydia forced herself not to step away, to control the trembles rippling underneath her skin. No, she didn't want to know the answer, terrified of what it might be.

She felt him assessing her with that razor-sharp perception he possessed, his own mind calculating, adding and subtracting the changes in her wrought by the years.

"You look well, Lydia."

"I am well."

A strange fog of memories began floating through her mind—things, people, events she hadn't allowed herself to remember for years upon years.

And there, in the forefront, her mother, a dulled, pale figure in her stark room of the sanatorium, the nuns fluttering about like blackbirds. Her hair, once so long, shiny, and thick, now cropped close to her skull, her skin white and papery. And yet when Lydia saw her for the first time in two years, the first thing she noticed was her mother's eyes.

The dark blue eyes so like her own had still contained a light—faded, dimmed, but there. And she knew in that instant what her father and grandmother had been hoping for during the long years—that the light might still illuminate the real Theodora Kellaway, the woman of laughter and warmth who had suffocated beneath the burden of her illness.

Lydia pulled her arms around herself as another woman came to her mind, a softer figure than Theodora Kellaway. This other woman smelled like apples and cinnamon. She wore her braided brown hair in a smooth coronet, spoke in a quiet, musical voice, smiled with her coffee-colored eyes.

Before she even asked the question, pain speared through the middle of Lydia's chest. Her fingers tightened on her arms, the woman's name pushing past her lips like a broken shard of porcelain.

"Greta?"

"*Sie ist tot.*" Joseph Cole spoke without inflection.

Shock froze her to the bone. Lydia swallowed a sob of sorrow and regret, backing against the wall as she struggled to put distance between them, not wanting to breathe the same air as him.

"W-when? How?" She didn't want to know, but she had to ask, had to absorb the knowledge as if it were a form of punishment.

"Consumption. Three years ago."

Lydia forced away the tears crowding her throat, hating the lack of emotion in Cole's voice but knowing that Greta would not have noticed anything was amiss.

I'm sorry, Greta. I'm so, so sorry…

"Lydia."

She turned to see Alexander come toward her again, though he remained a good distance away. Tension vibrated from him. She held up a hand to stay his approach, not taking her eyes from Cole, who stood watching her.

"Please." She whispered the entreaty both to prevent Alexander from overhearing and because regret stifled her voice. "Dr. Cole, please go. Please leave me alone. I don't want to see you again. I never did."

The faint smile disappeared from his lips, replaced by an iciness that she knew was borne from deep within his being. "Before you speak again, Lydia, I suggest you read my letter. Otherwise you might do something you will regret."

He stepped back, his gaze sliding from Lydia to Alexander and back again. "Congratulations on your engagement. I read about it in the *Morning Post*."

A sick feeling swirled through her gut. She watched Dr. Cole go, air from the open door washing away some of the thickness surrounding her.

Her heart throbbed with relentless pressure against her chest; her breath came short and choppy. Even her blood felt heavier, as if the concert of her body was determined to remind her that she lived. That she was alive, could inhale and exhale, could think and move and *be.*

Unlike her mother. Unlike Greta.

Alexander's strong arms caught her the instant before she collapsed to the ground.

The unopened letter lay like a flat stone on her lap. Alexander sat on the carriage seat across from her, his arms tight across his chest. Lydia could sense the questions simmering in his mind and his palpable effort to restrain them.

"Who is he?" Alexander finally asked. The question pulsed with urgency.

"No one you care to know."

"How do you know him?"

"He's a mathematician. A good one. Or at least he was. Years ago."

"How do you know him?"

"Could you... Alexander, I must go home."

"Why?"

"Please."

He rapped on the roof to gain the coachman's attention, then gave instructions to head to East Street.

Although Alexander remained silent for the drive, dissatisfaction and unease coiled through him. Lydia gripped the letter so tightly she thought she might tear it—and considered doing just that, ripping the paper up into a hundred pieces and tossing them outside. Horses' hooves, carriage wheels, wagons, dogs, pedestrians—all would trample over the torn pieces and crush them until they rotted and dissolved in the filth.

Because she knew the contents of the letter. Knew them as well as she knew the Pythagorean theorem. Knew them as well as she knew the contours of Jane's face, the different shades in the girl's hair. The color of Jane's eyes.

She preceded Alexander from the carriage and hurried to open the front door.

"Hello, Miss Kellaway. I've got seed cake fresh from the ov—" Mrs. Driscoll stopped in the foyer, looking past Lydia to where Alexander stood on the doorstep. "Oh, good day, Lord Northwood."

"Mrs. Driscoll, is Jane at home?" Lydia asked, trying to keep the urgency from her voice.

"No, miss. Mrs. Boyd took her to her piano lesson."

"Please tell me at once when they return."

Mrs. Driscoll looked from her to Alexander again, a line of confusion between her brows. "I'll...er...I'll fetch tea, shall I?"

Shedding her cloak, Lydia went into the drawing room, closing the door behind her to keep Alexander out. She sank into a chair beside the window, her heart pumping terror instead of blood through her veins. With trembling fingers, she turned the letter over, broke the seal, and unfolded the paper.

Her suspicion solidified into painful acceptance as she read the neat penmanship and tried to remind herself that she had feared this day for years. She should be grateful it hadn't dawned before now.

Every square matrix is a root of its own characteristic polynomial.

She refolded the letter and slipped it into her pocket.

Think, Lydia. Think.

The door opened and Mrs. Driscoll left the tea tray on

a table before departing. The smell of biscuits caused a swirl of nausea. Lydia tried to drink a cup of tea but managed only two sips before her stomach rebelled.

She grabbed a decorative bowl and retched, sweat breaking out across her forehead, her hands shaking as they gripped the porcelain edges.

"Lydia?"

Her heart plummeted. Tears stung her eyes, blinding her. Alexander's hand rested warm and heavy on the back of her neck.

"Lydia, go upstairs. I'll send for the doctor."

"No, I—"

"You're ill. If you don't—"

"No!" Her strident tone made him step back.

Lydia closed her eyes and breathed, trying to suppress the violent storm of emotions that would, if unleashed, drown all coherent thought. She fumbled for the teapot as Alexander took the soiled bowl out. Lydia took a drink, her stomach still roiling.

Alexander's booted steps moved almost soundlessly across the carpet. Lydia forced herself to look up. He stood with his arms crossed, his expression impenetrable but his eyes dark with both concern and frustration.

A crack split down the middle of Lydia's heart, jagged and sharp. She remembered when she had once believed Alexander capable of withstanding any truth, any confession she laid before him.

Now the time had come for proof—and Lydia thought for the first time in her life her theory would prove wrong.

She dug her hand into her pocket. Without speaking, she extended the letter toward him.

Alexander took the paper and opened it. His expression

didn't change as he read the contents—the contents Lydia knew by heart even after reading the letter only once.

Dear Lydia,

Congratulations on your engagement. I have anticipated the event, considering your acquaintance with Lord Northwood.

Through several colleagues, I have learned of his lordship's family history and the divorce of his parents. It seems Lord Northwood has been committed to putting the scandal to rest.

What would his lordship say, I wonder, if he were to learn of your secret?

A secret of such immense proportions that if it were divulged among his circle, his name would be damaged beyond repair? Moreover, it would destroy the credit of his entire family, which he has attempted so valiantly to restore.

I do not delude myself by thinking you've already told him. We must meet privately to determine the lengths to which you will go in order to keep your secret.

Alexander must have read the letter ten times before he finally lifted his head to look at her. A muscle ticked in his jaw, the cords of his neck tightening.

"What is this about?" he asked.

Lydia took the letter back, sweeping her gaze over it. Memories pushed hard at her consciousness, her heart waging a constant, unending battle with her mind, the desperate desire to belong to something, someone. To stop thinking. To start feeling.

"He wrote it," she said. "Joseph Cole."

"Who, exactly, is he?" His voice began to vibrate with apprehension.

"He was a professor at the University of Leipzig. My professor."

"And what secret is he threatening to divulge?"

He still watched her, wary and distant. Emotions swamped her—love, pain, fear, sorrow, guilt, regret. And yet as she looked at the man she so desperately wanted to marry, a strange sense of calm began to descend over the chaos, settling her heart, calming her blood. She drew in a breath and spoke in a steady voice.

"Alexander, Jane is not my sister."

"Not your—"

"She is my daughter."

Chapter Twenty-Six

A rustle of movement filled St. Martin's Hall as exhibition workers and curators worked on numerous displays. The light of dusk blurred the windows. Flames diminished in the fireplaces; lights dimmed in the huge candelabras.

Jane stood near a display of natural history educational objects. Glass cases sat along the walls filled with dried plants, animal bones, and various things preserved in glass jars. The tables bore remarkable cases of insects and butterflies, spread wings and beetle shells shimmering. She picked up a bottle containing the carcasses of several stick insects.

Her stomach knotted and pulled. She set the bottle down, glancing up at the darkening windows above the high gallery that spanned three sides of the great hall. She'd left Mr. Hall and Lord Castleford finishing their work on the Chinese display, promising to return within the half hour.

Jane let out her breath. She had no idea how she was expected to find Dr. Cole, if indeed he was here at all. She peered at a case containing locusts and silkworms. A shiver rippled through her. As interesting as she found insects, she didn't at all like seeing them dead beneath the glass, their bodies impaled with pins.

She moved away from the display toward a section beneath the gallery. At least two dozen floor globes—both terrestrial and celestial—were arranged beside a case containing numerous pocket globes. Jane twirled one of the celestial globes, studying the constellations, which were depicted as mythical figures and beasts.

Another celestial globe was made of heavy glass and sat upon an immense cast-iron stand and brass scale. Half-filled with blue liquid, the globe's surface was engraved with stars and the rings of latitude and longitude. Jane cupped the massive globe in her hands and tilted it within the half-circle bracket, watching the liquid sway inside.

"Hello, Jane."

The male voice, low and cultured, prickled against her skin. Her heart thumped as she turned to face the tall, slender man who stood near the back staircase, his eyes hidden behind the light reflecting off his glasses.

She swallowed. "You... you came."

"Of course. I said I would." He moved forward. The light slipped from his face, revealing his warm green eyes and aquiline features. "It's a pleasure to see you, though frankly I feel as if we've already met. As if we already know each other."

Jane smiled, her nervousness easing a little as she was finally able to put a face to the comments and riddles in the letters. He looked the way he wrote—elegant, clear, educated. His hair was blond, though dimmed by the twilight, a lock curling like a comma over his forehead.

He stepped closer until he stood on the other side of the globe. "I've been a bit concerned with your recent missives," he said. "It's evident that something has been upsetting you. I assume it has to do with this document of which you wrote?"

Jane nodded, her hand fluttering to the outside of her skirt pocket where the *acte de naissance* lay folded. She stole a glance at Dr. Cole. He was still watching her, a faint smile on his mouth, his eyes kind and curious.

"You had no idea?" he asked.

A lump clogged her throat. She shook her head. She'd apparently had no idea about anything. No idea that everyone she loved, her entire family, had been lying about her. Had been lying *to* her.

The emptiness in her chest widened to a gaping chasm. She stared at the surface of the globe, the engraved stars delicate against the thick glass.

"Why didn't you tell me?" she asked.

"I feared you'd stop writing if I did," Dr. Cole replied. "And I confess I didn't think you'd believe me." He paused. "Would you have?"

Jane shook her head again. Of course not. Of course she wouldn't have believed such an absurd thing. Papa was her father, not some stranger she'd been corresponding with for several months whose name she hadn't even known until a few weeks ago.

Except that he was. Every bone-deep instinct told her that he was. Even though his name wasn't on the birth certificate, she knew this man was her father. She could even see the resemblance in the shape of his face, the color of his eyes. Like hers.

This man was her father, and Lydia—*Lydia*—was her mother. The knowledge jumbled in her brain all over again, as riotous as a storm-tossed ocean.

She wondered if Lydia had ever planned to reveal the truth. If *anyone* had planned to. Or if they'd just expected to keep her in the center of a huge lie.

"Why didn't you contact Lydia first?" she asked.

"I knew she wouldn't want to see me," Dr. Cole replied. "We didn't part under the most... agreeable of circumstances." He shrugged. "I wanted to get to know you, and for you to know me, without her influence. I suspect she has nothing kind to say about me."

"Do you have anything kind to say about her?"

Dr. Cole reached across the globe, placing his long-fingered hand atop hers where it rested on the glass. His palm was warm, comforting. She tried to imagine what he might have been like as a father—but couldn't.

"Lydia is brilliant," he said. "She always was. I was surprised to learn from a colleague that she had all but disappeared from academia in the last decade. Her former mathematics tutors were astonished at her aptitude, even as a child. She was a prodigy. I was honored to have her as my student."

An unexpected sting of tears blurred Jane's vision. She knew that about Lydia, knew she possessed an unmatched intellect. She knew Lydia had so much to offer with her solutions and proofs and equations.

She knew Lydia could have changed the world... if she hadn't *disappeared* from academia, if she hadn't given up her public pursuit of mathematics.

Dr. Cole's hand tightened on hers. Too tight. She tried to squirm her hand from his grasp.

"At any rate, I consider it fortunate that you found the document," he continued. "Perhaps it's no coincidence that you found it just before Lydia is to be married. Maybe the truth was meant to come out now that she will no longer be living with you."

A thin but hard line of steel edged his words. Jane gave him a wary glance. He was still smiling, but something hardened behind his eyes like the first coating of frost on a window. A shiver ran down her back.

She managed to pull her hand away from his. "I'm sorry, but it's late. I'm expected back."

"Of course. May I see the document before you go?"

Jane pulled the paper from her pocket and unfolded it, staring at the mixture of printed French and swirled handwriting. "I don't know very much French, but there is only one name listed as parentage. Lydia Kellaway. No profession is given for her, though her age is listed as *seize*... she was...."

Jane shook her head to rid herself of the reminder that Lydia had been only five years older than Jane was now when she had a child.

"The address is in Lyons," she continued. "Both my father—Sir Henry—and my grandmother signed as witnesses."

"Interesting." He'd moved a little closer to her, his hand still resting on the vast surface of the globe. "Let me see if I can help you determine any further information. I'm fluent in French, you know."

He stretched out a hand. Jane started to extend the document, then stopped. She drew it back to her, holding it against her chest.

"Actually, I...I really don't need to know any more at the moment. It's time I spoke to Lydia about everything."

She took a step back. He took a step forward.

"Do you honestly think Lydia will tell you the truth now?" Dr. Cole asked, his tone both kind and slightly condescending. "Even if you confront her with the document, she has no reason to tell you the truth about your father. Are you quite certain my name is not written there?"

"Quite certain." Jane's fingers tightened on the paper, crumpling the edge into her palm.

"May I see it, please?"

"What for?"

"This concerns me as much as it does you, Jane. I've a right to see the certificate of my daughter's birth."

"Why weren't you present when the document was registered? Why are you not listed as a parent?"

"I was not there because Lydia left without telling me where she was going." A tension seemed to infuse Dr. Cole's body, dissolving the warmth in his eyes and replacing it with impatience. "Had I known where she was, of course I would have insisted upon being included."

"Did you intend to marry her?"

His mouth twisted in a manner that made Jane think of an uncoiling earthworm. "It is not your place to ask questions regarding my relationship with Lydia."

"It's my right to know the truth of my parentage." Jane wished she could somehow believe the truth was different, that Dr. Cole was not really her father. She wished she could believe something hadn't happened between him and Lydia. Something horrible.

She looked behind her, hoping an exhibition worker or curator would be close by. No one was there, and her view of the rest of the exhibit was blocked by a large display case.

Jane turned back to Dr. Cole. His expression was tight, the throb of a vein in his neck betraying his growing irritation.

"Give me the document, Jane."

She shook her head. Fear pushed against her chest. She didn't know why he was so keen on taking possession of the document, but she suspected that once she handed it over, she would never see it again.

Dr. Cole took two long strides forward, the suddenness of the movement like the strike of a snake. He reached to snatch the paper from her grip. Just as his fingers grasped the edge of the document, Jane yanked it from his reach. Thrusting it back into her pocket, she turned and ran. His low, guttural curse ripped through her ears.

Not daring to try to move past him, Jane headed for the narrow back staircase leading up to the gallery. As she passed the natural history display, she ducked around a diorama featuring mounted birds. Grabbing the document from her pocket, she shoved it behind the spread wings of an eagle before heading to the gallery with the intent of reaching the stairs on the other side that led back to the main floor.

Glass-fronted cases, desks, tables, and bookshelves packed the spaces of the gallery. As Jane maneuvered around them, she tried to look over the railing to find Mr. Hall, but there was no sign of him amid the massive displays.

Panic shot through her. If he'd gone home already... no. Mr. Hall wouldn't leave without her.

Jane quickened her pace, not daring to look behind

her as she skirted around a table piled high with scrolled maps. She was halfway across the gallery when her foot caught on something. She fell hard to the floor, a gasp jamming in her throat. Pain shot up her right wrist as she tried to break her fall with her hands.

Keep going. Keep going.

With a panicked sob, she tried to push herself to her feet. Then a man's shadow fell across her, long fingers curling around her arm. Dr. Cole spoke through gritted teeth, his grip tightening to the point of pain.

"Foolish girl," he hissed.

Jane tried to scream. No sound emerged before his hand clamped over her mouth.

Chapter Twenty-Seven

Alexander startled, taking a step away from her. Fresh, raw pain coursed through Lydia's chest. She averted her gaze but felt the shock that held him immobile.

"Your... your daughter?"

Lydia nodded, experiencing a sense of relief at having finally told him the truth. No matter how he reacted, at least she no longer bore the burden of such a secret.

"But Jane is—"

"Eleven. She was born when I was almost seventeen."

She lifted her lashes to risk a glance at him. He remained still, his hands curled into fists at his sides, his expression rigid.

"Tell me," he ordered.

"It is not a pleasant story." She paused. "Far from it."

"I don't care. What happened? Is *he* Jane's father?"

"Yes." Her fingers clenched on the letter.

"He didn't... did he..." Alexander swallowed, his fists tightening.

"No. No." Beneath her fear, shame began to simmer inside Lydia. She attempted to contain it, knowing she owed him the full story in all its sordid details. "It...it was a...a mistake, Alexander, a hideous one, but I was a willing participant. And I promise I will tell you whatever you want to know, but I must speak with Jane first. Please. I...I didn't think he'd ever find us again. I don't know if he's tried to contact her, if he would—"

Her voice shattered on the cusp of a speculation too horrific to name. She covered her face with her hands, dimly aware of the anger beginning to tear through Alexander's silence.

"Where did Mrs. Driscoll say she'd gone?" he asked.

"To her piano lesson with my grandmother." Lydia swiped at the perspiration on her brow. "I...It's imperative I speak with her—it's the reason I needed the locket back. All of this—"

"I'll collect her from Rushton's. You wait here. I do not wish there to be a scene at my father's house."

He turned and left. Lydia stared at the closed door. A bead of perspiration trickled down her neck, sliding beneath her narrow collar.

She went upstairs to her room, splashed water on her face, and fixed her hair. Nervousness twisted in her stomach. She went down the corridor to the schoolroom where she and Jane had spent countless hours together.

Jane's possessions and creations were scattered everywhere—paintings, dolls, toys, drawings, a world globe, books, bits of crochet, and embroidery samples.

Lydia picked up an old rag doll that Sir Henry had once given Jane for Christmas. The doll stared sightlessly back at her, one button eye missing, the stitches of its mouth beginning to tear.

"Lydia?" Wariness infused her grandmother's voice.

She turned. "Is Jane with you?"

"No."

Lydia frowned. "Where is Alexander?"

"I don't know. What is going on, Lydia?"

"He was on his way to collect Jane from her piano lesson," Lydia said. "Didn't you take her?"

"Yes, but she went on an outing with Mr. Hall after the lesson."

Lydia set the doll down and began looking through a stack of papers on the table—Jane's penmanship practice, several drawings, the start of a report about fireflies. She straightened several books and returned them to the bookshelf, bending to retrieve a wrinkled piece of paper that fluttered to the floor.

She started to fold the paper and place it back between the covers of the book, then stopped. Black ink spread across part of the page like a cobweb. Her heart thudded as she smoothed out the paper.

The neat handwriting blurred before her eyes. A wave of dizziness, of disbelief, swamped her.

No. No no no no no no...

"Lydia, what is it?" Her grandmother's voice rose with increasing alarm. Steeling her shoulders, Mrs. Boyd stalked into the room and grabbed the letter from Lydia's hand.

Lydia sank to a chair as her grandmother read the letter. The message was already branded into her brain, splashed with terror.

Dear Jane,

Lydia Kellaway was once a student of mine at the University of Leipzig in Germany. I suggest you ask her should you seek further elucidation.

Sincerely,
Dr. Joseph Cole

The paper fell from Mrs. Boyd's hand. The older woman lifted her head, all color drained from her face.

"What," she said, the word tight as a knot, "is the meaning of this?"

Nausea swirled through Lydia's belly again. She couldn't think, couldn't move. Did not know what to do next. "He... he's back. He's here. In London."

For an instant, Lydia thought her grandmother might strike her, but Mrs. Boyd merely pinned her with a glare as dark as the ocean floor.

"How long have you known?"

"I just found out."

"And what of this?" Mrs. Boyd jabbed her cane viciously at the letter, rending a hole in the paper.

"I don't know."

Pulling herself from a stupor of despair, Lydia stood. She began opening the desk drawers and cabinet, pushing aside boxes containing Jane's treasures. She fumbled through the low bookshelf, riffling pages of books in search of something she didn't want to find.

Her fingers closed around a crumpled stack of letters, each marked with the same distinctive scrawl. Lydia's vision lost focus; her head throbbed with a pain shot through with a dozen years of sorrow and regret.

She held up the letters. "Who delivered these to Jane?"

"Delivered?" Mrs. Boyd shook her head. "No one has delivered anything to Jane."

Lydia's grip tightened on the papers, crushing the edges into her palms as she read the topmost letter.

Dear Jane,

St. Martin's Hall is easily accessible. I will arrange to be present at the time you suggested.

I request that you bring the document with you so that I might see it, as you seem to believe it most categorically concerns me.

Sincerely,
Joseph Cole

Lydia lifted her head to look at her grandmother. "Where did she and Mr. Hall go?" she whispered.

"To see the preparations for the educational exhibition." Mrs. Boyd's frown deepened like a gash carved into a cliff. "Jane told me earlier that she wished to go, and Mr. Hall kindly agreed to take her. I've tea arranged with Mrs. Keene or I would have accompanied them, but—"

Lydia broke from her helplessness like a stone released from a slingshot. She shoved the papers into her pocket, pushing past her grandmother in the doorway.

"Lydia!" Mrs. Boyd's shout carried down the corridor as Lydia flew downstairs and out the front door.

She ran toward Baker Street and the cabstand, her grandmother's shrill call drowned out by the fear screaming inside her head.

Chapter Twenty-Eight

Twilight blanketed Long Acre, the front entrance of St. Martin's Hall concealed by a mass of traffic—pedestrians, carriages, carts, and wagons all swarming about like bees in a hive.

"Accident or something, miss," the cabdriver called. "Can see it from up here, looks like a cart crashed into something. Can't go much farther."

With a curse, Lydia pushed open the door. She tossed two shillings up at the driver and darted past the people clustered around to gape at the accident, shoving her way through a group of constables. She pressed forward, inhaling sharply when she saw Sebastian hovering near the entrance to St. Martin's Hall.

"Sebastian!"

He looked up, worry clearly etched into his features. "Lydia, what—"

"Jane." Lydia came to a halt before him. "Where is Jane?"

"I don't know. That's just it. She was with me all afternoon, then went to look at a display while I helped Castleford at the Chinese exhibit. When I went to find her, she was gone."

"*Gone?* What do you mean, gone?"

"I couldn't find her. I thought she might have been with Castleford, but it appears he's already left and none of the curators have seen her. I heard the commotion out here and thought she might have come to investigate, but there's such a throng—"

"Keep looking," Lydia ordered, heading for the front door. "Look in the classrooms and the library. Check the retiring room at the back as well."

"But where—"

"I can't explain now, Sebastian, *please*. We must find her!"

She ran into the entrance hall, her hard breaths echoing in the vast foyer. She hurried up the main staircase that led to the great hall, the length and breadth of which occupied the entire first floor.

Pushing through the doors, she went into the exhibition. Workers milled about the exhibition displays, the sounds of hammers ringing through the air even as people streamed toward the entrance to see the commotion on the street.

Lydia suppressed a fierce urge to scream Jane's name. If she was still here, if Cole was with her...God only knew what he might do to the girl if he knew Lydia was looking for her.

A shadow passed above her, moving across the window. Lydia peered up at the empty gallery, unable to discern much of anything through the dusk. Her heart thundered in her ears as she crept up the stairs to where the glowing embers of a fireplace illuminated a section of the gallery.

Her vision blurred, then cleared to sharp precision. Jane sat in a chair near the fireplace, one arm cradled close to her chest and her body trembling.

Lydia choked back a cry, an immense wave of relief sweeping through her. She fought the urge to scream for help.

A movement caught the corner of her eye. In the instant before her brain registered what was happening, a male hand clamped around her wrist. Pain spiraled up her arm. Cole jerked Lydia forward, his granite features mapped in shadows from the dying fire.

"Lydia!" Jane straightened, her eyes wide and frantic.

Lydia yanked her arm from Cole's grip and ran toward her daughter. She wrapped her arms around Jane and pulled her from the chair. Hugging the girl close, Lydia twisted to pin Joseph Cole with a glare.

"What do you want?"

His gaze on Jane, he replied, "How much is it worth to you, Lydia? How much will it be worth to keep the information from *him*?"

"Northwood already knows the truth. I told him."

Cole's smile appeared, as cold and sharp as a crescent moon. "You expect me to believe you would ruin your life like that?"

"Believe what you will. He knows Jane is my daughter."

"Our daughter. Perhaps you can convince her to tell me where the document is."

"What document?"

"The *acte de naissance* she hid," Cole said. "If she tells me where it is, this can all be ended very quickly."

No. It would never end. Lydia knew that to the core of her being. Never.

She felt the press of Jane's body against her side, the girl's hand clenching her arm. She met Jane's eyes. An odd understanding passed between them, something that spoke of regrets and sorrows that perhaps had some justification, some well-intended motive.

Lydia forced her gaze back to Cole. "Dr. Cole, why are you doing this?"

He looked at her with that clear, owl-like gaze that seemed capable of penetrating the deepest recesses of her mind.

"I lost everything, Lydia. First my position at the university. Couldn't find another job to save my life. Then Greta... you know how weak she was, how frail. She couldn't withstand the strain. Crumbled underneath it, really. What savings I had went to medical expenses, then, of course, to the burial."

Lydia wanted to clamp her hands over her ears to avoid hearing about Greta's death. "Why did you lose your professorship?"

A vague smile wreathed his mouth. "Ethics violations, of a sort. Can you imagine?"

"Ethics—"

"She was dead when I arrived. Shame they never believed me."

Lydia's breathing grew shallow, bile burning in her throat. "Who... who was—"

"The daughter of one of the history professors. Pity too. Lovely girl. I've no idea how many men she'd entertained in her rooms."

"And you... you—"

"They said she'd been strangled. They claimed I was a suspect, but they never proved I did the deed. Still, talk of the whole thing was enough for the education minister to see fit to dismiss me."

A door banged open somewhere. Voices rose from the lower floor like a flock of birds. Something crashed.

Lydia pushed Jane behind her, trying to make the movement inconspicuous. She wanted to shove the girl toward the stairs and the safety of the lower floor, but she had no idea if Cole was armed.

"It has been a year," Cole continued. "Then I read of Sir Henry's death and thought of you, so I returned to London. I wanted to know if you'd had the child. And when I found out about Jane, I wondered if she had your intelligence, your prodigious mathematical abilities. I thought that with you as her mother and me as her father, her genius might already be legendary. So I wrote to her."

A sick feeling swirled in Lydia's stomach at the idea that he had lured Jane into a correspondence. "What did you want from her?"

"At first, I thought she might have some novel ideas, different approaches to mathematics," Cole said.

"You wanted to mine her talents for your own purposes, didn't you?" Lydia snapped. "You thought she might provide you with some brilliant new theorems or identities. And you would have stolen them, published them as your own in a desperate attempt to regain your lost prominence."

He frowned. "That's not quite accurate. She is my daughter, after all, so by rights her theories would have been mine to begin with. Imagine my disappointment when I realized she possesses a rather ordinary mind. Comparatively speaking, of course."

Lydia clenched her teeth to prevent herself from contradicting his erroneous observation. "So what led to your current plan?"

"The news of your father's death," Cole replied. "I knew it would be a good time to contact Jane, and then I learned of your . . . relationship with a wealthy peer. If I can't have my reputation back, then a sizable amount of money might well assuage my disappointment. Enough so that I can live somcwhcrc clsc, pcrhaps Francc or Italy, in comfort for the remainder of my days."

He doesn't want Jane.

Lydia's greatest fear, the one that had haunted her for the last decade, eased a little. She didn't care what he wanted, what he did, as long as he didn't try to take her daughter away.

"If you get the money, will you go away?" she asked. "For good?"

"Perhaps. Though I will require the *acte de naissance* to ensure I can control the situation. With that document in my possession, with you knowing I have proof of Jane's true birth, I will know you cannot renege on your word."

"You cannot blackmail me forever."

"Actually, I can." Cole tilted his head as he studied her. "Why did you agree to marry him, Lydia? For the title and money? You've put both in jeopardy, haven't you?"

Lydia didn't respond, her throat constricting so hard it was difficult to draw in a breath.

"I will not lct you touch Lord Northwood." Shc stcclcd her voice and loosened her hold on Jane in the hopes her daughter would run. "Tell people whatever you want, Dr. Cole. I'll take full blame. You've no idea how things work, how they can be manipulated. Northwood can emerge from scandal intact if I'm the one who is vilified and liable. Then how effective will your blackmail be?"

Her words didn't appear to disconcert him in the slightest. "Suppose the revelation doesn't destroy Northwood. What do you think it will do to Jane?"

Lydia flinched. Cole smiled.

"I'm not a fool, Lydia. I know how much you want this kept secret, though I suppose your willingness to sacrifice yourself for your fiancé is admirable." He leaned forward to peer into Jane's face, lowering his voice to a gentle cadence. "It's quite simple, my dear. I will have either that document or you. Which shall it be?"

"You will not have Jane." A cold, deep voice lashed into the growing darkness. "Ever."

Alexander.

Lydia's mind registered his presence, his voice, even as her heart refused to believe it. And yet he emerged from the shadows, an ice-cold rage emanating from him.

"Lord Northwood." Cole raised an eyebrow, his expression wary but unafraid—as if he knew he was the person in control. "Perhaps you're the one who will prove sensible. The female mind is prone to emotional decisions, I've found."

Alexander moved closer, pulling Jane away from Lydia. He pushed her behind him to shield her from Cole. Without taking his eyes from the other man, he said, "Lydia, the carriage is at the Langley entrance. Take Jane and go."

Before Lydia could take one step toward her daughter, Cole moved as swift as a wasp, his hand clamping around Lydia's arm. Jane shrieked.

A gasp stopped in Lydia's throat, her body tensing to fight. The cold muzzle of a pistol pressed against her neck. Cole pinned her to him and dragged her toward the gallery railing.

"Miss? Miss!"

A flood of workers swarmed the floor below, staring up at the sudden commotion. Several men started up the stairs.

"No one move!" Cole shouted. "No one! I'll kill her."

The men froze. Alexander cursed and started forward, but Cole pushed the muzzle harder. Fear swamped Lydia.

Alexander stopped, his muscles bunched with tension beneath his coat. Behind him, Jane looked at Cole wide-eyed, then turned and ran. Relief over her daughter's escape overwhelmed Lydia's fear.

"Let her go, Cole." Alexander held up his hands in a placating gesture. "Whatever amount of money you want, you will have."

"No." Lydia flinched. Sweat trickled down her back, Cole's breath hot and harsh against her ear.

"Who's worth more to you, Northwood, the girl or Lydia?"

"They are of equal value."

Cole laughed. "Are they? Suppose I leave Lydia with you? Take Jane with me? I'd have myself quite a trump card, could bring her out any time as the daughter of Viscountess Northwood, the eminent—"

"Stop!"

Cole whirled, turning as Jane hurried along the length of the gallery, her hand outstretched. A piece of paper fluttered in her grasp.

"Let her go." She thrust the paper toward Cole. "And I'll give you this."

Cole stared at the girl, then gave a low laugh. "Perhaps I underestimated your intelligence, Jane. Even among this illustrious group, you might well be the smartest one here."

He held out a hand to take the paper, but Jane kept it from his reach. Determination hardened her features.

"First release Lydia," she ordered.

Cole shook his head. "Not until I have the document."

"How do I know you'll let her go?"

"You'll have to trust me. I am your father, after all."

"No, you are not."

A vibration of impatience went through Cole's body. "Give me the paper, Jane," he snapped.

Jane's eyes darted to where Alexander stood beside the fire. Lydia's heart jumped at his sudden movement. He hurled himself forward, his big hand coiling around Lydia's arm as he tore her from Cole's grasp.

The gun went off. Lydia stumbled to her knees. Jane screamed. A collective gasp rose from the crowd below, followed by a surge of movement.

Alexander plowed into Cole and slammed him against the gallery railing. The wood fractured and cracked. Cole grunted, swinging his arm back to catch Alexander on the side of the head.

Jane ran to Lydia. The document fell as she gripped Lydia with both hands and tried to drag her away from the brawling men. Lydia pressed a hand to her stomach, her vision blurring. She blinked and tried to focus, tried to...

"The girl!" a man shouted. "Get her away!"

Lydia pushed Jane toward the stranger's voice. The crowd below seemed to swell and shift like an ocean's tide.

A sickening thud echoed through the room as Alexander gripped Cole's collar and shoved him against the railing again. A bloody gash bloomed on Cole's forehead.

He cursed and kicked his foot upward, catching Alexander hard in the knee. The crack was enough to make Alexander loosen his grip. Cole tore away from him.

The gun. *Where was the gun?*

Lydia pushed to her feet, desperate, but Cole was advancing, closing in. He grabbed the gun from where it had fallen by the hearth. He swung it up, firing at the men advancing on the stairs, then toward the crowd.

People screamed. Doors slammed open and closed. Footsteps thundered.

Alexander crashed against Cole's back, bringing him to the ground. The gun went flying. Both men grunted, bones cracking.

Jane darted forward and grabbed the birth certificate. Cole twisted, breaking from Alexander's grip. He plunged forward and dove for Jane.

Lydia knew what was going to happen before it came to pass. Just as she knew she could do nothing to prevent it.

Horror flooded her as she watched Cole plow into her daughter, breaking through the splintered railing with a thunderous crack.

Unable to stop the forward movement, Cole shoved Jane aside before he crashed through the railing. With a shriek, Jane skidded against the floor as pieces of wood crashed onto the globe display below.

The crowd swarmed in a mass of confusion, shouts and gasps rising.

"Jane!" Alexander yelled.

He lunged for the girl, his hand clamping around her wrist just as she started to slide over the edge. He yanked her to a halt and braced one foot against a post.

Panic swamped Lydia. She stretched to reach for Jane's

other hand and sent up a million prayers of gratitude when her daughter's fingers closed around hers.

She looked over the edge. Cole had grasped a broken post to prevent himself from falling. Beneath them, a dozen globes gleamed, the round surfaces of earth and sky undulating in the twilight.

Fear and exertion contorted Cole's features. His legs thrashed in midair. The wood cracked again, jerking him downward.

Alexander and Lydia hauled Jane back to the safety of the gallery. Jane flung herself into Lydia's arms, sobs tearing from her throat and her body shaking.

Alexander reached his hand to where Cole still hung suspended. Cole's sheet-white face glistened with sweat. Alexander cursed and stretched farther. Cole released one hand from the post and tried to grab Alexander's hand. His legs kicked to find purchase. The post splintered with a noise like a fired bullet.

Oh, dear God.

Pressing Jane's face to her shoulder, Lydia stared down at Cole. His gaze, wide-eyed and panicked, met hers.

The post broke. With a cry, Cole fell, his arms flailing. His head smashed against a massive glass globe, a sickening crash splitting through the hall. Blood sprayed over the clear surface before Cole crumpled to the floor and lay still.

Screams rent the air as chaos erupted below.

Chapter Twenty-Nine

Commotion flooded St. Martin's Hall—shouts, thundering footsteps, the shrill noise of constables' whistles.

The throng from outside mobbed the foyer and lower floor, though whether the confusion started inside or out, Alexander didn't know. A man yelled for order. Women shrieked. Windows cracked under the impact of thrown objects.

Alexander pushed Lydia and Jane into a corner of the darkened gallery and prayed they would be safe. "Stay here. Do not move until I return."

Outside, police and a detachment of infantry swarmed the street, trying to restore order. Alexander helped pull the wounded out of the way, bile rising in his throat at the sight of a bleeding man lying amid the rubble. He grasped the man beneath the arms and dragged him to an empty doorstep.

"All right?" he asked. He yanked off his cravat and pressed it to the wound on the man's head.

The man nodded, his eyes glazed. Alexander yelled for a constable, then went back into the hall. Crowds of people surged through the displays and sent them crashing to the floor. Bird feathers floated in the air, musical instruments lay shattered, the model schoolhouses smashed. Alexander's heart plummeted at the sight of the destruction.

He pushed through the crowd to the globe display, where two constables stood over Cole's prone body. Bits of paper tore and glass crunched beneath Alexander's feet. He turned away from the congealed blood.

He searched the broken glass, the splintered wood. His fist closed around a piece of paper stuck beneath a globe of the stars. He shoved it into his pocket, then ran back out into the street.

They sat in silence amid the chaos. Shouts and noise flew upward from the lower floor. Several people ran past in the gallery, but Lydia and Jane remained concealed in the shadows of the hearth.

Lydia clasped Jane to her chest, Jane's arms wrapped around her neck. Her small body rippled with tremors.

Memories flashed through Lydia's mind of holding Jane as an infant, a toddler. All those years of watching her daughter grow and learn—her first steps, first words, her endless curiosity. Cherishing Jane's smiles and laughter. Loving every moment of time spent together.

She pressed her lips to Jane's cheek. How she wished her own mother had experienced such joy. And perhaps... perhaps in those first five years of Lydia's life, she had.

"I love you," Lydia whispered. "Whatever happens, please know that. I have and will always love you more with every beat of my heart. You are everything to me."

Her daughter didn't respond. Instead she sought Lydia's hand with her own and curled their fingers together.

Alexander wiped sweat and grime from his forehead with the back of his hand. Beside him, Sebastian hauled a woman away from the crowded street. Somehow his brother had found him, and they worked through the commotion together. They brought people back into the hall offices, yelled at others to get inside, lock the doors, close the shutters.

Over the course of several hours, the mob dispersed. Destruction lay in its wake—shards of glass and wood littered the streets, and broken wagons lay among scattered rubbish. Darkness fell in a heavy sheet as the noise began to settle.

Alexander dragged a hand down his scratched face. He and Sebastian returned to St. Martin's Hall. Fear tightened his chest as he went up the stairs to collect Jane and Lydia. They still sat huddled together near the hearth, pale but appearing unharmed.

Relief and gratitude streamed through Alexander, banishing his fatigue. He hauled Jane into his arms. Sebastian extended a hand to help Lydia to her feet, and they went downstairs.

"Oh, Alexander." Lydia's whisper of dismay cut through him as she saw the disaster that had once been the exhibition.

Outside, people still milled around the street, but the police had restored order and blocked off the entrance to the hall. Still holding Jane with one arm, Alexander pulled Lydia to him with the other. The tightness in his chest eased a little as her body pressed against his side.

"Lord Northwood." Sir George Cooke of the Society council strode toward him, his expression grim. "The police inspector is heading to Mount Street now. You'd best meet him there. Hadley is on his way as well."

With Sir George accompanying them, they returned to Alexander's town house, where the servants rose in a bustle of activity. A doctor was summoned, warm water and clean clothes procured, tea and brandy offered. Lydia sent Jane upstairs with the housekeeper to look after her and wait for the doctor.

"Preliminary reports, Lord Northwood, indicate that you are responsible for causing the riot." Police Inspector Denison peered at Alexander with a faint air of sympathy.

"Which," Lord Hadley added, "destroyed the interior of the hall and the Society's exhibition. We'll have to send word to the lenders and the foreign commissioners."

Alexander tried to muster up some concern at the ominous tone to the man's voice, but he was too tired. He rubbed his burning eyes.

"And?"

"We've got to conduct an investigation, my lord," Denison replied. "We've statements from several people who witnessed your altercation with Mr."—he consulted his pad—"Cole. They saw you push him over the railing."

"No." Lydia's voice sounded choked. "No, Inspector, that's not correct. That man was after my... my sister. Lord Northwood was protecting us both. He was trying to—"

"Miss Kellaway, no need for a defense at the moment," Denison interrupted. "More will come to light during the course of the investigation. However, I ought to warn you that the newspaper correspondents will be seeking people to give their account of events, and his lordship ain't appeared to be cast in a favorable light."

"Will charges be filed, Inspector?" Sebastian asked.

"I don't yet know, sir, but first the nature of the riot needs to be determined to see whether it's a misdemeanor offense or possible treasonous—"

"Treason!" Lydia repeated.

"Well, miss, I don't mean to suggest that's the case here, but with the war and all and Lord Northwood's... er... A couple of the workers remarked that he's got sympathies with the czar."

"As we know," Sir George added, "that is not a new charge."

Sebastian gave a hollow laugh. The inspector shifted with discomfort.

"That's all yet to be determined, sir," he said. "But his lordship will have to appear before the magistrate. And nothing I can do about the accounts people give."

Alexander exchanged glances with his brother. A single thought passed between them. No matter what the investigation yielded, their name would be linked to a deplorable situation.

He looked at the inspector. "How many people were harmed?"

"Last I heard, a dozen."

Lydia gasped. Sebastian swore. A rock sank to the pit of Alexander's stomach. He rose and gestured to the door. "Gentlemen, it's late. As I'm sure you know, we're all tired. If we can take this up tomorrow, I would appreciate it."

Lord Hadley nodded and picked up his hat. "We're informing the rest of the council, Northwood. We haven't made any decisions about a replacement for exhibition director, so you're still the one in charge. Best be prepared for the consequences."

The men filed out. Sebastian looked at Alexander, who gave him a short nod. Then Sebastian followed the men from the room.

The door clicked shut. Lydia's apprehension spiked. She twisted her finger around a lock of hair, pulling it hard enough to hurt.

Alexander strode to the sideboard and removed the stopper from a decanter of brandy. He poured two glasses and took a swallow from one before pressing the other into Lydia's hands. She stared at the amber liquid for a moment before taking a fortifying sip.

Alexander watched her, his expression brooding, a red scratch marring his cheek.

"Tell me," he said.

Lydia drew in a deep breath, knowing she owed him the truth even though it would mean the death of their relationship. Only one other person knew the whole story, and that person was now gone.

"Joseph Cole was the mathematics professor at the University of Leipzig." The past began to encroach upon her mind, all the hopes she'd had for herself, all the mistakes she'd made. "His father was British, his mother German. Dr. Cole had spent his childhood in London, then attended university in Berlin before receiving the Leipzig position.

"After I took the examinations, he expressed great admiration for my aptitude and agreed to take me under his instruction. He and his wife offered to provide me with room and board."

Silence stretched from Alexander, hard and cold. His knuckles whitened on the glass. "His wife."

Lydia nodded, shame curdling like bile in her stomach. "He was married. His wife..." She forced the name past her lips, punished herself with the memory of a soft, brown-eyed woman who rarely seemed to speak above a whisper. "Greta. That was her name. Greta. She was a good person. They'd met when he first accepted the teaching position.

"My grandmother had accompanied me to Germany. She wanted to find me a suitable companion, a chaperone, so that she could return and help my mother. She soon realized that Greta would serve well in that role, so my grandmother went back to London within a month. And Greta...it was so easy for her to be a companion. She taught me some German, ensured I wrote to my father and grandmother every other day. They had no children. I think she...she wanted to treat me like a daughter."

"What happened?"

Lydia's heart thumped hard against her ribs. An image of a younger Dr. Cole burned through the back of her mind, the man for whom she'd developed a dark fascination—elegant Dr. Joseph Cole with the brilliant mind and the cold, sharp eyes of a true intellectual.

"With special permission, I was able to take classes at the university, though I couldn't matriculate," she explained. "I didn't make many friends. There were no other girls, and the ones in the village didn't know what to make of me. The boys just thought I was an oddity. I spent nearly all my time with Greta and Dr. Cole. Then her mother became ill and she had to take a trip to Bremen. That left Dr. Cole and me alone. His elderly aunt came to stay at the house to avoid the illusion of impropriety, but she was frail and a bit forgetful. She spent most of her time in her room."

She shifted, still not looking at Alexander but aware of his unmoving, rigid presence. Her skin pressed against her clothes, sweat dampening her throat. She took another swallow of brandy.

"I was... I was taking a bath. He knew it; he'd seen the maid bring up buckets of water. He came into my room when I was..."

Her voice broke. She squeezed her eyes shut, the mist-filled memory congealing, forming behind her eyelids. Her initial shock giving way to wary intrigue as Dr. Cole approached the bath with deliberate intent. His fingers sliding over her ripe but untouched body, awakening her skin, her blood, her arousal.

"But he didn't... it wasn't..." Alexander's voice was strangled.

Lydia shook her head. "It would be easier if I could tell you he forced me. He didn't. He made an advance, yes, and perhaps he might've stopped if I hadn't... if I hadn't responded. But I did. I allowed him to do what he wished, and I... I liked it."

Her face burned with mortification, but she forced herself to continue as if this confession were penance for having enjoyed the illicit pleasures of her own body.

Long-suppressed memories seeped into the edges of her mind, the way Dr. Cole had shifted from a cerebral professor to a heated lover, the dispelling of her inhibitions like the shedding of a snake's skin. The freedom of her own nakedness, the delicious rasp of flesh against flesh.

"Before him, I'd never...I'd lived only inside my mind," she said. "Never gave much thought to corporeal matters. Certainly nothing like that. I was astonished. I... I didn't want it to end."

"But it did."

"Eventually. We continued even...even after Greta returned. When she wasn't home or in the middle of the night. Sometimes at his university office. If she suspected anything, I never knew. She treated me no differently, which should have made me put a stop to the whole sordid thing."

"How long did it go on?"

"Four, five months. Until I realized I was with child. I was terrified, of course. I told Dr. Cole, and it was like dousing a fire with cold water. In a very deliberate manner, he told me I would never be able to prove the child was his and that if anyone found out, I would be ruined. He took me to see a woman who supposedly could... could get rid of the child. I refused. Couldn't do it. He said if I didn't, I was no longer welcome in his house."

She looked down at her hands, realizing she was gripping the folds of her skirt. Her jaw ached with the effort of holding back a flood of tears.

"I knew my grandmother had gone to Lyons with my mother. They were staying at a sanatorium run by nuns. I had nowhere else to go. I certainly couldn't return to London. So I sent word to my grandmother to expect me, then took the train to Lyons. I...I never said good-bye to Greta."

"Did you ever see her again? Or him?"

"No. Not until today."

"What happened when you arrived in Lyons?"

"My father met me at the train station."

"Your—"

"He'd come to visit my mother a fortnight prior. I didn't know."

And then it was as if she were no longer in the room with Alexander. The smell of coal swept through the air, the screech of wheels against the train tracks, voices rising from passengers, porters, vendors selling their wares on the platform.

And there stood her father, waiting for her, unaware of her disgrace. His glasses perched on the end of his nose—the wire frames appearing so fragile against his features, his coat flapping about his legs like the wings of a crow. Lines of worry furrowing his brow, concern over his wife, his mother-in-law, his daughter.

"What is it?" Sir Henry had asked. "What's happened?"

She couldn't respond, could only fold herself into his arms with the dreadful knowledge it might be the last time he would ever want to embrace her.

And so it had been. But never—thank the good Lord a thousand times over, thank her father a million times—never once since the day Jane was born had Sir Henry Kellaway withheld his affection, his genuine love for the girl.

"Did you tell him?" Alexander asked.

"Actually, I told my mother." She gave a humorless laugh at the utter absurdity of the statement. "I don't know why. I hadn't seen her in several years. She was... they kept her on laudanum. I thought she didn't even know I was there, but I had a burning need to tell *someone* the truth. So one night I sat beside her bed and confessed all."

"Did she respond?"

"No. At the time, I didn't even think she'd heard me. But the next day she told my father."

"What?"

"She'd heard it all. Understood it, even. And she told my father what I'd told her. My father confronted me that night, and I had to confess a second time."

"What did he do?"

Lydia fell silent.

If p is a prime number, then for any integer a, $a^p - a$ *will be evenly divisible by p. The sine of two theta equals two times the—*

No.

She suppressed the proofs, the theorems, the identities, the equations. Suppressed everything that made any sense. Forced the dark memory to the surface. The side of her face bloomed with an old, latent pain.

"He was enraged. He..." She touched the side of her face, shuddering as memories ripped through her—the pain of the blow, her father's shock over his lack of control, her own fierce belief that she deserved any violence he chose to exact.

He inflicted no more—the one strike upon his own daughter was enough to stun him into immobility. For three days, he didn't speak to her, didn't look at her. Then one morning he and Charlotte Boyd called Lydia into a private room and explained in cold, blank tones that she would adhere to their plan or be left to fend for herself.

"It was my grandmother's idea," she told Alexander. "She said we would remain at the sanatorium for the time being. I think she and my father might have sent me off immediately if they hadn't realized I was the only person who'd gotten through to my mother—even with such a disgraceful secret. So my father told me to continue to sit with my mother and try to reach her."

"Did you?" Alexander asked.

"For several weeks, yes. Until it became clear her condition was worsening. My father spoke with the nuns about keeping me there during my confinement, and they agreed.

"No one else knew about my condition except Dr. Cole, and of course there was no danger of him telling anyone. So my grandmother said that after the child was born, we would tell people it was my mother's. My father donated a substantial sum to the sanatorium to ensure the nuns went along with that story. That...that drained his finances significantly. He was never able to repair them."

Her heart pounding with fresh trepidation, Lydia finally lifted her head. Alexander stood across the room, his gaze fixed on her. Wariness shone behind his eyes, but there was none of the censure or disgust she had feared.

"Go on," he said.

"After the birth, we remained in Lyons for another year. Then when my mother died, we returned to London with the story intact and unbreachable. Jane became the daughter of my mother and father. She became my sister."

"And you've kept the secret all this time."

"Yes. Although people knew my mother was unwell, they had no reason to believe Jane wasn't my father's child. If we hadn't told them, they still would have assumed she was the legitimate child of my parents. Even our distant relations believed that. Of course, we never wanted to change that assumption. And so we haven't."

"You've told no one?"

"My grandmother said that if anyone knew the truth, it

would cause irreparable damage to our family's reputation, and I would have to leave," Lydia said. "So I was allowed to serve as Jane's tutor, to continue my work in mathematics, though somewhat anonymously to lessen the chances of encountering Dr. Cole again. Of course, my grandmother has insisted on absolute propriety, irreproachable conduct. Considering the circumstances, I can't say I blame her. And so it's been for almost twelve years."

Until now. Until you.

He paced to the windows and back again. "Jane didn't know the truth?"

A wave of pain pounded against the numbness around Lydia's heart. "She... the locket, Alexander. There was another compartment behind the first. My father had it specially made."

Tears pushed against her eyes. "He'd placed a coin of good fortune inside the locket before he gave it to my mother. The coin was lost long ago, but the locket has held a key ever since Jane was born.

"I kept her birth certificate in a locked copper box, and I put the key inside the locket, in the hidden compartment. No one knew it was there except me." She glanced at him. "You had the locket for almost three months. You never noticed there was another compartment?"

"No. I didn't spend untold hours examining the thing. I've never even heard of a locket having two compartments." He frowned. "You didn't answer my question. Does Jane know the truth?"

Lydia's tears spilled over. "After you gave her the locket, she found the key. And she figured out that it belonged to the copper box, which has always been in my father's study."

Alexander was silent for a moment; then he cursed. "Christ. Is that why she went to meet Cole? Bloody hell, if I hadn't—"

"No. Don't do that. Not now."

The sound of his boots shuffling against the carpet drew her head up. He stopped closer to her. His hands flexed at his sides, tension lining his body like steel.

Oh, so many mistakes. So much pain.

"I'm sorry," she whispered. "So sorry."

"I... I was relentless, wasn't I?" Self-disgust laced his words. "Wouldn't leave you alone. Couldn't."

"In a secret part of my heart, Alexander," Lydia said, "I didn't want you to."

She stood, aching to touch him and knowing she could not. "But now you understand why a marriage between us can never be possible. I admit that for a brief moment, I believed it might work, but... well, that's a fool's errand, isn't it? And never let anyone accuse either one of us of being a fool."

Unable to help herself, she stepped to him and reached up to press her lips against his unshaven cheek. He turned his head, his mouth meeting hers in a kiss so light it almost didn't exist. And yet a thousand regrets passed between them with that single touch.

Lydia turned away, her heart cracking.

"I love you," Alexander said.

She made it through the door before the tears fell again.

Chapter Thirty

"Doesn't matter if the charges are proved or even legitimate, Northwood." Rushton stared at the fire. "It's an excuse to remove you from the Society council, from your position as director of the exhibition."

"It's an excuse to get rid of him," Sebastian said bluntly.

Alexander's stomach tightened at the shadowed gravity in his father's expression. Anger boiled in him at the realization that all his work for the past two years was coming to naught. That despite all he'd tried to do to restore his family's reputation, they would now be blamed for the destruction and injuries caused by the riot.

His father was correct. The truth didn't matter.

Did he care? Ever since Lydia had walked away from him, a hard, painful knot had formed in Alexander's chest. He thought about her every passing minute, dreamed about her at night and woke sweaty and aching. He'd analyzed the Jane situation from every angle, tried to find some way to place the full blame on Lydia, to vilify her...and only ended up ashamed of himself.

What could one say about a sixteen-year-old girl who'd lived a life of isolation and darkness, whose brilliant mind made her both a prodigy and an anomaly? A girl who'd lacked friends and a mother and a normal childhood? A girl who had succumbed to the grotesque manipulations of a man twice her age?

How could he blame her for any of that?

And how could he blame her for not telling him the truth when she'd been so adamant about not marrying him in the first place? She'd tried to protect him by declining his proposal, and he'd not taken no for an answer. Instead he'd manipulated her all over again to force her to change her mind.

He winced and scrubbed his hands over his face.

No. The only person he had to blame for this whole debacle was himself.

"Alex?"

He looked up at his brother.

"The police are looking into Cole's circumstances," Sebastian said. "Seems he was staying at a lodging house over in Bethnal Green. According to the owner, a Mr. Krebbs, he'd been there for almost five months. Krebbs claimed Cole had few possessions and said he had no kin. The superintendent doesn't expect they'll find anything of much import. Which is to your...our advantage. The official report will state that Cole died during an attempt to kidnap Jane."

"Doesn't affect the riot situation, though, does it?" Rushton asked.

"That's what they want to charge me with."

"I don't see how they can," Sebastian said. "It wasn't as if you were making a seditious speech or distributing anti-British pamphlets."

"Does it matter?" Alexander asked. "The council has been wanting me off the board for weeks, even before the war started, and likely out of the Society altogether. Why not claim I incited the riot that destroyed the exhibition and St. Martin's Hall? Like Rushton said, they won't care about the letter of the law if they've an excuse to get rid of me."

And while the council members wouldn't intentionally drag his name through the mud, they'd do nothing to stop it from happening.

Well, hell. He might as well marry Lydia, truth be damned, and live in scandal for the rest of his life.

He'd be a bloody earl one day, and if people wanted to gasp at his *shocking* behavior in public while they bedded their servants and mistresses in private...so be it. He'd have them all over for tea and give them both cakes and plenty of fodder for gossip.

Alexander looked at his brother. Sebastian would never let anyone else dictate how he lived his life. Why should Alexander?

"Lord Rushton." Alexander stood.

His father and Sebastian looked at him with faint surprise.

"Northwood?"

"Whatever happens," Alexander said, "I still intend to marry Lydia Kellaway."

Sunlight burned through a crack in the curtains. Jane pushed her hair away from her face and went to pull them open, allowing light to flood the room. She washed her face and hands at the basin, then paused at the table, where hot tea and a basket of muffins waited.

The door creaked open. She looked up from pouring a cup of tea to find Lydia in the doorway. Her sister...her *mother*...looked pale and drawn, her eyes wary. Grandmama stood behind her.

"May we come in?" Lydia asked.

Jane nodded. With a tentative smile, Lydia stepped inside. Grandmama went to sit on a chair beside the bed, her movements slow. "How do you feel?"

"All right. Tired but...fine." Jane sipped at the tea and picked up a muffin, then put it down when she realized she wasn't hungry. She returned to the bed, pulling the covers up over her legs. "Is Lord Northwood all right? And you?"

"We're both fine." Lydia settled on the edge of the bed and took a deep breath. "Jane, I—"

"Why didn't you tell me?" Jane interrupted, anger and hurt rising to fill her chest again. She looked accusingly from Lydia to Grandmama. "Why did you lie to me?"

"It's a long, complicated story," Lydia said. "But believe me when I say it was for the best. If you'd known...if anyone had known, you would have been taken away from me. This was the only way we could keep you with us."

"It's true, Jane." Grandmama sounded weary but resolute, as if she still held the belief of her strong convictions. "We did it to keep our family together. When my daughter fell ill, we did whatever we could to help her, even if it meant draining our finances. We traveled everywhere in search of a treatment.

"And when we lost Theodora"—she paused, cleared her throat—"to the ravages of that horrible illness, we had only each other left. My husband passed long ago, Sir Henry had no brothers or sisters, and Lydia...Lydia always thought she was more comfortable with her numbers and equations. She never realized how much she needed us."

Lydia stared at Grandmama, as if hearing this for the first time. Grandmama met her gaze, tenderness softening her features.

"So when we learned of Lydia's...situation," Mrs. Boyd continued, "we refused to allow you, an innocent child, to suffer. Especially when we knew that you might well prove to be Lydia's salvation."

A strangled sound emerged from Lydia's throat. Tears filled Jane's eyes as her mother's hand tightened on hers.

"It's true, Jane," Lydia choked out. "I never...I don't know what would have become of me if I hadn't had you. You gave me a purpose in life beyond numbers. You gave me hope and love and...I wouldn't change any of it. I would have lied to the devil himself to keep you."

"It was my idea, Jane, so you mustn't blame Lydia," Grandmama said. She gripped her cane and rose, then bent to press a kiss against Jane's forehead. "And it was all done to ensure you remained with us. With Lydia. Remember that."

She squeezed Lydia's shoulder and left the room, closing the door behind her.

Jane tried to imagine being raised in another house, with another family—and couldn't. She would only ever belong to the Kellaways. Only to Lydia.

"I didn't mean it when I said I hate you," she mumbled.

"I know."

Jane looked down and saw a crumpled piece of paper in Lydia's hand. "Is that..."

Lydia smoothed out the document, revealing the

swirled penmanship naming her as Jane's mother. Beyond the shadow of a doubt.

"It had fallen beneath one of the other globes," Lydia explained. "Alexander found it."

"What are you going to do with it?"

"Give it to you."

Jane looked at her. "Give it to me?"

Lydia nodded and placed the *acte de naissance* on Jane's lap.

"What am I to do with it?" Jane asked.

"Whatever you like. It belongs to you. I will never lie to you again. Not about anything."

Jane stared down at the paper that she'd pored over to the point of exhaustion, trying to believe, to accept, what she'd read. Now as she looked at the document for the hundredth time, she realized how fitting it all was.

There was her name, her birth date. The place where her grandmother Theodora had lived. Papa's name, Grandmama's name. *Kellaway, Lydia.* And a blank line where her father's name should have been.

Painful, but fitting. And right.

Jane swiped at a stray tear. "I'm sorry."

"What on earth do you have to be sorry about?" Lydia asked.

"For... for writing to... to him. Keeping it from you. I thought to tell you a number of times, but it was... well, it was a secret I had for myself. Something that belonged only to me."

"I understand. You've no need to apologize."

"Yes, I do. He told me... he said you had to give up your work after I was born. You could have done so much, Lydia, changed so many—"

"Jane!"

Jane looked up, startled, to find Lydia descending on her with all the force of a mother eagle. Lydia wrapped Jane in her arms and hugged her, pressing her cheek to Jane's hair.

"Never, *never* think I gave up anything for you. Never! I wanted you, Jane. You've no idea how much. Yes, I was frightened and yes, I made terrible mistakes, but once you were born—when I held you that first time, I knew my world had changed. I knew numbers and equations could never fill my heart the way you did. All I cared about from that moment on was being with you."

Jane's tears spilled over as she buried her face against Lydia's neck and breathed in the familiar scent of her. Her mother. For eleven years, she'd had a vague sense of longing for a mother, when all this time her mother had been right by her side. Always.

"I wish I'd known," she said. "I wish—"

"Would it have changed so much between us?" Lydia asked, her arms tightening around Jane's shoulders. "Would our relationship have been so different?"

No. *She* might have been different, though perhaps she wasn't meant to be. Perhaps she was meant to be exactly who she was.

Jane eased away from Lydia and looked at her, wondering why she'd never before noticed the similarities in their features.

"Did you love him?" she asked.

Sadness filled Lydia's eyes. She shook her head. "No. I never loved him."

"Do you hate him?"

"No. Because without him, I wouldn't have had you."

Chapter Thirty-One

Alexander's heart pounded so hard he felt it would burst through his chest. He'd waited for news of the riot to calm over the past week before approaching Lydia again, but the span of time had caused his emotions to knot into a disordered mess. He wiped his damp palms on his coat as Mrs. Driscoll bustled forward to lead him into the study.

Lydia rose from a seat beside the window, a guarded smile appearing on her face. His heart thumped harder. She'd never looked more beautiful, standing in a patch of fog-coated sunlight, wearing a black dress with a lace collar encircling her neck, her long hair captured in a ribbon. Her skin was pale, her blue eyes grave but not cold.

After Mrs. Driscoll left, Lydia stepped forward to clasp Alexander's hands, squeezing them tight. She smiled.

Oh, God. Could he possibly love her more?

"Hello." He couldn't manage another word.

Amusement flashed in her eyes. "Hello."

Alexander cleared his throat. "You've... you've been all right?"

"Yes. You? Talia told me the Society of Arts council has called a meeting for next week."

"To discuss what happened, yes. Lord Hadley asked two of the police inspectors to attend and give their reports of what happened that night."

"Why would the police... oh, Alexander."

"It doesn't matter, Lydia."

"It does matter! They can't charge you with something that wasn't your fault."

"They've been wanting an excuse to strip me of my duties anyway, so this is certainly convenient. Russian blood alone wasn't a strong enough reason for dismissal."

"But if there's no evidence—"

"They don't need evidence proving I was at fault. What matters is that there's no evidence proving I *wasn't*."

"Surely they know it wasn't until the gunshot that—"

"The police weren't there when that happened. All they've got are people's accounts. They don't really know anything."

Lydia caught her lower lip between her teeth and stared at his cravat for a moment.

"What are they saying?" she asked. "That you incited the riot by assaulting Dr. Cole?"

"Essentially. It's not a legal charge, but they'll either find a way to make it one or there'll be a report in the *Times* that'll do as much, if not more, damage."

"But there was a mob of people outside before you even arrived at the hall. There was already—"

"Lydia." He stepped closer to her, cupping the sides of her neck between his hands. He inhaled and let the clean, fresh-pencil scent of her soothe his frayed nerves. "It doesn't matter."

"You're wrong, Alexander." Lydia's voice rose a notch, her shoulders tensing. "All you've done, all you've worked for, they can't take it all away from you on some trumped-up charge. You can't let them—"

Alexander kissed her. He pressed his lips to hers and felt the pulse in her neck leap against his palm. Fierce satisfaction filled him when Lydia sank against him as if she could do nothing else, her arms sliding around his waist, responding to his kiss with both softness and heat. A little noise escaped her throat. He fought the urge to yank the ribbon from her hair and bury his hands in all that lush silk.

Lydia's hands flattened against his chest as she tried to put some distance between them. "Stop," she whispered.

He forced himself to step back, swiping a hand down his face. He had to make this work. He *had* to.

"Is..." His voice tangled. He swallowed and tried again. "Is Jane all right? Your grandmother?"

"Yes. Jane is... well, we need to figure out how to navigate this new territory between us, but she's not angry with me anymore. Still I think it will take time before she fully understands."

A tinge of sorrow appeared in her eyes as she turned to pour them both tea. She was silent as she handed him a cup, then added sugar and cream to hers. Alexander waited for her to settle on the sofa, then sat in a chair a distance away so he would be less tempted to touch her.

"What was it like?" he asked. "Acting like she was your sister when..."

Her shoulders lifted. "I became accustomed to it. I had

to. When my grandmother determined that's what we'd do, I was relieved. She and my father could have given the infant away, or sent us both away, and there would have been nothing I could do. So even though we had to lie, I was grateful I could keep Jane. And not just *keep* her—I was with her all the time. I never thought of her as Dr. Cole's child, only as mine."

She sipped her tea, looking out the window as if she were gazing at her past. "And during moments when I wished...when I *longed*...for her to know I was her mother, I had only to remember that she could so easily have been taken from me. But I think...I know I've always held something back from her. I've had to. With that kind of deception, I could never be everything I wanted to be to Jane. I could never truly be myself."

She blinked hard, her mouth compressing as she set her cup aside. "Even before Jane, I don't know if that had been possible. I was a strange child, Alexander. I found so much comfort in numbers, their purity, their comprehensibility.

"And though I will be forever grateful to my grandmother for insisting that my talent be nurtured, I also wish I'd learned to understand people as well as I did equations. Things might have turned out very differently if I had, though I still wouldn't have given Jane up for anything. But it wasn't until I met you..."

A tremble rippled through her voice. She paused, a mixture of sorrow and regret coloring her expression. "When I gave in to Dr. Cole, I did so because I wanted to *feel* something. I hadn't realized that ever since my mother took ill, I'd been buried beneath layers of calculations and theorems. I don't know what I expected, if

I thought we'd fall in love or have a brief affair. I didn't know if he'd leave his wife. All I knew was that I felt... awake. For the first time ever."

Alexander's jaw tightened to the point of pain. He hated, despised, the idea that Lydia—*his Lydia*—would ever have imagined she could find happiness with another man.

"But then," Lydia continued, "I realized how horribly wrong it all was. I was awake, but within a nightmare of betrayal and deceit. Both Dr. Cole's and mine. And even after Jane was born—especially after she was born because I was so afraid of making a mistake—I retreated back into what I thought was the safety of numbers."

She fell silent for a moment. "And for so many years, that was fine. I had Jane. I had my work. But then I met you."

She lifted her head, and those blue eyes fixed on him with such directness that he knew he was looking right into her bare soul.

"I didn't even realize until then that I'd retreated into a prison of my own making," Lydia said. "I hadn't considered what would happen to me, to Jane, once she came of age. Once she left home, got married, began her own life. I'd continue my work, of course, but then I realized it wasn't... it wasn't *enough*."

As Alexander continued to look at her, something cracked inside him, a feeling of simultaneous damage and growth, like a fresh shoot breaking through a hard, dry seed.

"What do you want, Lydia?" he asked, remembering the night so many weeks ago when he'd asked that very question in a desperate attempt to understand her.

For a long moment, they looked at each other, as if she,

too, was recalling that night, that kiss, that moment when everything had changed forever.

"I want my family to be happy," she said. "I want people to still admire my father's work, to respect all he did. I want my grandmother to feel as if all she's done has finally led to something good. I want Jane to live the life she wants, to—"

"No. What do you want for *you*?"

She didn't respond. He set his cup down and approached her. Nervousness twined through him.

"I know what I want," he said. "I still want you, Lydia."

She continued staring out the window. "Please, don't."

"I want to marry you. I don't give a damn what people say, what the Society outcome is, what—"

"You don't, do you?" She turned to him, frustration sparking in her eyes. "What about your father? Don't you think marriage to me will make him even more of a recluse? And Lady Talia? She's had a difficult enough time as it is, hasn't she? What will happen when people learn her brother married a woman who has an illegitimate child?"

"We don't have to announce it, for God's sake."

"So we marry and keep it a secret? What about Jane? Would she live with us as my sister still? And what happens if we're unable to prevent the truth from getting out?"

"No one else needs to know the truth."

"You would take that risk, keep that kind of secret, while knowing the truth could ruin you and destroy your family?" She stepped forward, her blue eyes hardening. "Didn't your mother keep a secret, Alexander?"

Anger coursed through him, sudden and swift. "My mother has nothing to do with this."

"But her secret is what caused your family's disgrace. Do you truly want to live like that?"

Old, hard feelings battered Alexander, culminating in a helplessness that caught him in a tight vise. His chest ached with it.

"I *will* fix this, Lydia." His eyes stung as he willed her to believe him.

She continued as if he hadn't spoken.

"And do you honestly think I would put your family, put *you*, in that kind of position? Subject you to such risk?" She stepped closer and put her cool hand against his cheek. Her blue eyes, filled with emotions he could not identify, searched his face. "This is why I refused your marriage proposal, Alexander. And I'm beyond grateful that we can finally be honest with each other, but that doesn't change my decision. I cannot marry you."

Her hand slipped away from him. Tears filled her eyes, making them look like the fathomless depths of the ocean.

"What do I want for me?" she asked. "I want a quiet life, like the one I..." She looked away.

"What?" Alexander demanded.

"Like the one I had before I met you." Her voice was so low he had to strain to hear her.

Alexander's fists clenched so hard his knuckles hurt. She was trying to hurt him, to drive him away. He knew that, and yet her words still hit him like rocks. "That life is gone, Lydia."

She swiped at her tears. "N-not for me."

"Really? Jane knows you're her mother now. Hasn't that changed everything for you?"

She flinched. Glad to see evidence of her disconcertion, Alexander backed to the door. He pointed a finger at her.

"The only life you can have now, Lydia—the only life we can *both* have—is the one we make for ourselves."

Chapter Thirty-Two

The great room of the Society of Arts building in the Adelphi bustled with people and voices. The Society council members and all union representatives had attended—whether out of curiosity or a sense of duty, Alexander couldn't say. Three police inspectors sat on the other side of the aisle.

Alexander sat beside Sebastian and Rushton in the front row. The council members presided over the meeting from a dais at the front of the room. Frowns creased their faces as they spoke to each other, consulted papers, glanced at Alexander.

"You ought to have shaved, at least," Sebastian remarked, his voice low in the din. He rubbed his hand across his own jaw. "I did."

"Bastian's right." Rushton looked at them both from the corner of his eye. "You look like a vagrant, North."

Although he didn't care, Alexander dragged a hand through his hair in an attempt to smooth it down. He'd hardly slept for the past five nights as he struggled to find a way to convince Lydia to give him a chance. But no matter how many ways he tried to find a solution, he knew she would not concede. Even if she wanted to.

He cursed beneath his breath and tried to focus on the council members as Lord Hadley stood from behind the long table.

"Order, everyone! I call the meeting to order."

Hadley waved his arms to indicate everyone should be seated. As the commotion waned, he cleared his throat. "As you all know, we have convened this meeting in order to address the issue of the educational exhibition as presided over by Lord Northwood. We have been aware for some time that his close ties with the Russian Empire, as well as his trading company, were perhaps at odds with the stated goals of the exhibition, namely to promote the supremacy of the British educational system and British industry and to continue to foster free trade with France."

Murmurs of agreement rose from the crowd. Alexander remembered that first time he'd told Lydia about the exhibition, when she'd sat in his drawing room and offered to assist with the mathematics display. If he'd known then how desperately he would come to ache for her...

I have a talent for mathematics.

She didn't know she also had a talent for stealing his heart.

"We have heretofore been willing to overlook Lord Northwood's Russian connections owing to his strong support of the Society of Arts," Hadley continued. "However, the recent onset of war has prompted us to weigh more carefully the value of his contributions versus the detriment of his... er... personal situation.

"The week before last, Lord Northwood was involved in an altercation with a gentleman who purportedly was attempting to kidnap a young girl, the sister of Lord Northwood's fiancée. The police have concluded, and we can all certainly agree, that Northwood acted to protect both his fiancée and the girl."

The girl. Alexander's chest squeezed at the thought of what might have happened to Jane. Such a bright, pretty girl, so full of hope and promise. He imagined Lydia might have been like Jane as a child if she'd been given the chance at a normal life.

"Several people claim to have seen him push the man to his death over the gallery railing of St. Martin's Hall," Hadley droned on.

Alexander shifted impatiently. Didn't everyone know this already?

"Others claim the man fell as a result of his own actions," Hadley said. "I do not know that either claim can be credibly substantiated, but suffice it to say that the police have not seen fit to charge Northwood with any crime in connection with this incident.

"Unfortunately, it sparked what we can only describe as a riot. A crowd had already gathered on the street outside St. Martin's Hall to witness an accident between two wagons, and the ensuing fistfight between the drivers caused further commotion.

"A number of people went into St. Martin's Hall to take shelter from the increasingly raucous fray, but upon witnessing the struggle between the two men, they, too, began to create an uproar. And when Dr. Cole plunged to his death... well, I'm certain you have all read the reports about the pandemonium that erupted following this tragic event."

"In addition to people sustaining injuries in the riot," Lord Wiltshire added, "the exhibition displays have been very badly damaged, several irreparably so."

"Northwood ought pay for that, then," called a man from the back of the room.

The council members exchanged glances.

Alexander stood, half turning toward the man. "I've offered to do so," he said. "The council has declined."

Hadley coughed. "We've been obliged to decline, sir, owing to the—"

"Not acceptable, Lord Northwood." A wiry man with spectacles rose from the other side of the aisle. "I am Henri Bonnart, the French commissioner to the Society. We cannot abide accepting monies from a man who owns a trading company based in the Russian Empire."

"*Merci,* Monsieur Bonnart," Hadley said. "However, the point of this meeting is to consider Lord Northwood's position as director of the exhibition and vice president of the Society of Arts. I'm afraid the police strongly believe his actions incited the ensuing riot, and in the absence of other conclusive evidence—"

"Lord Hadley!" A woman's voice rang out from the back of the hall.

Everyone turned. Alexander's heart pounded. Lydia strode through the door, her back ramrod straight and her expression resolute. Satchel in hand, she walked down the aisle toward the council.

Alexander stared at her for a second before realizing she was followed by a half dozen men carrying cases, books, large bristol boards, and rolls of paper. He recognized them as her mathematician friends—the men of the journal editorial board as well as Dr. Sigley and Lord

Perry, all marching behind her like a military regiment following their commander.

Lydia didn't spare him a glance as she stopped before the council. Color rode high on her cheekbones, but her voice was steady and firm as she spoke.

"Gentlemen, forgive the interruption, but I've something of great importance to impart. My name is Lydia Kellaway, and these gentlemen accompanying me are professors and mathematicians of the highest order. Upon learning of the pending charge against Lord Northwood, and knowing of its utter falsity, I asked my colleagues for assistance."

"Assistance with *what*, Miss Kellaway?" Wiltshire asked.

Lydia turned to her colleagues and gave a swift nod. The men assembled to the side, directly in front of Alexander, so they could be viewed by both the council and the audience. Two of them set up a stand and placed several display boards atop it, while another removed a stack of papers from a case and distributed them to the council members.

Mystified, Alexander looked from the men to Lydia. Not fifteen feet away, she stood watching him, color still flushing her pale cheeks but her blue eyes soft. She started a little as their gazes met. Alexander swallowed hard, clasping his hands together to prevent himself from going to her, grabbing her around the waist, and hauling her against him.

An unmistakable heat flared in her expression, as if the same thought had occurred to her.

Lydia. Lydia.

She gave a quick shake of her head and reached for a

pointer. She turned to the board, which was covered with a map of some sort, and delicately cleared her throat.

"This, gentlemen," she said, "is a diagram of the first floor and gallery of St. Martin's Hall on the night of the riot. My colleague Dr. Sigley has conducted extensive research on the dynamics of crowds, and he will explain how it is impossible that Lord Northwood could have incited a crowd to riot."

She smacked the pointer against the map. The audience shifted, rumbling a little with both bafflement and curiosity. Alexander leaned forward, his elbows on his knees.

Lydia nodded at Dr. Sigley. "If you would, please, sir."

"Delighted, Miss Kellaway." Sigley stepped forward to address the crowd. "Dr. Edward Sigley, gentlemen, FRS, DCL, FRSE, Lucasian professor of mathematics at the University of Cambridge, and editor of the *Cambridge and Dublin Mathematical Journal*."

He paused as if to allow everyone to absorb the illustriousness of his accomplishments. Silence filled the room, then was followed by murmurs of approval. Sigley nodded with satisfaction.

"I have conducted numerous experiments regarding the dynamics of crowds in relation to a flow-density relationship," he continued. "This can be written as..." He paused and scribbled an equation on the board.

"I beg your pardon, Dr. Sigley." Hadley held up a hand, a frown creasing his forehead. "If I may speak for my own colleagues, I would venture to suggest that we are about as interested in flow density as we are in women's fashion."

Several men barked out a laugh. Irritation flashed across Lydia's face. A large man with a bushy beard stood in the center of the room.

"Here now, my lord," he called. "Plenty of Society members are interested in mathematics, or at least know something about it. Part of the Society's division of subjects for the examination, isn't it? The professor here is talking about applied mathematics, isn't that right, Professor? We ought to listen to what he has to say."

A rumble of agreement rose from the audience. Alexander twisted around to see the man who had suddenly challenged the president of the Society on behalf of the mathematicians. Then he turned back to look at Lydia. She winked.

"Quite," Sigley replied with a nod of appreciation to his supporter. "Applied mathematics is pure mathematics, such as geometry or the properties of space, applied to establish the principles of statics and dynamics, which is what I speak of here."

"Good God, man, get on with it!" shouted a voice in the crowd. "What's this got to do with Northwood?"

The audience shifted again, more restlessly this time. Alexander and Sebastian exchanged glances. Sebastian looked rather worried.

Alexander returned his gaze to Lydia, who stood stiffly with her hands clasped, her white teeth biting her lower lip.

Look at me.

She did. A faint smile tugged at the corners of her beautiful mouth. Alexander allowed his eyes to sweep across the slopes of her shoulders encased in her stiff black dress, down to the curves of her breasts and waist. Even that first night, he'd known how lush and supple she was beneath her layers of clothing. Even then, he'd known he wanted her.

He hadn't, however, known how much he would love her.

Lydia flushed again, as if his gaze were a caress. Her hair was smooth and shiny beneath her hat, every strand pulled into an impeccable knot. Alexander wanted to yank all those pins out—damn them for confining Lydia's beautiful hair—and then feel the sweep of all that polished silk against his skin.

Christ. He shifted in his chair and tried to focus on the other mathematicians. That, at least, worked to dampen his arousal, but his awareness remained fixed on Lydia.

Dr. Sigley turned to his colleagues, and two of the other mathematicians stepped forward with charts. A third unrolled a scroll of paper covered with calculations.

"First," Sigley said, "in these studies, I have observed numerous situations involving large crowds. We can speak of the flow of information in a crowd much as we might speak of the flow of information in a pond. Suppose a lad throws a stone into the air. It lands at point *A*, and the dynamics of incompressible fluids dictate that the gravity waves spread out in a circular manner from the point of impact.

"Knowing as I do the equations that govern these dynamics, I could tell you when the first ripples from that stone would strike the shore. Now, here is where things get interesting. I could also solve the inverse problem. That is to say, if I came along some time after the lad threw his stone and merely observed the wavelets washing at my feet at some time, *T*, I could tell you very well where that stone hit the water even though I never saw it with my own eyes. I can make time move backward, if you will."

He stepped aside and nodded at Lydia, who wrote an

equation on the board. Alexander gave the numbers a cursory glance but couldn't keep his eyes from the graceful movement of Lydia's arm as she wrote, the studious concentration on her lovely features.

Warmth and pride filled Alexander's chest. He loved watching her mind work, knowing the complexity of the wheels and gears turning behind her blue eyes. Knowing that every other man in the room must be astonished by her brilliance.

Lydia turned to face the audience again.

"Therefore, we assert, gentlemen," she said, "that it is the same with the riot. A crowd is very much like a pond, a dense aggregation of particles that transmit information by colliding with one another."

"And we can solve the inverse problem as well," Dr. Sigley continued, pointing at the equation. "Though I was not there, I can state unequivocally that if Lord Northwood was indeed where you say he was at the time stipulated—and there are numerous credible witnesses who can corroborate this very thing, as I'm certain the inspectors can verify—then the laws of motion preclude his having initiated the disturbance that propagated through the medium at the nominal rate of fifty feet per minute—"

"What the devil is he on about, Miss Kellaway?" Hadley interrupted.

"My lord," Lydia said. "The very basic conclusion of Dr. Sigley's calculations is that Lord Northwood was not the slightest bit at fault for causing the riot. He was *here*." She smacked her pointer against the gallery on the map. "And the flow-density calculations, which you are all welcome to observe more closely, indicate the riot started *here*."

Another strike at the entrance of the hall emphasized her point. The audience was silent for a moment before a rumble began—questions, a couple of shouts, people standing to peer at the evidence.

"I'll be damned," Sebastian muttered.

Hadley stared at the map, then down at the papers Lord Perry had given him. The police inspectors approached the council table, lowering their heads to speak with the members.

A great deal of discussion and gesturing ensued, with Sir George Cooke approaching the mathematicians to point out items on the papers. Another council member began a discussion with Lord Perry, while the police inspectors scratched their heads and a couple of the other council members merely appeared bewildered. Union representatives from the crowd approached the dais to confer with the mathematicians and council members.

Lydia stood to one side, speaking with several men, her expression serious and confident. Alexander waited until she was alone for a moment before he stepped in front of her.

She lifted her gaze, her eyelashes like dark feathers against her white skin. Desire and...*more* simmered in her expression. He wanted to touch her. He wanted to kiss her. His fingers curled into his palms as he fought the urge.

"Why?" he asked.

She blinked, her gaze slipping to his throat. Her shoulders lifted in a shrug, though the casual gesture contradicted the multitude of emotions in her eyes.

"The calculations work," she said.

"That's not an answer."

"It's the only one I can give you."

"Beg your pardon, Miss Kellaway?" Lord Perry touched Lydia's arm to garner her attention and cast a faintly hostile glare at Alexander. "Your opinion on the ratio equation, if you please?"

Alexander stepped back and returned to his seat, not taking his eyes off Lydia as she moved to the board and commenced a discussion with two other men.

After a good half hour of buzzing and commotion, Hadley waved his arms about again. "Order! Everyone be seated, please. We've come to a sort of conclusion.... I think."

He waited for the din to settle, then cleared his throat. "We believe that Miss Kellaway and Dr. Sigley have provided compelling—if rather complex—evidence that Lord Northwood's actions did not, in fact, cause the riot to commence. Is that correct, Inspector?"

"Correct, my lord," Inspector Denison said, though he didn't appear entirely certain.

A rustle of movement came from the mathematicians, who turned to give each other handshakes and nods of approval. Lydia looked at Alexander and smiled in triumph.

He returned her smile because she was Lydia and he loved her for everything she was, all she had done for him, but caution kept him guarded.

"Yet while we can safely say that Lord Northwood is absolved of blame for actually inciting the riot," Hadley continued, "we cannot ignore the fact that he was involved in an altercation that ended in one man's death and that the ensuing chaos—whatever its origin—caused the destruction of the exhibition."

"Not to mention his connections with the Russian

Empire," Sir George added. "And we have been informed by Lord Clarendon that..."

Alexander stopped listening. He knew what was coming—a public announcement of his dismissal from the Society.

He looked at Lydia. She watched the council with wariness, one of her hands twisting and untwisting a lock of hair that had escaped from beneath her hat. Alexander almost smiled. He wondered if she knew she did that when she was nervous.

Sir George droned on—enemies, breaking of diplomatic relations, fleet in the Black Sea, the Ottoman Empire, French anti-Russian sentiment, acts of hostility...

As Alexander kept his gaze on Lydia, an emotion he couldn't quite name filled him. It overwhelmed his anger, his despair, his need for control, with a sense of expectation and hope. Of freedom.

He couldn't remember the last time he'd felt such things. He never wanted to see his family hurt again, but the duty of protecting them could no longer be his alone.

He looked at his father. Rushton stared at Sir George, his hard features set. Alexander had the odd thought that he'd never wondered if his father had ever been truly happy.

He put his hand on Rushton's arm. His father looked at him.

"Forgive me," Alexander murmured. He stood and addressed the council. "I beg your pardon, gentlemen."

All eyes turned to him. A buzz rippled through the crowd. Rushton tugged on his sleeve to try and make him sit down. Alexander pulled away and stepped to the front of the room.

"If I may?" he asked.

Hadley glanced at the other council members, who nodded.

"Go ahead, Lord Northwood."

"I would first like to apologize for the events of the night in question. People were injured, property destroyed. A man died. I was most categorically involved, and I am deeply regretful for the negative light this has cast upon the Society.

"For two years, I've worked hard as vice president of the Society to bring the exhibition to fruition in honor of the Society's one hundredth anniversary. No one wanted the exhibit to be an international success more than I did. However, in light of all this, I must resign my position as director of the exhibition and vice president of the Society. Effective immediately."

Gasps and shouts came from the audience. Hadley smacked his hand on the table. "Order!"

Alexander couldn't bring himself to look at Lydia. His mind, his soul, filled with images of a vast city where canals wound through crystalline squares and town house walls, where gardens bloomed amid crowded, bustling streets and wedding-cake palaces.

"I will be pleased to work for a time with whoever the council puts in my place," he continued, "to ensure a smooth transfer of duties. As has been pointed out numerous times, I own a trading company based in St. Petersburg. I believe now that is where I will be most useful. Therefore, I would have you all know that before the summer ends, I intend to leave London."

No.

Lydia suppressed a gasp of shock, her hand going to

her throat. Alexander continued speaking to the audience, his deep voice rolling like ocean waves. He was close enough that she needed to take only a few steps to touch him. Around her, the other mathematicians stirred and muttered, but she heard nothing beyond the roar of dismay filling her ears.

Alexander—*her Alexander*—wanted to leave? This brave, strong, proud man who could face down the world without flinching...now he was going to run away, leave London...leave *her*?

Her blood began to throb with anger and despair. She stared at him—his hair glossy under the lights, the strong column of his throat, the unyielding lines of his profile. Desperate love bloomed through her, causing her breath to stick in her throat.

With effort, she skirted her gaze from Alexander to his father and brother. Sebastian was grinning, while Lord Rushton looked somewhat perplexed. The council members bent their heads together and conferred.

Hadley cleared his throat. "Well, Lord Northwood, if that is your intention, then the council is forced to accept your resignation and wish you well on your journey."

The rumble in the room erupted into a sea of chatter as people surged forward to speak to the council and Alexander. A group of men surrounded him, several reaching to shake his hand and others to chastise him.

"Disgraceful, Northwood." One man scowled at him. "The lot of it."

"Good riddance to you," another representative muttered.

"Pay them no mind," a third man said, dismissing the naysayers with a shake of his head. "Most of us are well aware of the good works you've done, my lord. I agree with Hadley and wish you well."

Lydia turned to her colleagues, steeling herself against the urge to run to Alexander and... and what? She didn't know whether she wanted to hit him or kiss him senseless. Perhaps both.

"We'll take our leave, please, gentlemen," she announced. "Our work here is done."

They loaded up their books, rolled pages of calculations, stacked papers. Lydia snapped her satchel closed, grabbed her pointer, and strode toward the exit while trying very, very hard not to turn for one last look at Alexander.

"Lydia!" His urgent voice rose over the noise of the crowd.

Lydia's stride hitched as a brief hope edged past the despair, but then his words echoed through her mind. *I intend to leave.*

And why should it matter? He knew as well as she did their relationship could never be, so shouldn't she simply wish him Godspeed on his journey and cherish what memories they had?

Of course, her heart did not care what she *should* do. It only cared what she longed to do.

"Er, Miss Kellaway?" Lord Perry touched her elbow to indicate she needed to keep moving as the crowd rustled behind them. A wall of people closed between her and where Alexander stood.

Lydia swallowed, gripping her satchel tighter. She straightened her shoulders and continued to the lobby.

"Lydia!" Frustration filled Alexander's voice.

A tremor shook her. She quickened her pace, trying to

conceal herself within the circle of her colleagues. She could not face him, could not allow him to see how the mere thought of him leaving nearly broke her heart in two.

"Gentlemen!" Sebastian's voice now, lifting over the cacophony. "Gentlemen, drinks served in the meeting room!"

The voices surged in appreciation as the men began making their way across the hall. Unable to help herself, Lydia glanced back once as the crowd parted in front of Alexander.

He pushed forward, his fists clenched, his expression determined. Their eyes met across the distance, and the dark frustration radiating from him prickled the hairs at the back of Lydia's neck. Her chest constricted as she turned away.

Dr. Grant pulled the door open and held it while she hurried into the entrance hall. Her colleagues bustled around her, their voices humming with confusion and concern over the haste of her departure.

"Is the carriage ready, Lord Perry?" Lydia stopped, searching the crowded street in front of the building. "Please, we must hurry—"

A curse sounded behind them, followed by the bang of a door.

"Lydia!"

She froze. The other mathematicians turned, their stances guarded as Alexander stalked across the hall. His expression clouded, his hair disheveled and hanging over his forehead, sweat beading his brow, he looked like the devil himself come to collect her soul.

Several of the mathematicians crowded closer to Lydia in a semicircle of protection. As Alexander neared, she schooled her features into an impassive expression, even as a swarm of emotions rioted through her.

"Lydia." Alexander stopped, his chest heaving. An instant passed as his gaze swept over the other men, and then he made a visible effort to regain his composure. He took a breath and exhaled, dragging a hand through his hair. "Gentlemen. Lord Perry, Dr. Sigley, my deepest thanks for your efforts on my behalf."

"Glad to help, my lord, though you ought to know assisting Miss Kellaway was foremost in our minds."

"As well it should have been, Dr. Sigley." Alexander straightened, his gaze going to Lydia. Her heart fluttered at the sensation of that mere look, urgent and insistent. "I... a moment alone, Miss Kellaway?"

The mathematicians rustled around her. At least two of them puffed out their chests in warning.

"Lydia." Her name was an entreaty. "Please."

Although her resolve was beginning to crack, she tried to muster the courage to withstand him. To withstand her own overwhelming desire to surrender.

"I've no idea why you need to speak with me alone, Lord Northwood," she replied, surprising even herself with a tone that would have chilled a penguin. "You indicated quite clearly to the entire assembly that you've no wish to continue your work with the Society or fight to restore honor to your name, which we"—she indicated her colleagues—"worked for several hours to help you do. Lord Perry even canceled a lecture so that he could meet with us at Dr. Sigley's office to formulate our evidence."

Beside her, Lord Perry made a noise of agreement, narrowing his eyes at Alexander.

"I don't—," Alexander began.

"*Moreover*," Lydia continued, pulling her satchel in front of her like a shield, "since you've made plans to return to Russia, there is no further reason for us to—"

"Lydia, be quiet, for pity's sake," Alexander snapped. "I did not say I wished to return to Russia *alone*."

She blinked, her heart stilling for an instant. "Well, what else—"

"I did not say that because I don't intend to."

"You don't?"

"No." He took another breath. "I want you and Jane to come with me."

Lydia gasped. She took a step back as if to evade the desperate hope in Alexander's words, the hope that slipped into her blood and warmed her to the core. The mathematicians shifted and muttered. She took another step back and bumped into Dr. Grant.

Alexander did not take his gaze from her face. Lydia pressed a hand to her chest, the wild beat of her heart thumping against her palm, traveling the length of her arm. She turned to her colleagues.

"Er...excuse me, gentlemen, please. Alexander?"

Her mind whirling, she led him to a spot beside the staircase. She closed her eyes, drawing in a breath and blocking out the images, the *promise*, his words evoked. Then she turned and gave him a mutinous glare, slapping him hard on the arm.

"What are you going on about, you foolish man?"

Alexander rubbed his arm, amusement flashing beneath his desperation. "I'm going on about our future. I want you and Jane to come and live in St. Petersburg with me."

"Are you mad?" *Why would her heart not still at those words, at the expectation in his beautiful eyes? Why was hope coursing like brilliant light through her blood?* "I can't live with you in Russia."

"Why not?"

"Because I can't marry you, Alexander!" Speaking the words aloud diminished the gleaming emotions that had begun to shine through her resolve. She sobered. "Haven't we been over this time and again? Nothing has changed."

"Why did you bring your troupe of geniuses to the meeting, then?"

She stared at him, her mouth opening and closing as she struggled for detachment. "I knew they could assist me with proving your—"

"No. Why did you bring them? Why did you want to see me absolved?"

"I didn't want you to be blamed for something that wasn't your fault," she replied. "I know how hard you've worked. You don't deserve to have it all cast aside because you tried to save Jane and me."

"So you felt you owed me?"

"Well, in a sense, yes, but—"

"Why else did you do it, Lydia?"

Lydia let out an exasperated sigh and stared past his shoulder at the opposite wall. What did it matter if he knew the truth? It changed nothing. Why not allow him to leave with at least the memory of what they meant to each other, even if a future together could never be? *Especially* since that future could never be.

"Lydia."

"Oh, all right," she snapped, swinging her gaze to his. "I still love you, Alexander. I wanted to help you because I still love you and I couldn't stand the thought of those men belittling your character in front of such a large audience, and you there with no one to defend you. All right? I've said it. Is that what you wanted to hear?"

"Most definitely."

He gave her a wide grin, his happiness searing her with a love so potent it nearly took her breath away. Hope brighter than the sun glowed in Alexander's eyes. He gripped her hands as if restraining himself from pulling her into his arms.

Lydia tightened her hands on his in return, loving the sensation of their fingers clasped together, his big hands engulfing hers. Yet she was unable to prevent sadness from clouding her pleasure.

"It still doesn't matter, Alexander. Loving you with all my heart, everything I am... it changes nothing."

"Marry me."

She clutched his hands, praying for the strength to resist the beauty of everything those two simple words encompassed.

"Please stop," she whispered. "If you want to run away—"

"I'm not running away from anything," Alexander said, his voice threading with renewed urgency. "I'm running toward something, and I want to go there with you and Jane. Don't you see? It's the answer to our dilemma."

Wariness flashed in her. "Going to a foreign country?"

"No. Going home." His throat worked as he swallowed, the strong lines of his features edged with nervous tension. "Do you remember that night you told me we always have a choice? You were right. For too long I've let other people's decisions, circumstances, dictate my life. No longer. Now I'm making the choices I want to make. And I choose you."

"I can't—"

"You can," he insisted. "It *will* work, Lydia. I promise you. Make a life with me. Please."

Her heart pounded so hard she heard the beat in her ears. She knew then why he'd come to this decision—in St. Petersburg they could live among people who knew nothing of their past circumstances. The reputations of both their families would not suffer further. They could live in freedom. Even hope. Joy.

Oh, God. Her mind worked frantically, shifting through all the arguments, weighing the risks, discarding the doubts. It was true. He was right—they could leave London together and start a new life in a city that belonged to Alexander, a place of white nights, troika bells, and cherished memories. A place that could be theirs alone, a place where they could live a life of their own making.

Was it possible? Was happiness within their reach? Could she trust him, trust *herself*, enough to take such a leap of faith?

"Choose, Lydia," Alexander whispered.

"I...I choose Jane," Lydia finally said, then put up a hand when he tried to speak. "I choose Jane *and* you, Alexander. I choose us."

A huge smile broke across Alexander's face. Happiness flooded Lydia's veins and overflowed into her heart. He grabbed her and pulled her to him, lowering his mouth to hers.

She gave a squeak of surprise as he kissed her without restraint, claiming her as his, surrendering to her. The tension in her slipped away, her body relaxing against his as the kiss seemed to go on forever...until they both remembered where they were.

Alexander grasped Lydia's shoulders, his gaze searching her flushed face, his dark eyes filled with love and hope.

"I love you," he said. "More than life."

"I love you," she replied, and smiled. "More than numbers."

Alexander chuckled. Lydia's blush deepened as she glanced toward her colleagues, who still stood near the doors. All watching them.

Alexander cleared his throat and stepped away from Lydia. An awkward, embarrassed silence filled the lobby.

"Er...quite well done, Lord Northwood," Dr. Sigley finally said.

Dr. Grant snorted. Another man clapped his hands, and then all the mathematicians started chuckling. Even Lord Perry, who appeared a bit gloomy at first, soon joined in the laughter and scattered applause.

Alexander grinned and looked at Lydia. Her eyes sparkled with amusement as she tilted her head toward the mathematicians.

"Perhaps they would be interested in my theories of love after all." She slipped her hand into his, knowing she would forever cherish the warmth of his gaze, the touch of his fingers. "In the end, I think we'd all choose love, Alexander. Every last one of us."

Chapter Thirty-Three

Lingering scents of the wedding breakfast filled the house—spiced apples, wine, galantine. Flowers bloomed from crystal vases, a few bright petals dusting the carpeted floors. Sun streamed through the curtains and bathed the drawing room in a golden glow.

"I have been contemplating it for the past two weeks," Lord Rushton said, his brow furrowed. "It was all very interesting, what the professor imparted, though I confess to still not understanding one word."

"I'd be pleased to explain it in more detail, my lord, if you would—"

"Never mind, Lady Northwood." Rushton waved his hand in dismissal. "I'll take your and Dr. Sigley's word for it."

"Very wise, Lord Rushton." Mrs. Boyd nodded her approval.

Lydia caught Alexander's eye from across the room, as he sat playing a game with Jane. He winked at her. She smiled, her heart filling with so much love, so much gratitude, that she felt as if she were swimming in radiance.

For so long, her soul had been tight, crumpled, like a piece of clean white paper crushed into a ball. But now every time she sensed Alexander's warm gaze on her, every time he touched her, she felt herself unwrapping, smoothing out. Releasing.

"Lydia, did Alexander tell you one of the most prominent mathematicians in St. Petersburg is a woman?" Talia asked. "You ought to meet her straightaway."

"Our brother Darius might be acquainted with her," Sebastian said as Alexander and Jane approached the group around the hearth. "He's not a very social sort, but he knows a number of people. You will not lack for companionship."

"Perhaps he might provide you with the names of suitable piano teachers so Jane might continue her lessons," Mrs. Boyd said.

"Must I?" Jane made it sound as if her grandmother had asked her to dig a well. Sebastian grinned.

"Knowing Darius, he's more likely to want to discuss insect species with you." Talia gave Jane a smile. "I plan to visit you there as well. Are you looking forward to the trip?"

"Oh, yes." Jane brightened. "I've always wanted to travel, you know, but we've only been as far as Brighton. This will be tremendously exciting. And Lord Rushton has agreed to take care of my fern while we're away."

The happy anticipation in her daughter's voice made Lydia's heart sing. She tightened her arm around Jane. Just a short time ago, she would not have imagined possible a future of hope and promise and freedom. A future in which she could be Jane's mother in every sense of the word, could give the girl everything Lydia never had.

Over the past two weeks, a lovely calm had settled over Lydia's soul, secured by the knowledge of her and Alexander's love and devotion. And somehow, too, by the knowledge that this life on which she was poised to embark was the life her own parents would wish for her.

A life in which she would never be alone again.

"We will likely return to London in a few years' time." Alexander put his hand on Lydia's shoulder and squeezed, as if he sensed the emotions tumbling through her. The heat of his palm burned through her clothes to warm her skin. "Once things have settled."

"Yes." Rushton's brow furrowed deeper. "This will not ignite another public scandal."

"It certainly will not, my lord," Mrs. Boyd replied. "Especially considering how hard Lord Northwood has worked to restore your reputation."

The earl slanted her a glance.

Mrs. Boyd thumped her cane for emphasis. "It is an impressive man who takes the reins and does what he can to rectify a perilous situation. Lesser men than Lord Northwood might have hidden themselves away. You are to be commended for raising such a strong-minded son."

The earl frowned.

"After all," Mrs. Boyd continued, "what is more important than looking after one's family? And when Lord and Lady Northwood leave London, I trust you will carry out your duties with the honor and dignity that befits a man of your stature and position who—"

"Mrs. Boyd." Rushton interrupted the woman's sustained lecture by slamming his large hand against the mantel. "I thank you for your very strong views on the matter."

Northwood coughed. "Mrs. Boyd, if you wish to remain in your house, I will ensure it is fully staffed. Perhaps you would also consider retaining a companion."

"Perhaps." Mrs. Boyd nodded again, looking to where Jane sat beside Lydia. "As for Jane, I expect you all to return on occasion so I might see her. And I might not be adverse to making the trip myself once or twice, provided suitable accommodations are arranged."

"I do wish you'd come along," Lydia said. "I don't like the idea of leaving you here alone."

"For heaven's sake, I will not be alone, Lydia. I have my work, my circle of friends. And quite frankly, it seems to me that Lord Rushton might do well to engage himself in meaningful Christian good works, for which I am pleased to offer my assistance." She nodded at the earl. "Please take no offense, my lord."

Lord Rushton looked as if he indeed took a great deal of offense, but Alexander spoke before his father could bluster.

"We plan to leave before the end of the month," he said. "I expect to have things settled with the Society by then."

"Excellent." Rushton straightened both his spine and his lapels. "You've produced an unconventional idea, Northwood, but a good one. Well done."

He nodded at Talia and Sebastian to indicate they should all take their leave. As the party prepared to depart, Lydia approached Lord Rushton. He looked at her with kindness and took her hand.

"My son once told me you are like no one he's ever met," he said. "I must say I've rarely heard a truer statement."

"We've only room left for truth, my lord," Lydia replied, covering his hand with her other one. "And the truth is that I'm honored to be part of your family. I love your son with all that I am."

She glanced at Alexander, who was watching her with a smile so filled with love that her heart somersaulted, a riotous combination of joy and expectation spilling through her.

"The girl." Rushton's voice was gruff. "Jane. Take good care of her. I've become quite fond of her."

He gave her hand a brief but tight squeeze, a gesture that told Lydia all she needed to know. She embraced Talia and her grandmother, then bent to gather Jane into her arms.

"I'm glad you married him." Jane hugged her tight. "It'll be an adventure, won't it?"

"Of the very best kind."

After everyone had left, Alexander moved forward, and then Lydia was in his arms, her face against his shirtfront, the warm strength of his body solid against hers.

Jane was right. Their future in a new country would be an adventure—complex, unpredictable, exhilarating. Like her relationship with Alexander. Like life.

"Are you happy?" he whispered against her hair.

"Completely." She looked up at him. "Are you?"

"For the first time ever."

His weight lay heavy and delicious on top of her. His fingers gripped her hips. The coarse hair of his legs abraded the soft skin of her inner thighs. His breath heated her shoulder. Her breasts pressed against his chest. His shaft throbbed inside her.

God.

Lydia clutched Alexander's back, her face buried in the side of his neck. His scent filled her head. She shifted, a moan escaping her throat as he pushed deeper. A low curse rumbled from him. She tightened her legs around his thighs. Her hands slicked down his back, smoothing over taut muscle and skin.

She arched her hips upward. Sensations crashed through her, centering on the juncture of their union—the pulsing, the yielding flesh, the spiraling pressure. He tightened his hold on her hips, then pulled back and thrust forward. Again. Again. Oh, glorious loving... *again.*

She moaned. Panted. Writhed. Then felt his body begin to tense, his long muscles coiling and flexing against her hands, his hips pushing...

"Oh, wait..." She gasped, shifting to ease away from him, her hands moving to seek his erection. "Wait, I... let me..."

He stopped, still embedded inside her. He planted his hands on either side of her head and lifted himself to look down at her, his eyes simmering with heat and the need for release.

"Lydia." His voice was hoarse, thick with desire. "We're married."

"Yes, but..." She stared up at him, her gaze sliding over the sweat-damp angles of his face. The underlying meaning of his statement pierced through layers upon layers of love and urgency, striking her right in the middle of the heart.

Her breath caught in her throat. "You mean..."

His lips brushed her damp forehead, stirring loose tendrils of hair. He encircled her wrists with his big hands, pressing her arms to the sides of her head and immobilizing her. Then he thrust into her again, so powerfully that her whole body shuddered.

"Alexander..."

He responded with another push, another pull, an enthralling rhythm that had her blood burning and her need intensifying.

"Take me," he hissed against her throat. "All of it."

Her eyes stung with tears. She gripped his back, parted her legs wider, feeling that unmistakable surge toward bliss. And beneath the exquisite sensations, the pure carnal pleasure, anticipation sprang to life. Hope, love, and happiness swirled in her blood and merged into an outright joy that spread through her entire being.

"Take me," he repeated, his voice barely more than a growl.

"Yes." Lydia gasped, her hips bucking up against him as pleasure began to cascade through her body, shimmering and flowing. "Yes, I will... I want..."

"Now." He thrust fully inside her as his body began to shake with release, his shaft pulsing.

"I feel it." A cry ripped from Lydia's throat. "Oh, yes, I... I feel it..."

She pushed herself closer to him, clutched him against her, pressed her cheek to his shoulder. Brilliant colors of purple and blue swept across her mind, reds and yellows surging through her blood as her husband spilled his seed into her body and made her his all over again.

Afterward, he pulled her into the crook of his arm and stroked a hand through her tangled hair. Lydia closed her eyes and breathed. She placed her hand on his chest, feeling the rhythm of his heart, and for a moment she imagined that her own heart beat in perfect unison with his. A sense of wonder lit within her as she realized there was still so much about him she had yet to discover. Still so much they had to share and plan.

"You were right," she murmured.

"Was I?" His voice was deep, lazy with satisfaction. "About what?"

"There's a story written by Mrs. Mary Shelley." Lydia shifted to look at him, propping her head on her hand. "It's about an alchemist who drinks a potion that will grant him immortality. But he drinks only half the bottle and then wonders what is one-half of infinity?"

"A question for the ages," Alexander mused.

Lydia gave him a light tap on the nose. "But the question," she continued, "is meaningless. Infinity isn't a number. It can't be measured or multiplied or halved by some mathematical calculation. It's a concept, an idea of something that goes on forever. Without end. Without boundaries."

She pressed her lips to his cheek and stroked a hand down his chest.

"That's what you were right about," she said. "I've tried to quantify attraction and desire, to develop differential equations to explain the relationships between men and women. But it's impossible. Life and *love* are immeasurable. They cannot be quantified or calculated. Life extends beyond death in ways that we will never comprehend. And love... love is as complex, as boundless, as infinity itself."

"Mmm. You are brilliant indeed, Lady Northwood." He slipped his hand up her back. "Brilliant and beautiful.

You'll cause a sensation in St. Petersburg. Though I will never let you forget that you said I was right."

Lydia smiled. "I'd expect no less of you."

Alexander's thumb moved to caress her neck, sliding back and forth in an echo of the way he had touched her that first time in his drawing room.

"And I love you infinitely," he said, cupping her nape as he drew her closer. "Forever."

As their lips met again, Lydia's heart filled with a love powerful enough to banish all regrets. She knew then that her future had begun during that first midnight encounter. Warmth, light, and hope had bloomed within the shadows and flourished into this lovely place of here and now.

A place where infinity was as real and substantial as her husband's touch. A place where, in moments of extraordinary beauty and good fortune, one plus one could equal . . . one.

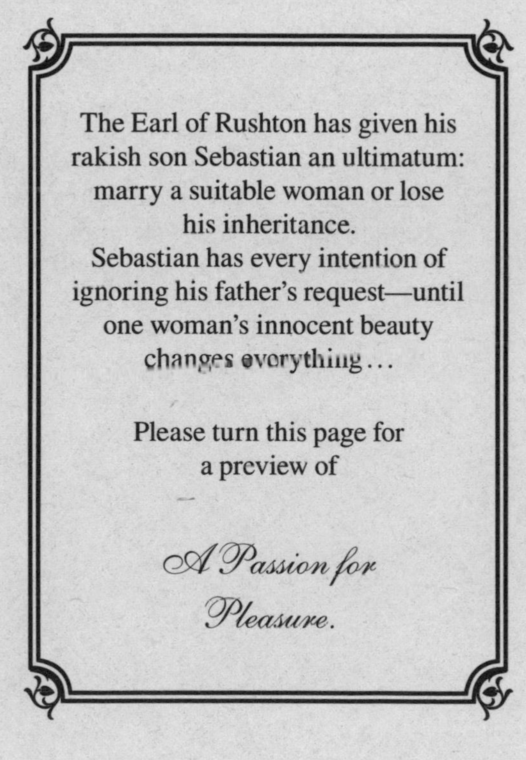

The Earl of Rushton has given his rakish son Sebastian an ultimatum: marry a suitable woman or lose his inheritance.

Sebastian has every intention of ignoring his father's request—until one woman's innocent beauty changes everything…

Please turn this page for a preview of

A Passion for Pleasure.

Chapter One

She was carrying a head.

Sebastian Hall squinted and rubbed his gritty eyes. He blinked and looked again. Definitely a head. Cradled in one arm like a baby. A woman's head with coiffed brown hair, though at this distance he couldn't see her expression. He imagined it to be rather distressed.

He watched as the young woman crossed the empty ballroom to the stage, her steps both quick and measured, her posture straight in spite of her gruesome possession.

Sebastian pushed himself away from the piano. The room swayed a little as he rose, as if he were on the deck of a ship. A hum, seasick-yellow, droned in his ears. He dragged a hand over his face and scrubbed at his rough jaw as he crossed the room.

The woman didn't appear to see him, her path set unswervingly on her destination. A basket dangled over her left arm.

Sebastian cleared his throat. The guttural noise echoed in the vast room like the growl of a bear.

"Miss." His voice sounded coarse, rusted with disuse.

The woman startled, jerking back and losing her grip on the head, which fell to the floor with a thump and then rolled. A cry of surprise sounded, though in his befuddled state, Sebastian couldn't tell from whom it had emerged. He looked down as the head rolled to a stop near his feet like the victim of an executioner's ax.

A perfect waxen face stared up at him, wide, unblinking blue eyes, pink mouth, her hair beginning to escape a smooth chignon.

After a moment of processing this turn of events, Sebastian bent to retrieve the head. The woman reached it before he did, scooping it back into her arms and stepping away from him.

"Sir! If you would please— Oh."

Sebastian looked up into a pair of rather extraordinary eyes—a combination of blue and violet flecked with gold. Something flickered in his memory, though he couldn't grasp its source.

Where had he—

"Mr. Hall." She tucked a stray lock of brown hair behind her ear, hugging the head closer to her chest. "I didn't know you would be here."

She frowned, glancing at his wrinkled clothes, his unshaven jaw and scuffed boots. For an uncomfortable moment, he wanted to squirm under that sharp assessment. He pulled a hand through his hair in a futile effort at tidiness, then experienced a sting of annoyance over his self-consciousness.

"Are you..." He shook his head to try to clear it. "I'm

afraid this room is closed in preparation for Lady Rossmore's ball."

She tilted her head. "You don't remember me."

Oh, hell.

Out of sheer habit, Sebastian attempted to muster a charming smile, though it had been so long since one had come naturally to him that his face felt like pulled clay.

"Well, far be it from me to forget a woman as enchanting as yourself. Your name has slipped my mind, though of course I remember...that is, I must be out of my wits to—"

"For pity's sake." She seemed to be trying hard not to roll her eyes. "My name is—was—Clara Whitmore. My brother and I both took piano lessons from you years ago when we stayed in Dorset."

Sebastian struggled to make his brain work as he looked at her round, pretty face, her curly brown hair pulled into an untidy knot. A streak of grease or oil smudged her cheek. She looked like a thousand other ordinary women—a shopkeeper's daughter, a clerk, a schoolteacher, a milliner's apprentice.

Except for her eyes. And a tiny black birthmark punctuating the corner of her smooth left eyebrow, like the dot of a question mark.

"Does your father reside in Dorset still?" Sebastian asked.

"No, I'm afraid that property has been long abandoned." Her eyes flickered downward, shading her expression. She shifted the head to her other arm. "So, Mr. Hall, I've continued to hear great things about you over the years. You were at Weimar last summer, were you not?"

The admiring, bright pink note in her voice clawed at

him. His fingers flexed, a movement that caused tension to creep up his arm and into the rest of his body.

"Yes." His voice sounded thin, stretched.

Clara blinked, a slight frown tipping her mouth again. Her eyes were really the strangest shade—a trick of the light, surely. No one had eyes that color. He certainly didn't recall having noticed them when she was his student. He didn't even recall having noticed *her.*

Discomfort pinched Sebastian's chest. He wouldn't have noticed her back then. Not when women had flocked to him with bright smiles and hot whispers. Among such birds of paradise, Clara Whitmore—even with her unusual eyes—would have been a plain brown sparrow.

She still is, he told himself.

He straightened his shoulders, glancing at the waxen head with an unspoken question.

"My uncle is debuting an automaton tomorrow evening at Lady Rossmore's ball," Clara explained. "Well, I'm debuting it on his behalf, as he was called out of town rather suddenly."

A surge of comprehension rolled through Sebastian as the pieces began locking together in his blurred mind.

"Then you are Mr. Granville Blake's niece," he said. "I'd expected...that is, Lady Rossmore said he might be here."

"He'd intended to be, but owing to the circumstances, I'm to carry out his duties." Clara touched the automaton's head, drawing Sebastian's gaze to her long fingers. "This is Millicent, the Musical Lady. Part of her anyhow. She plays four tunes on the piano."

"How"—*ridiculous*—"interesting." Though he'd heard Granville Blake dabbled in all sorts of mechanical toys and automata, Sebastian was interested in only one of the man's many projects.

And now he apparently had to be interested in the man's niece as well.

"You oughtn't be here alone," he told her. "Especially at this hour."

"We've permission to set things up," she replied. "This is the only opportunity we have to assemble Millicent and her piano. And I'm not alone. My uncle's assistant Tom is just outside loading the remaining crates." She glanced behind him to the piano resting beside the stage. "Will you be performing at the ball?"

His jaw tensed. If Lady Rossmore had not told him Mr. Granville Blake would be in attendance, Sebastian would have spent the following evening wreathed in the smoke and noise of the Eagle Tavern.

"I will be in attendance," he said, "but not performing."

"Oh. Well, I do apologize for the interruption. I didn't even know anyone else would be here. Once Millicent is assembled, we'll leave you to your work."

Work. The piano was all the evidence she needed to assume he'd been working.

He was about to respond with a sharp tone—though he had no idea what he'd say—when a needle of rational thought pierced the fog in his brain.

At the very least, he needed to be civil to Clara Whitmore if he wanted to learn more about her uncle's projects.

Or perhaps he should be more than civil. Women had always responded to his attentions. Even if now those attentions were corroded with neglect, Miss Whitmore didn't appear the sort who had much to judge them—or him—by.

"Would you care for a currant muffin?" She opened the basket. "I thought I'd better bring something to eat since I don't know how long Tom and I will be here. I've also got apples and shortbread..."

She kept talking. He stopped listening.

Instead he stared at the curve of her cheek, the graceful slope of her neck, revealed by her half-turned head. He watched the movement of her lips—a lovely, full mouth she had—and the way her thick eyelashes swept like feathers to her cheekbones.

She looked up to find him watching her. The hint of a flush spread across her pale skin. With a sudden desire to see that flush darken, Sebastian let his gaze wander from her slender throat down across the curves of her body, her tapered waist, the flare of her hips beneath her full skirt. Then he followed the path back to her face.

There. Color bloomed on her cheeks. Her teeth sank into her lush lower lip. Consternation glinted in her lavender eyes. He wondered what she'd look like with her hair unpinned, if it would be long and tangled and thick.

"I...er...I should get to work," Clara went on, ducking her head. "Tom will be in momentarily, and there's a great deal to do. Please, take a muffin, if you'd like."

Sebastian rolled his shoulders back. A cracking noise split through his neck as he stretched. He realized for the first time that day he'd almost forgotten the headache pressing against his skull.

"Thank you." Again he experienced that wicked urge to provoke a reaction. "I'm not hungry. Not for food."

Her lips parted on a silent little gasp, as if she wasn't certain whether to be offended by his suggestive tone or to ignore it altogether. Expressing offense, of course, meant she'd have to reveal that she had recognized the implications of his words.

She gave a nonchalant shrug and shifted, then held Millicent's head out to him. "If you please, sir—"

"I please, Miss Whitmore." His voice dropped an octave. "Often and well."

He was drunk. Or recently had been.

That didn't explain why Clara's heart beat like an overworked clock, or why the rough undercurrent of Mr. Hall's words heated her skin, but at least it explained *him.*

She tried to breathe evenly. She couldn't recall ever having had *this* reaction to him. She remembered him leaning over her shoulder as he demonstrated the position of his fingers on the piano keys. She remembered the assured tone of his voice as he spoke of quarter notes and major scales...but he'd been distant then, a brilliant pianist, a dashing young man who attracted beautiful women, who would keep company with kings and emperors.

Now the distance had closed. He stood before her close enough to touch. He had aged, diminished somehow. Had he...fallen?

A tiny ache pierced Clara's heart. Sebastian Hall had always been disheveled, but in a rather appealing fashion suited to his artistic profession.

I've no time to fuss, his manner had proclaimed. *I've got magic to weave*.

And he had, with kaleidoscope threads and fairy-dust needles. At dinner parties and concerts, Mr. Hall spun music through the air and made Clara's blood echo with notes that had never before moved her.

Not until Sebastian Hall had brought them to life.

Sleeves pushed up to his elbows, hair tumbling across his forehead, he'd played the piano with a restless energy that could in no way be contained by the polish of formality.

But now? Now he was just…messy. At least three days' worth of whiskers roughened his jaw, and his clothes looked as if he'd slept in them for even longer than that. Dark circles ringed his eyes. He appeared hollowed out, like a gourd long past Allhallows Eve.

Clara tilted her head and frowned. Although Mr. Hall's eyes were bloodshot, they contained a sharpness that overindulgence would have blunted. And his movements—they were tense, restless, none of his edges smeared by the taint of alcohol.

She stepped a little closer to him. Her nose twitched. No rank smell of ale or brandy wafted from his person. Only…

She breathed deeper.

Ahh.

Crisp night air. Wood smoke. The rich, faintly bitter scent of coffee. Clara inhaled again, the scent of him sliding deep into her blood and warming a place that had long been frozen over.

"Miss Whitmore?"

His deep voice, threaded with cracks yet still resonant, broke into her brief reverie. Such a pleasure to hear his voice wrap around her former name, evoking the golden days when she had been young, when William and their mother had been alive and sunshine-yellow dandelions colored the hills of Dorset like strokes of paint.

She lifted her gaze to find Mr. Hall watching her, his eyes dark and hooded. Her face warmed.

"Sir, are you…are you ill?" she asked.

The frank question didn't appear to disconcert him. Instead a vague smile curved his mouth—a smile in which any trace of humor surrendered to wickedness. A faint power crackled around him, as if attempting to break through his crust of lassitude.

"Ill?" he repeated. "Yes, Miss Whitmore, I am ill indeed."

"Oh, I—"

He took a step forward, his hands flexing at his sides. She stepped back. Her heart thumped a restive beat. She glanced at the door, suddenly wishing Tom would hurry and arrive.

"I am ill behaved," Mr. Hall said, his advance so deliberate that Clara had the panicked thought that she would have nowhere to go should he keep moving toward her. Should he reach out and touch her.

"Ill considered," Mr. Hall continued. Another step. Two. "Ill content. Ill at ease. Ill-favored. Ill-*fated*—"

"Ill-bred?" Clara snapped.

Sebastian stopped. Then he chuckled, humor creasing his eyes. An unwelcome fascination rose in Clara's chest as the sound of his deep, rumbling laugh settled alongside the delicious mixture of scents that she knew, even now, she would forever associate with him.

"Ill-bred," he repeated, his head cocking to the side. "The second son of an earl oughtn't be ill-bred, but that's a fair assessment. My elder brother received a more thorough education in social graces." Amusement still glimmered in his expression. "Though I don't suppose he's done that education much justice himself."

Clara had no idea what he was talking about. She did know that she'd backed up clear across the room to the stage. He stopped inches from her, close enough that she could see how the unfastened buttons of his collar revealed an inverted triangle of his skin, the vulnerable hollow of his throat where his pulse tapped.

A prickle skimmed up her bare arms, tingling and delicious.

Sebastian kept looking at her, then reached into his pocket and removed a silk handkerchief. “May I?”

She shook her head, not certain what he was asking. “I beg your pardon?”

“You have”—he gestured to her cheek—“dirt or grease.”

Before she could turn away, the cloth touched her face. She startled, more from the sensation than the sheer intimacy of the act. Sebastian Hall’s fingers were warm, light and gentle against her face.

He moved closer, a crease of concentration appearing between his dark eyebrows as he wiped the marks from her face with the soft handkerchief. Clara’s breath tangled in the middle of her chest. She stared at the column of his throat, bronze against the pure white of his collar, the coarse stubble roughening the underside of his chin.

She didn’t dare raise her gaze high enough to look at his mouth, though she wanted to. Oh, how she wanted to. The urge made her fingers curl tight into her palms, made a strange yearning stretch through her chest.

The muscles of his throat worked as he swallowed, his hand falling to his side. He stuffed the handkerchief back into his pocket.

With his attention turned away from her, Clara noticed the weariness etched into the corners of his eyes, the brackets around his mouth, the faintly desperate expression in his eyes that had nothing to do with alcohol and everything to do with fatigue.

Fatigue. That was it. Sebastian Hall was bone-deep exhausted.

He met her gaze.

No. The man was exhausted past his bones and right into his soul.

Before she could speak, Sebastian stepped back, turning toward the front of the room. Tom pushed open the doors and maneuvered a trolley loaded with four crates. He glanced up, his face red with exertion. "Almost done, miss."

Clara hurried to meet him. They conferred briefly about how best to organize the various parts of the machine; then Clara turned back to the stage. Sebastian Hall was gone.

THE DISH

Where authors give you the inside scoop!

♥ ♥ ♥ ♥ ♥ ♥ ♥ ♥ ♥ ♥ ♥ ♥ ♥ ♥ ♥

From the desk of Rochelle Alers

Dear Reader,

I would like to thank everyone who told me they couldn't wait to return to Cavanaugh Island. And like the genie in the bottle, I'm going to grant your wish.

You will get to revisit people and places on the idyllic island while being introduced to others who will make you laugh and cry—and even a few you'd rather avoid. It is a place where newcomers are viewed with suspicion, family secrets are whispered about, and old-timers are reluctant to let go of their past. Most inhabitants believe what happens in Sanctuary Cove, Angels Landing, or Haven Creek stays on Cavanaugh Island. Angels Landing—or "the Landing," as the locals refer to it—takes its name from the antebellum mansion and surrounding property that was and will again become a crown jewel on the National Register of Historic Places.

In ANGELS LANDING you will meet newcomer Kara Newell, a transplanted New York social worker who inherits a neglected plantation and a house filled with long-forgotten treasures and family secrets spanning centuries. Kara finds herself totally unprepared to step into her role as landed gentry, and even more unprepared for the island's hunky sheriff. Her southern roots help her adjust to the slower way of Lowcountry life, but she finds herself in a quandary when developers concoct elaborate schemes to force Kara into selling what folks refer to as her birthright. Then there's hostility from newfound family members, as well as her growing feelings for Sheriff Jeffrey Hamilton.

Jeff has returned to Cavanaugh Island to look after his ailing grandmother and to assume the duties of sheriff. His transition from military to civilian life is smooth because, as "Corrine Hamilton's grandbaby boy," he's gained the respect of everyone through his fair, no-nonsense approach to upholding the law. However, his predictable lifestyle is shaken when he's asked to look after Kara when veiled threats are made against her life. When Jeff realizes his role as protector shifts from professional to personal, he is faced with the choice of whether to make Kara a part of his future or lose her like he has other women in his past.

So come on back and reunite with folks with whom you're familiar and new characters you'll want to see time and time again. You will also get a glimpse of Haven Creek, where artisans still practice customs passed down from their African ancestors. Make certain to read the teaser chapter from *Haven Creek* for the next installment in the Cavanaugh Island series.

Read, enjoy, and do let me hear from you!!!

Rochelle Alers

ralersbooks@aol.com

www.rochellealers.org

♥ ♥ ♥ ♥ ♥ ♥ ♥ ♥ ♥ ♥ ♥ ♥ ♥ ♥ ♥

From the desk of Christie Craig

Dear Reader,

Have you ever stared in the mirror and had yourself a mini identity crisis? Felt unsure of who you really were? I have, and that was the inspiration for BLAME IT ON TEXAS. But for my heroine, Zoe Adams, her identity crisis isn't so mini.

Imagine seeing a childhood picture of yourself splashed across the TV screen on an unsolved mystery show, which claims you were kidnapped from some highfalutin Texas millionaire family. Imagine learning that your corpse was supposedly discovered shortly after you were kidnapped. Imagine it, when all your life you've had some strange memories that didn't make sense.

With Zoe's parents—or people she thought were her parents—deceased, she's certain of only one thing: She's not dead. (Although, after her fiancé ran off with another woman, taking her heart with him, she hasn't felt too alive.) So Zoe does the only thing she can: She takes a leave of absence from her job as a kindergarten teacher, packs up the only thing that matters in her life—her handicapped cat—and hightails it from Alabama to the Lone Star State.

Her search for answers lands her in a whole lot of trouble, too. When someone starts taking pot shots at her, she winds up under the protective arm of a sexy commitment-phobic PI who is more than willing to play bodyguard. Between Tyler Lopez, his family and friends, and all the zany characters she meets while working at Cookie's Diner, Zoe learns that who you are isn't so much about your birth name or who your parents were. It's about whom you let into your life and whom you love.

From Texas-sized flying cockroaches and ticked-off clowns, to games of strip Scrabble, writing the story of Zoe and Tyler was the most fun I've had doing something that wouldn't get me arrested. The chemistry between these two characters lit up the page from the moment she dropped three plates of food on him. Hot grits and sunny-side-up eggs never looked so good. I hope you enjoy the story of two people stumbling their way through life's bumpy roads and landing smack-dab in the lap of love.

I love hearing from readers, so please come visit me at www.christie-craig.com; find me on Facebook at https://www.facebook.com/christiecraigfans; or follow me on Twitter at @Christie_Craig.

Laugh, Love, Read.

Christie Craig

♥ ♥ ♥ ♥ ♥ ♥ ♥ ♥ ♥ ♥ ♥ ♥ ♥ ♥ ♥

From the desk of Nina Rowan

Dear Reader,

Confession #1: I'm terrified of math. I have been a math-o-phobe since first grade, when we learned basic addition and I had to count on my fingers to make sure I was getting the answers right. Confession #2: I still count on my fingers. Confession #3: I'm way, way beyond first grade.

Math and I have never found a groove. I'm okay with some numbers (2 and 5 are polite acquaintances of mine, if not exactly friends), but others make me nervous (7 is somewhat flinty, and 9 is plain evil). I never memorized the multiplication tables. I still can't do long division. My son is now a first grader and completes his math homework faster than I can check it.

So what provoked me to create a heroine who is a brilliant mathematician? Lunacy, of course, and maybe a little bit of "Ha! I will confront you, Math, even though you scare me." At least in writing about a mathematician, I could channel my fear into creating what I hope is a unique and memorable heroine.

If there is one thing Lydia Kellaway, the heroine of A STUDY IN SEDUCTION, does not fear, it's numbers. Equations comfort her. She enjoys theorems, series, postulates. She understands them. They understand her. And I loved the idea of a Victorian woman who has a harmonious relationship with math and who is renowned for her extraordinary intelligence.

The seed of Lydia's character came while I was researching nineteenth-century Russia and discovered information about Sofia Kovalevskaya (1850–1891), a prominent Russian mathematician who made major contributions to the field.

Despite the barriers she encountered in academia, Sofia earned a doctorate summa cum laude from the University of Göttingen, becoming the first woman in Europe to hold that degree. Personal and professional struggles did not prevent Sofia's success, as she soon became the first woman in Northern Europe to hold a full professorship at the University of Stockholm. She published numerous papers, edited a mathematical journal, and received the competitive Prix Bordin from the French Academy of Sciences.

While Sofia Kovalevskaya inspired my idea of a heroine who is a mathematician, I wanted Lydia to be a unique character in her own right. I loved that she could immerse herself in numbers and find comfort in equations, but what did that mean for the other parts of her life? What would happen if Lydia had spent her years in lonely isolation, with only numbers as her faithful companions, and then was suddenly forced to confront the exact opposite of intellect—the pull of lust?

After her destructive early experiences, Lydia lives in safe comfort inside her head...until Alexander comes along to wreak havoc with all his hot Russian sexiness. He is fascinated not only by her body, but also by her brilliant mind. Writing about how Lydia's affinity with math affects and changes their relationship was both a challenge and a pleasure.

Confession #4: I'll never overcome my fear of math. Words I love, but numbers I'll merely tolerate. I'll always carry my portable calculator, and when my son's math homework gets beyond me (which it soon will), I'll either study with him or recruit someone else to be the homework helper. I'll keep working at multiplication, especially the 7s and 9s, but in the meantime I take a small measure of comfort in Sofia Kovalevskaya's remark to one of her teachers: "I was unfortunately weak in the multiplication table."

Happy Reading!

Nina Rowan